D0014704

THE
WHOLENESS
of a
BROKEN
HEART

K A T I E   S I N G E R

T H E

W H O L E N E S S

of a

B R O K E N

H E A R T

RIVERHEAD BOOKS

A member of Penguin Putnam Inc. • NEW YORK • *1999*

This is a work of fiction. Any resemblance to persons living or dead is purely coincidental.

The author gratefully acknowledges permission to reprint the following: definitions from *The American Heritage Dictionary, Third Edition,* © 1996 by Houghton-Mifflin; adapted and reproduced by permission. "Love is a Rose" by Neil Young, © 1975 by Silver Fiddle; all rights reserved; used by permission of Warner Bros. Publications U.S. Inc., Miami, FL 33014. An adaptation of Orvin Marcellus Blanding's "Questions for My Father," first published in *Knowing the Light Will Come,* the 1987 *Mosaic* anthology of stories and photographs by students at South Boston High.

Grateful acknowledgment is made to *Lilith* and the *Jewish Women's Literary Annual/1997,* where previous versions of portions of this work appeared; and to the Western States Arts Federation, the Ludwig Vogelstein Foundation, and numerous individuals whose financial support made this work possible.

RIVERHEAD BOOKS
a member of
Penguin Putnam Inc.
375 Hudson Street
New York, NY 10014

Library of Congress Cataloging-in-Publication Data

Singer, Katie, date.
The wholeness of a broken heart / Katie Singer.
p.   cm.
ISBN 1-57322-147-3
1. Jews—New York (State)—New York Fiction   I. Title.
PS3569.I5445W48   1999   99-33149 CIP
813'.54—dc21

Printed in the United States of America
1   3   5   7   9   10   8   6   4   2

This book is printed on acid-free paper. ∞

Book design by Judith Stagnitto Abbate/ABBATE DESIGN

with love

————

to Sallie Bingham and Bob Levin
whose faith and passion
embraced me while I wrote

to Rebecca Green
my much cherished sister

to the memory of Esther Usdin and Mary Krasovitz
and for the conversations with which we continue

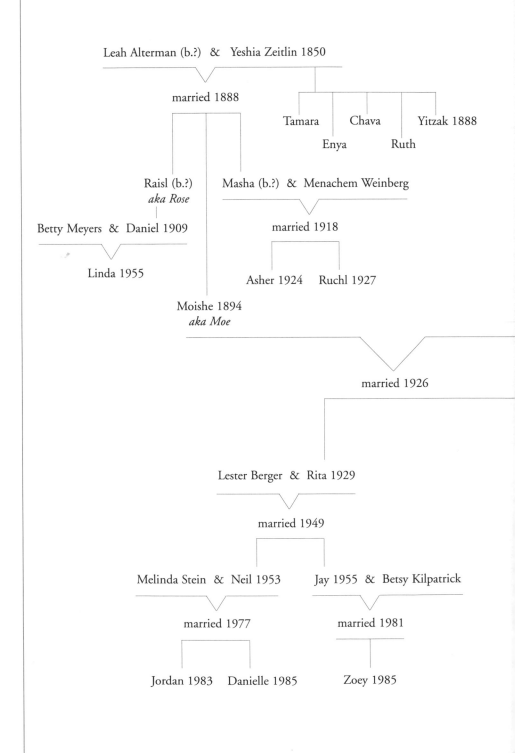

Leah Alterman (b.?) & Yeshia Zeitlin 1850

married 1888

Tamara   Chava   Yitzak 1888

Enya   Ruth

Raisl (b.?)
aka Rose

Masha (b.?) & Menachem Weinberg

married 1918

Betty Meyers & Daniel 1909

Linda 1955

Asher 1924   Ruchl 1927

Moishe 1894
aka Moe

married 1926

Lester Berger & Rita 1929

married 1949

Melinda Stein & Neil 1953

Jay 1955 & Betsy Kilpatrick

married 1977

married 1981

Jordan 1983   Danielle 1985

Zoey 1985

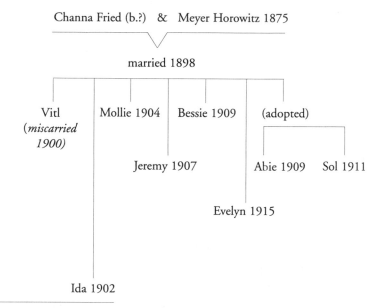

Channa Fried (b.?) & Meyer Horowitz 1875

married 1898

Vitl
(*miscarried 1900*)

Mollie 1904

Bessie 1909

(adopted)

Jeremy 1907

Abie 1909   Sol 1911

Evelyn 1915

Ida 1902

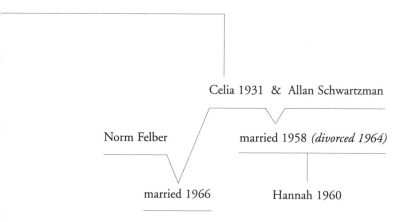

Celia 1931 & Allan Schwartzman

Norm Felber

married 1958 *(divorced 1964)*

married 1966

Hannah 1960

AUTHOR'S NOTE

M AM E-*loshn*—Yiddish—the mother tongue of East European Jews, evolved from a combination of German, Hebrew, and Slavic languages. And over a millennium, Yiddish speakers freely adopted words and phrases from the language of the country in which they resided—Latvia, Lithuania, Poland, Hungary. Yiddish has always been written with Hebrew lettering. (Ladino, the language of Sephardic Jews, was and is spoken by those with roots in Spain or Portugal.)

The Institute for Jewish Research (YIVO) and the Library of Congress have different versions of transliterating Yiddish. For example, *challah* is commonly spelled with the Library's version; YIVO spells the word *khale. Chutzpah,* another word known to American English users, is spelled *khutspe* by YIVO.

I have kept the spelling of *Ach!, challah, chutzpah,* and other words and names as they are commonly known; but in other cases, I have used the YIVO standard of Yiddish transliteration.

Rabbi Zusya taught:

God said to Abraham: "Get thee out of thy country, and from thy kindred, and from thy father's house, unto the land that I will show thee." God says to man: "First, get you out of your country, that means the dimness you have inflicted on yourself. Then out of your birthplace. That means, out of the dimness your mother inflicted on you. After that, out of the house of your father. That means out of the dimness your father inflicted on you. Only then will you be able to go to the land that I will show you."

—MARTIN BUBER
Tales of the Hasidim: The Early Masters

Es iz nitto a gantsere zakh vi a tsebrokhn harts.
There's nothing more whole than a broken heart.

—YIDDISH PROVERB

1 9 7 0 - 1 9 8 0

HANNAH

born in 1960
in New York City

MIDNIGHT, midwinter, northeastern Ohio.

Like ghosts or angels, the towering trees that border and adjoin much of Shaker Heights are taking on snowy garments for morning. These elms and oaks and maples loom over brick and aluminum-sided houses with three or four or even eight bedrooms. They frame the apartment buildings, too, for the widows and single mothers. My family lives on the east side, furthest from Cleveland. Young honey locusts line our street, with stakes in the ground to ensure they grow straight.

I'm awake in the dark. My ten-year-old skin feels like the thin layer of ice on the Shaker lake, near our house. I leave my room and go to my mother's. I lift her comforter, the heavy lip to her bed.

Without questions, she takes me in.

Against her hot body I slide my cold one. I nestle my back against her breasts; I tuck my feet between her thighs. I weave our fingers and bring her warm hand to my chest. In the cradle of her body, my chills subside. I feel warm enough to breathe again.

My mother's body smells like the color olive. Like moist dirt. Like orange peels just beginning to turn in our garbage pail. What gives her this strange smell? Over and over, her scent draws me back to her.

I sleep through this night, knowing I will melt in Mom's heat. By dawn, my gown is soaked with our sweat.

"Change quickly, love," Mom whispers. "I don't want you late for school."

MORNINGS, my mother does not come downstairs until I've made the coffee and the newspaper is on the kitchen table. She walks past our living room sofa, thinly striped in velvet greens, beiges, and orange-browns. It looks out toward the front doorway—not toward our two olive-green chairs on the room's other side, which face our dining room. Her small captain's desk, which holds drawers full of private papers, is right next to the doorway, without a chair.

The dining area is small, just between the living room we hardly use and our family den. Here, in the den, Mom examines her plants before she walks back through the dining room to enter the kitchen. Wide thresholds, not doorways, mark the transitions between rooms.

In the kitchen, Mom toasts a slice of bread, spreads cream cheese and blueberry preserves on it. She pours coffee into a blue Dansk mug, sits. While she reads the stock market quotes, she drinks her coffee and eats her toast. Done, she refills the mug, lights a cigarette. Quietly, I spoon the oatmeal I've prepared for myself into a bowl, and watch her read first the bridge column, and then the front page. I try not to read over her shoulder.

After two cups of coffee, Mom leaves the front sections of the paper on the table, made of thick, butcher's block wood. I take the paper with my oatmeal to our dining room. We have a round cherrywood table in here, which can be extended to seat eight people, and chairs to match. Mom folds our laundry on this table. The chandelier is brass, with hand-blown goblets. The walls are painted off-white. Here and there hangs a still life of flowers or a seaside painting that once belonged to my grandparents. Like those of the living room and the stairs to our second floor, the dining room's carpet is a fine, thick wool, the color of rust. Mom says it warms the whole house; and she's proud that the men who installed it appreciated her unusual good taste.

I curl up beside the dining room's heating vent to read quickly and eat while I keep warm. Daddy will be downstairs soon, dressed for work, wanting the newspaper sections with his coffee. Mom takes a pencil, a pack of cigarettes, and the crossword puzzle into the bathroom, where matches always lie next to the soap. She runs cold water while she sits on the toilet in a blue velveteen robe, its skirt pulled up around the seat, and works the crossword puzzle. She taps her ashes into the sink. The running water washes them down.

Until she is out of the bathroom, we do not speak.

I AM Celia's only child, born in Manhattan, in 1960. She named me Hannah, after her mother's mother, Channa Fried Horowitz, who died a few years before I was born. Mom doesn't speak much about Channa (the *ch* pronounced not as in *church,* but with a throaty *h*—as in *ach!*), which is what she called her grandmother; and whenever she does I can tell they'd adored each other. Mom smiles, and her eyes get sparkly. Naming a baby after someone who's died is a Jewish tradition. But Mom *really* did it because she wanted to be reminded of her grandmother.

Just after my fourth birthday, Mom divorced Allan Schwartzman—my father—and moved back with me to Cleveland, where she was raised, where her parents still lived. He's a social worker, Allan. He did not want their marriage to end. My mother refused to discuss the matter with him. She wanted a speedy divorce, and she made him go to Mexico to get it.

When I was six she married Norm Felber, a pharmacist. He doesn't talk much. I call him Daddy, which pleases my mother. When I was ten he adopted me, and I became Hannah Felber. That made him and Mom happy, because before he married Mom, he got the mumps. So besides me, Norm can't have kids. Allan, who had visited me twice a year since the divorce, stopped calling our house, even on my birthday. That's good, because he and Mom never got along. My friend Karen thinks it's strange that I just stopped thinking about my true father. But Mom's enough for me. And I like the quiet house we have with Norm.

We have a pretty normal life, I think, though I know my mother isn't typical in Shaker Heights. Our vegetables often come from the Stouffers outlet in Solon, where Mom buys frozen cauliflower or broccoli au gratin in bulk; but nearly every day she bakes a new dessert from scratch—brownies, rugulach, chocolate whipped cream pie. She lets dishes pile up in the sink; clean laundry can lie in a wrinkled heap on the dining room table for days. Once or twice a year, exasperated with her own housekeeping, she hires a woman to come weekly to scrub the floors and iron the clothes that overflow from the basket in our front hall closet.

Usually, in the late afternoon, before her help's bus is due to arrive, the two of them will sit at the kitchen table to ponder their notions of God. Just under the butcher block, Mom slides her hands into her blue jeans' pockets. Quietly, she says she's agnostic. While the woman cautiously forms her response, Mom stares at the woman's eyes, into the pause.

The women have dark skin, dark like the shadows in caves. I don't think their children are the black kids I go to school with, but I'm not sure. As if their bodies are deep wells, their words bubble up slowly. I listen from the next room, glad my mother has a friend for this little while. Mom rarely likes other adults, because they lack interest in philosophical matters. With these ladies, though, I think she feels met.

But after two or three Thursdays with Martha, or Retta, or Jean, Mom will curl her lips inward, then stretch them back out and say, "I just don't like paying someone to do my dirty work." She tells each woman she won't need her anymore. Through my disappointment that she won't continue those conversations, I admire her, her admission of her own mess, her willingness to live in it.

My mother takes public transportation more often than not, and prefers solitary card games and weeding the lawn over watching TV. She doesn't own a lipstick, and she never goes to a beauty salon. She has thick, wavy hair, slightly gray. She's proud of its color, which turned from dark brown just after I was born. She cuts it herself in a style I can only call short. She eats two candy bars a day between meals, and she's still a perfect size ten.

Twice a year, on their birthdays, my mother and her sister Rita talk on the phone. Aunt Rita lives on Long Island, in a house much bigger than ours. She has two boys, both older than me. "Oh, they're impossible," Mom says, into the phone, which sits on one of the built-in bookshelves in our family room. I know she is speaking of my grandparents. "Impossible," she repeats to Aunt Rita. I sit just a few feet from her on the Stickley daybed,

newly reupholstered in a mustard-colored plaid to match the den's brown shag
carpeting, with homework covering my lap. I wish I knew what makes Gram
and Grampa so hard to take.

Sundays, Daddy drives us to my grandparents' house, a mile away. Mom
carries the business sections from the *Cleveland Plain Dealer* and *The New
York Times,* which earlier that morning were delivered to our front door.
Grampa wants them for the stock market quotes.

"Celia," my grandfather says—only that—just as we walk in. Sometimes
his sister, Aunt Rose, is sitting in a wing chair when we arrive, just a few feet
from the doorway. She was born in Russia, just like Grampa. When she lived
there, her name was Raisl. Now she lives on top of a toy shop on Taylor
Road, near the house where Mom grew up.

Mom always nods to Rose when we walk in, and so do I. I've never
heard her speak. Her face is scrunched, like dried-up fruit.

Mom puts the newspapers on the hall table, which Grampa bought in
Europe before she was born, and which has real gold on its legs. This table
attracts clutter, including a used hand towel beside the newspapers Mom has
set down, though there are many beautiful things on it: Hebrew prayer books
sandwiched between marble bookends carved as bears; a metal lamp with a
flute player at its base, and a fringe carved out of the metal shade; a royal blue
elephant designed like a tureen and filled with shells, each large enough to re-
quire two hands when they're held. Many of the things here are antique and
handmade; because the house is so dark, they're hard to notice.

Mom follows Grampa's broad, slow-moving body to the spare bedroom.
Through the closed door, I try to make out the meaning of what they say,
what they hide from the rest of us. I hear my grandfather's Yiddish accent, his
gruffness now soft from old age, and the edge in my mother's voice, coming
out of her arched back. I think these conferences are about money matters. I
don't think Mom *likes* Grampa, but when he asks for her opinion, she feels
some kind of satisfaction.

Daddy heads past the dining room for the TV in the den, to watch the
end of a ballgame. That leaves me with my grandmother, Ida, until her sister Mollie arrives by taxi. Mollie is my grandmother's unmarried sister. She
offers Gram a bag of pears or grapefruit when she walks in—payment for Ida's

meal and the company of her family. Aunt Mollie has recently retired from working as the secretary to a judge downtown. She wears a knitted suit to our Sunday dinners; she dyes her hair to keep it brown. Gram's hair is white, her dress a plain blue—and usually covered all through dinner by an old apron. The pants and once-white, buttoned-down shirt that Grampa wears are old and stained. Our Felber family comes in jeans.

"My neighbor, that nice young woman who just finished nursing school," Aunt Mollie begins, "well, her fiancé just broke off their engagement."

"Oh?" Gram replies, interested to hear more.

"Yes," Aunt Mollie continues. "Nancy's beside herself. Some days, she feels too ashamed to go outside."

While Aunt Rose sits quietly in the living room, Mollie stands at the kitchen's alcove, telling her sister what news she has. I bring to the dining table the dishes Gram has prepared—cabbage soup or kreplach in chicken broth, pot roast or stuffed peppers, potato kugel, applesauce. Because we each have individual tastes, she often cooks the same dish two ways. The kitchen is dark, even with the ceiling light on. The windows look out to the neighbor's brick wall; the floor is bluish gray. Since she has such little cupboard space, Gram keeps her used grocery bags in a pile on the floor. There's an empty package of vacuum bags there, too, and a big bowl for making pastry dough and noodles.

Gram hands me a plate of potato pancakes. *Es iz nito a gantsere zakh vi a tsebrokhn harts,* she says.

"I suppose," Mollie says.

I catch my aunt politely eyeing the pancakes, their edges brown and crispy. I look up to Gram, then to Aunt Mollie. Their long bones make them both tall as trees, and they wear high heels, too. "What's that mean?" I ask. *"Es iz nito a gantsere . . . ?"*

"Uhh," Gram says, tasting the cole slaw she's marinated all day, pausing to come up with a clear translation. "Something like there's nothing so open as the rift in a broken heart."

I tear a pancake in half, give one side to Aunt Mollie and take the other for myself.

Aunt Mollie lingers over her pancake. "I'd say it means there's nothing more whole than a broken heart."

Gram gives a simple shrug, hands me a bowl of applesauce to put on the table.

"Ma—your namesake Channa—used to use that expression a lot," Aunt Mollie tells me.

"Mmm," Gram says. "Now, *she* had a big heart."

"Yes," Aunt Mollie says, nodding in my direction. Neither she nor Gram will say so directly, but they want me to know I am lucky to be named for Channa—and that they're glad I got their mother's name. "She had a big heart for *everyone*. For our neighbor, Mrs. Fels, who hardly spoke English; for the mailman, our teachers—for everyone. And everyone loved her back."

"Does that mean she had a broken heart?" I ask, feeling especially short with these tall ladies.

"What kind of a question is *that?*" Aunt Mollie glares.

Gram lets out a grunt. "Call everyone to dinner," she says.

Grampa and Norm sit at the head and foot of the boxy, mahogany table, which this evening bears one narrow leaf. Aunt Rose sits next to Norm. There's a mahogany hutch for Gram's tablecloths and good silver, and the chairs are also large and chunky. Gram and Aunt Mollie take seats at the side closest to the kitchen; Mom and I take the other side. With the backs of our chairs up against the hutch, Mom and I have no room to move.

We say the food is good. Aunt Mollie asks about the books I read in school, and if we've heard about an upcoming television program on Emily Dickinson. "More slaw," Grampa says, speaking for the first time.

"Uhh," Norm says, "the roast, please."

After our meal, unless I volunteer, Gram cleans up by herself. My mother will have no part in picking up, and Aunt Mollie never enters her sister's kitchen. Aunt Rose is still stoney and quiet. "Go on, Hannah," my mother says, reaching for another pecan roll, scarcely looking up from her second reading of the *Times* business news. Mom likes her mother's cooking, though Gram's complaint that we never take her out with us—shopping, or for a movie—irritates her. She thinks Gram doesn't have much to say that's positive.

"Go on," she says again, while I pick at the crumbs on my plate. "Give Old Ida a break."

As I rise toward Gram's sink, feeling the warmth of my new, brass-buckled belt and red plaid blouse, my two braids keep neatly at my collar bones. To Mom, I give my "thanks a lot" expression, my rolled eyes.

M y grandparents' house is laid out much like ours, only they also have two bedrooms downstairs, and their den and kitchen are smaller. One night at their house, where I've been sent while my parents go to a movie, I go from the den through the dining room to look for a snack. I open Gram's fridge and search for ham.

Mom keeps our ham stocked in the meat bin. She likes it scrambled in eggs, or on toasted rye with mayonnaise and a slice of cold tomato. I look everywhere, but can't find anything in Gram's fridge wrapped in white deli paper—only kugel and a tongue in Pyrex dishes, each covered by a plate.

Finally I return to the den, where Gram waits for our Scrabble game to resume. I sit in Grampa's orange chair, in the deep dent in its seat. Grampa has been in bed for at least an hour. His tray table is beside his chair, cluttered with a butter knife covered in dried-up jelly, two plates with toast crumbs, a coffee cup, and a newspaper folded in half. Against the window ledge, Gram's violets sit neatly in a row.

"You don't have any ham," I say.

"Of course not."

I scrunch one side of my lip toward an eye.

"Ham's from a pig, Hannah. It isn't kosher."

"What's kosher?" I ask.

"You don't know what *kosher* is?" She looks disturbed.

"Gram, I'm only ten," I say. "How should *I* know everything?"

Gram sighs, a sigh that matches the room's old mess. "There are Jewish laws for your diet," she says. "They keep you healthy. I don't follow all of them. But I don't mix milk and meat. And I don't have *pork* in the house."

While Mom drives me home the next morning, I tell her we shouldn't eat ham anymore, because we're Jews. She curls her lips in a smile: she adores me, even when I request things she doesn't like. "Okay," she says. "I'll buy lox then."

A few weeks later, though, she switches back to ham. "Lox is a luxury we can't regularly afford," she announces. Her voice has authority; the rules of our house are hers to make. Quietly though, I decide not to eat pork again.

MY best friend's name is Karen Caplan. We're both in our school's modern dance club. Anyone can join the club, which our gym teacher, Ms. Hirsh, runs after school. We make up our own dances and perform them twice a year, in the gym. The dance club is mostly black, and Ms. Hirsh is glad our programs have variety: Karen and I like choreographing to "Switched-On Bach," while the black girls prefer Aretha Franklin. After rehearsals, we like to compare the lard in their mothers' cookies with the butter in ours; and Karen and I admire that they already have boyfriends. She often walks home with the other dancers, because they all live in an integrated part of town; I walk alone, toward a section that is mostly white.

Karen and I are both short girls with short brown hair; but hers is straight, and mine is curly. Her nose has a bump in its middle; mine is plain. We both have small breasts. Karen has a brother older than we are, already off at college. Her father teaches philosophy at Cleveland State University. I like her mother, who bakes the desserts for a catering company, and sometimes gives me a cake or a pie to take home to my family. Mrs. Caplan has an accent, because she grew up in France. Sometimes, when I'm at their house, we'll all talk French so I can practice what I learn at school. Once, Karen told me, "My mother barely survived." Somehow, I knew she was talking about the Holocaust.

At Hebrew school on Saturday mornings (which I asked to attend after Gram told me our religion's dietary laws, and after Aunt Mollie gave me a copy of Anne Frank's diary—even though Karen doesn't go, and Mom says she would *never* join a temple because they're all just interested in money), we learn the Hebrew alphabet and the meaning behind the Jewish holidays. We also see movies made by Nazis. Adolph Hitler filmed the rooms he filled with Jewish hair and jewelry. He filmed the people who lined up before the

gas chambers, naked, thinking they'd be taking showers. *Are any of these peo-*
ple our relatives? It's hard to tell, when people are naked and their heads are
shaved, if we look alike. We see their dead bodies, the bones like dried birch
sticks, bulldozed into trenches other Jews have dug.

After the movies, which we kids have filled the auditorium to see, a
teacher stands in front of us, and says things that I don't hear. We're all too
dazed to talk. There are probably two hundred of us in this room, which is
still dimly lit. *I think I sort of look like Anne Frank, and she kept a diary, too.*
As we file back to class, Jenny Fein asks if I'm going to Ken Glickman's party
that night. I've heard that people smoke grass at Ken Glickman's parties,
which makes me uneasy; I've heard that David Jacobson and Ken are
friends—and that makes me sort of want to go. "I'm babysitting tonight," I
tell Jenny, "for my favorite kids."

When the carpool brings me home, I tell Mom we watched those movies
again.

"Uh huh," she says. "That's rough."

I can barely eat the macaroni and cheese she's prepared.

"Don't let it get you down, love," she says. She starts a cigarette, and suggests we go to La Place after lunch, a new mall in Beachwood.

I say, "Okay," but I am thinking about Karen's mother, Mrs. Caplan. I've
looked for a tattoo on her arm, like the Jews in the movie, but she always
wears long-sleeved shirts. And Mrs. Caplan is a little plump, not skinny like
the people we saw through the concentration camps' barbed wires. What
happened to her in the war? I wonder. I wonder if even Karen knows.

I think our mothers could be friends. Mrs. Caplan likes to talk about cur-
rent events, she has good taste in fabric, and she's always looking out for a
good sale. Their house is similar to ours, but cleaner. But Karen and her
mother fight as much as Mom and I get along.

At La Place, Mom brings pants and sweaters made of fine cotton and
wool to dressing rooms flanked with mirrors, then rests on the upholstered
chairs in the lushly carpeted rooms. While I bare myself and bring the new
clothes down over my head and my new breasts, my eyes still in the dark,
Mom watches me.

"Smashing," she says decisively, as I roll up the pants, which are always too long. "You'll have to get them." Or, "Take it off, love. That's not you." She observes me with the kind of look that honeymooning couples give to Niagara Falls. I love her gaze; I bathe in it.

AFTER I start junior high, my mother reserves her Friday nights for playing bridge with Henrietta Leeder. One dry, windy, autumn afternoon in University Heights, a suburb next to Shaker, a few years before she and Mom became bridge partners, Henrietta's three children were raking leaves on their front lawn. Suddenly, the leaves caught fire: in a spontaneous chaos, without warning, the blaze appeared. The two younger ones, a boy and a girl eight and ten, were engulfed in flames. They died from inhaling the smoke. There was no reason for this tragedy, no culprit but dry wind. The firemen sobbed with Henrietta and the rest of her family, right there on her lawn. A tinge of smoke hung in the daylight. The trees were untouched.

"The gods can be cruel," Mom says, when she tells the story.

She's moved by Henrietta's life, pleased to be close to her. The life of someone whose children died so unreasonably has depth and meaning; and once Henrietta begins to venture out again, Mom is proud to give her an ordinary evening of cards.

My mother returns from her bridge games and tells me, "She does her makeup in such a lovely way." Normally, the wearing of makeup is considered gaudy and vain. But on Henrietta, Mom admires it.

One night after cards with her friend, my mother removes her trench coat and hangs it neatly over a chair before she greets me. I lie on the living room's striped sofa, feeling grown up in the matching maroon sweater set Mom wore in the fifties, as a college girl. I'm reading *Gone With the Wind*. Daddy is already in bed. Mom says, "Hi," then clears her throat. I fold my book together and give her my attention.

"I want you to know why I don't display photographs of you like other parents," she says somberly. "It's because static images serve mainly to remind one of the dead."

A chill ripples through me, but I don't let it show. My body is unusually agile, even wiggly; but I can also sit very still. I do so now, with Mom. I'm not sure I agree with her idea. Somberly, though, I nod.

As if I've concurred with her, Mom continues. "I don't want photographs on a mantel if I can see a person, or talk with them on the phone."

I nod again, more slowly. I understand the gravity of her feelings, though the idea sounds strange to me.

A half hour later, just as I turn out my light, Mom appears at my bedroom doorway. "And when I'm dying," she says, her voice floating into the darkness of my room, "you are to get as far away from me as possible—no matter what I might beg for then."

"Okay," I say, in a tone that sounds as close to promise as I can muster.

Then Mom walks away, toward her own room. "And," she says, returning with an afterthought, "do not attend my funeral."

"Okay," I say again, figuring it's going to take me a long time to get to sleep tonight. It doesn't occur to me to ask what she's talking about.

AFTERNOONS, when I return home from the eighth grade, I go to Mom's room, where she's been napping, and climb into Daddy's side of the four-poster bed. Like most of our furniture, the bed is a Stickley. It's covered by an Amish quilt, and has matching cherrywood dressers—one for Mom, and one for Daddy. There's a black-and-white TV on a plastic stand from Norm's bachelor days. Between the TV and Mom's closet, there are usually a pile or two of dirty clothes or other things Mom needs to put away. I wonder sometimes why her housekeeping is so sloppy, whether the mess protects us from gods looking for a clean house to stir.

I bring a snack we can share, maybe chocolate chip cookies and milk. Mom's in a padded bra and white underpants that go up past her belly button. Her smell, as always, is nearly intoxicating. It seems to come from deep inside the sheets.

I tell her that in the library, I learned that Mark Twain is not the author's real name. Other writers, too, have used pen names when they published their books. "You still want to become a writer?" Mom asks.

"I do," I say, nodding at her recognition of my innermost desire, and feeling my face light up. "Writers can change the world. When President Lincoln met Harriet Beecher Stowe, he made a joke that she started the Civil War with her book, *Uncle Tom's Cabin*. But really he wasn't joking."

Mom bites her cookie, and twinkles her eyes. I know she's proud of me. "When I publish my stories," I say, "I'm going to make my name Hannah Fried." Before she married, Fried was Great-Gramma Channa's name.

"How'd you know Channa's maiden name?" Mom asks, retrieving a crumb that's fallen under the covers into her lap.

"Gram told me," I say.

She nods, my cue to go on. I tell her about the fight Karen had with her mother before she left for school: in their laundry pile, Mrs. Caplan saw a pair of Karen's underwear soiled with menstrual blood, and she started calling her nasty names in Yiddish. Karen knows her mother loves her, but she can be really mean sometimes.

While I share my stories, Mom smokes in a recline, just upright enough to keep an eye on the length of her cigarette ash. "Well," she says, "for most people, mothering's not so easy."

We both know, of course, that for her it is.

EVENTUALLY my mother has to get out of the house. "Out of this bloody bed," she says. So when I am fourteen, she begins working as a substitute teacher in the Cleveland public schools. One day when Mom returns home after I do, clearly exhausted, she asks me to squeeze her a glass of orange juice. She makes her way to the family room. I notice that her dress is unzipped in back. "Mom," I say, "your dress . . ."

"I know," she says. "It's the least of my worries. Just bring me the o.j., love. I'll be on the La-Z-Boy."

"What happened?" I ask, handing her the juice, seating myself across from her, on the daybed.

"I just spent seven hours with twenty-eight children, each with enough energy to turn the world upside down. I got there just before the bell had rung, and already the room was in chaos. All I could do was stand in front of them and keep whispering, *'Can anybody hear me?'* until they got quiet."

I imagine her students, sixth-graders just two years younger than me, ill at ease with my mother's gentle demeanor, startled by her whisper like when a baby's finger caresses your thigh. I imagine them bewildered. I imagine them more awake today than they'd been in a long time.

Mom takes another sip of juice, closes her eyes, and leans all the way back in the recliner with her dress still unzipped. I know she wants to be alone now.

I go back to the kitchen and plan a menu. I stir minced garlic and dried oregano into hamburger meat and form it into patties. I put potatoes in the oven to bake. I chop up a head of broccoli and put water in the steamer. Once Daddy gets home, I can have dinner ready in fifteen minutes.

O N C E every few weeks, late into the night, after our parents are asleep, Karen and I meet to do homework at our own kitchen tables. Our telephones are turned up, off their hooks, so we can each hear the other's calls for help. Sometimes, on a Sunday afternoon, we'll study at her house or mine.

"Does your mother smoke weed?" Karen asks, breaking my attention to a play by Lillian Hellman.

"I don't think so," I say. We are fifteen, sitting across from each other at my kitchen table, working on English papers. Mom has gone upstairs, to nap. She's never said so, but I don't think she's comfortable around Karen. When Kim Johnson comes over, Mom will stand at my bedroom door, and proudly watch us choreograph a short duet. On three-day weekends, she often suggests I invite Jane Fitzgerald over, for a Monday afternoon marathon of triple solitaire. Mom will bake brownies with walnuts, and splurge on Breyer's ice cream, too. She'll stop smoking to speed through her decks, pointing out cards she'd like Jane or me to play. Jane and I slink back to our chairs, our rhythm lost while she wins, again and again, and declares, "That's all there is to it, guys. You can't beat me."

This afternoon, Karen persists. "The way she sucks on her cigarettes looks like she's smoking weed."

"No," I say, feeling the ache of a new pimple on my cheek, certain that Mom wouldn't smoke marijuana. "No way."

"Well, when did her eyes get crossed?"

"I don't know," I say. "They seem okay to me."

But Karen's question startles me, because I've never noticed anything strange about my mother. I can't imagine she's smoked marijuana, since *I* never have.

Now, I wonder if Karen has tried it, and I watch Mom more closely. When she inhales from her cigarette, she pulls the smoke into her parted lips and spirals it down a passageway to her pelvis. From the bottom of her torso, she retrieves the smoke, then blows it out with brutal grace. It disperses around the room in long-suspended clouds that curiously make me wonder about sex.

I look through the clothes in her closet: a pair of corduroys, a few T-shirts, sneakers. A plain, denim dress by Oscar de la Renta, a gray tweed pantsuit by Yves St. Laurent, a green blazer by Calvin Klein. These are the outfits she wears to the furniture store, where she works now as a bookkeeper. In a zippered, plastic case, she keeps a strapless black dress and sling-back pumps with a delicate strap around the ankle. Where does she wear this gown? If she and Daddy go out—this happens maybe a few times a year—they go to a movie, in jeans.

I watch what Mom wears. I watch for what she doesn't wear. I can make her Calvin Klein blazer look like it fits me by putting on a bulky sweater underneath. She lets me wear it like this, and gives me her favorite necklace—two strands of perfectly chiseled turquoise that she bought at an auction of Indian jewelry. While I dress, I wonder if the jacket looks too big; I worry that the necklace is too grown up.

But then I come downstairs, and Mom says, "You look sensational."

MIDWINTER Sunday afternoons, we tuck ourselves under the covers of Mom's bed. She lies in her slip, smoking Pall Malls, and dreams up my summer adventures. "I've got it," she says after a few minutes of meditative quiet, her voice sure as a man's. "You could go to Europe as an exchange student. In France or Switzerland you could use your French."

"Wow," I say, thinking of photos I've seen of the Alps, and wondering if their food is as good as my French teachers describe.

"You give me five hundred dollars of your babysitting money," Mom says, "and I'll pay the balance."

"A deal," I say, grinning at her faith in me, and her offer to let me travel so far away, alone.

Just before I leave, Mom tells me I'll also owe her letters. "At least two a week," she says, pulling a tray of butter balls from the oven.

"Oh, Mom." I tip my head adoringly, feeling like an adult in my newly short haircut, my curls framing my head like a soft bowl.

"At least two a week," she repeats, placing the hot cookies on a plate, sprinkling them with powdered sugar, pouring herself a fresh cup of coffee.

NEAR Lausanne, in a small French-speaking Swiss village, I live with a family that grows and butchers rabbits, some of which they eat. The others they sell. They have two young boys. On the outside, the house is just like the tourist pictures, with red and blue awnings. It's high up on a mountainside, and surrounded by trees. Inside, the house is tiny and dark. The family sleeps in the two bedrooms upstairs, while I have a private room behind the house. From the front door, I can see the village below. A trolley goes up and down three times each day.

I think these people hosted me because they wanted a babysitter for their sons. I feel uneasy, but I agree to take the boys walking each morning, down our dirt road to the meadow at its end. I bring a picnic of bread and cheese, and I read a children's story, in French. Afternoons, I take the trolley down the mountain into town.

One day, I walk into the tiny watch shop in the center of town, just to look. The woman behind the counter says *"Bonjour"* with an accent that sounds familiar, not Swiss. She says she has seen me on the bench in front of her store, writing. "American?" she asks.

"Oui," I say.

The woman smiles warmly, then brings her arms out from under the counter, and folds them over her large breasts. One arm has a tattoo. After staring for several moments, I lift my eyes, and I meet her sad face. *"Juive?"* she asks. "Jewish?"

I nod, grateful to have been recognized so far away from home. "Tova," she says, putting her hand on her heart and giving me a big smile. She looks just like the ladies behind the counter at Lax & Mandel's kosher bakery, on Taylor Road in Cleveland Heights.

"Hannah," I say, smiling back, feeling my eyes light up.

"Ach!" she says. *"Gut, gut!"* She comes out from behind the counter and wraps her round, short body around my small frame.

"Come again," she insists. "I'll get for you a kosher salami."

I wonder if I should write Mom or Karen about my new friend, but I don't think they'll understand: Tova keeps kosher and doesn't work on Saturdays, which is way too religious for Mom to take her seriously. I have lunch one day with her and her husband, then visit their shul. The building is simple and plain, unlike any synagogue I've seen in Cleveland. Wooden chairs that don't all match are lined up in rows and divided by a curtain. Tova explains that one side's for men; one side's for women. The walls are soft and yellow. The ark that holds the Torah is dark mahogany.

Sunlight comes in through the windows we crank open for fresh air, and then Tova and Ruven and I take seats. We just sit quietly, peaceful, for nearly a half hour.

When I return from my travels, I notice my mother's increasing attention to the needs of our lawn after she gets home from work. She sits on the grass in her oldest jeans and a vertically striped maroon and white T-shirt. She pulls at the weeds. She picks them with her right hand, then passes them to her left fist until she has a large clump. The clump goes into a brown paper bag. When the bag fills, she dumps the weeds into a large plastic bag in our garage. The bag says, "Keep Shaker Heights Beautiful."

Her rhythm mesmerizes me. She looks satisfied, though she's hardly moving. Evenings and weekends, I look out from the window near my bed, where I sit writing in my journal or reading books like *East of Eden*. I can watch her on the lawn from here. I know not to disturb her but to wait, suspended until the moment she returns to the house and we can talk again.

Then school begins, and the weather turns too cool for Mom to work on the lawn. She comes inside. Like an admirer of a sunset or a beautiful painting, her eyes beaming with pure, unobstructed delight, Mom keeps her gaze on me. When she finds me writing past midnight, the light from my room disturbing her sleep, she comes to my door, smiles approvingly, then closes it without speaking.

I menstruate now, a mysterious event so painful it takes me to bed. Each month while I suffer, Mom reminds me to "lie still."

"If you fight the pain," she says, "it only makes things worse." She brings me a heating pad. Later, when she notices blood on the sofa I've just risen from, she quietly says, "Hannah," casts her eyes on the stain, and simply suggests we turn the pillow over.

Sometimes, Mom and I just sit quietly on the daybed in our den. With thin needles, she knits bedspreads of fine, undyed cotton she orders from France. She knits hundreds of five-inch squares, each with graceful bumps and ripples, each taking five or six hours to make. Sewn together, they form geometric patterns. When I am in pain on the dentist's chair, I think of my mother's knitting and feel comforted.

Daddy is often upstairs, maybe in a bubble bath or watching TV, while we sit downstairs. I hold my journal in my lap, twirl a pen slowly in my fingers, and listen to her needles bump each other. I can't write while Mom sits so close to me, but sometimes I can doodle.

When my mother asks to see my journals, I hesitate. In these notebooks I write about the things we don't talk about—my irritation with Norm, who spends all his time watching TV; short story ideas; and for two months now, Karen looks the other way when we pass in the hall. She keeps her chin stiff and high. I know it'd be useless to call her—this strange wall between us feels too hot to touch. It started just after I got back from Switzerland, after Karen told me she thought of asking her mother if they could see a psychiatrist. I don't know what that has to do with me, though I'm afraid we'll never again be friends. We're in high school now, and both in the dance club; but we never perform the same dances.

The idea of Mom reading about these experiences terrifies me; but it gives me a thrill, too. For a few moments, I think I'd rather keep my writing to myself. But then Mom puts down her knitting and says, "C'mon Hannah. Let me have it."

She's only an arm's length away. I turn the notebook over, move to the living room sofa, and wait nervously for her response.

"I'll pretend I didn't read the part about how you can't wait for college," she says, smiling coyly as she hands the book back, "to see what kind of life you'll make without me."

I blush. I'd forgotten writing that.

"And my God," she adds, rolling her eyes upward, "you're so introspective."

Sitting so close to her, I can't figure out how to ask why this is a problem, or what I might do to change.

A few months later, when Karen and I find ourselves alone in the girls' locker room, showering after a dance rehearsal, the buildup from our not speaking lets go as soon as the water sprays. We soap each others' backs and squeal. "What's going on in here?" Mrs. Morrison asks.

"We're just happy," I say. "It's been a while since we had fun together."

Even though Mom seems to think being introspective's a problem, at least I can have a good time with my friend.

ONE February day in my senior year, when all of Cleveland is coated with ice, Mom and I bring groceries to Gram and Grampa's house. In harsh weather, my grandfather will not drive; and Gram has never learned how. Mom steers our gold Nova to the end of their long driveway, then we carry in the bags of food through the back door. At Gram's invitation, Mom sits down for a slice of warm apple pie.

I am seventeen now, an eager driver. "Give me the keys," I say, "and I'll turn the car around. I'll get it to face the right way for when we leave."

I bring the front seat closer to the pedals. Carefully, I drive forward and back on the cement patch adjacent to the driveway that's meant for turning our cars around. Earlier today, Grampa hired a teenage boy to shovel it. As I maneuver, the car slips into a steep mound of snow.

Mom and Gram hear the car's wheels spin deeper into the ice. Gram opens her back door, only a few feet from our helpless car, and steps under the awning to see what I've done.

"My God," she moans. "Grampa paid *eight dollars* to clear the drive! He'll be back from his afternoon walk in *ten minutes!*"

I climb out of the car's passenger side, my mouth tucked under my scarf to hide the nervous smile I can't suppress. I head to the garage to retrieve Grampa's rusty shovel.

While she raises a fork of pie to her mouth, Mom looks over Gram's shoulder. "I'm not up for dealing today," Mom shouts to me. "Not with Grampa. Not today." She fills her mouth with moist apples and walnuts while my grandmother turns back inside.

"Celia," I hear Gram say, bending over to slide a foot into a plastic bag before she puts it into a boot, "get your coat on. We have to help Hannah."

"Not today," Mom repeats from her platform at the back door. "You guys handle it." She watches me carry the shovel toward the car. She sucks her fork clean, then gives me a grin as wide as the driveway.

I grin back. Despite Gram's fret for this bind we're in, I love the way Mom beams at me. I can't stop grinning—even as I notice, perhaps for the first time, *Mom drinks me in with crossed eyes.*

IN 1978, I leave Cleveland to attend the University of Michigan in Ann Arbor. I take classes in literature and history, my favorite subjects; but sitting in lecture halls doesn't give me the intimate attention or exchange of ideas I crave. The night before an exam in U.S. history, I read the *Encyclopedia Britannica Junior*'s account, since I haven't read any of the books on my syllabus. When I get a B+ on this exam, I write Mom, "If my history professor thinks I know enough just from reading a children's encyclopedia, then I flunk my history professor. My plan now is to take as many classes as I can each semester, and get my bachelor's as soon as possible. Meanwhile, I'm happy reading novels and writing in my journal."

When I'm back home in Shaker Heights for Thanksgiving, Mom and I sit quietly on the daybed, talking while she knits. Daddy has gone to bed early. I tell her I'm thinking of moving out of the dorm, and into my own studio apartment. I don't like the dorm; I feel like a sardine in there. "Sounds great, love," she says, clicking away at her needles, wondering what kind of apartment I'll find.

We have Thanksgiving dinner at Gram and Grampa's with Mollie and Aunt Bessie, their sister, who's about to head to Florida for the winter. Back home, Mom and I return to our den for more conversation, and to decide which shops we'll visit the next day.

Karen is at Ohio State, majoring in dance. We talk every few weeks on the phone, and we planned, during our last call, to spend this Saturday together. But she calls Thursday evening, just after our dinner at Gram's. "Can you come here," she whispers, "now?"

"As soon as I can," I say. I hang up the phone, wondering if I'll be able to help.

Mom looks up at me through the eyeglasses she has just begun to wear. *"Nu?"* she asks.

"It's Karen," I say. "She's in some kind of trouble. I told her I'd come over." Already I'm looking for my coat and searching through Mom's purse for keys.

"She's always begging your attention," Mom says. "If it were me, I wouldn't go."

"Mom," I reason, startled by her response, "I'm her friend—I want to go."

"I suppose," she says. "But be back by eleven. Otherwise, you'll be tired tomorrow, and no fun."

"Okay," I say, taking a pecan roll that Gram wrapped for me in tinfoil for my ride, wondering what it is Mom doesn't like about Karen.

I pull into the end of the Caplans' driveway, near the garage, so I can enter the back door. Karen's there to greet me, even before I knock. Her face looks heavy and old. "Take off your boots," she whispers, "so my mom won't get upset." I do, then follow her quietly upstairs to her room. I hang my coat against the back of her desk chair. We sit cross-legged, facing each other, on her twin bed.

"I'm scared," she says. Her face, usually animated and expressive, is stuck now, like a mannequin without a smile.

I nod. I keep my eyes intent on hers. Karen had a nose job over the summer. Seeing her surgery fully healed for the first time, I wonder why she looks less beautiful with her nose smooth and small.

"I can't handle sex," she says. "I can't handle dorm rooms. I can't handle being away from my mom. I don't really like my dance classes."

"You can't handle sex," I repeat, wanting to grasp what she's saying, to find a way in. "You can't handle the dorm. You can't handle being away from your mom."

Karen nods again. She's in a trance I wish I could break. We hear Mrs. Caplan vacuuming downstairs, but I don't think Karen's annoyed by it, as I am. Her father is working in his study. Her brother lives in Berkeley, California, now; he won't be home for this holiday.

"You're scared," I repeat.

"I haven't felt anything since I got to OSU," she says. "Except I miss Ms. Hirsch."

I nod, slowly. Ms. Hirsch was the first person who told Karen she could dance. Just a week after we finished ninth grade, she was diagnosed with cancer of the ovaries. She died in October, a month after we started high school. She'd just turned thirty-four.

Most of our town kept quiet about her death. People said it was awful; beyond that, that there was nothing to say. We kids found our own way to grieve. Karen and I liked sitting quietly at the top of Thornton Park with her memory, then running down the long slope used in winter for sledding. Running took us to speeds beyond our control; the force of the wind whipped smiles back into us.

Karen's eyes are hard now, like thick blue glass that won't break. Her lips form a straight, thin line.

"You're afraid," I say, realizing as I speak, "you might want to join her."

She just keeps staring at me. She doesn't even nod. But I know her answer is yes. The November air feels thin. The tree towering over Karen's bedroom window is bare, even of snow. For as long as I can stand it, we sit quietly in this terror. I remember a warmer day on this very bed, when Karen's eyes found and lingered on a spider while we talked. She took it into her hands, led me to the nearest door so I could open it, and let the spider out.

I hear myself ask where she keeps notebook paper.

"In the bottom drawer," Karen says blandly.

"Let's make a list," I say, "of things you can do back at OSU." *Get therapy*, I write; *choreograph something, even if you perform it for just a few people. Keep a journal.* "And once a week," I say, knowing, deep inside, that this list is really pretty flimsy, "let's write or phone."

When I hand her the paper, Karen says she feels better. She gets teary and wipes her eyes. "When you're away, do you miss your mother?" she asks. I know she's wondering if she is the only one of us who feels so strange.

"I do," I say. "But you know, I haven't been happy in the dorms, either. It's too noisy there for me to write. And I don't like having a roommate. I just decided to move out and live alone. I want to cook for myself, and have privacy to write—in quiet."

"Oh, God, Hannah. You're so grown up. I feel like such a wimp."

As I drive through the cold Cleveland night, back to my mother's house, her Nova reeks of gas. I roll down the window, feeling the cold air blow in, preferring the chill to the noxious odor. *Once I do have my own apartment, I hope the solitude will allow me to rest.*

BACK in Ann Arbor, I find a studio in the attic of an old Victorian house. Weekends, I wait tables at the Coffee Cup. I like reading the poetry books I find at Shaman Drum, a second-floor bookstore on State Street, and writing portraits of people I meet at work. Once a week, I make an elaborate dinner for my friend Julie Kaufman, a dropout who likes to read philosophy. We met in a modern dance class before she quit school. And I begin another journal, one my mother will never read.

It's night now, long past sunset. I sit on the loveseat in my own, one-room studio. Through the windows I see into the apartment across from mine. People my age are sitting on a balcony, playing music and smoking dope.

I am nineteen years old. In my window's reflection, I glance at the Paul Klee poster on the wall behind me. I can see myself, too. I wear a gray sweatshirt with the sleeves pushed up almost to my elbows, and Levi's. I have a small, dancer's body, and can sit in a tight ball with this notebook propped up against my knees. I have short, dark curls. My eyes look sad. My mouth is small and might be angry. My face is round and young. I'm not part of that crowd on the balcony. I don't really want to be.

It's been several months since Karen told me she's ambivalent about being alive, maybe even suicidal. I got a great letter from her today— she said she feels like her old self. She's started liking school, though she's still having a hard time with her mother.

Maybe I'm just spoiled, having had Celia Felber as my companion all these years.

I am still a virgin.

There's a guy who works at Shaman Drum, the bookstore. His name is Hal Riley, and he talks with me about "the merchandise." I don't think he's Jewish. Does that matter? He talks sort of like an urban cowboy, but I think he's a softie underneath. He has brown hair, almost red, straight past his shoulders. I kind of wish he'd ask me to a movie.

Maybe it's time to test my women's lib?

I send Mom long letters each week, and at least twice a month she writes me back.

Dear Hannah,

I still think about your visit last month, the exuberance with which you came back here after your afternoon with Gram and Grampa, looking through old family pictures. I myself of course don't give a damn about ancestral stories; but I'm so proud of your interest, proud, too, of myself—that you could have an experience different from my own and that I could take pleasure in it, see the good of it. I feel this even when you don't have a clue about how impossible Moe and Ida are as parents. Father can barely walk now. This is disorienting for me, to see this man who all my life has been a veritable force of nature walk slowly and timidly. I don't think he should be left alone.

Mother has become, in a nutshell, an absolute bitch. Yesterday, she phoned to tell me she didn't think Father could take her to her dental appointment. I knew she wanted my help, but I get a lousy ten days' vacation each year. I did not exactly want to take a half-day of my vacation time to run her errands.

"Take a cab," I told her.

I might as well have called her a tramp, to suggest such impersonal help. We hung up with a bit of tension. I didn't sleep.

So, dammit, I took the afternoon off today, just went to the house and picked her up. She was surprised to see me, but that was it. I am left with a terrible let-down feeling which I'm still trying, hours later, to cast off.

Moral of the story: maturity is accepting that which one cannot change, yet trying to change oneself (for the better or for a growth process). I am foggy on this. Will have to think more about it.

But anyway, my love, your vitality still reaches me, and makes you more wonderful a person than I ever imagined I could mother. Just last week I saw Mrs. Unger at the supermarket. I can't tell you the pleasure it gave me to see her shock when I told her you're living alone, your best friend is a dropout—and that I'm so proud of you.

Truly, I am very proud. And I don't give a damn that nobody else understands.

I love you,
Mama

I GO home to Cleveland every couple of months for long weekends of talking and shopping with Mom. I visit Gram and Grampa, too, to sort through photographs in the bottom drawer of the cabinet in their living room. Gram sits at her kitchen table, eating a little piece of kuchen and working a cross-word puzzle, while Grampa tells me the names of the people in the fading images: Mom and Aunt Rita when they were children; Gram and Grampa in their grim wedding portrait; a couple and a young boy, fashionably dressed for the early thirties. "Who's this?" I ask.

"Masha," he says matter-of-factly, "my sister."

"I thought Aunt Rose was your sister. How come I never heard about Masha?" I ask.

"She perished in the war."

"How do you know?" I ask, memorizing her name and her story.

"Ve just didn't hear again from Masha. Not Menachem, either."

"That's her husband?" I ask, of the man next to Masha.

"Ya, and der son, Asher. Also, dey had a little girl after the boy."

"Why didn't they come over when you did, or when you brought Aunt Rose?" Aunt Rose died when I was eleven.

"Didn't want to."

"I never heard of Masha," I repeat. "How come?"

"What's to say?" Grampa asks. His voice seems numb. He is eighty-six now, still broad and muscular. But his stubble, his slowness, and the brownish-yellow stains just under the collar of his old shirt make him seem vulnerable. While I sit with photographs fanned out before me like a deck of cards, I wonder how much is still unsaid.

Grampa shuffles back to the kitchen. "I need prune juice, Ida."

"Oh!" I hear her rise from her chair, place a plate in the sink, and head toward the TV. "You and your prune juice! Get it yourself!"

Grampa returns to our display of photographs looking like a pillar of stone. I glance up from my place on the floor, meet his dark eyes. Neither of us smiles. He returns to the Queen Anne chair beside the cabinet, seats himself, and responds perfunctorily to my last questions.

Just as we've gathered the photos into a pile, Mom arrives to bring me home. She says hello; I stand to leave. To greet her, Grampa nods. I hold our stack of carefully arranged pictures in my hands—a treasure I will guard for-ever, even as I put them back in his drawer. "I love you, Grampa!" I say.

"You do?" he asks. While Mom walks nonchalantly past us to see what pastry Gram has, Grampa's eyes light up. *"Ach!"* He beams, embracing me with the forceful strength of an athlete my age. "I'm glad of that!"

THE middle of August 1980, just a week after my visit with Grampa, Mom phones at dawn. "Gram found Grampa on the bathroom floor when she woke," Mom says. Her voice has an intoxicated quality, as if she is a little thrilled to be the messenger of this news. "She couldn't rouse him. He's passed away."

"Oh, Mom," I moan. I curl into my nightgown. I just want to be held.

"Uh huh," Mom says. "This is rough. And there's a lot to do. How quickly can you get here?"

"Um," I say, "I don't know. I'll call you back once I know the bus schedule. I'll try to be home before dinner."

AT the funeral, Mom tells the rabbi (who is new to my grandparents' temple), he might talk with me to learn about Moe. "She spent time with him, going through pictures," Mom says. I notice her pride in me; I notice the stiff arch in her back.

Gram moves among us at a steady pace, nodding to her friends and neighbors. She will live forever, I think, despite her disappointments. That evening, while Mom and I make sandwiches from a platter of meats and smoked fish, I realize that the people who attended the funeral know only *Gram.* "Did Grampa have any friends?" I ask. "Or even business associates?"

"No," she says, somberly. "Grampa always found reason to cut people off, especially people he liked."

"Why?" I ask. *He never cut* me *off.*

Mom shrugs. "I don't know," she says. Without thought of a chair, she bites into her sandwich.

"Listen," Mom says, changing the subject. "Ida shouldn't be alone now. I can't say I blame Aunt Rita for already returning to Great Neck; I can't say

I'm not pissed about it either. But this is beside the point. What do you think of a week with Old Ida?"

I know she's asked only because she doesn't want to do it, but still I feel honored by the invitation. I feel that Mom's recognized my maturity. Besides this, the Coffee Cup can get by for a week without me; and school doesn't resume for ten more days.

IT'S eleven o'clock when Gram finally plops on her chair in the TV room. "I feel so strange," she says.

"How so?" I ask.

"I don't know," she says. "Maybe like I've lost some weight."

We sit, not turning on the TV, not talking much. Her neighbors' lights go off. "I guess it can be pretty dark at night," Gram says.

"Are you tired?" I ask.

"You mean do I want to go to bed yet? No."

"I could give you a massage," I say. I've been reading *The Art of Massage* at the bookstore, and wanting to try the strokes they show.

"No," she says curtly. "I'll just have a hot bath."

"Okay," I say, at once disappointed and relieved that she's turned me down. "I'm going to bed."

"All right," Gram sighs, "I'll see you in the morning."

I sleep in the guest room. Some evenings, Mom and Norm join us for dinner, which I usually prepare. The ladies from Gram's card club stop over a couple of times, and the rabbi pays a visit. Mostly, in the quiet of Grampa's absence, it's just the two of us.

One morning, while combing through the drawer with the old pictures, I spot a well-worn leather binder. I take it in my hands and open it slowly, aware there may be things in it I should not be privy to, deciding, with each slow second of opening, that I want to know what's in here.

Grampa's naturalization papers slip out. I see the telegram that came from Russia the day he and Gram married, and a few newspaper clippings about the money and time he gave to Zionist organizations. Mostly the pages are filled with poems Grampa either wrote himself or copied down. The papers smell and show signs of age. I want them.

Gram's in the den, repotting an African violet that has outgrown its tiny pot. "Can I have these?" I ask, afraid she'll say no.

"But what'll you do with them?"

"I don't know," I say. "I just know I want them."

Gram shrugs. "I suppose," she says.

Later, Mom and I drive to the thrift store to give away Grampa's one good suit. I tell her about the papers I found, and that Gram said I could keep them. "I'm not sure I want you to have them," she says sternly.

"Why not? The binder's just got quotes and poems he wrote down. Listen—" I say, taking the book out from my backpack. " 'You can cuss him out till you have nothing but holy thoughts left in you,' " I read; and

Strange am I, and wild, and new.
Oh, can your loving have me free,
when out of the dark I come to you.

"That's one's called 'The Unborn,' " I say.

"He did have a sensitive side," Mom sighs. "And he was also a bastard, Hannah," she says, accelerating to drive through a yellow light. "Don't forget it."

I RETURN to school and waitressing, and to writing in my journal. In the middle of January 1981, I wake early one morning with a dream so strange it stays with me until I write it down.

Mom dies and lives as a ghost. I go to Gram's closet to write Mom's eulogy, and make myself free.

When I tell my new friend, Julie, the dream, she says it sounds like I'm blessed by an angel, because the dream tells me where to go for help.

"Help," I say, mouthing the word as if I'm still in the veil of the dream. "Because I'm not free now."

A MONTH after my dream, I go home again, to Cleveland. As my ride drops me off in our driveway, Mom peeks out the front door. If we had tails, they'd wag. We beam at each other as we make our way to the kitchen, then embrace.

"Oh, Mom, you'll never guess!" I say, hugging her longer than I usually do, noticing her familiar awkwardness while I hold on. "Marie Delaney, the writer who edits the *Ann Arbor Weekly*, wants to publish a poem I wrote about Channa!"

Mom looks confused. "Channa? My grandmother? When did you write a poem about *Channa?*"

"Oh, a while ago," I say. "Gram gave me a photograph of her that week after Grampa died." I barely take a breath to tell her my other good news— "And yesterday, Marie, who comes to the Coffee Cup, offered to work with me on my writing!" My happiness spouts out of my ears, out of my skin.

Mom shakes her head slowly, smiling a reserved grin that does not mirror my own. "These kinds of things aren't for me, my love." She reaches for her Pall Malls.

I give a simple shrug just as Mom leans back against the kitchen counter to light up, and Norm comes into the kitchen from watching TV. A large company recently took over his pharmacy and laid him off for two months. He's just returned to work.

"Hi, Daddy," I say.

"Hello, old girl." He gives me a quick grin, then opens the freezer for ice cream.

"I hear you're not a housewife anymore," I say.

Mom lets out a strange sound—a grunt someone might make if they were on the toilet.

"Nope," Norm says. "Not anymore."

"Mom?" I ask, "are you okay?" Usually at this juncture—with Daddy returning to TV—my mother and I begin a conversation at the kitchen table that continues at least until midnight. But now, without answering my question, Mom wraps herself tightly in her bulky, gray cardigan and heads upstairs.

Something's wrong. Helpless, I follow her out of the kitchen with my eyes. The air here has distinctly changed. My heart has turned small and tightened. *Is it stopping?* My neck has stiffened.

"Daddy?" I ask, wandering into the den, certain that my calling him a housewife is the cause of our changed air. "Did I say something wrong? Did I offend you?"

"Nope," he says. "That's what I was." He takes a new, remote control gadget, aims it at the TV until he finds a station he likes. I linger in the den, dazed. I'm dazed, but I also feel wide awake. "Maybe she was expecting you'd be a reporter with a real job," Norm says. "Not a poet." His eyes stay fixed on the screen.

I make my way to Mom's room. I'm drawn there, though my body has become heavy like a piece of furniture. The bedroom door is open a crack; through it I see a red glow, her cigarette's tip. She's pulled down the shades. I can scarcely make out the silhouettes of what are still my familiars: Mom's long, mahogany dresser, the four-poster bed, the blue robe that wraps her body as she lies propped up on pillows.

"Mom?"

She inhales deeply on her cigarette.

"Can I come in?"

"Housewife," she mumbles. "How dare you." Her voice is guttural, low. Her bedroom, strangely, is clean. There are no piles on her dresser or beside it, and the TV is new. The nightstand beside her holds only a lamp, a phone, and a clean ashtray. She holds the cigarette pack and matches in her hands.

I stay near the doorway, afraid to enter the room any further, let alone move to my place beside her. I've fallen from her grace, and I know it.

Mom inhales another puff.

"Mom," I plead, "I just asked Daddy if I offended him. He said, 'That's what I was.' I don't think he feels disrespected at all."

"I see." She speaks like she is an interrogator of war crimes and whatever I say cannot be believed. Her gaze is on the blank TV. She doesn't turn to look at me. "I don't respect you anymore," she says. "So I no longer respect my-self."

She exhales a long beam of smoke, stubs out the cigarette, and leaves us completely in the dark.

THE next morning, I stay in my bed as long as I can. I smell her coffee and smoke, then hear the toilet flush. Heavy with fear and lack of sleep, I slip a flannel shirt over my nightgown and button it. I tie the drawstring of my sweatpants. She's not in the kitchen, which gives me a moment's relief. While I fill the teakettle with fresh water, I notice how flat and rigid my body is, standing parallel to the stove.

Mom lies in a limp, blue heap on the family-room sofa. I stand at the room's threshold, gripping both hands around the warm mug. Mom's eyes have a glossy sheen. Her mouth hangs open.

"Mom?" She looks like she might be in a trance.

"What?" She moves her head a slow inch to look at me directly and glare.

"Last night . . ." I'm fumbling.

"No more," she says. She speaks slowly in a monotone driven by will or fatigue, maybe both. "You will have to leave. You will have to take your things."

"What?" I ask. My voice alerts me to my meekness and strength. "What do you mean?"

"I mean get out of my house. Today would be best. If not today, then to-morrow."

"But, Mom," I say, resting my mug on the bookcase just inside the room, intending to spark rational discussion.

"There's nothing to talk about," she says. Her lips quaver, and she puts her hands to her face to cover her tears.

For a few moments, I just watch her. *What do I do now?* some voice within me wails. *She's disintegrated.*

Pack your bag, another voice whispers. *Phone for a cab to take you to the bus station. Go home—to Ann Arbor.*

IN the evening, I stand in the dark near our front door, waiting for the taxi that will turn into our driveway and take me away. Mom lies upstairs in bed, her door shut. Daddy has poured Stouffers' beef stroganoff—boiled in a plastic pouch—into a bowl. He sees me getting ready to leave. "Take care of yourself, old girl," he says. He takes his dinner to the family room and turns on the TV: this rift will not be his affair.

I zip up my down jacket to prepare for the cold outside; I straighten the handles of my suitcase so I can grasp them easily once the cab arrives. I look down the street, entirely dark, then scan our living room, as if looking might break the numbness I've begun to feel, and help me come alive.

My eyes rest on my mother's desk. I walk over to it, open the bottom drawer. Just as headlights beam through the large front window of our house, I spot the manila envelope that I know holds photographs of Mom and her grandmothers—Leah and Channa. I take the envelope from the drawer, and slide it into my purse. I pull on my gloves, pick up my bag, and head toward the driveway.

LEAH

born c. 1869

in Dvinsk, Latvia

A GROYSE *gedile hot mir getrofn.* A big deal it happened to me. I hit the jackpot. *Ikh bingeborn gevorn.* I got born.

In Dvinsk I got born, with the name Leah Alterman, Vulf's daughter. Thirty-five versts from Riga we live. The Czar, he owns our land, he tells what we can keep on it, what we can't keep. Just four goats and some chickens means a lot of trouble. The Czar's men come whenever they want, spit on our scholars, take the women to the fields and roll on us, make us dirty like animals, like them.

Children give a little bit of joy, sure. But after fourteen winters, I've seen plenty die before they get to their first day of school. Girls we sometimes lose before they can mind the littler ones. Winters are cold, very cold. We have the one stove only, and two beds for all the children, eight of us, plus a little mat made of hay. Because I'm the only girl who lives, I get the mat. Sure, it's hard for me, to be the only girl. Some nights, so cold they are, I bring in a goat to share my mat, keep me warm.

My dear father, my tatte, he works in the tannery. He gets a little bit of rubles from it. My brothers go with him, of course. In the summer we sell eggs from our chickens at the market. In the fall we trade our extra for apples. Tatte, he likes my tzimmes, my stew, even without raisins. On Shabbes he takes my brothers to shul, to study Torah with Reb ha-Cohen.

Mamme and I, to wash the linens and the clothes, we carry them with the scrubbing board to the lake. In winter, we wash through a hole in the ice.

Sometimes on the way back, my brothers' pants turn to ice. A whole verst it is—nearly a mile. We get home, I fork hay to the goats, Mamme starts the cooking. On the string near the stove, I put the laundry to dry.

Night and day, we haul water from the cistern out back. To cook and wash the pots for eight people means a lot of buckets. On the days we bathe, *vey iz mir.* You don't want to hear what I have to say about that.

My mother is a *shtilinke,* a quiet one. Which is to say she doesn't complain much. What else is to talk about, but complaints? She works all the days. She eats a little, she sleeps a little, she goes back to work. She has Shabbes of course. After blessing the candles, she whispers each of our names, so God is reminded of us. So, then she has a day for rest.

I think we are a pretty family. Dark eyes we have, dark curls, and sturdy bones. If you take a look behind the eyes, anybody can see, my tatte and my brothers are sharp, good with the books. Me, I am a short girl. But from all the water I haul, I have good muscles—like a donkey. And, when our new goat won't let her baby nurse, I'm the one who clears her teats each morning, and gets the little kid to drink from my bowl.

Like I say, I am the only girl who lives. The one before me, Golda, had only two years. The one after my brother Avram, Sora, she lived through a bad, bad winter, then took sick in the spring. She had maybe ten winters, and the best giggle in all of Dvinsk.

So, even though I'm a girl, to Mamme, I am a blessing. I am her help.

WHEN I am nearly an old maid, nineteen winters, a neighbor girl whose aunt is Yente Malke, she says there's a man with an eye on me. For a few days, while I cook and wash and haul the water, I have little birds in my bosom. Like dreams. I wish for a man with eyes that tell me to him I am beautiful. A man who will buy from the Yiddish book peddler, and read books with me after sunset with help from candles. For this I wish.

Then my father tells me, ya, in two weeks I will have a wedding.

"Who is it?" I ask him.

"Who is it? It is a man," he says. "A good man, a wise scholar. You'll see."

Mamme is quiet, quiet. I think, for her this is not so easy. She thinks she will be alone with the work now. "Mamme," I say. "I will live near enough, right? We can still go together to the lake, right? And it will be a while before I have babies. So I can still help you at the market, too."

"We'll see," she says. Tatte has left the room.

The night before the wedding, Mamme and I are alone, making the challah. Mamme is heavy, sad like the dough after you punch it down. We each braid a long loaf, put them in to bake. Where Tatte usually sits, in our one chair with arms, she sits. So, I sit too. I think, maybe she has a blessing for me. I know talking for her is not easy. So, I wait. My heart feels like a flower, wide open. I wait to hear something nice, something beautiful.

But then with a fist she pats her mouth. "Leah, Leah," she says. Little tears come down. "It's Yeshia Zeitlin your father arranged for you to marry. The scholar."

I don't know the name. Mamme, she keeps looking at me, not talking. Her eyes are dark like an iron skillet with a thin layer of oil. I smell the challah just then, giving the air a bit of sweet.

"Yeshia Zeitlin . . ." I say. With his name on my lips, I recognize. *"YESHIA ZEITLIN?! Yeshia Zeitlin has five children!* A widower he is—from a wife dead only two months!"

Mamme nods. "The oldest is Tamara, your age. You know her, ya? She'll be your help."

My hands, my heart too, they turn to nervous fists. I want to shove Mamme out of Tatte's chair. I am ashamed to say it, but maybe you can understand. I have nothing but a womanish brain after all: I want to shove her out so *I* can sit in that chair with arms. So if I live twenty years more, at least I'll have this little bit of comfort for my memories.

YESHIA, he isn't my dream. I think he knows it, because he says thank you a lot. Otherwise, with me he doesn't have much to say. He lives seven years after we marry, long enough for his younger ones to mind me as their mother. Long enough to leave me three children of my own, not counting the one that dies before it gets born. Long enough to see I can make the goat's milk into cheese and sell it at the market, like his first Mrs. Zeitlin.

M O I S H E , he is my boy. Raisl is my first, then Masha after Moishe. From when Moishe was a baby, four years old, even three, he comes to help me without my asking. So many boys, especially that age, their help makes more work. But Moishe, his help helps. This boy will carry the logs to the stove from the outside, pile them neat yet. At the market, he calls out, "Goat's milk cheese! My mother made it! If you buy some, she gives me a slice of her challah, so buy some!" With Moishe around, we have plenty of fun. Plus, we can sell anything.

The day Moishe turns seven, Yeshia is dead only two winters. Yitzak, the only boy of the first Mrs. Zeitlin, he can do a little fixing of watches. Not all watches, but some. From who knows where, Yitzak brings me walnuts, a quart of sour cream, and apples—treasures. "For kuchen," he says. "For Moishe's birthday."

But Moishe says, "No. Bring it to the market, Mamme. We should call it something special, sell it at Tamara's stall. We'll get good prices." Yeshia's daughter Tamara, she got married fast after I came to live in her tatte's house. She got pregnant fast, too. So, now she and her husband have a business of selling cloth she gets special from Riga.

"With chutzpah such as this to fill a boy of seven winters," says Chava, Yeshia's oldest daughter not yet married. "Where does he put the Creator? Send him already! To America."

Moishe already has put my pastry board on the table, and the bucket of flour. Of course, he hears his brother and sister talk about him. He puts his fists on his hips, and he turns to them and he says, "Another hard winter, I don't want. I'd rather have a chicken next winter than kuchen today. So, let's get cooking. For the market."

We all laugh. Except for Moishe, my taskele. I pull him to me for a special squeeze. Sure. It's not just me who admires this boy.

But where does it come from, such ambition? Not from the rebbe, I think, and not from his father. Not from me.

ONE day just after he is bar mitzvah, my boy says to me, "Mamme, I want we should build another room. We'll make an inn for the people who are traveling. Tomorrow, I'll go to the mill for wood planks. I can make it a nice room. Yakov Levinson says I can rent his cart to bring back what I buy from the mill."

He tells me this just before sunset on *Erev Shabbes,* the beginning of Sabbath. He tells me our landlord, Mr. Ilyitch, has given permission to this deal—and next month, he'll raise our rent. So, I am putting out on my table the cloth my parents gave me at my wedding, and I have a puzzle. "Could be good," I says, worrying already we have more rent. "But it's Shabbes, Moishe."

"Ya," he says. A "Ya" like to him this is no big deal. Onto the table I put the silver candlesticks the first Mrs. Zeitlin got when she married Yeshia. Usually when I get this far in making Shabbes, I start to feel it. The flowers sewn into the white cloth, the shine from the silver, just to look on them makes me feel like a queen. A queen who could rest for a day. When I lift my hands to bless the candles, to myself I always think, for a whole day I don't have to move an inch.

With this plan in Moishe's head, I look on him like he is *meshugge.* He looks back at me with eyes that have room only for what he plans. He tears a piece of Raisl's fresh challah for himself, dunks it in my pot of borscht, fills his mouth. Chava and her next sister are married now, in their own little houses. Raisl and Masha have gone to bring a bit of cheese to my mother for Shabbes. Raisl, I think she has a crazy dream to marry Menachem Weinberg, our young doctor in Dvinsk. Masha, she is too young for dreams.

I sit on a chair. "I'm stunned, Moishe," I says. My feeling is not like the night I learned I would marry Yeshia. No, that night the shock I got lit me up with angry fire. I use that fire still—to move my bones. To cook and wash and stay awake the nights the children are sick. But this shock, it comes over me like cold water from a bucket. In a whisper, I say again, "It's Shabbes."

Moishe's voice has muscle like a horse. "Not for the men at the mill who sell the boards to build a new room," he says.

"I didn't say, for those men. They're *goyim!* For you, it's Shabbes. For me."

"I paid already Yakov Levinson to use his cart," he says. And he takes from my pot of borscht again.

I just sit. Always he eats like this, and I don't mind. This day, I mind. But what do I have to do about it? For Moishe, his matter is settled. For me, Shabbes is nearly here.

Vey iz mir. He will use the rubles my brother gave him at his bar mitzvah to buy at the mill his boards. Can you imagine that? To give a boy money at the time he's called to read the Torah? Yeshia, if he knew, would roll over, I'm sure. The man who's called to read who gives money to the *shul!* I don't say anything when Chaim, my brother, gives him these rubles. What could I say? I could say something. Maybe it's my biggest sin that I kept my mouth shut. But what do I know?

What I know is Moishe thought to take this money and build us a room to rent. Because some nights, now that we have trains coming through Dvinsk, we have people stopping here on their way to America. At the station, Moishe knows they ask for supper or a place for their bones to rest. I see the tight knot what gets made in Moishe's belly every time he hears the train whistle. Because to him it means he loses a ruble.

Only thirteen winters, my boy has, and a mind what gets happy when he fills his pocket with rubles. Sure, rubles are nice. But I have a bad feeling for all of this, even though, of course, we could use extra money.

I get up from my chair to put on my Shabbes dress. "It's your rubles, Moishe," I says. "What you do with your rubles is your own decision."

Sure, sure, maybe I sound smart. Like I have let my son become his own man. But for me, something has come undone—like shoelaces I thought I tied tight enough to last all day, then I find out no, they're good as noodles.

After the children go to bed, I notice a strange thing: one Shabbes candle burns out halfway, from a wick stuck in the wax. I think: the *Shekhinah,* the Divine Presence, has left our house early. It worries me, let me tell you. It will be something to live with.

Emes is nor bay got; un bay mir a bisl. The truth of it rests with God alone. And a little bit with me.

———

THE next day, when Moishe has all his boards, and he's ready to find strong men to help him build his new room, I put my worries into making a big cholent for him, and an apple kuchen, too. But so excited Moishe is, with his dream coming true, his new boards and nails, he doesn't even notice the smells coming from the kuchen, or the sweet smile on Raisl's face. She braided the pastry herself, took it from the oven exactly when it's done perfect. But Moishe doesn't want dinner this night. "Mamme," he nods, taking off his coat, taking a challah roll from the basket Masha puts to him. "Raisl," he says; "Masha." And off he marches to settle with another helper boy before the light is gone.

In this moment, I am glad to have daughters with me in the kitchen. Even if I don't talk, I think they know my feeling—that this boy who is maybe the favorite of each of us doesn't have ears for his mother right now.

Like a happy little army, four boys come to us the next morning. Moishe, he comes to the kitchen for apple kuchen for each boy, which the night before he was too excited to eat. He doesn't even ask me can we feed them! Of course, I would say of course. But he doesn't even ask!

A yung mit beyner he is, my son, a powerhouse. I hear one of the Steinberg boys say it, after Moishe tells them all what to do, and he is yet younger than this Steinberg boy.

Raisl and me, we are in the kitchen when Moishe takes the pastry. Once he leaves we make a big bowl of chopped liver and another of cabbage salad. We hardly talk. We slice the bread we'd figured would last us till Shabbes, spread onto it chopped liver. I hear myself mumble, "It panics me."

I see how Moishe's chutzpah has set us all in motion—the helper boys, Raisl, and Masha, and me, those boards going up so fast. *"Redele dreyt zikh,"* I think, "the wheel—the world—turns itself." But Moishe, with his little bag of rubles, he makes it turn faster.

This is my panic.

IT'S past Sukkot, the holiday of the fall harvest. I walk to the market through bitter air. "Nice to see you," says Rivke Plotkin when I arrive to her stall. "With that scarf, you always look nice."

Rivke has a round body, with soft curves—little dips and valleys what can take troubles and hold them. Our mothers had us in the belly at the same time. She also helped me birth my babies. From Rivke I buy goat's milk when I don't have enough to make cheese.

"Thanks," I says. I know she likes this scarf, the color of blood. My mother sewed it up when I left her to marry Yeshia, he should rest in peace. I'll never know how she got it, cloth so warm and soft. Well, I have a feeling Rivke has something on her mind. I don't say much back to her.

"And *mazl tov,*" she offers me, "that Yeshia's girls are all married."

"Ya," I say. "It leaves me with only Moishe and Yitzak and my own girls."

"My boys are making their plans," she says. She keeps her eyes down as she ladles her milk into my jar. She moves slow.

"What?" I say, like I am a fool at the beginning of learning. But of course she is talking about something what I don't want to hear.

"Leah, we have to talk about it," Rivke insists, "the Czar's conscription. Every Jewish boy must serve his army."

I look on Rivke with blank eyes, because I know it's time to stop pretending I will not lose my boy. Again she says, but more slowly, "Every Jewish boy must serve his army. For twenty-five years. The Czar gives each boy a baptism, then makes him work like a slave."

Like it wants to run off screaming, my jaw sticks out—but it's stuck to the rest of my face. Then I get my words out. *"Got meiner vu bistu?* God— where are you? *Vu bistu?!"*

Rivke, she stops her work, she shows me her wet eyes, her scared feeling, then looks quick to the ground. Rivke. She got married before me by three winters at least. She has five sons. I like also to count her girl who got born dead, the one the rebbe said would have no name or funeral because she didn't live thirty days. I helped with that one's birth. And I got such anger for Reb ha-Cohen when he said that stupid law, anger what helped Rivke get hers. But now, she looks frail like a chicken with its neck on a log. Winters, I've seen her manage, and the days of potatoes only. She even has a husband who sometimes drinks on holidays besides Purim. But now, her candle burns low.

"My husband won't leave," she whispers. "He won't leave his mother. It means in a few weeks I won't see my older boys again. To America or Palestine they'll go, without us. A place called South Africa they also talk of." The way she holds her arms to her bosom, they look like sleeping babies.

"Maybe, Rivke, in another country our boys will know freedom. The kind for what we just have dreams."

"Ya, maybe," she says. "But right now I spit on freedom. Right now all I think is because of that Czar, I won't meet the girls who will be the mothers to my grandchildren. And the grandchildren—who knows if I'll even get to know their names."

"A curse to the Czar!" I say. *"Oyf doktoyrem zol er es oys gebn*—May he have gold enough to fill ten ships, and may he spend it all on doctors!"

Of course, I feel *rakhmones* on Rivke, compassion. For me it is not my worst time. Yeshia's son Yitzak talks with a dream for France; the girls' husbands think if they move to Riga, it will not be so bad.

My own, my Moishe, he is a baby yet—too young for the Czar.

IT passes, a quick year with Moishe, Raisl, Masha, and me. Yitzak has gone to France. The inn does well for us. Since we have the railroad station, Dvinsk is a good place for travelers from Polotsk or even Minsk to rest from their long journey to the new worlds. So, we have a business.

Moishe, his body gets big and strong. For the son of a scholar, he sure has shoulders. Like an ox he gets. He has muscles coming from out his *tefiln,* his prayer straps. And you can see the muscles through his coat. It's a strange thing to me—because Yeshia, his body was like a bird's. Like most men who sit all day in shul, reading.

One day maybe a year after he is bar mitzvah, Moishe takes my cheese to market and meets a Mr. Diamont visiting from America. Zionism this man talks, we should make a Jewish state. And meanwhile he tells my son, "Who should mind if you do business on Shabbes?"

When Moishe tells me such ideas, my heart pounds! I think, God should mind! Your father, he should rest in peace, should mind! And *I* mind!

I mind, but I say nothing.

My son comes home from the market. All my cheese he's sold. He practically sings it that Mr. Diamont talks smarter than our Reb ha-Cohen. The rebbe's ideas aren't modern, and Moishe says he wants to be a modern man. It pains me, to hear about a man who says if you want, you should work on Shabbes—and that this same man should interfere with the work of God and make a scheme for a Jewish state.

Well. From Mr. Diamont Moishe buys himself a pair of spectacles. He looks smart, even if I don't like the notions in his good-looking head. My son looks now like a man you don't want to cross. I see Perle Fineberg, my cousin Kayla's daughter, with eyes on him at the market the next day. Out loud I hear my own voice say it: Moishe is a man. Inside, another voice: *at the next roundup, the Czar will take him.*

Raisl is by now a young woman with a little dowry, a kind smile, and a lot of hard work in her hands. A real good Jewish woman. She's pretty, too, Raisl. Long hair she has, dark. She keeps it usually in a braid on her back. Her cheeks—rosy. Like her name. Raisl bakes the bread for the inn and makes the cheese we sell at the market. I cook, Masha keeps the rooms clean. Masha is just like Yeshia—she likes books. When the Yiddish book peddler comes, it's her holiday.

And Moishe. What would I do without Moishe? He brings in the buckets of water from the well we share with the Eisenbergs and the Solowitzes, just out back. He splits the wood. He can tell people about the trains that go to Riga. He talks to the Czar's men when they come asking about our accounts. And he makes my heart sing when he eats my apple pie and likes it so much. He makes happiness for the girls, too—he reads Raisl's poetry and says he likes it. And he's the one who gives Masha the rubles to buy her books. Yeshia's girls each have babies now. For them, Moishe always has treats. Even if he sometimes does business on Shabbes, he still makes our hearts sing.

I remember what all I said to Rivke two winters before, and what she said back to me. We mothers, we'll never get to see freedom or the grandchildren from our sons. *Ach!* I know more than one woman who poked in her son's ears, then dunked him ten times in a well to make sure he'd go deaf. For a deaf boy, the Czar's army has no use. I take to standing still, thinking about this, when I should milk my goats, or bring water to the house, or clean the root cellar.

Feh. I have a mind like a pot of tzimmes: a mess full of thoughts.

So, it comes Moishe's time to get a physical examination from the Czar's men. For three weeks he eats only water and a bite of bread here and there. Such a good job he does—he makes himself very sick. He gets so skinny, it makes me weak to look on him. I almost wish he would let the Czar take him already so he would at least have skin to pinch. I am so worried, you can't imagine.

Well, he goes for his examination. And to the Cossacks he is a healthy Jewish boy with muscle plenty enough. To the Cossacks skinny cheeks don't matter a thing. They just wants Moishe in their army. To do their hard labor.

Moishe is not just sick now, he is shocked, too. Because he had no doubt his plan would work, and he would stay with me and maybe build another room. He comes home for his last night of me to feed him, and of course he is too sick to eat. Anyway, I don't have sweet-and-sour fish, his favorite, because I also was sure he would be with me until I died. But now, he is headed to Siberia.

It's a dark hour, let me tell you. I put him to bed early. "But Mamme," he says, "I want we should talk about the accounts."

I tell him no. For me it will be better he should go into the world a healthy man. I will learn the accounts on my own. I am strong about this, and he is too weak from skinniness to fight me.

I leave him at the bed and go to the kitchen to prepare him a sack. My heart is heavy like a bucket of water I have to pull up from the well. Rivke's words I remember. When I tell her my troubles, she smiles on me and says, "God will provide." Then she smiles to make me smile. "If only God would provide until He provides."

Moishe, his words I remember also. "If prayers worked," he says, "the people would pay you to do them."

Well, anyway, I tip my eyes up—to Him. "In case you didn't notice, Mr. God," I say, "I need help. A big help!"

Then who do I see in my doorway but a Cossack what had bought from us a loaf of bread the week before. I figure he has something to tell me. Ha! I have things to tell him, too. But of course I keep shut my mouth.

"I hear, Mrs. Zeitlin," he says, "that your boy will be joining the army soon."

"Right," I say.

"I could arrange something else for him, if you like."

He smells so dirty, this man. Every word from him sounds *treyf* to me, like a lie. He has a belly that comes way out. I know it's full of pigs and beer. I close the door to my house so I can hear better what he has to say. "I could arrange for your son to take the boat to America," he says. "Next week."

A few days before, this would not have been good news. But now, my heart takes a leap. Of course, to him I don't let on.

"What would this be, such an arrangement?" I ask him. Like we are in something of a business.

"To enjoy your daughter's company," he says, "tonight." He has a grin so full of dirt, a casket it could cover. "The older one—you call her Raisl, ya?"

My body gets hot fast like a stove with too much pitch. I'm not shocked, no. I have lived by now a long time. And now I feel a storm rising in me, a fury I can't calm down. Because a stupid soldier has given me a choice: Moishe or Raisl. I have a fury because—God who curses me—I'll have to make it.

The dog, he grins like he doesn't have a doubt in his stupid head. I leave him to wait outside while I go back into my house. Raisl, she is in the kitchen still, scrubbing pots and making the bread.

I pass the bed where Moishe sleeps. Ya. He's got his troubles. What good will it do for him to hear me think? Let Moishe sleep. I see our extra room for travelers, empty.

To that Cossack pacing outside in the cold night, I whisper, *"Zoll er krenken un gedenken.* May he suffer and remember."

Raisl now. She never asks for anything, always has a nod and a shy smile for me in our kitchen. Of course we never keep track of girls' birthdays, but she is almost eighteen winters. A ripe fruit. A quiet fire, waiting. Like me when I got married. Because she is such a help, Raisl, I have held off the matchmaker.

I think Raisl is about to ask me, how is Moishe. But quick, I hear words spill out of me first. "The soldier who likes your breads is here. If you go to the renter's bed with him, he says Moishe can go to America."

What have I said? I have given her *the stupid Cossack's question!*

Oh Raisl, Raisl. She is sweet, and smart, too. She knows what a night like this will mean for her. I don't think it shocks her. The shock is I am the one asking. Like my mother shocked me, the night she said my father arranged for me to marry Yeshia the next day, and become a mother to his five children.

I don't see even a little glare from Raisl's eyes. She makes her lips tight, she bows her eyes and her chin a bit. "All right," she says. She doesn't look on me. I am grateful, that makes it easier. But maybe not. If she could get angry, it maybe could help her. She takes off her apron, all floury. "In fifteen minutes the bread will be ready," she says. "You should take it out."

If one good deed leads to another, to where would an *aveyre* lead—a sin such as this?

MOISHE, I don't tell him this deal I arranged. In 1909, when I say goodbye finally, it's like seeing him go to his casket. I figure I'll never look on him again. So, what good will it do him to tell what I asked Raisl? That's what I think.

Well. I didn't know Raisl would get pregnant from such a deal. I didn't know Moishe would turn his thoughts against his favorite sister when he found out she had a baby, and think that she was *treyf,* unclean—for being a woman with a son but no husband.

In 1929 he comes back to me an American man, rich and married, traveling on Shabbes no less. We live in Riga now. We came here after the war. Masha has married Menachem Weinberg, the doctor. Raisl had her eye on him once. Raisl and her son Daniel and I live with Masha's family in an apartment of three rooms. Moishe, he has a fancy suit with stripes and a vest to match, shiny shoes, spectacles made from gold wires, and no beard—a razor he takes each morning to his face! "Moe" he wants I should call him now, not Moishe.

"So, Moe," I tell him, "This is your nephew, Daniel, my grandson. You know just after you left, Raisl married a nice Jewish man, Daniel's father. But then her husband went to America, and he doesn't even write her what city he lives in. If not for Dr. Weinberg, and Tamara and her husband, who have a grocery shop here now in Riga, I don't know what we'd do to get by."

Moe, he shrugs. Like he's heard plenty of stories like this. Plenty of nice Jewish girls whose husbands forget about them once they get to America. He shrugs, and then he offers we should all go back with him. "All the books you could want," he tells Masha, swooping her baby boy into the air. "In the libraries, they're free. What with all the bookstores, you can make your own library. Plus," he tells Tamara, "we have restaurants what serve kosher food." Then, to me he gives a mink stole. To Raisl he hardly says hello.

Masha, Tamara, their husbands, they want to stay here. "It's good enough for us here," they say.

"It's safer there," Moishe says, like he knows something we don't know.

"We know it's hard here," I says. "We know, and we manage."

"You want we should leave Mamme?" Masha asks. "I got a nice boy, and Ruchl here. It's too much trouble for me, America."

But Raisl says, "I want to go. Daniel and I will go."

Moishe, he looks at her like she just made an insult on him.

So, I take my son aside. I tell him the truth about Raisl, her son, and the Cossack. And then it is my turn for a shock. "I knew it from the day I left for America," he says. "The Cossack told me himself, the day he signed my papers."

He has eyes on me like a madman. His mouth he fills with my kuchen. I made it extra—extra walnuts, extra raisins. Cinnamon and sugar, of course. Well. It doesn't make his heart any sweeter, all this extra.

"Moishe," I say. "Such bitterness you have. And for your sister, not for the Czar!"

He glares at me. "She shouldn't have done it," he says. "I could have found another way!"

To myself I think, look who talks. His way, to make himself skinny, didn't work. Such a chill goes through me, I can't tell you. I pull around me the shawl of mink he brought, tight. *A shande un a kharpe*—a shame and a disgrace, I think: this is what I raised. A man who can buy mink in America to warm his mother's shoulders. But in his heart he has ice only—for the choice I made that bought him freedom.

THREE

1981-1982

HANNAH

I N Ann Arbor, I walk to Kerrytown, the farmer's market, for avocados and red leaf lettuce, Dover sole and fresh dill—things I've never seen in Mom's refrigerator. I buy a stem of purple flowers—the saleswoman calls them on-cidium. I walk back to my studio, trading the handles of my canvas bag from one hand to the other. Then I take the whole sack into my arms like a baby. *Is there something I missed in the last twenty-one years as Celia's daughter? Something about the way the world works? Something about* her?

I sit on the steps of the university's Angell Hall to let my groceries down for a minute and watch the few students who are out walking this weekend morning. It's February. The sun is bright, and the air is cold. I wrap my arms around myself and rub, then curl my head into my lap, covering my ears with the insides of my arms. My jaw is clamped tight. My spine feels like a series of rusted hinges.

Just feel cold, for a moment. Don't do anything. Don't even rub.

This voice arrives in my head like a radio tune from nowhere. It speaks with a gentle steadiness, as if it's been counseling me for years. *Who are you?* I wonder. I lift my head, and the day's brightness stings my eyes. A young girl, maybe seven years old, walks in front of me, her mittened hand clasped in her mother's. They walk through the cold air in a synchronized stream of red scarves and blue down jackets. As they leave my view, I hear Mom's stony voice. *"There's nothing to talk about."* Compared with the gentle whisper I just heard, hers is distinctly harsh. *"I don't respect you anymore, and so I no longer respect myself."*

Mom, Mom, what do you mean?

Consider those photographs of your great-grandmothers, the ones you stole from your mother's desk.

GOD! I feel like screaming, *What's it going to take to patch this thing?*

Antsy to move again, I stand up to head home. *Let it cook ten years,* the gentle voice in my head declares. *Ten years.*

Isn't that a little excessive? Mom and I have never really fought.

I turn onto Monroe Street. *There's a lot you haven't noticed yet.*

As if in response to my questions, a flock of birds circles over my head, then settles on the telephone wire behind my house. Like schoolchildren, they're lined up in a neat row, waiting for class to begin.

AT the Coffee Cup, a woman with an old, thick polyester coat, a shopping bag, and bright red lipstick sits down at my station. Her frizzy, salt-and-pepper hair reminds me of Mom's. "My true good friend," she asks me, in a throaty voice with a broad smile, leaning slightly against the counter. "Is my credit good here? Have I paid my monthly bill?"

I look into her sparkly eyes, and smile back. "I'll ask Van," I say.

Just as I turn toward the grill, he hands me the B.L.T. for my customer in number seventeen. "My answer's no," he says, matter-of-factly. "And she can't sit at the counter unless she buys something."

My woman overhears Van's "no," laughs richly, then leaves.

My eyes linger on her as she heads toward the post office. Kathy, another waitress, catches my wandering eyes. "What's happening?" she asks, while we sort dirty dishes and silverware into the proper tubs.

"Do you think she's crazy?" I ask, feeling my eyes begin to tear. I have been wondering what craziness looks like.

Kathy's got long brown hair, tied back in a ponytail. Her face is kind of flat, like a cookie, with raisins for eyes, and an almond nose. She's not much taller than me, but she's almost six months pregnant. In front of her mushrooming belly, I feel especially little. "That woman's in God's hands," Kathy says. She puts her arm around my shoulders and gives me a squeeze.

I nod my head slowly. She's not going to answer my question, and I'm not going to press her for an answer.

Kathy is three years older than me, twenty-four, grown up enough to shake her head and smile like a mother. "You ought to be proud," she says, "of how compassionate you are."

My eyes scrunch down toward my chin as I look back at her kind face; then I hear my customer in number eleven holler for coffee.

Dear Mom,

Every enthusiasm, every success and failure, every ripple of insecurity and feeling of offense, every celebration I have experienced, I have wanted to share with you. Not only because you're my mother, but because your perceptions are so keen, and your compassion's been so large.

Mom, please call or write me. I need you.

Hannah

"I love you," she replies, on a half sheet of unlined typing paper. "I can't see you. Don't ask me to talk about it."

APRIL passes, then May. Every night after waitressing and classes, I watch sunsets from my third-story windows.

"You are the saddest-looking woman I've seen all week," Tyrone says, after I take his order for coffee and a donut. He reminds me of Sharon Johnson's boyfriend—she was a dancer in my club at Shaker Heights High. Tyrone's body is large, dark-skinned, slow-moving with quick eyes. Usually, when he sits at my station, he likes to boast about his harem; and I like to contest his usury of women. But he has also told me recently that when he broke up with his girlfriend of two years, he also lost her young son. *That* got to him. "Let me walk you home tonight," he says kindly.

I shrug, say, "Okay." I like Tyrone. As soon as the Coffee Cup's door closes behind us, I begin a nonstop monologue about all the customers I had today who went on and on with their tales of woe—and left me no tip, or a minimal one.

"Ain't it the truth," Tyrone says, patting the top of my head with his large hand. "Everybody asks for coffee. But really they want someone to listen to their stories."

"Yeah," I say, realizing by the warmth of his hand that I'm one of the ones aching to be heard.

"I'm not going to come up," he says at my door. I feel a pang of disappointment, then relief. "For us, that wouldn't be right." *Does he know what I can handle, and what I can't handle?* I nod, still feeling a little sad to return alone again to my small apartment.

I know I'm hungry for friends, but I don't really know how to tell people what's happened to me. I don't really know what has happened. My mother adored me; now, we don't even talk. I know other people have fights with their mothers, but I wouldn't call what we're in a fight. I don't know what I would call it.

WHEN the phone rings at nine-thirty the first evening in June, I leap out of bed to answer it. Phone calls always surprise me, and now I've taken to going to bed early—I like to rise with the sun and write. Besides, evenings are my loneliest time. Going to sleep early shortens that dark stretch.

"Hannah?"

"Yes." I don't recognize the warm voice.

"It's Marie Delaney."

"Oh, hi," I say, aware of the suspicion in my tone. I push my curls away from my face. My hair is shoulder length now, too short to tie back, too long to stay out of my face. I'd called Marie months ago, soon after she'd offered to look at my writing, left a message, and never heard back.

"I apologize for taking so long to return your call," she says. "My father got sick, and I went to Boston to help him."

"Oh, I'm sorry," I say, warming up to her again.

"He's better now," she says. "And I'm glad to be back in Ann Arbor. I haven't forgotten about taking a look at your work. Would you like that?"

"Yeah," I say, revving up, despite the late hour. "That'd be great."

MARIE'S house is a bungalow of three rooms on Ann Arbor's west side. When she opens her door to greet me, I notice her bones are large and sturdy. Her brown hair is in a long braid. She wears a large green T-shirt, and lets it hang out over her jeans. I figure she's at least thirty, maybe thirty-five.

We walk through her front room, lined with books; a few framed pictures rest on the shelves, and there's a large desk here, too. In the kitchen, poetry books are stacked on the counter near her phone. The table we sit at is large and round, made of dark wood. Two pink tulips tilt away from the table's center, toward us. Marie offers me a selection of herbal teas—chamomile, peppermint, even licorice. I choose licorice, a kind I've never tasted. Marie pours hot water into our mugs while my eyes wander around her kitchen, catch the butcher-block counter behind us, the knives lined on a magnet above it, a row of large jars filled with different kinds of beans, and grains shelved beside them.

"So let's see a poem," Marie says.

Out of my blue backpack, I pull a folder. "It's called 'The New Moon,' " I say. It's about my first period. I had terrible cramps, and Mom told me not to fight them; she said that fighting would make the pain worse.

"Why don't you read it aloud?" Marie asks. When I finish and look up for her expression, her chin is in her right hand. She taps her lips with two fingers, but this doesn't hide her smile. "You are a poet," she says, practically blessing me.

I feel myself blush.

"And I'm not telling you anything you don't already know about yourself," she says.

I nod. I am so young compared to Marie, and my body is so much smaller. *But I am a poet—just like her.* I look over her large, round table and think, *Someday, I'll have a big table like this.*

Marie puts her mug down, and gently raises her eyes to meet mine. "You're about to graduate, yes?"

"I have two semesters to go," I say. "Maybe three."

"What are your dreams?" she asks.

"I want to write," I say. "Or teach." The words come out thoughtfully. I wonder if she can tell from the poem that my mother won't speak to me. "I'd like to work with people who like to tell stories."

Marie tips her head and nods. "I got a call last night from a friend in Boston. She runs a program in Cambridge for women who are learning to read. She mentioned that she wants to expand the writing program. I have a hunch you'd make a great writing teacher. I have a hunch you'd have great fun at it." Her voice sounds like Mom's when we schemed my summer adventures: steady, with a kind of enthusiasm that makes the world feel inviting.

"Wow," I say, with a smile blossoming on my face so widely I feel silly. "But I won't have my bachelor's until next spring at the earliest."

"I wouldn't dwell on that. Just shoot for this, if you want it."

Biking home, I pass the market, then Angell Hall, and turn onto Monroe Street feeling like a queen. It's time to call Mom. I have news to share.

There's a letter from her waiting when I get home.

Dear Hannah,

> *I hate Cleveland—I always have. So Daddy and I will move to Seattle in September. It will also be good for me to get away from you. I don't mean to hurt you in saying this, but the truth is you don't need me—and I can't handle that. I will leave your belongings with Gram.*

She signs it *Mom*—without *love*—and includes their new address and phone number.

I run my thumb against the white sheet's edge. My fingertips slide over her new Seattle address. Then I reach for my notebook and a pen, taking them into my hands like food that might save my life. *Can anybody hear me?*

ONCE I learn I can graduate in the spring, I take out another student loan, sign up for an extra class, and cut my shifts at the Coffee Cup to three a week.

The restaurant gives me a social life, not just an income. A lot of the customers work for the post office, or in businesses downtown. I hear their stories while I take their orders and serve them food; and they notice my moods. It's easier for me to talk with my customers than with other students, though I'm not sure why.

Tuesday evenings, I go to my friend Julie Kaufman's communal house for a meal. They have a party there, once a month. But I don't see the fun in drinking or listening to loud music. I'm never sure if the person I'm talking to is drunk or high, and I can't hear anyone well enough at those parties to have a conversation. Sometimes, Julie comes to my apartment for dinner, or we go for a walk in the Arboretum. She likes to read books by Martin Heidegger. When I tell her about my mother, she asks if I feel at home in the world. "I'm not sure," I answer. "I think I am, but I'm not sure." And I wonder if Julie thinks I'm strange—because I can't shake my sadness.

Each month, when my period comes, I get violent cramps. They feel like grief, though I had periods like this before I lost my mother. Nearly every night, I dream of her: *stainless steel bricks are strapped to her feet, keeping her from floating away as she wants, while a white-haired woman insists I need a good school.* Saturdays, I bike to the farmer's market and back, write in my journal, and roast a chicken that lasts me nearly all week.

Especially while I'm bicycling, I like to imagine myself teaching and living in Boston.

But Boston is across the country from Seattle.

If calling Daddy a housewife took her away from me, I ask myself, is there a word that would bring her back? I've never really felt close to Daddy. But he's devoted to Mom. I guess she's devoted to him, too. This Sunday afternoon, in the middle of January, I think of phoning Mom. "That's a ridiculous idea," I tell myself in the middle of a paper about Paule Marshall's *Brown Girl, Brownstones,* a novel about a mother and daughter who don't get along. She's never phoned me, even to ask, How are you? I whisk dirty clothes out from my closet, separate them into whites and colors, rip the sheets off my bed: I'll go to the basement, do laundry.

When I come up, I think again of calling her.

I stand at my kitchen window, watching the street three floors below, nervously re-tucking my T-shirt into my jeans for a crisper fit. It's the same color green as one of Marie's T-shirts, but I don't let mine hang out like hers.

I take the phone from the receiver, then dial her new number.

"Hello," Mom says, in a voice that sounds normal—quiet, reserved, slightly controlled.

"Collect from Hannah," the operator says. "Will you accept the charges?"

"Uh," she says, with an expulsion of breath that makes me think that air has escaped the earpiece.

Several moments pass.

"Ma'am," the woman says, "we're waiting. Is it yes or no?"

"Mmm," Mom says.

I see the blond woman from the second floor leave our building with the man I figure is her boyfriend. I turn my back to them.

"Ma'am?"

I knew it. I shouldn't have called. I certainly shouldn't have called collect. But I have barely enough right now for food and rent, *and she's my mother, and she has money.*

"All right," Mom says. She speaks with disdain. Once the operator disconnects, Mom tells me, "This is humiliating, a collect call. Don't do it again."

As if they're sealing off the questions inside myself, my lips close in on each other. "Okay," I say, barely opening my mouth. "How are you?"

"Fine."

"How's your house?"

"Fine." She clears her throat. "We like it very much." I get the feeling she's speaking in a dark room.

"How's Daddy?"

"He's fine."

Silence. I don't know how to talk. Outside, the sky is filled with dark clouds I haven't noticed before. I lovingly hold the phone at the side of my face, hoping it might come alive, snake around, and embrace me. *Would Marie know of writers besides Paule Marshall who've written about mothers and daughters? I need other women's stories.*

"Look," Mom says, "this isn't going anywhere. I don't trust you, and so I don't have anything to say."

My body might float away or evaporate, it feels that strange. I swallow my tears. Like a hurt three year old, my voice is just above a whiny whisper. "Well, I wanted to talk to you."

"So, we're talking."

"I'd like to visit you, see your new house."

"Uh huh." She speaks mechanically, as if our sentences are transactions.

"I could come early in the summer. For four or five days."

"How would you pay for it?"

Oh God, I cringe. I nestle the side of my head against the kitchen's corner cupboard. I have to say I want something from her.

"I was hoping you'd pay for it. I'm at the limit with money. I'm still in school."

Silence again.

"I'll have to think about it," she says.

It's snowing when I hang up the phone. I cover my wool socks with plastic kitchen bags, like Gram does, then slip them in my boots. Over my turtleneck, I layer on a sweater, a down vest, and my poncho, and head out the door. As I walk toward the Arboretum, the snow conceals my tears. At the base of the Arb, I lean against a tall oak, watch snowflakes dissolve in the Huron River, and rest.

THERE'S a letter from Mom in my mailbox two weeks later. I make myself a cup of tea and set it on the small table next to my bed. I tuck myself under the covers to read.

Hannah,

I'll come right out and say that we will loan you half the fare. My thinking is that to give you the money would place strings on you and distort our relationship further. Daddy says we should give you half. I

*feel this offer of a loan is a compromise between his position and what
I really prefer—that you pay your own way.*

*However, I will not compromise on the length of your stay. Anything
less than a week would be ridiculous. It'll take at least a few days for us
to get even remotely comfortable with each other, and then there's more
to do in Seattle than you can imagine.*

We certainly hope you come.

Mom

I hug my pillow and wrap it and myself around the navy afghan Aunt
Mollie crocheted for me years ago. *What do* you *really want, Mom?* I want to
make a sound, but nothing comes. *I miss you. I'd like to see you. How could
you doubt that?*

Who could understand me now? Karen Caplan has become one of Ohio
State's star dancers. Her teachers want her to audition for a modern dance
company in New York. I'm happy for her; but now six months can go by
without our being in touch. I get out of bed, take a look at myself in the long
mirror inside my bathroom door. I still have pimples here and there, and my
tiny breasts could be a high-school girl's. But my eyes are dark and sincere. I
squeak a smile at myself. "It's going to be okay," I whisper.

*If she wants me to come for at least a week, that means she wants me to come.
Right?* When I first returned to this apartment a year ago, after the weekend
Mom told me to leave her house, I tacked a black-and-white snapshot onto
my bulletin board. It was one of the pictures in the manila envelope I took
from her desk without asking. October 1962: while my mother beams at me,
the photographer captures Celia's radiant profile. I am nearly three, looking
directly at the camera. *It sure* looks *like she loves me.*

I return to my bed. Her letter has slid under my blankets. From the
sheets, the controlled, elegant lines of her writing peek out. I don't want this
paper for a bed partner. But I'm so stiff and tired, I can't move her letter away.

"AUNT Mollie?" I say, practically gleeful that someone has accepted my collect call. Months ago, when I told her I was happy to be writing and wait-

ressing, that I looked forward to the possibility of teaching in Boston, Aunt Mollie said, "I don't exactly understand it, why such a smart girl like you would plan for a job that might never happen. But it's not for me to decide. So, I'll be happy for you. You sound happy." She feels like a friend.

"I told Mom I want to visit her," I tell Mollie now, "and she says I can come, but I have to pay for it. She says she'll loan me half the fare."

"But Celia has plenty of money!" she shouts. "And you're a student! What is she trying to prove?"

"I don't know," I say. I feel a sudden wave of hunger, though I just ate dinner.

"Well, if you want to go, I can pay for it," she says.

"Really?" I say. I'd called Mollie because she knows Mom; because Mom's behavior might sound weird to her, too. I hadn't expected her to offer me money.

"Yes, really. Celia takes after her father too much. *A toytn baveynt men zibn teg, a nar, dos gante lebn,*" she says. "You mourn seven days for the dead, a lifetime for a fool. And we have too many fools around here.

"When your mother and Rita were girls, your grandmother used to borrow money from me so they could have things like tennis lessons. They ate lamb chops off painted plates served by a maid, but Moe wouldn't give money for tennis lessons. So Ida borrowed it. She paid me back every time—slowly, but all of it. So Moe wouldn't know.

"With Moe, a person just couldn't need anything *he* didn't figure you needed. Which left out a lot of things. I always thought Moe really was crazy for your grandmother; and Ida could've wrapped him around her finger. She should have gotten what she needed or left him, simple as that."

She pauses for a moment. "I guess I shouldn't talk, Hannah. I never married. So what do I know?"

Mollie, my mother once told me, fell in love with a man just after she got out of high school, before Gram had married Moe. He was a kind man; he had a simple, successful business selling office supplies, and he adored her. But he wasn't Jewish. On top of that, Ida hadn't married yet, and Ida was the elder sister. So my great-aunt turned down the man's invitation to make a life with him.

Now, Moe's dead, and Gram and Mollie are two old women alone in Cleveland. Their sisters, Bessie and Evelyn, spend their winters in Florida. It's no secret that Gram and Mollie bug the hell out of each other. And they do it every day, too, because that's how often they talk.

"I think you know a lot, Aunt Mollie," I say.

"A gezunt oyf dayn kepele," she says. "It should be a blessing on your head."

"EXPECT me sometime in June," I write Mom. "And don't bother about loaning me any money. I'll pay my own way."

I think of enclosing a copy of one of the mythology books I'm reading now for my senior seminar. When I read the myth about the goddess Demeter and Persephone, her daughter, who were separated for such a long time, it felt like I was reading about Mom and me. But I just fold my note into the envelope, and lick it to make the seal.

APRIL. I turn on my electric typewriter and type:

ABOVE THE LOVESEAT

Above the loveseat in Gram's apartment hangs a portrait of my great-grandmother, Leah Zeitlin. My grandfather, Moe, hired someone to draw it from a photo he had taken during his visit back to the Old Country in 1930. The portrait is done in a fine lead pencil, precise enough to look like a photograph, large enough to take up the big wall above the loveseat. Leah sits in darkness, with a shiny mink stole wrapped around her shoulders. From somewhere outside the picture comes a light that bounces off her eyes. When I was a girl, spending Sundays in my grandparents' house, her black eyes came at me like bullets.

I roll the paper up high over the typewriter carriage, read the paragraph back to myself.

If I stared long enough at her portrait, would Leah talk? I roll the paper back down, and begin again to write.

Once, when I was seven, maybe eight, my grandfather came to our house and placed two dollar bills into my small hands. "Such a lucky girl," he smiled, pinching both my cheeks, "with a zaydie *who will take her to Woolworth's!"*

I got into his big, green car and sat alone with him on the front seat as we drove to the store. "In the Old Country, I once built a whole room with two dollars. So now we'll see what such a lucky girl as Hannah Felber does with her money."

He found a space right in front of the store and parked. I felt exuberant with our adventure, too. I slammed my door shut like he did, then slid my hands into my pockets.

The two bills were no longer there.

"Grampa," I cried, "the money's gone!"

He waved his fists in the air. "Trombenik! Ne'er-do-well!" he shouted. People began to stare at us. "Zoln vaksn tsibeles fun pupik! Onions should grow from your navel!" (If onions grew from my navel, I'd be a corpse, buried in dirt.)

I'm sure he didn't hear my apology, or see the terror that entered my body. After Grampa's outburst, we got back in the car. He would take me home.

Just as we turned into my driveway, he swung his head toward me like it was a bowling ball speeding down an alley, into my face. He smiled—a smile I felt travel through his whole body. "Hannah," he said, "my mother made such apple pies! High like mountains she made them. Ach—they were good!"

Does Grampa know his mom had bullets in her eyes? Did she shoot him with those bullets and make him crazy?

Maybe I got shot.

Because I love him.

On the bulletin board above my desk, I have a photo of Leah with her son—Grampa Moe. This one was taken in 1930, on his return to

Riga, after he'd become an American. Gram once told me when he came back with that picture of him and Leah, and its inscription, Mother wishes us long life and happiness and that you bring a brother for Rita, *she got an eerie feeling. That trip, he'd offered to buy tickets to America for whoever would come back with him, to Cleveland. His mother didn't go with him as he'd wanted, nor his favorite sister Masha, nor his half-sisters and their families. Only Rose came, his older sister, and her son.*

"Like an omen," Ida once said, "I had a feeling that the ones who didn't leave with him wouldn't have long lives." Gram also told me they gave Moe a small handful of apple seeds to plant in America. "We had already enough fruit growing in the yard," Ida said, as if the telling gave her a sour taste. "I suppose it was a nice gesture, but what use do I have to wait for apple seeds to make trees?" Gram scattered the seeds at the side of the house, but didn't live there long enough to see if anything grew from them.

Anyway, no brother came for Rita—my mother did, with fine features that replicate Leah Zeitlin's. They're both angry, hawk-eyed women with finely chiseled features. But Leah's anger keeps her on the ground, and moves out. My mother's rage begins way back, behind her eyes, and smolders. It doesn't shoot out like Leah's does. Instead, without notice, she might explode.

I take the paper out of my typewriter, go to the kitchen for a slice of the banana bread I made last night, and then I have to get out of the apartment for fresh air, away from the questions I can't answer. It's a Sunday afternoon, a few weeks past the spring equinox. I can bike to the Arboretum and be back for my dinner shift at the Coffee Cup.

At the river, I lay down my bike, and squat against my favorite oak, its green buds sparkling above me. The ground is covered with dark, old leaves, moist from last night's rain. My hands still buzz from writing. I close my eyes, and let my fingers swirl in the composting layers of old leaves.

I hear a man singing—I think it's a Beatles song, but I'm not sure. I sit up quickly, annoyed that my rest is interrupted. As I head to retrieve my bicycle, I spot the singer further up the river, with a notebook in his hand. It looks like Hal Riley from Shaman Drum, the bookstore. "Hal!" I blurt out, as if I'm sure it's him; as if we're old friends.

He looks my way and squints: he doesn't recognize me.

"It's Hannah," I say, "Hannah Felber. I come to the bookstore."

"Oh, hi," he says, still turned toward me.

Framed by budding trees, Hal stands tall in an olive green, flannel shirt; his hair is long enough for a short ponytail, and he has a thick, golden beard. I wear a navy sailor top over jeans, and silver earrings made in Israel that Karen gave me when we graduated from high school. New barrettes hold my hair off my face, which has two new pimples today.

We walk toward each other cautiously. "How often do you come here?" I finally ask.

"Not often," Hal says.

I nod.

"I just finished a long paper," he says. "I came here to celebrate."

I nod again. I know Hal's doing a master's degree about the lyrics of Neil Young. He wants to return to Detroit to teach juvenile delinquents in a new school he wishes had been around when he was a teenager. He told me these things the last time we talked, probably a month ago.

Around his collarbones, muscles swim like minnows, then disappear to parts I can't see. "I just finished a paper, too," I say. My body feels lit up as we stand with the trees and the spring air and look at each other. He's not Jewish, I think, as if I'm talking to Aunt Mollie, but I like him. I slip my hands into the pockets of my jeans, as if I could tuck away my nervousness. I don't really have much experience with men.

"What's your paper about?" Hal asks.

"It's a story, really. I called it 'Above the Loveseat.' "

Hal winks at me, which I'm not sure I like. I think men only do that with women they think are young. I'm twenty-two already, but he might be almost thirty. "It's not what it sounds like," I say, then change the subject. "What were you singing?"

Hal grins at my daring: he likes me. " 'Hey Hey, My My,' " he says, "a Neil Young song."

"Oh," I say. "I don't know it." *Maybe if he came here alone to celebrate, he doesn't have a girlfriend.*

"I know it just enough to sing it when I think I'm alone in the Arb," he says.

I giggle. He speaks slowly in a rich, sandy voice that makes me think of motorcycles, and I feel a distinct desire to wrap my arms around him. I've wanted to be close to other guys before, but they've always felt too far away, out of my reach.

"Oh!" he says, tapping his head lightly in recognition, "I remember you now—you're the one always checking out the new poetry titles."

I smile so warmly my pimples might not matter. "Ya," I say. "That's me."

"Olga Broumas," he says, naming my favorite poet.

"Yeah," I say, taken that he remembers. "And you write about Neil Young's lyrics."

Hal giggles, pleased, I think, that I've remembered.

"Um, I have to get back to town right now," I tell him. "I wait tables, and I've got the dinner shift tonight."

"Oh, sure. Where do you work?"

"The Coffee Cup."

"Really? I was roommates with a guy who washed dishes there."

"Who?"

"Mark something," Hal says. "This was probably six or seven years ago."

"Before my time," I say, a little more crisply than I'd like—I've got to get to work. But I want to keep talking with him. "Um, I roasted a chicken yesterday," I blurt out. "I've got enough leftovers to feed about four people. Would you like to come over tomorrow, like for dinner?"

Hal's smiling warmly at me, as if he knows I'm a novice at this, though I've figured out by the way his eyes haven't let go of mine that he doesn't mind. "That sounds great," he says, squeezing his notebook between his elbow and his hip while he slides his hands into the pockets of his Levi's. "Sure."

I scribble my address on a blank sheet in his notebook and pedal away to the Coffee Cup with enough energy to take me to Detroit.

———————

MARIE tucks our chairs back under her kitchen table while I return "Above the Loveseat" to a folder in my backpack. Before I swing the pack over my shoulder, she reaches to embrace me. "This writing your way through the riddle with your mom, Hannah—I like reading it. You know, I didn't have an easy time with my mother, either. I don't know if any woman does."

I want to melt into her maternal embrace, but instead I step back with a question that feels foolish to have to ask. "What's love?"

It's strange to ask Marie such a serious question, because she's wearing her lime green plastic pumps today. Once, she proudly told me she got them at the drugstore for only $3.99. But they look so uncomfortable. Mom would surely dismiss a woman in such impractical shoes.

Marie's large hips remind me of statues of Greek goddesses. When she walks, I think of water rolling over a boulder.

"That's not the question," Marie says.

We stand now in the alcove at her front door. I hold my backpack at my feet, not yet ready to slide it over my shoulder and bike home. I want to tell her that this Friday I'm going to see *Ordinary People* with Hal. It'll be our third date. Tuesday night, the last time we were together, he made me dinner. I told him about my mother, that she won't really talk with me anymore, that I'm going to visit her soon. "Sounds like you were partners or something," Hal intuited. "Like lovers. And then she left you without saying why. She doesn't sound like a regular mother to me." We'd been sitting on his sofa, and as I began to cry, Hal pulled me toward him. I curled onto his lap and said that sometime soon I might like us to spend the night. "You let me know," he said. He knows I'm still a virgin.

"The question," Marie says, looking directly into my eyes, "is what *blocks* you from love? What blocks you from loving?"

My head tips to the side, perplexed. Marie brushes a hand slowly over my head and then rests it on my shoulder. "Love's here, right here," she says. "Just like you have stories that live inside you, and you write them down. You don't ask, 'What's a story?' You just play with it. Same as love."

Earlier, when I'd read Marie a vignette about what Mom's body is like while she's propped up in her bed smoking, my own body had arced stiffly; I'd stopped breathing as I read. "Hannah Felber, your body is not two pieces joined by a belt!" Marie had exclaimed. "You've got to *breathe!* And make the bridge between the top half of your body and the bottom. Between the woman in you who's sweet and tender, and the woman in you who's a bitch."

She was seeing something I've always felt but never articulated. I took in a long gulp of air.

FOUR

_1890 - 1902_

CHANNA

born c. 1880

in Koretz, near Kiev

I HAVE maybe ten winters at the funeral of my Bubbe Sarah, my mamme's mamme. A little army of Cossacks rides up on their horses into Koretz, our quiet shtetl south of Kiev. To Bubbe's grave they ride, just after Tatte and my uncles lower her into the ground. One soldier, he throws into the hole his empty bottle of vodka. The clunk of the bottle on the casket and the laugh what comes from the man's belly make me think our earth goes down deep. Like a pot of cholent, it holds everything.

I see this soldier is a bitter man. *Un es kukt oys az keyner hot im keyn mol nit a glet geton.* It looks to me like no one has ever touched this soldier gently. To look on him makes me feel sad.

Mamme, though, she gets a mad like a noisy cough she can't hide. With four boys, three girls, me the oldest, and Tatte of course, she has her hands full enough. To hide a feeling she has no time. Like normal, she sits shiva for Bubbe Sarah, but all week I watch her get hot inside her skin. And this is where the story of my life begins. Because this is when I see Mamme and I see the world from different heads. By the end of this week I am scared that her mad on the soldier will take her up to smoke.

The first day after we sit shiva, she says to Tatte, "To live with more of this, I won't. We should pack our things and say goodbye and go to America. A fixer of furniture like you should do very well; and even in New York the people need matzos and wine for Pesach. I'll do my little business there. I won't have to watch the graves get spit."

Mamme, she has most of the words in our family. Tatte, he has the yesses and the nos. But always he does what Mamme wants. He tells everyone she has a good mind.

"So, sure," he says. "We should go to the new country."

Mamme, she has everything ready in three weeks. Since Daniel and Devorah got born, our littlest ones, she moves like a horse on fire. I can remember when she used to rest from her work and sing a little. But not any more. She keeps her mind to feeding us and cleaning. Now she has also the work of leaving Koretz and moving to America.

It is maybe two months before Pesach—Passover—Mamme's season for business. She sells her wine and matzos early, and trades what she has left to Mrs. Avrum. Mr. Avrum has a mule and a cart what can carry us to the trains in Kiev. Tatte, he makes us a trunk. Mamme, she wraps our mezuzahs and Bubbe Sarah's candlesticks in a tablecloth from her wedding, squeezes them into the trunk with two pots and her chopping board. Tatte, he has his box of tools, of course, and his holy books, and a kiddush cup so old no one can say.

Mamme shows me how to make a knife hop, so my small hands can chop onions and carrots while I keep an eye on Daniel and Devorah. Mamme has her work to get ready.

Just one month before Pesach, we are almost ready to leave. Tatte says I should come with him, to say goodbye to the *mishpokhe* tree. What's a *mishpokhe* tree, I wonder. What's a family tree?

Mamme says, "I need Channa to mind the children, Dovid. So I can wash the linens."

"Anya," he says. "To mind the children, she can always do this. To say a proper goodbye she cannot always do. Let her come with me. The linens will get their cleaning. The children will get minded."

"*Ach,* Dovid," Mamme says. "You make like it's Shabbes. Today I want to clean the linens. I don't want you should take Channa now. But you're right! She should say a proper goodbye. So take her."

My heart makes like a grasshopper when she says it, because I love time alone with Tatte. With Mamme, sure, I like it okay, carrying water from the creek, rocking Devorah who cries so much, keeping the fire a fire, carrying water—the time I have with Mamme is all the time, like ground underneath. I miss it that she doesn't have time for fun anymore. Tatte, he works at other people's houses during the days, fixing their tables, and he can also make an outhouse, or a shed for chickens.

When Tatte is near me, I know I have a place in this world, a home in his heart. He's near when the sun comes out from under the edge of the world and starts making shadows; when it slips back down again, into the dark—and makes colors swirl on the hills, colors what look like babies falling to sleep on a mother's breast. Every morning, every night—when light and darkness mix—Tatte and me have a trade of smiles.

Maybe because I'm with Mamme so much, I don't notice her smiles so easy.

To get to the tree, we have to walk first through the cemetery. At the grave of Bubbe Sarah, we stand quietly. Tatte says a prayer. "We're going to America," I whisper to her. "From now on, if you want us, that's where we'll be."

Since Bubbe Sarah's funeral, the trees have made buds, little bits of green. The cemetery looks like a painting, with all the different colors of green in the baby leaves.

Through the graves we walk. The wind plays with my hair like a pesky kid. Tatte, sometimes he puts a hand to a gravestone and strokes it, as if it's a new baby's head.

Down to the river we walk, past the graves, to a tree dead on its side with a branch sticking up like an arm to heaven. The way Tatte puts his hand to it, I know it's our *mishpokhe,* our family. For a long time he keeps his hand on the limb. He moves his thumb over it, back and forth. This tree, it knows secrets from Tatte's heart.

"Come, sit with me, Channa," he says.

So we sit on his tree. We sit so we can see the river. *"Vey iz mir!"* I say. "That water moves fast!"

"I think maybe you know the river from summer only, when it's slow and quiet. But in spring, around Pesach, it gets angry with extra water," Tatte says. "The snow that melts from the hills gives it the extra, and makes it move fast.

"So," he says. He pats the tree. It has no bark, this tree. It looks like a big bone—smooth skin, very dry, almost white, like a bone I saw in the field once. "So," he says again. "You want to hear about my friend here?"

I nod. I feel like a queen. I must have a lot of *mazl,* I think, a lot of luck that I should see how much my tatte loves a tree—when, who knows, maybe the rebbe would say to put your heart to a tree, it's *meshugge, crazy.*

"An apple tree it was, my *sheyne meydl,"* he says, calling me his beautiful girl. "An old apple tree that watched over the cedar and pine trees what got planted when Mamme and I got born."

I look to the cedar and pine behind us while we sit. Ya, I know about these trees, and I heard about the match my grandfathers made, that Mamme and Tatte should get married. Somewhere it is written, when you arrange a match while the man and the woman are still babies, you should plant a cedar tree and a pine. At the wedding, you take a branch from each tree—to make the *chuppe,* the canopy.

"Well," Tatte says, "the bubbes thought, if they planted near a fruit tree, it would give our family luck. Also, at the wedding, we could eat apple kuchen. So, near this old apple tree, they planted the cedar and pine.

"By the time I went to school, I knew already the way to these trees. I used to go and sit with them. I got so happy to see the apple blossoms come out, and then the little green balls what turned into red apples. They were such good apples—sweet, with a little bit of sour. My tatte, he made a hole in the ground, and a big wood box to fit in the hole. And there we kept what I picked from this tree through the winter. Most years, we had apples enough until almost Pesach, and for Mamme's family, too." Tatte looked to the river while he talked, but each word went to my bosom.

"By the time I was bar mitzvah," he told the river and me, "I knew how to prune—how to keep the dead branches from sucking the living ones; how to cut the branch that grows too much fruit, and keep the tree balanced.

"The summer Mamme and I had passed seventeen winters, we had our wedding. We took branches from the pine tree and the cedar for our *chuppe,* and Bubbe Sarah and Mamme made apple kuchen for everybody.

"A few years later, you had two winters, just after Yom Kippur it was, we had a big storm—crazy lightning what wouldn't stop for a whole night. You were quiet, Channa, but awake. Mamme, she was big already with Yehudis; it was hard for her to sleep. I was a little scared. What if Mamme should have her time in a night like this? But like a Shabbes bride, full of the *Shekhinah's* peace, you were a teacher for me this night. The more you get quiet, you seemed to tell me, the more you hear the storm. And the more I heard, the more beautiful it got. Between thunders, I could hear the animals making their soft noises. The more I listened, the more everything fit, peace and thunder, soft and storm. You were just a baby, just starting to talk; but already you knew this.

"After Yehudis got born, a few weeks later it was, I went to our apple tree, to tell her we had a new baby. This is when I saw she was dead on the ground, flat except where her roots curled around the earth. In her fall she brushed on Mamme's cedar tree—you see how it has less branches on the one side?

"Like I had lost my mother, I cried and cried.

"Mamme, somehow she knew something had happened. She left her cooking, and she came with you and Yehudis all the way to our tree. When I saw Mamme, then you and Yehudis, well, I didn't hide my tears. Mamme cried, too, because she had made her quiet times alone with this tree and its fruit. You girls thought we were pretty *meshugge*, grownups crying in a field waiting for spring. So you cried, too. Sometimes you laughed at us."

Tatte gets up from sitting to stand on the tree. I stand with him. We can see up the hill to the gravestones of our shtetl. Tatte puts his hand to my head. He touches it soft, then goes back to sit on his tree.

"So," he says, "our tree was dead. But for a couple years, some branches still made leaves. And then Mamme's cedar tree, with half its side cut off— still it grew! It made me wonder, when I came to visit, what's dead, what's alive? Sometimes, it's not so clear to me. I couldn't understand. I saw roots torn out of the dirt, like guts of a chicken. Still, after Pesach, it had green leaves coming out.

"Well, now we leave for America—*di goldene medine,* the golden land. I don't want to go. English they talk over there, not *mame-loshn.* I hear you have to be a rich man to live near an apple tree. Ha! This I really don't understand. To know an apple tree you just have to live near enough to walk to it and carry your pruning tools, ya? But I heard it from Mr. Caplan who has a son in New York. *Nase venishma,* I suppose. That's what the rebbe says. We do now, we understand later."

THIRTEEN years I have, Mamme figures, by the time we have finally our own apartment on Cherry Street. Up till then we lived with Mamme's cousin Sadie's family, in a tenement of four rooms for both families. Let me tell you I like it when the Fried family gets its own! Chairs and a big enough table for the bunch of us we have, and meat and dairy dishes, too. We have enough finally so that when Shabbes comes, we can really make Shabbes.

To get steady work, it took Tatte a year. He cuts cloth to make new shirts for the rich American men. From dark to dark he works, in a very tall building, in a room what has no windows, and a lot of noise from sewing machines and bosses with mean eyes what watch the people cut and sew. Tatte got the job cutting the cloth because the machines make him nervous. Well, every week we have money from his cutting, and after a few months this apartment where Mamme has her own kitchen and beds enough that each child can sleep.

I have by now learned a little English. "I love America!" That's what I like to say—when I sweep our kitchen floor and dance with the broom. In the Old Country, sometimes we went hungry. In America, to eat, we have enough.

One day Mamme says she's had enough of me around the house, talking English to myself, making up songs and dances with the little ones. "Time for a smart girl like you to go to school," she says.

So, I go. P.S. 122, they call it. For three blocks, I make a walk down our street to get to the school. Into a first-grade class with Miss Fisher I get put. The room has long rows of little desks, and a blackboard up front with words on it already. I can't read a one. Near the window, Miss Fisher points me to a table with a chair a little bigger than the others. The other kids are like my brother Hankus, maybe six or seven. Already they know English better than me. Some of them got born here. They all stare on me like I'm a grownup, a grownup too old for their class.

My hands squeeze together, tight. I don't want to make rude to Miss Fisher, but I want to leave. It's not my American dream in here. I have five or six winters more than these children. I see a girl put a sweet eye to a boy with some freckles. I can tell he likes her back, because he gets red in the cheeks. What am *I* going to do in a class with young boys?

So I decide to tell Mamme: to this class, I won't come back. I look out the window as much as I can and still be *mentshlekh,* polite. A yiddishkeit girl I will stay, a yiddishkeit girl who can't read English.

MAMME wants me to make a good American. That's why she sends me to buy our groceries, and to pay the rent to our landlord, Mr. Goldberg. It's my favorite thing, to take the BMT down to Mr. Goldberg's office near Coney Island and give him the fourteen dollars for our three rooms on Cherry Street. Mamme usually gives me ten cents extra, and my friend Tova comes along.

Tova, her family lives in the tenement below ours. She is also from the Old Country. She has red hair what everybody looks on; but Tova, she has a mind like a boy's. She wants to go to school. Her father says no. He is at shul during the days, just like in the Old Country, while her mamme washes the laundry of men not yet married. Once each month, Tova and me make ourselves a lunch of pickled herring and boiled carrots, and take the subway to pay Mr. Goldberg, our landlord. We walk on the boardwalk and look out to the great ocean. And I remember our tree, over on the other side.

THE years pass. I help Mamme with the cleaning and the cooking like a grownup, and I mind the young ones. Tova tells me what she hears from her older brothers about free-thinking ideas, Socialism. I still think about Tatte's stories that day by the apple tree. How you have to prune to keep a good balance. I think about this when I see mothers with ten little ones to feed and only one loaf of bread for three days. And I wonder about rich American girls with ten dresses to wear: how do they choose when they have so many?

But I love America! You can go to the bakery, to shul, to the night lectures. You can get a job and make money, eat hot dogs, make yourself a business, make yourself a teacher. You can go to the park with flashing lights and rides in the dark. Just from the choices, you can get dizzy.

T AT T E says he could get me a job at his factory. I am seventeen. My pa and me, we don't have walks together like we did in Koretz. He doesn't have the same happiness when he leaves in the morning, or when he gets home. On Shabbes, he looks a little lost. Living in a big city and working inside all day without wood or his fixer's tools makes him confused and sad. Still I feel like a star around him, like a good egg.

When Tatte tells me I could work at his factory, we make faces that remind me how we used to smile on each other. "Sure," I say, "I'll try it."

Could be good, I think, to make money a little, and spend time closer with him. But also I feel nervous. Because if I don't like his factory, well, I don't want Tatte to feel more hurt. I wouldn't want to tell him I don't want what he has to give me.

Anyway, I go. To Cohen's Shirtwaist Company on Hester Street. Tatte has a friend with a daughter my age, Bernice Horowitz, and somehow he manages it that I work near her. She puts the buttons on the shirts, and makes sure threads don't hang. A finisher, Bernice is. From her, I learn how to make my machine go slow or fast, how to put thread in, and how to sit with the noise.

It makes me dizzy really, to work in a room with a hundred women and a hundred machines. I feel like I am part of something big, like I work in a big ship—but I live in a little box, closed up. Is this big factory a good or bad thing? I wonder. Is all the stitch-stitch noise good for us girls?

Well, I don't know. But I feel sad to do this work. I feel proud, too.

Only a few weeks after I have my own machine, Bernice takes me to my first union meeting. There's a big fight about what should a man do if he sees the boss is nasty, but he's scared to make a report because he doesn't want to lose his job. Everybody shouts at the one man who is scared to lose his job. One man, maybe only two years more than me, and his accent still thick, he says, "Let this man say what he has to say." He speaks quietly, this man, but everybody listens, then lets the lonely man talk.

"My cousin," Bernice whispers into my ear, nodding to the man who makes us listen.

My eyes light up. Bernice sees what's in my heart. She squeezes my hand. She says, "I can make an introduction."

THE first few times Meyer and I meet, we are shy with each other. Only Bernice talks. But one day, when we leave the factory, Meyer asks would I go with him to the Jewish theater. In America, they call this a date. Mamme and Tatte, they like it, that in America people don't make their match with a yente, but with their eyes and hearts.

A man of ideas Meyer is, a Socialist. Like other boys trying to make themselves American, he shaves his beard. Already I am five years in this country. Still, a shock it is, to see the whole face of a man, not just the eyes. A lot of parents get upset with the shaving. You know, that their boys take razors to their faces. I love it to see the sun glow on Meyer's cheeks, and his nose. And he's tall, Meyer, and he has a real sweet smile. He will always be a kind man, and fair. I bet he and Tatte could make friends.

One day, we walk along the river. Meyer walks with his hands behind him. I throw some old challah crumbs out to the sea birds. "Channa," he says, "I know you have troubles like anyone else, but always when I look on you, you look like you are glad with your life."

I smile, sure. Because then I know he wants a life with me.

Mir hobn gehat zeyer gute gefiln eyner tsum tsveytn. We have good feelings one for another, Meyer and me. So, we get married.

EVEN before my first monthly came, I could cook for a big family. But now, my big dinners have no place to go. Except to my husband of course. And even though Meyer likes my cooking, dinner enough for ten people he can't eat.

Every month, I bleed like I did before I got married, and I know, again I'm not pregnant. The Bible's Channa, she had a lot of talking with God before she got herself a baby to love. She also thought she would be a barren woman.

It's three years since I married Meyer. I still work at the factory, and while I finish the shirts, I dream of babies. Then, what do you know, I miss my monthly! *Oy!*—I feel wonderful, with something to give my heart to, something that takes my care. After four months with this baby, Meyer says his work makes us money enough, I should prepare myself for the baby. So, I tell the boss, "I quit."

Still, I get up early with the smells. We live on Cherry Street, just two blocks down from my mother, on top of Hershel's Fish. Some people complain, but I like those fish, mixing in the air with the carrots and the onions, and sometimes the river's smell. Sure, sometimes I get a dizzy feeling. It's not so terrible.

After a little cleaning and something to eat, I march down the stairs from the third landing, down and out. Normally, I like to talk. But now that I'm pregnant, I keep to myself. Even near Meyer or my mother, I don't have much to say. I figure around Rosh Hashanah, the baby will come. I walk each day to the East River to watch the birds, and to see how the waves change.

What do other women do the first time they're pregnant, when they've got no children or job to put their chutzpah to? Maybe God wants it that you have some time alone with Him. My mother had eight altogether; and all these years, I've never seen her alone, taking a walk just to talk to herself.

After visiting the seagulls, I walk back to the shops to buy a chicken or a fish, a head of cabbage. Besides my mother and Meyer and my sister Devorah, I alone know I have a baby with me. I'm a big woman, you know. It's hard to see my belly has something in it more than borscht and kuchen.

Well, something must look different. Because people come out from their shops to me, like Mrs. Bafmudsky who sells the breads her husband bakes. She says, "Mrs. Horowitz, excuse me, but I see you coming through here in the afternoons with such a kind smile, and I want you should know it's like a mitzvah you do for me, to walk by my little shop with the happiness of a young wife."

I smile to her, I ask for a loaf of her rye. *"Libe iz vi puter, s'iz gut mit broyt*—Love is like butter," I say. "It goes well with bread." I feel full of grace—that my simple things to say make people smile.

Then one night, I have a dream. My grandmother and the Cossack who threw on her grave the bottle with no more vodka, they are both still in the Old Country. They say I have a girl, I should call her Vitl. *Life,* her name means, vital. I am five months along now. I feel such a peace from this dream, and from remembering an old woman named Vitl from Koretz. She made a good challah—with raisins.

The next morning, Meyer and I have our together time, in the bed. Then we have bread also without talking, just smiling, sweet. Meyer, he takes from me his lunch of boiled potatoes and a boiled egg. I cover them with a little sweet and sour sauce from the fish we had the night before. Only our eyes talk. When he gets home, it will be Shabbes.

After he leaves, I take my walk to the river. I feel like the waves are watching me—not just me watching them.

I come home, I make dinner, I wait for Meyer.

In this apartment on Cherry Street, we have our own room. With another couple just married, the Feldmans, we share a kitchen and the toilet. Meyer knows Mr. Feldman from his union. This weekend, they have gone to a fancy place for Mrs. Feldman's sister's wedding, outside the city. The girl is marrying a rich man.

So, we will have a Shabbes of just ourselves. I scrub the floor, I clean our little closet. I braid our extra challah dough around chopped walnuts and apples, a little cinnamon and lemon juice—I make a little kuchen. I set the table with the cloth we got at our wedding, and my candlesticks. Finally I sit at the table to wait for Shabbes and for Meyer. On an old dress, to make it fit my big belly, I stitch.

Suddenly, like a giggle, something slips out of me. I look quick in my panties and see blood. I know right away it's Vitl's soul, off to the Other World.

My legs get soft and take me to the floor. Still I can't see anything in my panties but the bit of blood. "What's wrong?" I ask, to the walls. Over and over I mumble this, hoping God will answer. An hour later, just after Meyer gets home, out comes her little body—a small bird without feathers—onto our bed.

I feel so confused. I have just made *Shabbes*. How does such a pickle fit with Shabbes? I have this thought in my head like it's a whole army not going anywhere.

Meyer, he spins around to the hallway for our neighbor to fetch the midwife. She comes quick. But already I have lost a lot of blood. By the weight of my heart, you'd think different. It gets heavy like a rock, when the rest of my body feels like one of those balloons from Coney Island what fly away when you let go the little string. While the midwife checks to see that everything is out from me that needs out, Meyer goes for a walk to I-don't-know-where.

Finally, the midwife talks. "With rest, you'll be all right," she says. And she puts her bag of medicines back together.

Just then, Meyer walks in, and he starts to talk a fire. Slow and hot, his words come out: "How can this happen?" He asks her like she is the one responsible.

"Meyer," I whisper.

But he is too upset to stop. *"Tsu fil far ir,"* he says, glaring at the nice lady who I think has seen a husband like Meyer before. "Too much for her to have worked in a sweatshop."

"It happens sometimes," the woman says. "Sometimes it just happens. Don't worry yourself."

This only makes Meyer more upset. But he takes a look on me and sees I've had enough. Over our chest our drawers holding our linens and clothes, he bends his head forward, like he's praying. From the top drawer he takes two dollar bills. "Please," he says to the midwife. "I know it's Shabbes. I don't know if you take money on Shabbes. But for your trouble, you should have it."

Meyer. Even in my weakness, I can see he doesn't have a place to put his feeling. The union is God to him now, Socialism. What comfort does the union give a man with his baby dead before he gets to hold it? I give a prayer to God, to give Meyer a place to put his mad. "Even my husband deserves to be upset sometimes," I whisper to Him.

I tell the midwife I want to go to the river. Meyer, he looks at me like I am *meshugge*. The midwife, maybe she understands, but she says, "Not for five days."

So, I wait. I wait five days in our little rooms. Mamme comes when she can, and Devorah, who is not my baby anymore, but an American girl of twelve—a real smartie she is. They wash my linens, they bring food already cooked.

After five days, to my bench I go. When I get there, the waves are so big! Big like monsters—and loud. I can hardly hear the army what has taken over my thinking. You know, thinking I should not have scrubbed the floor for Shabbes—maybe it's what killed the baby; or, I should not have bought herring from a new man.

I can't sit. I feel thunder, thunder what has turned in my heavy heart all week, and I stand up. "You, Vitl," I hear myself shout. "What nerve you have! What nerve you have to leave me before you sit on my lap! Before you taste my kuchen! You take all the love words I give to my belly and then you leave me! How could you do such a thing to me? Tell me—*mayn ziskeyt,* my sweetheart—what do I do with this love?"

I have tears I didn't know I had. I shout, I cry, and when I am done, my big mad is gone to the waves. They swallowed my tears like a baby swallows milk.

"So, this is what I know," I say to the river, "from being a woman. A woman with a child she can talk to but not touch." I say it without even moving my lips, with tears only, what roll down my cheeks. Some people nearby, they look on me with pity. Maybe they think I am a poor, crazy woman. Well, maybe I am.

For my arms, I have nothing. For my heart, I have my daughter's name. So, I can call on her. And also, I have a river with waves that roll to me, over and under, and take all my words.

Ya, and for this day, this what I have, it's enough.

NATURE, she gets insistent you know, she don't let up. It's like God has a long spoon in me, down to my privates, and He stirs. Again I get pregnant. It's like the beginning of soup when a pregnancy starts. My heart gets soft, and I feel the weight of water and salt, like something's cooking.

I still have some days with a word or two for Vitl.

Into the choppy water of the river I shout, "At least in your City of Souls you could know a baby what would stay around to lay on my shoulder and crawl through my kitchen! You tell me—what do I do with this love?!"

How I scream at her, *oy*. It feels good, too—like she hears me, even with the waves swallowing my feelings. Vitl, she is always near.

And with this new baby, I have a big joy, so strong it hurts sometimes. When I smile I feel like a fancy car with those strong beams that light up the dark like two full moons.

Mrs. Kassenstein, she sees it. "Are you carrying?" she asks me. She makes the question with her lips only. With a smile, I nod. Mrs. Smolinsky of Mr. Smolinsky, the butcher, she sees the question and the answer, too. She's a kind heart; she, too, gives me her smile.

Ay, a good feeling this is, that the women on Cherry Street should know my secret. All the way home, I sing. Mamme would say it's early yet for people to know, I should watch for the evil eye. Ya, maybe. But what could I do—tell Mrs. Kassenstein that I don't carry a baby? And why should I hide happiness?

No. While I cook dinner, make the bed, walk to the butcher, I like to sing.

MEYER, he knows all the talking I do with our girl Vitl. Maybe he also talks to her. At night he holds me so gently I can really rest. We have a window near our bed, and if our heads are in the right places, we can see stars. "It's good looking up to the darkness," Meyer says. "With eyes to those stars, we'll get a blessing."

Ya, Meyer, he's a good man. Still, with this new baby, already I feel scared that it, too, will leave me with my arms empty. One night Meyer wakes with a strong dream. "Channa, do you sleep?" he whispers. "I have a dream."

His dream says a fire comes after the sun is down, into our dark rooms. It makes our place light and warm. But if you turn on the electric lamp to see this fire more clearly, you won't see anything. This fire you see best in the dark.

I am big then, seven months already. When he tells me this dream, tears come down his face. They look like threads from his sewing machine spools, unraveling. So, it's tears what keeps us sewed together, I think, when Meyer's crying gets like a kid's, a kid what don't hold back. "Oh, Channa," he says, "what if this one we also lose?"

For a little bit I just hold him, as well as I can with my belly so big. I put a hand to the side of his head. And I tell him, "Meyer, I think your dream is a good thing. This one can keep warm through darkness. It's a girl, I think. We'll call her Ida. That's a sturdy name for an American girl."

FIVE

1982

HANNAH

I SET my luggage on a floor of wide wood planks, just inside the front door of my parents' house in Redmond, a Seattle suburb. It's the end of June. "So," my mother says, slowly folding her arms under her breasts. "You've never seen a view like this one."

We look out a long wall of windows to the coastal mountains. "It's pretty startling," I say.

"Right," she says, moving us down a hallway and pointing to her guest room. "Now. I've put towels on the bed, and we're meeting the Felbers for dinner at six."

"Who are the Felbers?" I ask, following her back to the front of the house. "I thought *we* were the Felbers."

Whatever's happening here—entering Mom's house like I'm a guest, the grand view, dinner at six—it's way too fast for me. We haven't seen each other for a year.

Out of the corner of my eye, I glance around the living room at plants twice as large as any we had in Shaker Heights; a deep brown velvet couch fronted by a coffee table, its top a slab of petrified wood. The walls are covered with Native American rugs and baskets. We had these in Cleveland, but kept them in a storage closet that Mom and I occasionally opened to ooh and ahh over privately. I think she hid them because she feared Grampa's response, especially if he learned how much they cost. I sensed that if Mom really wanted something, she could buy it; and sometimes she did. But these purchases were rarely displayed. "I prefer sharing it just with you," she once said about a Pakistani quilt with mirrors in it which she bought from a woman who traveled to Asia, then sold her treasures out of her home. "It makes them sacred."

"What do you mean—'Who are the Felbers?'" Mom's tone is nearly shrill.

I feel tempted to cross my arms under my breasts, too. But then I'd feel like I'm in a boxing ring. "Just what I'm asking, I guess."

"Daddy's brother, Rob. Rob's wife, Lois. Their daughters: Lynda and Darlene." She knuckles both hands into her hips as she spouts off these names, then raises a corner of her upper lip. She's disgusted.

"Sorry," I say. "I thought they still lived in Cleveland."

"No," she says, with enforced civility, "Bellevue."

"Bellevue?" I tip my head, confused. "Isn't that a residential place for mentally ill kids?"

She clears her throat. "Bellevue, Washington." She spells it out. "B-E-L-L-E-V-U-E. The next town over."

"How long have they been here?" I persist, despite the clear message that she does not like explaining any of this, does not like my not knowing it, either.

"They've been here a few years."

I nod. Rob and Norm didn't speak much when we lived in Cleveland. They said hello at their family's funerals and weddings. Sometimes, at the supermarket, we ran into Lois. I vaguely remember Mom telling me a few years ago that they'd left Cleveland.

I don't sense room to ask more questions, though I've got plenty of them: *Who have you become, Celia? When did the Felbers start to matter so much? Why did you want me to spend a week here?*

We stand in her living room, staring silently at each other, while Norm straightens the TV's rabbit ears in the den. I get the feeling Mom could stand here forever. But I can't. "I'm going to lie down for a half hour," I say, "maybe take a shower."

Mom nods but doesn't say anything. Her eyes have become reflective, like she's in a trance. I nod back, slowly, wondering if she's okay. We're suspended in the silence between us for several moments—until Mom says, "I'll water the plants, then."

"Good idea," I say. I lift my bags and head down the hallway toward the guest room.

OVER dinner at the Sizzler, Lynda and Darlene, who are thirteen and eleven, tell the waitress they want an adult menu, not the kiddie one. "Kids are treated like fake people," Lynda says once the waitress fills our yellow-tinted glasses with ice water and leaves us to decide on our steaks. "Like, there's no place for me to earn money, except babysitting." She wants to buy records and earrings.

"I know a place," my mother says, beaming at her the way she used to beam at me. "It's a blueberry farm. You get up to sixteen cents for every honest pound you pick. The more you pick, the more money you make. We'll go Saturday. Uncle Norm'll go with us. And Hannah, too. Right?" Her eyebrows raise in a question to which she has assumed our answers. Then she dabs a jumbo shrimp with cocktail sauce, and bites it. "If you work as a family and pool your blueberries, everyone makes more money," Mom adds.

For respite, I go to the ladies' room. Alone in front of its mirror, I loosen my belt buckle one notch, and draw a deep breath.

I ENTER the kitchen with a clear intention: to fill the distance between the girl I am around my mother—and the woman I am in Ann Arbor.

Over a big T-shirt and shorts, I'm wrapped in the shawl I bought from a woman in my Contemporary Writers seminar. The shawl is a delicate plaid of grays, soft browns, slate blues. This morning, especially, it comforts me like a baby blanket.

"Good morning," I say.

"Hi," Mom says casually. "I thought we could go downtown today," she suggests. "Go shopping."

She's in her blue morning robe, on her second cup of coffee, looking through the paper for midsummer sales. Her plate of toast only has crumbs.

"That sounds okay," I say, sitting across from her at the table.

"I won't go downtown with you in that shawl, though. You look like an old lady."

When did she start fighting about such stupid things? "I don't have to wear the shawl," I say. I reach for an orange from her fruit bowl, and begin peeling it, while she returns to the paper. "Mom, are there any bookstores near where you want to go?"

My mother sneers. "When you visit people, you spend time with *them.*"

"I like seeing what different bookstores carry," I explain calmly, trying not to be swayed by her disapproval. "I've heard the ones in Seattle are really good. I'd really like to see what they have on teaching writing." When I phoned her a few days ago to tell her my flight number, I told her that I got the job teaching in Boston. It won't pay as much as a regular teaching position, but I'll have a lot more freedom to be creative in class, and more time to work on my own writing. "I could probably scout out what I need in an hour," I say, thinking she might like some time alone or in a bookstore herself.

"When you leave here, you can have all the bookstores you want!" Mom pushes away from the table, rises to the coffee pot, and pours herself a fresh cup with her back toward me. "Oh, do what you want," she spouts, turning around suddenly. "You have no idea what it takes to mother somebody—somebody like *you!* You are so Hannah-oriented!"

Without speaking, I go to the velvet sofa in the living room, taking my journal with me. I prop a pillow behind me so I can sit upright and stretch my legs. I put the notebook on my lap, lay the shawl over the length of my body.

I close my eyes. I remember the roses Hal brought me before I left—one in celebration of my new teaching job, the other to wish me a good trip. I had dinner all ready when he arrived, but it took us more than two hours to get to it. While I put the flowers in a vase, he stood behind me, smelling my hair and brushing his lips along the backs of my ears and the nape of my neck. "Hi, Hal," I said, melting like a butter stick in August. "Are you hungry?"

"Mm hm," he said. We took hands and walked to my bed. "You look so pretty," he said, running his fingers through my curls while I lay on top of him. *Who taught me to lay my body on a man's, swirl my fingers around his biceps and through the hair on his chest? How did I know to lay back and do nothing but enjoy his soft lips on my breasts? I've never even seen Mom and Norm hold hands.*

One evening last weekend, we drove in Hal's red Volkswagen Beetle to the Arb to watch the sunset. "Climb up," he said, once we got on the trail, "onto my shoulders. I want you to see life from high places."

"If I do that," I'd said, feeling my eyes glow and my grin widen while I got a foothold on his right hand, "you might get macho ideas."

"Wouldn't that be grand," he beamed. "To make my shoulders a podium for a feminist's soliloquy."

I drummed Hal's forehead while he held firmly onto my thighs, just above my knees, and spun me around until I squealed. "Before you go east," he said as he let me down, "I want to take you to the sand dunes." He spoke definitively, as if this trip would be our farewell. In August, two months from now, I will move to Boston; and Hal will return to Detroit to teach junior high.

"And then what?" I asked, crawling down from his shoulders.

"And then I'll make you the best spaghetti dinner you've ever had."

I couldn't tell if he knew he'd avoided my question. "Hal," I asked, patting his chest, "and then what'll become of *us*?"

He put his hands in his pockets and fidgeted. "I don't know, Hannah. We'll be pretty far away from each other."

I looked him squarely in the eyes, hardly noticing I had to look up nearly a foot to do so, aware I wasn't quite ready to hear that he doesn't plan to make his life with me. "I have more to say about this," I said. "I'll want to talk about it when I get back from my mother's."

"Yes, Ma'am," he said, saluting me, my dictatorial tone, then scooping me back over his shoulder and whirling me around until I giggled again.

Here on Mom's sofa, I also think of Nancy Sullivan, who'll be my boss at the Wild Women's Center in Cambridge. Nancy was in Ann Arbor a month ago to visit Marie and interview me. We talked about Paolo Freire, the Brazilian philosopher with radical ideas about education; about Paule Marshall, Olga Broumas, and Tillie Olsen—writers we both love.

Nancy told me about the Center, which offers a GED program for women, most of whom are mothers. Their ages range from late teens to late sixties. A new grant will allow Nancy to hire me to teach writing classes.

By the time I left my apartment yesterday, the petals from one of Hal's roses had extended themselves. The other had yet to bloom.

After I've been in my notebook for about a half hour, Mom enters the room. "This sofa is not for reclining on," she says.

I don't budge. "You knock everything I do," I say. I take her momentary silence as acknowledgment.

"Look," she says, "you may find this hard to accept, but you're a visitor here."

"That stings," I say.

"Sorry," she says. She turns and goes slowly toward a corner of the living room. From behind a tall palm, she pulls out a foot-long brass tube. She twirls it like a baton, but in slower motion. "It's a kaleidoscope," she says. She moves it upward, toward a skylight, then places it several inches away from a glazed eye.

I P U T the last of our dinner dishes into the washer while Mom sits at the kitchen table, eating a second slice of chocolate cake. If everything's out in the open, I think, we'll be okay. I should just come out with my question. I don't want mistakes. I need the right words—the ones that can help us get past a secret she may have harbored my whole life.

"Mom," I say with a voice so steady I'm sure that asking her this question will make things easy and open between us again. "You once said you were married at twenty-eight." I look into her eyes as kindly as I can. "You turned twenty-nine in January 1960. If I was born in February 1960, that would make you pregnant at the wedding."

I stand three feet from her, my side to her side, drying my hands. For months, I've wondered if she married Allan just because she got pregnant, and if she's turned against me because of some festering anger toward him. Maybe I look like him, and that bugs her. Mom and I stand now like somber, similarly charged magnets pushing away from each other, knowing we can attract only if one of us turns around.

She shakes her head suddenly, as if it's tracing a narrow zigzag, and laughs. "My God!" she says, rolling her eyes, taking a swig of coffee, and turning toward me in one motion. "You think you weren't wanted! That's the most hysterical thing I've ever heard!"

I laugh, too, nervously. Tension's been broken, though there's no warmth in the air. "I didn't say *that,* Mom. I've never wondered about being *wanted.* I just wonder if I was *planned.*"

She crushes out her cigarette. "I was married in December of fifty-eight, when I was twenty-seven. You were born a year later, in February." She picks up her Pall Malls and matches, and leaves me alone with the remains of her chocolate cake.

NORM is our driver. "I always let Daddy choose whether or not he wants to drive," Mom says, pleased with herself. Norm looks straight ahead, both his hands gripping the top of the steering wheel. Then Mom begins a list of instructions, turns and roads that will get us to the highway. "Okay! OKAY!" he finally shouts, "I get it! I know how to get there!"

We arrive at the Felbers' house, and Lynda and Darlene tumble into the back seat with me. I sit between them, silent and disgruntled despite their admiring glances. Soon Norm turns into a mall and says he'll hold a table at the deli while "the ladies" head to Safeway to buy snacks for the berry-picking adventure to come. I want a Granny Smith apple, not a candy bar. "No," Mom says. "Everyone will want one, and they're too expensive."

"I'll pay for it then," I say, knowing as I speak that my solution crosses one of her unmarked boundaries. Mom's glare and quavering lip let me know *I've offended her again.* I catch Norm's grimace, his head swiveling. He gets out and locks the car while Mom heads toward Safeway with Lynda and Darlene. I walk with Norm toward the comfortable smells of the deli.

———————

THE farm has rows and rows of blueberry bushes. When we arrive, a middle-aged woman in khaki Bermudas explains that we must pick a minimum of ten pounds to earn any money—ten cents a pound. "If you pick thirty pounds," she smiles, "you get twelve cents a pound. Fifty pounds makes fourteen cents." And so on.

I hardly pay attention. As I take the tin bucket she hands me and follow her down a long row that she admits has already been picked over, I notice clusters of Vietnamese families stooped beside the bushes, picking and releasing berries into buckets at mechanical speed. Aside from the overseer, we are almost the only Caucasian people here.

The five of us take our places. After twenty minutes, I still can't find a comfortable squat. I have picked just enough to make a meager layer at the bucket's bottom. "This is absurd!" I scream. "*Totally* absurd!" I might never have appreciated before what goes into a small box of blueberries at the supermarket; but isn't there an easier way to harvest this fruit?

Daddy, Lynda, and Darlene look up from their picking to check out what's happening with me. Mom stays focused on her work, which makes the others return to their berries. I haven't stopped my picking either, despite my outburst, until I hear myself scream again, "Aren't there machines for this?"

My mother, her head bent toward her bushes, glances up at the others. "Just ignore her," she says, an irrepressible smile on her lips.

"Are you enjoying this or something?" I ask. "I mean, are you trying to say you don't think this is absurd?"

Mom continues her picking. Norm does, too. Lynda and Darlene look to me, then to my mother, forgetting the bushes in front of them.

"This is a ridiculous way to make money!" I scream, after another five minutes, glad I've found some way to release the tension between Mom and me. "If it *is* the only way to make money, money's not worth it! Unless you're the one passing out buckets!"

"You're a goddamn Commie!" Mom shouts.

"What's a Commie?" Darlene asks.

Mom gives the blueberry bushes a coy smile. "It's someone who has no concept of reality," she says, and then she cracks up.

I'm laughing now, too. I laugh so hard I accidentally tip my bucket over. While I land on the ground, soothed somehow by our mess and the soft gray clouds above us, Norm and the girls start laughing, too. *Maybe this blueberry picking is worth it; maybe we're finally back to normal.*

RIDING home from the farm, I feel more at ease than I have since I arrived. Lynda and Darlene sit on either side of me in the back seat while we eat berries out of a small box on my lap. "Your cheeks have blue streaks," I tease Darlene.

"That rhymes," Darlene says.

"It does," I say.

"Hannah," Darlene asks, "do you mind being short?"

"I don't," I say. "On an airplane, I only need two seats if I want to curl up and nap. And I can always find good sales on clothes."

"Hannah, where do your pimples come from?" Lynda asks.

"That's pretty simple, really," I say, taking her question without a hint of offense, and recalling a story Karen Caplan and I once made up. Mom and Daddy don't turn around for our conversation, but, quietly, they listen. "There was a family of Eddies and Freddies, and they lived up north, on my forehead. They wanted to go south for the winter, so they did. They brought all their kids with them, and all their old people. And along the way to my chin, they picked up some cousins on the West Coast. Oh, they really like all these vacation spots, you know?"

Lynda touches a blueberry to her forehead before popping it into her mouth with a hearty giggle.

"Could you get rid of them?" Darlene asks.

"Maybe, but I don't like to take drugs."

"Drugs?" Darlene's eyes bulge out in panic.

"You know, pills," I say.

She nods, pauses. "What about creams?" she asks. "Clearasil?"

"Maybe," I say. I smile at Darlene with a motherly feeling I sometimes had for the kids I babysat, in Shaker Heights. "Are you thinking I'd be prettier if I didn't have pimples?"

Mom suddenly turns around to point out Lynda's window, behind Daddy. "Oh, look! Mount Rainier's out today!" she exclaims. "And there isn't a cloud nearby."

I shift from the fluid pleasure of storytelling to feeling like I'm in a movie theater with a frozen screen. I don't say anything. When we drop off Lynda and Darlene, I barely manage to tell them goodbye.

BACK at the house, Mom doesn't want me to make a vegetable pie because it's too much fuss. It requires some ingredients she doesn't keep on hand. I give her an angry, questioning stare. "Our values are not the same," she says, as a way of explanation.

"Ma!" I plead, "What are you talking about? I can take the car to the grocery store and be back in twenty minutes. But you don't let me give to you. You won't let me cook. When I have a precious conversation with two sweet, curious girls, you cut it off with a line about a stupid mountain."

"What do you want me to say?" she asks in a tone filled with venom. "That your pimples are *offensive?* That you're *ugly?* That that's all anybody notices about you?"

We stand in the dusk-light, both of us facing the kitchen's wide window, the sun setting over the coastal mountains. Whatever strength I felt while voicing my plea has dissolved. Her presence feels like an old sweater whose holes might not be worth repairing. I feel unable to move, and resistant to seeing us like this. After several minutes, Mom turns from the window and faces me, slowly enough that I know to meet her eyes.

"I loved you too much when you were growing up," she says. She has arched her back and raised her chin slightly, as if to brace herself from collapsing. "We were too close."

I remember when she protested Aunt Mollie's saying this, probably ten years ago. What changed her? That—I can't say. But I see now the main thing Mom's done with her life is mother me. Maybe she just wants out. She started a new cigarette.

"So then we need this," I say. "Some separation."

"No," she says, pushing her teeth against her lips, groping for control. "Nobody could need this."

It's my last night in Seattle. Mom and Daddy have gone to bed. I sit on the new sofa with one of Mom's knitted squares on my leg. Tucked in side its ripples and smooth valleys, my fingertips find comfort and pleasure. The house is quiet.

I dream of staying here, as if I could find the old way back to the affection between us. And yet I can hardly wait until morning, when a plane will take me away, to the rest of my life.

I am never so full of contradictions as when I am in my mother's house.

THE last weekend in July, Hal and I drive five and a half hours to the sand dunes west of Traverse City, just outside Glen Arbor. The following Friday, I'll spend two nights in Cleveland with Gram and Mollie. And a week after that, I'll move to Boston. Hal and I haven't talked about our future since the week before I went to Seattle. Once we're snuggled in bed at the motel tonight, or maybe while we're walking the dunes, I'll tell him I'm prepared to fly to Detroit every other month. I don't know how I'll get the money; I only know I'll want to see him that much.

At Sleeping Bear Point, we walk the entire afternoon, looking out in all directions and seeing nothing but sand and a few other couples. There's also beach grass and other small plants, even occasional cottonwood trees. These amaze me—plants growing in sand. The air is easy, not windy, not too warm. Hal takes my hand and swings it. "Oh, Hannah," he sighs. "Let's meet like this once a year for the rest of our lives. Let's write each other into the contracts when we marry other people."

"What are you talking about?" I ask, letting go of his hand. "What other people?" I stop and face him. We are so small, compared with these dunes. *Doesn't he want to bring my head close to his?*

Hal slips his hands into his jeans pockets, just like he did that day at the Arb. "We wouldn't last, Hannah," he says. "You have too much traveling to do. I'm just your first lover."

A gust of wind blows sand into my mouth. "Isn't that for me to decide?" I cry, crossing my arms over my breasts. Hal puts his large hands on my shoulders. "I mean, what *am* I to you?" I ask.

"You're wonderful, Hannah. You're an awesome woman."

"So then, why are you so ready to leave me?"

"It's you who's leaving Michigan, hon—I'm just moving to Detroit."

He's avoiding my question. My leaving Michigan and his leaving me are very different matters. "I'd thought we'd visit each other," I say. "Like once a month. I thought we wouldn't be leaving each other at all." As I speak, the anxiousness in my voice tells me that the intimacy Hal and I have enjoyed won't continue. I will be a single woman when I get to Boston; I just won't be a virgin.

Because I'd expected to sleep naked beside Hal, I didn't bring a night-gown. Cuddling with him through the night has been one of my favorite things about being in a relationship. Tonight, wearing the T-shirt I had on all day, I form a tight curl, and keep to my side of the bed. When Hal reaches out and lays a hand on my back, I turn my face toward his, just a little.

He's got his T-shirt still on, too. He scoops me into the pouch formed by his own curved position. "I'm sorry, Hannah," Hal says, in that voice I can't stand, that voice bent on both of us knowing he's seven years older than me. "You know, with my first girlfriend, I was convinced I'd marry her." He makes a quick, small swirl on my shoulder blade, withdraws his hand, and turns away to sleep.

I stay awake all night, as I normally do when I sleep with Hal; but this time I'm not drunk with the glow of a man's body near mine. This time I'm sad to be so alone, and angry that Hal hasn't really said why he doesn't want to stay with me.

We drive home the next morning with the windows open. The highway noise gives us a comfortable excuse for not speaking. I like it actually, the silent soaking in of each other's presence as a way to bid goodbye. Then Hal starts to sing:

> Love is a rose, but you better not pick it
> Only grows when it's on the vine.
> Handful of thorns and you know you've missed it
> Lose your love when you say the word mine.

"Linda Ronstadt," I say, more pleased with myself for knowing this fact than indignant at Hal for singing it.

"She sings it," he says, "but Neil Young wrote it."

RIDING the bus to Cleveland the next weekend to visit Ida, I feel jittery, like I did when Mom first stopped talking to me. It's a panicked feeling that keeps my face stony. *Hal Riley isn't going to be my life partner; I have no life partner.* And why does this jitteriness feel so intense when we were only lovers for a few months?

"Hi, Gram," I say, wrapping my arms around her wide girth as we step into her living room, welcoming her firm response to my hug. "Here's for you." I hand her a pint-size plastic container.

"Thank you," she says tartly. "What is it?"

"Ratatouille."

"What's that?"

"Eggplant and zucchini, green peppers and tomatoes, basil, oregano, and garlic. I made it for my lunch on the road, and I made extra for you. It's good with an omelette."

"Well, I like eggplant. But I hope you didn't put much garlic in, Hannah. I don't like garlic."

"You can be a *hanna-pesl,* Ida Zeitlin," I say. "I give you a present and you complain about it before you even taste it."

"Yes," she says, closing the subject.

Her apartment isn't familiar to me yet—Mom moved her into this complex of elderly Jews just before she left for Seattle, when Gram was widowed barely a year. I offer to put the ratatouille in the fridge, so I can see what she's made: chicken soup, tsimmes, and applesauce. Even though food hasn't appealed to me much since my weekends with Mom, then Hal, this looks pretty good.

Leah's portrait still hangs above the loveseat. Old Channa's sad and loving eyes shine through a framed photograph on the bedroom vanity. I feel comforted by these pictures, though my first hours with Gram are trying. I hiccup too much, she thinks; I dress like I don't care about how I look. I use too much soap when I wash dishes, and the friends I speak of—Julie, Karen, Marie, and Nancy—are all girls.

"*Women,*" I finally say, exasperated by her criticisms. "Not *girls.*"

"*Ach,*" she says. "You talk like a *phudnik.*"

"What's a *phudnik?*" I ask.

"A *nudnik,*" she says, without even a hint of a smile. "With a Ph.D."

I t ' s Sunday noon, Gram's hour for phoning Celia. "Go pick it up—in the bedroom!" Gram insists, waving her hand toward me while she sits in the kitchen, waiting for her daughter to answer. I do as she wants: maybe with Gram's help, Mom will open up to me again.

In the month since my visit, Mom and Norm have been to Reno, Nevada. "Oh, we just loved it," Mom says. "We had a ball. An absolute ball. The food was so cheap, you wouldn't believe it. And I won fifteen dollars gambling, but of course I let it go at that. Norm gets nervous around me when I gamble."

She goes on like this for another five minutes, maybe ten, without asking anything about Gram or me.

I feel deflated after hanging up. "I don't have much hope," I say dejectedly to Gram as I return to the kitchen, surprised to hear myself so open with her. "She's turned into such a selfish person. I can't imagine she'll ever be nice to me again."

"You have to be careful, Hannah," Gram says. "*Az men khazert tsu fil iber vi gerekht men iz, vert men umgerekht.* Protest long enough that you are right, and you will be wrong."

"I never heard that before," I say, as if her expression's newness will make it irrelevant.

My grandmother shrugs, and fills in a new word on her crossword puzzle.

I stand from the table to get dressed for the day. Karen's in town, too. She's preparing to move to Washington, D.C., to join a modern dance company there. We're having lunch.

"Uh, Hannah," Gram calls, just as I head toward the bedroom, "would you help me clean the hall closet today? It's got boxes of old papers I don't need anymore. But I have pictures in there, too. You might like some."

"I suppose," I say, noticing that I begrudge her like Mom did when I was young.

"Also, I thought I could wash your shawl. It's so pretty, you should keep it clean. I've got a nice soap for handmade wool. By tomorrow you can wear it again."

"Okay," I say, quietly taking in the difference between her response to my shawl, and Mom's. "You know, Grampa and I went through your pictures before he died."

"Well, I just need help, Hannah."

"All right," I say. "But wait until I get back from lunch with Karen."

When I emerge from the guest bathroom in a plain red T-shirt and belted cutoff jeans, Gram's carefully rolling my clean, wet shawl into towels so that it won't dry out of shape. She rolls the towels tightly, with a slowness that allows great care, then hangs the shawl on her laundry rack. "So," she says. "Tell Karen I say hi. And bring me back a little bag of mandlebread."

KAREN sits in the back corner booth at Sand's Deli, slouched over her journal. She wears a gray sweatshirt; her hair is coiled on top of her head in a braided bun. She looks up slowly as I approach the table. I see her slender neck, and notice the dancer in her. She folds her notebook together and puts it on the seat. She barely smiles.

I lay my jacket on a nearby coat rack, then hesitate before I slide into the booth. But she's not going to get up. We're not going to hug hello.

"Hi," we say.

Her boyfriend left for Washington last week, she tells me somberly; yesterday he found a place for them to live. He's a painter, and will probably have to wait tables to pay his share of their rent. Her mother doesn't like him, though she can't say why.

I've been traveling so much in the last couple of weeks, I've almost been able to forget the angst in my belly. Now, in the face of Karen's dark slowness, I'm alerted to it; I feel driven to talk fast and cover up what I feel. "My teaching job starts in Boston in a month," I blurt. "And I don't know anyone but my boss in the whole city. That's what's scaring *me.*"

Karen says, "Uh huh," and nibbles the matzo ball in her soup. "How are you and your mom?"

"Yeah," I say, rolling my eyes. "I just saw her and Norm."

"Norm?" Karen asks.

"My stepfather," I say. *Maybe just for this moment, we could both believe I'll manage without him, without my mother, too.*

I don't say anything about losing Hal.

IN her front hall closet, Gram points to an old trunk I've never seen. "It was my mother's," Gram says, "or *her* mother's, I should say. From when they left Russia."

I grasp a short leather strap that was once a handle and drag the trunk into the foyer. We lift its top. "Yeeesh," I wince, recoiling at the pungent odor of mold. "Ooo, Gram. That smells."

"Oh, come on, it's not so bad. Everything is wrapped in plastic. Just take it out and close the lid. And get me a chair. And the wastebasket."

When I return with her requests, Gram has a stack of photographs in her hands. "Here," she says.

The picture on top is a four-year-old girl: Mom. I plop onto the chair I just brought over. "Oh Gram," I blurt. "She looks like a little angel."

"Plenty of people sure thought so," Gram says. "I suppose she was an angel. A strange one, but still an angel. You know, except for one girl she knew before her accident, Celia never had a friend."

"Hold on, Gram," I say. "Let me get another chair."

When I return, Gram starts right in again. "I suppose I wasn't a very warm mother. But I just couldn't find ways. Not with Moe around." Gram speaks matter-of-factly, like she's a detective, trying to figure out a puzzle. "She did have a nice rapport with my mother, Channa. And then there was Leonard."

"Leonard?" I ask.

"Her first boyfriend. I liked him quite a lot. He died just when I thought they'd be announcing an engagement."

"I never heard of him."

"Well, I'll tell you about him some day."

I feel dizzy as Gram talks, and I say so.

"Maybe you need to eat something," she says, and heads for the kitchen. When she returns with a bowl of chicken soup, it's just what I want. I take several spoonfuls—and then my skin begins to tingle and burn. I feel like weights are pressing against my body. It feels difficult to move my head, or my arms. Gram's inside the closet now, pulling out old shoeboxes stuffed with papers.

"Gram," I say, in a slow, heavy voice. "Wait."

She sets the boxes on the floor, sits back on her chair. "Maybe you want to cry before I tell anymore?" she asks.

With the large base of her bowl warming my thighs, the clear broth lapping at the edges of its rim, I do.

1 9 1 7 - 1 9 4 1

IDA

born in 1902
in New York City

THE summer after I turn fifteen, 1917 it is, our second summer in Cleveland, my mother and I are up to our elbows in hot water, canning tomatoes. It's late August. Bessie and Evelyn, the littlest girls, my sister Mollie has taken to the park to keep them out of our way. But my brother, Jeremy, and my cousins Abie and Sol keep coming in with their clothes sopping, soaked like fish. One of the neighbors has set out buckets and a hose so the kids can cool off. Between the canning and all the water the boys bring in, the kitchen floor looks like the start of a stew.

It's a big kitchen, bigger than we had in New York. We left New York because Pa's work got so sporadic. His brother Irving said in Cleveland a tailor could work year round. Pa didn't like it, leaving his union, but he has to feed the lot of us. So we packed up and took the train. Evelyn wasn't yet six months old when we made the trip, and she hollered the whole ride—while a group of soldiers traveling on their way to the war overseas was trying to catch a little sleep.

I wipe a puddle of water from the floor. "This kitchen will never be clean," I say. Ma hears me, of course. She's wearing the dress Pa made her just after Passover, a navy shift with red and beige flowers. It goes on over her head. He made it, I think, because finally last spring Evelyn stopped nursing, and so Ma could wear a dress without buttons.

"Ya," Ma says. And then she shifts her round body to mine. "Ida, *ikh hob nayes vos ken iber kern di velt,"* she says, "I have news to turn the world upside down. *Ikh hob nokh a mol farshvengert.* Again I've conceived."

I turn my face toward her. I have an urge like a rocket running through me to take the tomato I just peeled, make like I'm a baseball pitcher, and smash it on the wall in front of me. Ma just scrubbed that wall the week before.

Well. I won't do it. But my hands, all red they are, go to my hips. I keep my face toward hers, I put my lips together and lock them. And I suppose you'd call the eye I give her a mean one. I feel an invisible kind of shawl come around my whole body, a wrapper that puts me in my own world, sealed off from the rest.

This moment will stick on me my whole life. Because here's where the world turns for me from a hard place to an impossible one. I adore my mother. Just from chores she can make me feel good. "Oh, Ida," she'll say, "why don't you cut the salad? When you do it, it tastes the best." Or "Why don't you dust, *sheyne meydl?* Just give it a swish-swash."

But right then, because she's pregnant again, I have to leave the kitchen. *I have to get out of the house.* Because I can't stand to be near her.

I DON'T have to say, do I, what it means for me that Ma has another pregnancy, a new baby due in March, just before we'll all be getting out of school. Evelyn is almost three now, the youngest, just out of night diapers. We also have Abie and Sol living with us, my Uncle Isaac's boys. Ma took them in when we got to Cleveland—their mother died from tuberculosis. The boys are eight and ten, sweet, sure. But with them we make nine people altogether, and we have only three bedrooms for the lot of us.

A new baby means that whatever dreams I have of going on picnics with my friend Pearl Fishman I can forget. Also there is a bookkeeping class I want to take, so I can get a good job after high school. I'd like to help my parents, and I want a little money of my own.

My dreams aren't so wild. Oh, I have a crazy one of becoming a doctor who invents a foolproof method of birth control. But mostly I'd like a taste of the world beyond housekeeping—though I don't have the foggiest notion of what that might be. Bookkeeping, of course, is a lot more practical; and I'm a practical gal.

Well. Two weeks pass from the afternoon when Ma tells me she's pregnant again. The whole time, I don't talk to her. It's not a plan or anything, I'm just steaming mad, and afraid if I open my lips to her I'll speak things that'd make the situation worse. Like always, I get the groceries on my way home from school; I make a dozen chopped liver sandwiches every day and pack them into lunchbags, or maybe a hard-boiled egg salad. On Thursday afternoons I take each rug in the house to the backyard and whip out the dust.

If Ma is nearby, I feel that extra layer wrap around me, fresh. If Pa is near, I lower my eyes a little. I'm mad at him, too, I suppose. I know what it takes to make a baby; I know what it takes not to make one. I don't see why they can't stop doing it. I know they have a love marriage. That's not hard to see. But can't they find other ways to love each other than make babies?

These are my useless thoughts.

After I wash the dinner dishes—sometimes I can get my sister Mollie to do them without me, but tonight she's nowhere to be found, probably lost in some book—I walk out of the house and around the block, to cool off. For company I stop by Pearl Fishman's. She knows what's going on at my house, and even though she probably would prefer talking, she lets us walk in silence. She's a good friend, Pearl.

Later, after everyone's asleep, I go to the washroom for my moonlight bath. That's what I call it. Ma calls it my private *mikve*, which of course you don't take until marriage—to encourage the woman's seeds to sprout, after her monthly. Ma jokes I take enough baths to end up with more children than her; or that once I marry, I won't have to bother going to the *mikve*, because I do enough as a young maid.

That is not my intention.

I turn the light off when I slip into the tub. I soak up the quiet as much as the warm water. I soak up the darkness, too, I suppose. I see the moon through the window; it's a tiny bathroom, but it has a window, big enough for me to watch the night. They say at Rosh Chodesh, the new moon draws inside herself. In that dark moment, you can't see anything but its loneliness. That's how each cycle starts, moves on to a full circle, then returns to emptiness again.

I don't remember when I started taking these baths. We were still in New York; but as soon as I began, I knew I needed them. Going to my own quiet place, so dark it's like nothing, no names, no effort, I feel quiet and still, even with a world war going on. A bath can carry me through the next day.

Anyway, two weeks have passed since I spoke a word to Ma. Tonight, just after I drain the water and pull my gown overhead, someone taps on the door. I know it's her. I glance at the moon, nearly full. I feel my lips tighten. When I open the door, Ma squeezes in. We just stand there a moment, in the dark. Then she talks. "I need help, Ida, tomorrow. So, I ask you. But if you don't want with what I ask you, then please, I want you should say it. Okay?"

I nod. I have my arms crossed over my chest. I feel like a horrible person, and quite frankly, I don't care enough about that to make myself different. No: I don't have an ounce of desire to take my arms down. I don't want to see, either, that Ma looks like a ghost. Like a leech has sucked all her blood away.

Her eyes catch onto the moon. So, we have another moment of quiet. I don't mind. After a while she looks to me again. "I wonder would you stay home from school tomorrow, watch Bessie and Evelyn, and also make Shabbes. Mrs. Kaminsky tells me, down on Woodland, she knows a man who can make me an abortion. Today I made my mind up to do it. Pa knows I'm pregnant, but I'll wait till my body is healed again to tell him this. Mrs. Kaminsky says she can finish her Shabbes making by two o'clock and come meet me. So I'll have someone to walk me home."

An abortion. Pearl's Aunt Saura gave herself one three years ago, and she didn't live to tell about it.

Everything is pretty closed in for me now. I'm inside my seal, and our washroom is tiny for one person, let alone two. I feel sick, whirly. I sit on the toilet, more like I melt onto it. I can't tell what's what. I feel like I'm the one pregnant, like I'm the one who decided on an abortion. I start to cry. I worry I'll wake the others, but I can't control myself. *"Dos moyl ken nisht zogn vos iz oyfen harts,* Ma," I say finally, after my long cry. "The mouth can't tell what's in the heart."

Ma puts a hand to my head, which brings more tears. "It's too difficult to be a woman sometimes," she says. So then I sob against her belly, with that baby growing inside.

Ma's face and her eyes are so kind on me, especially with the moonlight. I notice, too, how much sad she has in her. "It's not what I wished for, that you should have an abortion," I say.

"I know, *sheyne meydl,*" she says. "And I know that if I have another baby you might never leave this house."

"Ya," I say. "But an abortion—it's not what I wished for."

"For what did you wish?" Ma asks.

"I don't know!" I cry.

Ma strokes my head, hands me a tissue.

"I'll stay home for you," I say. And with her tissue I wipe my tears away.

JUST before Pa gets back from the factory, and my sisters and the boys are all playing outside, Ma walks into the kitchen. I have a big hot pan of kugel in my hands when she leans on the door and opens it. When I see her I don't dare take my eyes away, even if it means burning my hands. She looks nearly dead. Maybe, I think, if I keep my eyes to her, she won't slip away. You know, die on me. She moves heavy like an elephant, but her face looks white like a ghost.

We get her into bed and decide we'll tell the others she's taken sick with flu. Whatever that so-called doctor did to her, he says the baby won't come out till tomorrow. If we say she has a bad flu, we figure she can have a day in bed.

This time, it's me who says, "It's difficult to be a woman sometimes."

"Ya," she says. She gives me a little smile, moves one arm over her head, then the other, so I can pull her dress off. She's gotten so doughy, Ma has, big. When she was pregnant with Bessie, no one had known. "Ida," she says, as if to comfort me, "Vitl's here."

Vitl. That's the girl Ma miscarried before me, her angel in heaven. "The whole day," Ma goes on, "Vitl has said, 'Whatever you choose, let's keep talking.' She knows either way for me would not be easy. She says this soul I carry can manage, either way.

"*Ach.* My big scare was if I put away this baby, Vitl would stop her talking. And if she stops her talking, I will turn completely *meshugge.* But even when I was up on that man's table, she talked. '*A brokhe oyf dayn kop,*' she said to me, 'a blessing on your head.' And 'This too shall pass'; and 'Breathe gently, the world can hold this too.' "

Once her clothes are off, Ma falls to sleep, and I tell the others we'll have Shabbes without her. So—I light the candles that night. I feel Vitl nearby. I'm not jealous of her. But sometimes I feel jealous of Ma, that she has Vitl to talk to. Maybe, I think, the one she put away today, maybe I should talk to that one. Maybe it has words for me. I even wonder should I give it a name, this baby I had not wanted to come into this world.

I have these thoughts and then the next thing I have is to make sure Pa can have a little Shabbes, even with his worry about Ma. I'm sure he knows something's up with her, because she's never taken a rest like this, on account of a flu, at our Shabbes meal no less. And Evelyn's soup needs to cool off before she takes that spoon to her mouth, and if Abie takes too much kugel, he'll get sick. He doesn't take so good to potatoes.

Well, I don't have a name for that baby. But I think of it, and I think of it as mine, too.

In 1920, I graduate from the Longwood High School of Commerce, right when women get the vote. Ma and my friend Pearl and I, we think it's nice we can have a say in matters of the world. Ma thinks this even though she has never learned to read. But to tell you the truth, I don't see how a man in a fancy white house in Washington, D.C., could know what I need. Margaret Sanger is a popular woman now, the birth control lady. Some politicians say the information she prints is sin, but I don't see it that way. Maybe it's thinking of those men that makes me march Ma out of the house to cast a ballot for us, since I'm not yet old enough. They let me in the booth to help her mark an X next to the name of James M. Cox, the Democrat, even though Warren Harding has been our senator since we got to Ohio.

For Pa it's like a holiday, to hear his wife made a vote, even though our candidate loses the election. Pa. I can't say I know much what his insides are like, but I like him. On personal matters, we're kind of shy around each other. Maybe it's because we're the two people closest to Ma. We both know her insides, and in that way we know each other's, though of course we never confide anything. "Who knows," Pa says, while we sit the night at dinner, admiring Ma's special glow, "how the world will get better now that women have say-so."

THE Sunday after we graduate, Pearl and Sophie Frankel and I make a picnic at Garfield Park. We bring kaiser rolls and pickled herring, boiled beets from Sophie's garden, cole slaw with bell peppers in it. I bring Ma's old, large table-cloth, spreading it out so the bunch of us can sit together under an old oak.

We all have our dreams, none too different from the others. We each want to meet a nice, handsome, professional man. I'm especially interested in the professional part. Because I see how hard a time my parents have, even with their marriage a love marriage. So I wonder if money might make the difference.

I've got a job now, bookkeeping at the Gordon Hat Company. My sisters do the chores that were mine before I started working, and if I give Bessie a quarter for the week, she washes my stockings.

By 1924, Pearl is married and pregnant. We still visit, usually on Saturday afternoons. I buy new clothes for my sisters sometimes, I have dates occasionally. It's a gay time, I guess.

Before I know it, I'm twenty-three. An old maid.

NINETEEN twenty-six it is, and the Gordon Hat Company is moving its business to Columbus, where the boss has more family. Well, I take myself to Eisen's Employment Agency, and they send me to Zeitlin's Plumbing Supply. A bookkeeper is needed.

It's spring, just after Passover. Zeitlin's shop is at West Sixth and St. Clair, maybe a half mile from the Terminal Tower. While I walk over, I feel full of something, something like the peace I get when I take a moonlit bath. I like walking in a big crowd, in that downtown air filled with cars and cement and noise, and men in suits. But then someone bumps his elbow accidentally into my ribs as we cross a street, and it jolts me. Suddenly I feel like a tender girl on her way to a new job, alone in the big world.

I look out to Lake Erie and see the moon still hanging in the blue sky. It's a comfort, believe me. I shut my eyes for a moment and stand quiet, just so I can feel that sweet pull between the moon and me. I know the part of me that's always soft can be tender on a busy street, too.

I appreciate all that bustle then. It's offered itself to me, like a dance partner almost, pointing out my own grace.

This is my thinking when I walk into Zeitlin's Plumbing Supply. Ha! A *balagan* it is—chaos. If I say the downtown streets offer me a challenge, well, I don't know if there's a word for what the shop presents. There are hardly any windows, so it looks like night in here, even at nine o'clock in the morning. The place is full of men, buying the pipes and toilets and God knows what else they'll need for the day. I recognize Mr. Zeitlin right away, because he wears a suit with a tie in this mess, if you can imagine. The customers are in overall-type clothes. I can tell he has an eye for fine fabric and well-cut clothes. He's a large man, though not much taller than me. He has the broadest shoulders I've ever seen, and he wears spectacles fit for a professor. He must be a force to reckon with.

I've worn a pale pink dress for my first day, and a white handbag. My dark curls are soft and short around my face. I stand out like a tall daisy in a garbage dump, I imagine. All the men get flustered and stop their talking and poking through the bins of short pipe things. Mr. Zeitlin is the most flustered of all. He just stands still and stares at me.

I've captured him, like a photographer would. This almost makes me giggle, because Mr. Zeitlin doesn't look like the kind who ever stands still. I stand there knowing that my womanly softness is now the hub of this store. I give all these men, their wrenches and such, a place. *A frof ken fartrogn a ganse velt,* I think. A woman can carry a whole world.

Finally our Moe Zeitlin moves his mouth, makes words. "Miss Horowitz?"

I look straight at him. "Yes," I say. My back stands strong as any man's in the shop. The more I meet Mr. Zeitlin's eye, the stronger I feel. His feathers are ruffled, though. He just stands still in front of all of us with his jaw hanging open.

This whole bit doesn't last more than a minute of course. Moe Zeitlin does not waste time when he could be working, flustered or not. "Let me show you to the back," he says, "the desk for the bookkeeper."

So, I follow him. And get introduced to the tiny office some other girl just left the week before in order to get married.

Not long after that, he takes me on a few dates—if that's what you want to call them. Moe comes up to the house, nods to my parents and sisters and cousins like he's shy—ha!—and takes me for a drive in the country. He has a big green Packard, big enough for six people. Once he even takes me to a Chinese restaurant in Shaker Heights, a fancy suburb where they don't let in too many Jews. They serve shrimp and lobster, even pork. I'm miffed, to tell you the truth. But of course, I don't say anything—in fact I don't talk at all. I learn Moe's thirty-two, eight years older than me. He got to America when he was just fifteen. Seventeen years alone he's been, without a woman, tied up in plumbing supplies so he can make his fortune.

He sends money back to his family in the Old Country, where he has all kinds of sisters and nieces and nephews. *"Mentshn,"* he declares, with a face I haven't yet seen smile, "good people." He regards his mother very highly, and his sister Masha. Of course, he hasn't seen either one since he was a teenage boy.

It touches me, to be honest, to have a man show me pictures of nieces and nephews he's never met. He has a little story about each one. He managed to send Masha's boy a wooden train, and he knows a song a little girl likes. I still wouldn't say I *like* him, Moe Zeitlin; but I appreciate his family sense.

He recognizes my appreciation, I suppose. On our fourth date, he comes to pick me up for dinner, I get in the car. *"Mir darfn khansene hobn,"* he blurts. "We should marry. Would be good."

I can't say I'm surprised, but still the idea comes into my lap like a case of canned beans. For several minutes, I can't budge an inch. Finally I turn to him. "I'll think about it," I say.

I get out of the car and nearly slam the door. "Enjoy your evening," I say. "I'll see you at the shop, Monday morning."

So, again I fluster him.

I don't have to tell you I'm not crazy about Moe. Ha, crazy. I don't have the foggiest notion how to hold a conversation with him about bookkeeping, let alone making a home, or any of that sweet stuff they have at the movies between people in a romance. He's like a machine, Moe. He tick-tick-ticks to run his shop. Whatever he has to say he does in as few words as possible; and if somebody else should take awhile to explain something, he just turns away when he tires of listening. I see him do this even with customers, even customers with a lot of money to spend.

My father, however, when I tell him of Moe's proposal, has plenty to say. "A rich businessman wants you for his wife," he says, like God has picked me to be queen of the human race. "It's good, Ida, that you have such *mazl.*" When he notices *I* don't feel so lucky, he also says, *"Nor a shteyn zol zayn aleyn.* Only a stone should be alone."

To me this is *not* the point. But I hold my tongue. I want a love marriage, sure. Yet I know none of my sisters will marry until I do, and there are four of them after me. My father has struggled so hard to feed the lot of us, and here I have an opportunity not to struggle. What good would it do to say that Moe Zeitlin doesn't make my heart go pitter-patter?

Ma, I think she understands my predicament. "Whatever you decide will be right," she tells me. Then, "Go walk. The girls'll do your chores."

Monday morning at the shop, I fill a drinking glass with water so the tulips he's brought for me won't dry up. "All right," I say, thinking these flowers are probably the only romantic gift I'll get for the rest of my life, "I'll marry you. But the wedding meal has to be kosher."

What are you doing, I hear some voice pestering me, *marrying a man you don't even like?*

I realize, I don't know. But I think also of something Ma once said when we heard about a man two doors down from us who stole from his boss, who was also his wife's brother, because he wanted to start his own business. Pearl's mother said this man was lower than a rat. But Ma, she said, "Everyone is worthy of affection. Everyone is a human being."

"Including Moe Zeitlin," I tell that pestery voice—as if the challenge of this realization will carry me through my next fifty years.

Then my lips come together and tighten against my teeth. Just like a wrench around a pipe.

————

We have the wedding in a party room just built by the Katz family. To me it's a little odd, marrying in a party room and not a temple. But that's where Moe wants it, for reasons I don't ask. I learned real fast about reasons: reasons are what Moe says are reasons.

There's roast beef enough to feed all of China, plus plenty of vegetables, fresh fruit, and kuchen. I have never seen so much food in my life—and I've seen a lot of food by now, having helped Ma cook for the nine of us since I could hold a knife. The meal is kosher, just like I said, though when I went to set up our kitchen, Moe said, "Forget kosher. In America there's no reason for kosher."

No reason? *Kashrut* has reason! It's a way to mix what goes well together, and separate the things that don't—starting in the kitchen. Plus, I want Ma and Pa to feel comfortable eating in my home. But I keep my mouth shut, to Moe. When I tell Ma my dishes will be separated by everyday and special, not meat and dairy, she's the one who surprises me. "Well," she says, "I suppose the world changes. I suppose we have to change, too."

She's a great lady, my mother is. I hope my children will admire me the same as I admire her.

Back to the wedding—my dress has hundreds of white feathers sewn into it; my bouquet is a fan of long ones. Moe gets a tuxedo, and one for my father and even my brother. It's a spectacle, people say.

I suppose. All these bird feathers do for me, however, is make me wish I could fly away. It just doesn't feel right, so much fanciness. Ma sees my feeling. *"Er iz a ferd,"* she says, when we have a moment alone. "He's a horse. An animal." She puts a hand to my shoulder. *"Mit a gut harts*—with a good heart." And also she says, "He has a feeling for something special." You know—meaning me. I take her words like water before a long walk in the desert.

After the dinner, I change into more casual clothes. Eve and Ezra Feigenbaum, who Moe knows from business, wait for us at Moe's car with their daughter, Sadie. She's carrying a little suitcase. This is when I learn we'll have an escort for our honeymoon, eight years old no less.

I feel pretty darn mad that this is happening, without my opinion even considered. But the truth is I'm also relieved to have Sadie join us. I haven't yet been alone with Moe for very long, and I can't say I look forward to it.

We drive to New York, all three of us in the front seat. I haven't seen the City since I was a girl, and I've never seen the parts that need money: restaurants, department stores, hotels, Broadway. Moe books us a big room at the Plaza Hotel with a window to Central Park, a canopy bed, and even a telephone. I suppose such fanciness should make anyone feel like a queen. But it's too hard for me to enjoy the pleasures Moe's money can buy when Moe is the one nearby, buying.

We have a sofa in our suite, and if you take off the pillows, it makes a bed for Sadie. I realize he brought her along because he's nervous about sex. So, I have a giggle to myself. I figure for at least my honeymoon I won't have problems. But later that night, when Sadie goes to the bathroom, ach. Moe rolls over on me—so quick I let out a yelp like I heard a kitten do once when my cousin went after it, a tiny yelp you can't be sure anyone hears but your own kind.

I say, a woman should have a door from her honeymoon suite that lets her walk out scot-free, if that's what she wants.

In my case, if there is such a door, I don't see it. Rage spreads through me like red ink on white cloth. I feel like I'm on fire. I feel dazed, too. Because I hear Ma saying, *"He has a good heart."* Somehow, I know this is true. I know, also, this craziness is the best Moe has to offer. And marriage, for me, will be making the best of *that*.

RITA comes in 1929, just as Moe's money is speeding up the stock market like there's no tomorrow. Then Moe wants a boy, after Rita. "If it's a boy, it's a boy," I tell him. "If a girl comes, it's a girl. What does it matter?"

Course I know what matters. A boy he can use at the shop.

The spring of 1929, he wants to take a loan out on the business, build a warehouse for fancy bathroom fixtures. But the banker turns him down. You can't imagine the ranting and raving he does about this—until he finds a bank that will do what he wants. Right away, he transfers all his money from the old bank to the new one.

Well. In the fall, his old bank goes under with the crash; the new one stays solvent. Moe walks around like he's Master of the Universe.

Just a couple of months after the crash, in December 1929, he goes back to the Old Country to see his mother. Now this is fun, just me and the baby. When Rita sleeps, I sleep. We eat when we feel like it. She has a friend already, Pearl's girl, Nora. I can call Pearl and have them both over for a morning or an afternoon while her boy is at school and her husband's at his bakery. Also I learn there's a kosher butcher who'll deliver to my house. If I'm not home, the Irish girl who lives in our attic will pay him and put the meat in the icebox. So. I won't have different dishes for *milkhik* and *fleishik*, dairy and meat; but our meat will be kosher, and I won't serve cheese kuchen for dessert on nights we have meat! I feel proud, honestly, that I've found this way to keep a Jewish kitchen. The nights I have Mollie over for dinner, I beam like a car in the dark.

These are uneventful days, and I love them. So different from with Moe. With him, every five minutes he yells something crazy—"Rita has been playing near the newspapers! Why does she play near my papers?" Or he storms into the kitchen while I fix a meal, asks, "Why do you use two chickens for soup just because you have your parents and your sister coming to dinner?" If I go in to bathe before bedtime, to relax, he can scream through the door like there's no tomorrow. "A good cook," he shouts, "could do it with half a chicken!"

He interrupts me at any moment, wanting answers. Constantly he goes on like this. Constantly.

But then he'll take a bag of unshelled walnuts, and make a game with Rita of spilling these nuts from the bag to the bowl and back. It's nice, to see a father play with his daughter. The trouble is his attention span is not as long as the baby's, only ten minutes or so.

Well. In Riga he gets a photographer to take pictures of him and his mother, Leah. One of these he uses for a postcard. Such serious faces you never saw. She wears the mink shawl he brought her for a present. *"Mother wishes us long life and happiness and that you bring a brother for Rita,"* his picture says, on the back.

Fine, fine. Say what you want, I think, changing a diaper or putting a load into the washer. I'm not happy yet with you; a brother for Rita won't change anything. And I can't do a thing about making your seed into a boy. So send your postcards to God, not me.

He comes back in the middle of February with his sister Raisl—another one with a serious face. We call her Rose, a name that doesn't match her at all if you ask me. Unless you're talking about a rose that's dried up. Even before we married, Moe didn't talk much about this sister. About Masha who likes books and married the town doctor, he talks. But about Rose, all I get from him is that her husband left her early in their marriage, when their boy Daniel was still small. By now Daniel's a young man, about twenty, I'd guess. He's come too, of course, to America.

Rose gives me their mother's Shabbes candlesticks. I put them on the dining table, polished, so something in the house has a sparkle. Moe gives the photograph of their mother to a customer with a kid who can draw, and pays him a few dollars to paint her up large as life. Over the fireplace mantel, he hangs the portrait.

So, we have his mother's face and two more people in the house for a while. Rose cooks; Daniel helps Moe at the shop. I kind of like their company, to tell you the truth. They both want to learn English, and with Rita just taking to words, we can have a good time while everyone learns a little vocabulary. Wet. Dry. Eat. Nap.

After two months Moe says he's had enough. What's the problem? We have an extra bedroom even. I think Moe just doesn't like Rose. And I think he didn't like leaving behind his mother and his other sisters, especially Masha. Masha and her doctor husband have a little boy, Asher, who is five or six; and Ruchl might be three. He makes a good living, her husband. He doesn't need America.

Well. Moe won't join our talking game. In fact, he won't talk at all to his sister or Daniel. Once I notice and ask him about it, he turns a deaf ear to me, too. "Moishe Zeitlin!" I finally holler one morning while he gets dressed. "We have things to talk about! Rose needs to see a doctor, and she and your nephew both need a real class in learning English. You're going to have to give us some money for these things!"

But he won't.

I don't know how a person can shut himself off from the pleas of another, especially when it's his wife, no less. But at bedtime, in our room, whenever I begin to discuss Rose or Daniel, he just turns into bed with his back to me, and lays his head on the pillow I plumped up, like I don't exist.

It's during these days I conceive again. I feel this small stone growing in me, absorbing not only my husband's craziness, but mine, too.

Soon enough, Moe gets an apartment for Rose and Daniel on top of a toy store on Taylor Road. It's two rooms. Even when you put them together, the whole place is still only as big as a closet. She's grateful, but I feel ashamed. We could afford nicer than this. I have a feeling that maybe in Riga he tried for Masha to come and for Rose to stay with their mother. It gives me a bad taste. When I ask him, he looks at me like he did my first day at the shop: he doesn't know how to talk. If he would talk, I wonder if he'd just explode.

Ach. It's all craziness, what I think and want.

Less than a year after they come back from the Old Country, in January 1931, my second girl is born, Celia.

Through the whole labor, I moan and cry. I feel like an oboe, with small holes and big ones, making lonely, strange sounds. I heard a radio show once that told all about that instrument, and I liked it. Anyway, when Celia comes out, she takes so long to cry, the doctor gets a little concerned. But she can't be fazed, Celia. Or if so, she hides it. All through getting born she doesn't make a sound. When the doctor spanks her finally, she whimpers a little bit.

I take her to my breast right away. I want her little chest against mine, so I can feel the in and out of her feathery breathing.

She's not a boy like Moe wanted. She's Celia. For a few days I won't let him in my room. She's so delicate, so sweet, I'm afraid he'll hurt her. He can be gruff, Moe. I ask the nurses to keep him away, tell him something, I don't care what.

Rita kicked and scratched me to get into this world. She came out fighting, and took to nursing like a hungry horse takes to fresh hay. From eating, she can't be stopped.

Celia is different. She would've liked staying in my belly forever. If she got pushed out, well, she's not the kind to fight city hall. So in that way, I suppose, she's like me.

I take her to my breast. My milk comes easy; it had with Rita, too. But Celia won't have it. She won't drink. I do everything I can think of—I give her my finger to suckle, then my nipple, fast. I lie flat for her, drape a warm cloth over my breasts to make them warm before I put her little body upside down, over my shoulder . . .

Nothing works: she will not take my milk. Finally the doctor says it's time to use a bottle. "After all," he says, "we don't want her to starve."

I feel like a failure, frankly. My milk is the best love I have to offer, and here my child won't have it. What can I do? I know she needs milk, to survive. I know she needs love, too; and that'll have to come from some part of me I don't yet know about—not my breasts.

So I ask for the formula, and I tell the nurse to let Moe in the room. I can keep him away only so long. Oh how she screams when he comes in! And he gets shy. He takes off his hat and enters the room s-l-o-w-l-y. Like he's a guest, not the father. When the nurse brings the bottle in, I hand it to Moe, and then I give him Celia. I giggle a little, to see him so sweet and helpless. He's not so bad with her.

AFTER Celia is born, Moe works even harder at the shop, if you can imagine. Maybe because she's a girl he figures he'll have to carry the business on his own, and so he'd better make good. Maybe it's because the news from Europe spells trouble. We all know a war is coming. I keep a cool eye: I can be calm through just about anything. I can live with the devil. It didn't take me a year with Moe before I learned that.

We write and send money and telegrams to Leah and Masha as usual, but we rarely hear back from them. *What else can we do?*

At work, Moe can dig his hands into things. He has a lot of energy, and he puts it in the business, like a sort of madman. He insists I am the only one trustworthy to do the books—which means going to the shop with him four, sometimes five days a week. We're out the door by six A.M. Because I have help in the house, I'm a lucky woman, I suppose. Our Irish girl stays with the children on the days I go to the shop. Rita talks by now. And Celia, she's six months when I start back at Moe's books, the quietest baby you ever met. More like an old man than a baby.

I feel crazy that my sisters and I had more time with our parents than Rita and Celia have with us. Because I want to give them some fun. But it's twelve-hour days. Usually we don't get home till six-thirty. It makes me think I'm a bad mother, that I can't convince my husband the girls need me more than his books do. Once I suggested I could do them at home, and he didn't talk to me for two weeks. Then last spring, on my mother's porch, I complained to Mollie how I hate the shop—I was dreading the summer heat in that back room. Well, Moe heard and came out from reading Pa's papers. He came out and slapped me, a red mark to each of my cheeks.

Ma was out there quick as a light switch, took him into her bedroom to say who knows what. When she came out she told me, "He won't hit you again." I don't know what she said or did, but I knew I could believe her. I wasn't prepared, though, when Moe didn't talk to me for the next month.

My heart is so torn up, confused. I dwell on Moe being only fifteen when he left his mother, and having almost twenty years after that without a woman. Then I got sent to be his bookkeeper, and he got a wife out of me, too. On top of such a lonely life, he gives himself the job of saving his family from the Nazis. From all those Yiddish newspapers he reads, he gets a clear picture of what's coming to the Old Country. A clear picture that makes him go crazy.

"*Ver veys,*" my mother says to me, "Who knows? Maybe he needs you more than the children do."

Yeah, maybe. Whenever I think these things, it helps me feel a little soft for him. I figure he doesn't have much room in his head for the cares of a woman with two babies, even if they are his own.

I know he's crazy, mixed up. But I learn to live without talking. I have tough skin. And if I should leave him, what good would come of it? We'd be shunned without a man in our house, and poor as the dickens.

I have to admit, I don't have the gumption it would take to leave this marriage. For whatever comes, I'll grit my teeth and give it my best.

———

P E O P L E say Celia has a special beauty—*aza sheynheyt iz in der velt nit tsu gefinen*—a beauty not of this world. I see she's pretty, sure. But the Other World part I don't see.

As she gets older, I see there's something strong between Celia and Moe, something deep, like reverence. But I simmer with a strange feeling whenever I glimpse them alone. It's nothing I can put my finger on, but his looking at her makes him a little drunk.

A spetsyeln farbund hobn zey, I tell myself, a special knot they have. A place not mine to enter.

O N E day after Moe's return from a road trip to sell plumber's things, I find a box on his closet floor. Inside, there's a painted plate of a nude lady. She's lightly draped in chiffon the color of seafoam, and a swan is sticking its beak in her direction. I'm not a prude; I know the human body is a beautiful form. But when Pearl stops by to borrow an egg, not a half hour later, she notices something is not right with me. I feel ashamed, I realize, about the plate.

"I imagine," I say as I show it to her, "with all those years alone he had, he's got all kinds of manly desires."

With compassion, Pearl looks at me. When her hand rests on my shoulder, I don't move it away.

A week later, Moe brings this plate out to hang. April it is, 1941. The war is going full force now. Moe says we need something beautiful to look at, to keep us going through a dark hour. We haven't heard from Masha in a long time. Her last letter came a year ago. She wrote that their mother died, quietly, in her sleep. "All right Moe," I say, feeling my jaw tighten as I talk, "do what you want."

But then he takes that lady and puts her above Celia's four-poster bed, with a green, paisley duvet covering the down comforter. She's got a vanity with a mirror, too; but I'd be surprised if she ever sits at it. "What are you doing?!" I ask him. "Celia is a ten-year-old girl! What kind of crazy notion is in your head?"

He ignores me, of course. He just hammers his nail in the wall, then tips the plate to his satisfaction. I see I don't have a chance to win this battle. I get an idea to take my rolling pin and bash it into his head. The girls are with Mollie today, a Sunday. She took them to dinner downtown, for a treat. I have a vision of them walking back into the house, seeing their bloody father on the Persian rug in Celia's room. Well. I can't imagine any good would come of that.

Ach. I need a better imagination. Because once Mollie drops off the girls and leaves, Moe says, "Celia! Have I got a surprise for you. In your room."

What's a mother to do in such a situation? Even through her shyness, Celia gets excited. Who wouldn't? And it's strange for Rita, too, because she doesn't have anything coming.

My head gets all tied up into knots, trying to figure something that will make all this go away.

"Ida, you and Rita stay down here," Moe says.

I want to protest, but I just swallow my words. Rita says, "I'm going outside."

Normally, Moe would raise a canary at such talk, her playing outside alone at night; but this time he doesn't say a word. I can't say the idea thrills me, but in that moment I don't want to impinge on her freedom. "Twenty minutes," I say, and I get a nod back from her.

"It's a dark hour with the war, Celia," he says, while we all climb the stairs. I follow quietly as I can. I'm not going to let her alone with him for this. "But a beautiful girl such as you should know you give me something I like to look on through this war, more beautiful even than this woman." Then he flicks her light on.

"Nemesis, she is," he says. "The Greek goddess of destiny."

I feel sick to my stomach. *What in God's name is he saying to Celia—to her mind?* A ten-year-old girl wants a new doll maybe, not a nude woman! And we're *Jews*—not Greeks! *Moe Zeitlin,* I want to scream, *we're just not going to look on things your way! And what good could it do to give the burden of beauty to a child—during a war yet?!* But I just stand there frozen, with a mind rattling off a hundred things I can't speak.

Then, God forgive me, I catch a wave of fear that Moe is doing more than talking crazy. *That he is touching Celia in her privates.* I know right then and there—*Celia will be wounded, maybe even crazy, her whole life.* My knees get weak. I reach for the vanity chair so I can slump onto it, but I land on the floor. Quick like a madman, Moe loses his eye on that plate—which doesn't budge from my fall—to see what's the matter with me. Celia slips out of the room.

For months after that evening, the only way I can fall to sleep is with prayers that my daughter knows somehow her father means well. That there's a lot more to the world than the way he sees it. That she knows I love her with my whole, imperfect heart, and a mind that can't figure how to feed two girls and house them without a man's help. Other than praying, I can't think of what to do.

I HAVE a hard life in a big house, and I live with it. You know, a woman doesn't have places to pound out her anger nowadays. Cutting vegetables takes a fine hand. Tearing plastic wrap off a chicken, seasoning it, and popping it into an electric range just doesn't satisfy like wringing a neck and plucking feathers. For laundry, you just push buttons. My mother, she used to go down to the basement every Monday with the clothes and linens of seven children and Pa and herself, too, and not come up till dinner. Sometimes if I opened the door, I'd hear her singing. Sometimes her voice sounded more like a moan, or a wail. She'd be tired when she came up, sure; her fingers would be thick and bright red. But she came up with a lighter heart, like she'd scrubbed her burdens out with the dirt.

The way I work now, I sit at a desk at Moe's shop, or stand at my kitchen sink, or at the cutting board. Whatever hangs in the air goes into my hips and my legs, until my body is as heavy as old wood. The older I get, the heavier I get.

Old wood gives a hot flame if you burn it. Maybe it's why I hold on to my anger, and don't fight the days Moe won't speak to me. Because if I let it out what I really have to say, this whole house would catch fire.

SEVEN

1982 – 1983

HANNAH

I FLY to Boston with Old Channa's pastry board, my six-year-old Smith Corona typewriter, and two duffel bags of clothes. I've already mailed ahead six boxes filled with kitchen stuff, linens, and books.

Fastening my seat belt, anticipating my new job, I feel like the world's luckiest college graduate; and I've woken every morning of the last two weeks with the runs. Julie came over a couple of times to help me pack, and even brought over hummus sandwiches with alfalfa sprouts and tomatoes one night—but I could barely eat. I felt too scared of all my changes.

Hal only called once, to say I'd left a sweatshirt at his place, and when he came over with it, he stepped inside my door, then pulled back quickly from our hug. His pulling back so quickly seemed mean—we used to have hugs that lingered. Or maybe he was just being honest.

Julie has a new man in her life, a musician who wants her to move in with him. That's all she talks about. I don't even know if she noticed how scared I am, and how crazy I feel to be so scared. Because really, I'm very lucky to get this work teaching in Boston.

Over the rumble of the plane's engine, my mind replays the list of its fears. *Boston's such a big city! I've never even been there. I'm moving alone. What if I hate the job? What if Mom loses my phone number? I mailed it to her in a letter. Maybe I should have called her. Maybe I should have tried for a job closer to Seattle.*

This litany let up yesterday, briefly, when Marie came to drive my boxes to the post office and presented me with a blank journal and a box of pens. "True home," she'd said, glancing at the gifts, then smiling at me. "For a writer." The last time we met to talk about my poems, I told her that Ann Arbor's been my home since my mother stopped speaking to me, and that she's been my anchor here. Now that I'm moving to a new city, I'll be lucky— and on my own again.

Marie held me firmly against her large bones as we bid goodbye, then took my face in her hands and whispered, *"Go! Impose yourself on the world!"*

I swallowed her command like a good meal. I even felt worthy of her faith in me. Now I look out of the airplane's window. I see patches of orange and yellow, trees beginning to turn. *It's a new season.* I reach for my backpack and pull out the manila envelope with the photographs Gram gave me when we cleaned out her old trunk. I sift slowly through the pictures, then open my notebook and write a new poem about Mom.

It's strange that Mom is *always* my subject—even after I've had my first romance, even as I'm moving to a new world.

THE taxi brings me through a long tunnel. My duffel bags are piled on the seat beside me. When we emerge into a maze of highways, the pace of the city makes me spin.

"You have lucky stars," Nancy Sullivan declared when she phoned to say she'd found a furnished, rent-controlled sublet for me through a woman who's moving in with her boyfriend for a six-month trial. "I know people who spend their lives looking for rent control." I hold onto her words as we cross the Charles River, filled with sailboats.

My apartment is on Inman Street in Cambridge, seven blocks from the Central Square subway, a twenty-minute walk from Harvard Square. It's in a four-story brick building constructed in the twenties, flanked by two trees that must be just as old.

The taxi driver lets me off. I find two keys in an envelope in the mail slot, where they are supposed to be, unlock the lobby door, then eye the stairwell I'll have to climb, bags and all, to my entrance on the third floor.

It's six o'clock when I open my door. Rays of sun douse an old rug in the center of the main room. There's a loveseat under the bay window; a rocking chair beside it; a desk against the inside wall. The wall opposite the bay window makes the kitchen: a row of appliances and chopping space, with a small dining table. The hallway begins at the front door. It's lined with bookshelves, a pale blue bathroom, and a small bedroom at the end.

Nancy has left me a note with a map of Cambridge on the table. Within three blocks there's a women's bookstore called New Words and a natural foods grocery, Bread & Circus.

I hang up my clothes in the bedroom closet, put the typewriter and my *American Heritage Dictionary* on the desk, open the kitchen cupboards to see they've been emptied, along with the bookshelves, as Nancy said.

I head out for Bread & Circus, delighting in my new neighborhood's trees. I'm in the store maybe five minutes when a young boy begins howling near the cashiers. I stand in the produce section, in front of the lettuce, unable to choose red leaf or bibb. When another customer reaches for a head of romaine, our eyes catch in the boy's howl. I glimpse his mother at the checkout. She has a red coat, a neat, blond haircut, and a stone face. Her shopping cart is packed. I want to offer something, something soothing; but I just stand and stare at them until the cashier returns the mother's credit card, and the mother wheels her wailing boy and their groceries out of the store.

Home again, I curl into the shape of an egg on my living room rug, and angle myself to get the most of the sun's last shine for the day. It's just me and my boxes on this rug.

When I emerge from my shell, the cradle my hands made for my head, I reach for the loveseat, pulling it by a leg out from the southern wall. I stand and slide the small bookcase there; before, it was tucked under the window. I push the desk to the window: I'll have a view of Cambridge treetops while I write. The loveseat's still waiting for a new spot. I maneuver it toward the dining table: if I have guests, they can relax near me on the loveseat while I cook.

Standing at my cutting board with broccoli, trout, and my favorite knife, I turn around to scan my new home. My own interior feels aired out and set in motion.

T H E Wild Women's Center is on Lawrence Street in Cambridgeport, just beside a small playground and basketball court, ten blocks from the Charles River. Cambridgeport's residents are a mix of families, artists, and recent college grads; West Indian immigrants, African Americans, Puerto Ricans, and working-class whites. Across the river, in Brighton, Southeast Asians have recently settled. Women from that neighborhood come to school at the Center, too.

From my apartment, I can walk to the Center in thirty-five minutes. If I time it right, I can take a bus from Mass. Ave. down Magazine Street to Lawrence, and save fifteen minutes. The Center is in a nearly hundred-year-old, periwinkle blue Victorian house, its name modestly painted on a sign that hangs over the front door. I admit to myself I'm here at least in part because of how much I like the Center's name.

I wear green corduroy pants, a yellow blouse, and a red plaid vest. To look older, I need such tailored clothes. And Mom used to say, when she subbed in the Cleveland public schools, that starting off on a conservative foot was the way she gained her students' respect.

I walk up a few steps to the porch and enter a cozy living room with two slightly worn sofas and a tall bookshelf. There are two other rooms on the first floor: the childcare room and a kitchen. The second floor holds a classroom with a round table surrounded by folding chairs, and Nancy Sullivan's office, where there's also a desk for all the teachers to share. On the third floor, a dozen wooden writing desks form a haphazard circle; another tiny room holds two overstuffed chairs.

Nancy has given me two groups of women nearly ready to take their GED tests; each meets three times a week. "I want these ladies writing," she says. "And I want you all to have fun at it."

She gives me a quick pat on the back. "I'll be in my office working on grant proposals if you need anything. I'm sure you'll do extremely well."

When she leaves, I think at least one of us must be crazy. I've done a lot of reading and writing in my time, but I've never taught a class!

I take a seat at my room's round table and wipe a crusty spot on my vest with spit while I wait for my students to arrive. *I'm not prepared enough. I don't know anything about teaching, I just know I like to write in my journal.* I hear the husky voices of women coming up the stairs, giggling, teasing one another. It sounds like someone had a good date over the weekend. Once they stand at the door to our classroom and see me sitting with my open journal at the round table, the women get quiet as nuns. The xeroxed article I intend to hand out and the class roster are piled neatly on the table, giving me purpose and maturity. But surely these women also see how tiny and young I am. *How new at this.*

The students take chairs, averting their eyes from mine. They are all different ages, shapes, colors. They take their seats delicately, like we're in a porcelain room that could break. I ask each one her name.

"Marianne Donnelly," the one beside me says.

"Marianne Donnelly," I repeat, turning so our eyes can meet. She has a stocky build, skin pale as mine, short black hair, a thick Boston Irish accent, a chipped front tooth that doesn't keep her from grinning. I think she might be nineteen.

"Belle Jimenez." She looks twenty-five, maybe two or three years older than me. She has an athlete's body, a creamy, light-brown complexion, muscles rolling out of her T-shirt like fast balls, and a Spanish lilt.

"Saundra Naylor." She has a deep, rich voice that matches her dark skin. Under the table, I see her hand rest shyly on a bulging belly. She must be forty. She doesn't want our eyes to meet.

"Marianne Donnelly, Belle Jimenez, Saundra Naylor," I say, the repetition giving me the group's attention and reinforcing my memory.

"Kunthea Rath." She won't return my smile; but she's not afraid to look me in the eye or nod to let me know she is serious about the work we will do together. I can't tell her age. She's small and as delicately built as I am; the stack of books in front of her is piled high and neat.

"What kind of a name is that?" Belle Jimenez blurts, "Kunt Rat!"

I don't think Belle knows how belligerent she sounds. Her smile is toothy and warm, but her bluntness cuts like a knife. And I like her, maybe for the sassiness of her smile.

"Kunthea Rath," I say. "It's Cambodian, yes?" I look at Kunthea to confirm what Nancy told me when we went over the Center's makeup.

Kunthea nods.

"I think it's a beautiful name."

"Huh," Belle says, as in, "I think it's stupid."

I want to rest my hand on Kunthea's arm, but she is too many chairs away. I meet her eyes kindly, hoping she'll give Belle a chance.

Velma Langley, the next woman, could be twenty or thirty-five. She sounds Jamaican; but I realize she could be from some other West Indian island, or a place I've not imagined.

I nod with a reserved smile toward her. "Velma Langley," I say.

There are twelve students in this class. I distribute an article I got from a class I took in Ann Arbor on the history of women's work in America. The women are with me, sort of, for a while as I read it aloud; this is the way school's supposed to be, and they're here to be good students. Then I ask if someone else would read. The air turns stiff, as if a soundproof wall was suddenly erected and I am now the only one hearing my words. No one volunteers. I decide to keep reading, wishing someone would call the article stupid, so I'd at least have a voice to interact with.

Nancy had warned me, they're slow readers. But they're all so alert to my every move, the tonal changes in my voice, it's hard for me to believe that.

With half the number of students, I might find a way to sit individually with these women and learn what they'd really like to do. Instead, I suggest, "We could write our own articles. We could start by interviewing women we know who have interesting jobs."

"That's boring," Belle Jimenez mumbles, after a long ten seconds of silence.

Saundra Naylor says, "Uh huh." In just two syllables, she's shredded my idea.

The rest keep their eyes down and away from me while I finish reading the article in a weary voice. I dismiss the class. Gathering my papers, I feel a sore throat coming on.

Marianne Donnelly walks with me back to the office so she can use the phone. "So how do you like us?" she asks.

I hope her question is at least a little friendly, not just a test. "Well," I say, appreciative of the interaction. "I'd prefer a smaller group." *How does anyone teach without draining themselves—especially when most teachers have twice as many students as I have? Is it possible to leave a classroom feeling exhilarated?*

"Wait till November," Marianne says. "Half of them will have dropped out."

H O M E now. I need to get off my stuffed chair and put the chicken I left marinating this morning in the oven, reheat yesterday's potato kugel, sauté some broccoli.

I catch a glimpse of myself in the mirror and I'm surprised: I feel so alone, but I look okay, comfortable. I lay out tomorrow's clothes: a navy skirt and a periwinkle blue, ballet-neck T-shirt. Despite my acceptance of Marie's dare—to impose myself on the world—my clothes are so preppy.

There's determination in my eyes, and plenty of sadness. I have no friends in this new place, and I can't even call my own mother to moan about it. I let this thought linger as I sit down to a whole, perfectly roasted chicken, potato kugel, broccoli sautéed in olive oil and garlic—and National Public Radio.

Why do I always cook enough for three or four people?

I W A K E with my arms wrapped around one of the down pillows Mom gave me when I went off to college. The tiny buttons that close my long johns down my center feel like a sensuous trail. I feel my skin move under these buttons. My hand brushes over my breasts, and I feel a little tingle. In the bathroom, I see a new red mountain pushing to explode at the surface of my cheek. I feel so exposed.

At school, I tell my students: "Write 'I am the one who' at the top of a blank page. Then keep writing until you get to the bottom." It's an exercise Marie recently suggested I try in my journal. Like a steamy kitchen, the room heats and swells while everyone writes. I look into each woman's eyes as I collect her paper; each looks back and lets me know her story needs respect and care.

"I am the one who wants to be loved," Belle's paper says. "I am the one who need help but don't show it."

"I am the one who wants to write about her life," Marianne writes, "from when I lost my mother at the age of ten."

"I am the one who is all way praying to the Lord," Saundra says. "Because that's what my grandma done, and she the one who razed me."

Hazel Cotton, an infrequent visitor to our class, twenty-two, with the cutest pixie shape that a pregnant belly only complements, writes, "I am the one who is having a baby girl. So I want to right some storys for her."

"I would love to read your stories," I scrawl in the margins, almost shaking from the trust they've given me. "Please write back." These women want to write the stories that I want to read, I realize—stories that tell what being a woman and a mother are all about.

October 1982
Dear Hannah,

> *Think of you all the time.*
> *I'm at my usual loss of words. Very frustrated, very angry, very empty. Would like to return to our meaningful relationship. Can't cope with your letter writing, your lack of letter writing. Realize you have no need for me and I cannot open any door and so I withdraw.*
> *Wonder if you have filled this emptiness I feel or closed the door forever. Can only wait it out. Can't take your indifference. Can't be what you want me to be. Can only be myself. Hope you have not lost any of your creativity, your freshness, your desire to be loved and to love in return.*
> *I'm here, as always,*
>
>   *Mom*

She's hurting. That's clear. And she writes as if I'm the one who started this no-talking thing. It sounds like she doesn't know that I'm hurting, too. Three nights in a row, I phone Seattle. Each time, Norm answers and tells me Mom's asleep.

"But your time, it's only four in the afternoon. Could you wake her?" I finally ask him.

"I don't think so," he says. "I'll tell her you called, don't worry."

"Will you tell her I'd like to talk with her?"

"Sure I can," he says. "But she's pretty set she doesn't want to talk with you." Norm sounds mostly annoyed with me for disturbing him. I realize I don't expect much from him; maybe I never did—even though I've called him Daddy all these years.

"Look," I say, exasperated, "I just want to tell her hello." *Hello. I got your letter. I carry it around in my journal. I'm teaching, and I love it.*

"Hannah," he says, "I'll tell her. And I'm sorry, but I just don't know if she'll talk with you."

I ARRIVE home from Bread & Circus just as my neighbor is heading out her door. "Hi," she says, in our dimly lit hallway, "I'm Annie Kingston." She's tall—probably five seven at least, probably in her late twenties. She has long, straight, blond hair; a warm, Scandinavian face.

"Hi," I say, putting my groceries down in front of my door so I can allow for a proper introduction. "I'm Hannah Felber. I just moved here from Michigan."

"Welcome," Annie says warmly. Her outfit is made of a silky maroon fabric that drapes her like a sort of Roman toga.

"I like your outfit," I say. *But she wears pink neon lipstick.*

"Oh, thanks," she says. "It's Moroccan. I heard you're from Ann Arbor. What made you move here?"

I look up at her, keenly aware of my petite frame, my dark eyes and curls, my tailored navy skirt and white blouse. "I'm teaching," I say. "At the Wild Women's Center."

"Wow," Annie says. "That sounds neat."

I bob my head a bit. "I like it," I say. "So far."

"Mm," Annie says. Beginning at the top of her forehead, she runs a hand through her hair. It touches me that such a striking woman would have a nervous habit; and it makes me like her, actually.

"What do you do?" I ask.

"I'm in theater," she says. "I'm an actress with the A.R.T.—the American Repertory Theater. I'm off to a rehearsal right now."

We hear my phone ring. As I scramble to unlock my door, we bid each other a quick goodbye.

"Hannah?" Gram asks, while I turn on a light in the kitchen. "Why haven't you called me?"

"I'm sorry," I say, not because I mean it, but because it's polite. "I've been overwhelmed. My classes have started."

"What do you mean overwhelmed?"

"I've got about twenty-five students who have really wonderful stories to tell," I say. Explaining myself to Gram is tiresome, like my long day. "But not all of the writing assignments I've given them so far have worked. I'm trying to come up with assignments that are, you know, more creative than 'How I Spent My Summer Vacation.' "

"Well, what kind of stories do you want to *read,* Hannah?"

"Oh, Gram, I don't know," I say, raising my left shoulder to hold the phone against my ear so I can use both hands to put away my groceries. I want to get dinner started. "I want to read stories about what their lives are like. You know they come from a bunch of different countries, and a lot of them are mothers."

"So," she says, "you like family pictures so much—do something with family pictures."

"Such as?" I can't help noticing the irritated tone in my voice.

"I don't know, Hannah. Ask them to describe some family picture, so someone who doesn't have the real picture could imagine it," Gram insists, overriding my irritation.

"Maybe," I say. I don't want to give her credit, for some reason—though this is really a wonderful idea.

"What've you got to lose?" Gram harps.

"All right, Gram. I said I'd try it."

"No, you said 'Maybe,' " she harrumphs back.

"Hey, Gram, I just met my new neighbor," I say, changing the subject. "Her name's Annie Kingston. She's an actress."

"Oh?"

"Mm hmm," I say. "And she seems nice."

"Well *that's* good, Hannah."

"Yeah," I say. "I think so, too."

"CLOSE your eyes," I say. "Imagine a photograph of your family, and describe it for someone who's never seen the picture." I hand each woman a blank sheet of paper, noticing that the room is already quiet—a sign that the assignment's a good one.

Estelita Cabral, who has been to class only twice in two months, whispers to me in halting English, "No write." She's from Cape Verde, an island off the west coast of Africa, where people speak Portuguese. I don't know how long she's been in Boston, but by the scrawl at the top of her paper, I see that in English, she can barely write her name. "Do you have a friend here?" I ask, wondering how she got to my class, knowing she'll need lots of tutorial time.

"Nobody knows me," she says. She has large gray eyes that don't close. Her soft, well-curved body—seems to float in sadness.

"Meet me at my office after class," I say. "I'd like some time with just the two of us."

But she doesn't show up.

IT's a Saturday afternoon in March. I'm reading Joan Chase's new novel, *During the Reign of the Queen of Persia*, cooking a stew of brown rice and lentils, taking breaks to dance in my living room. Rays of sun linger now on my floor for a few hours each day. *The floor is my lover.* I give my weight to the wood boards, roll and arc in the golden light. At the beginning of the month, the woman I've been subletting from decided to let me have the lease. So I'm now the proud tenant of a rent-controlled apartment in Cambridge, Massachusetts.

The phone rings. I still don't get a lot of calls; certainly not on a Saturday afternoon.

"Hannah?" a familiar woman's voice asks.

"Yes."

"It's Ellen Katzman."

"Wow, Ellen—hi!" I say. Ellen lived about a block from Karen's family. She was a year ahead of us in school. She went to Georgetown University to study political science; I heard from Karen that she stayed in Washington after she graduated, and got a job in a senator's office. She offered Karen her living-room floor when Karen auditioned for her dance company nearly a year ago. Karen had a new boyfriend there, and she was getting along well with her mother, too. I wasn't surprised when our conversations grew further and further apart. I just didn't know how to tell her I wanted her to listen to me—not just for me to be supporting her.

"I have bad news," Ellen says somberly.

"Okay," I say, scanning my desk under the bay window with the new Phoebe Snow record I just bought on it, and my dining table, covered with papers for school.

"Karen committed suicide, Thursday."

"Ohhhh," I gasp, bringing my free arm around my face and head, as if to shield myself from a blow. I moan from my gut, then dip to the floor in a squat, and rock myself.

Ellen waits silently until I am ready to speak.

I sit back up. "What do you know?" I ask.

"She just broke up with her boyfriend, and she wasn't really making enough money to support herself. She moved into a house with a few other dancers in Maryland about a month ago. The last time I talked to her, maybe a week after she moved, she said she felt there was no *reason* for her dark moods. They didn't come from a concrete, tactile place—and the mystery of that scared her. She left a note that said the therapists she saw didn't believe her feelings. They tried to convince her she was okay."

"Oh, God, Ellen, you know, we talked about all this while we were in college. But then she was feeling better."

"I know," Ellen says. "You know the dance company really loved her. She was doing really well. But then she broke up with Chris, and something snapped—even though she was the one who initiated their breakup.

She said she loved him, but she knew it wasn't right for her to stay with him."

"How did she die?" I ask, walking myself and the telephone cord over to the table, so I can sit on a chair.

"Carbon monoxide poisoning," Ellen says, her voice just above a whisper. "In her garage."

I double over and let my head fall between my knees, keeping the phone to my ear as best I can. I imagine Karen asleep in the fumes, resting. *In poisonous fumes, her face would be contorted, uneasy.*

"So STUPID!" I blurt, sitting upright with a jolt. "When did she become STUPID?!!"

"There's one more piece," Ellen says. "The funeral was Friday. We both missed it."

Suddenly, I smell a burnt odor: I've forgotten the lentil stew. The bottom layer is crusty and charred. I'm sure that no matter how hard I scrub, this pot will forever show dark marks outlining bits of rice and beans.

Once Ellen and I say goodbye, I realize I have to get out of my apartment. I throw on my down vest and head for the Charles. On the Mass. Ave. bridge, which the subway traverses, I can moan as loud as I want, and no one will hear.

"Mrs. Caplan? This is Hannah, Karen's friend."

"Ohhh, Hannah," she says. "Hannah." When she starts to sniffle, I join in.

"Ellen Katz called me," I say, though I'm sure she's figured out I've been told about Karen's death.

"You were Karen's best friend. Her very best friend."

I don't know that I deserve to be called that for the kind of friend I was in the last couple of years, but I don't protest.

"I'm really sorry she's gone," I say. "I'm going to miss her so much." *I always figured we'd get closer again. I just didn't know when.*

"*Oui,*" she says. I sense her holding back tears. "Are you still in Boston? That's the last I heard."

"Yes," I say.

"I should have called you," Mrs. Caplan moans. "I should have told you about the funeral."

"It's okay," I say. "I'm glad we're talking now."

She's silent for a long moment, then asks me what I'm doing.

"I'm still teaching writing. I like it."

"That's good. And how is it with your mother?"

Her question pierces me. Karen must have told her. I'm grateful to have my grief out in the open. I even like Mrs. Caplan knowing my relationship with my mother turns out not to be perfect. But if I tell her how hard a time I have with Mom, where will that take us? "It hasn't changed," I say quietly. "We still don't talk."

"Uhn," she moans again, as if this news hurts her in the same place that Karen's death now occupies. "I'm so sorry to hear that."

I don't hide my tears. "Mrs. Caplan," I say. "I called to comfort *you*. But you're comforting *me.*"

"I guess it works that way sometimes. Listen, call me Becky, okay?"

"Okay," I say.

"And keep in touch with me. That's what you can do to comfort me."

"GRAM," I begin, feeling whimsical or a little crazy that I'm calling her before eight A.M. as I ready myself for school, "you've lived eighty years. Tell me, how do people get by?"

It's a month since Karen's death, and despite the fact that I love my job, I wrote two new poems this week, and I have a neighbor I like well enough to invite for dinner, I am waking up at three o'clock each morning, unable to sleep. I have itchy, red lines at the folds over my eyelids. I keep remembering the smile Mom gave me in the Cleveland bus station just after I met Marie and Norm had returned to work—two years ago. *"I don't respect you anymore,"* she said the next day. *"And so I no longer respect myself."* Each morning, I wake with this memory. And when the phone rings on Saturday afternoons, I panic: someone could be calling with horrendous news.

"Well," Gram says, obviously pleased to be asked her opinion, "my mother got by better than anyone I know. She used to talk to the baby she miscarried before me. Vitl, she called her."

"What do you mean?" I ask.

"Just what I'm saying. My mother talked to Vitl. She'd ask questions, Vitl would give her answers."

"But Vitl was dead! I mean—she never got born!"

"Sure." Gram seems to think such conversation is logical, and practical, too. "Look," she says. "When you don't have to run off to work, I'll tell you more about her."

"I'd like that," I say.

"Sure," Gram continues. "I could tell you about Vitl, about my mother, even about Celia."

"Oh," I blurt, feeling something like affection for Gram swelling in my chest, noticing the bowl of grapes on my kitchen table, and sliding a bunch into my lunchbag.

I hang up the phone hungry for arms that would wrap and hold me. A man's arms.

When I open the lobby's front door to the cool spring air, my body feels like a Mason jar of captured fireflies. I buzz, electrically awake, thinking I could fuel a rocket launch.

EIGHT

1926-1941

CHANNA

THE first time I see Moe, I think on that Cossack who threw on my grandmother's grave his bottle of vodka. The way he walks into my house looks the same to me as that soldier man at my Bubbe Sarah's funeral. He's not big on words, but he has a mission. Ida, when she tells us, "He wants to marry me," I can see she wants to have a sweet feeling for him. But she doesn't. This is her suffering.

Meyer of course, when he hears it that Moe Zeitlin of the downtown plumber's shop wants to marry Ida, he says he's never heard such good news. Sure, because she is getting on, twenty-four already. And this Moe has a good business. He's a Socialist, Meyer. But when he looks on a man with money in his pocket, he thinks, *I klug, i sheyn, i men ken gut zingen.* This man, he is also wise and handsome and probably he sings well, too.

It's true, right after they marry, Moe buys a big house, to give Ida a nice American life. I'm sure he knows it, what a dignified woman he got himself. But yet, except in his leather book, where Ida says he writes down poems, the kindness Ida has doesn't have a place with him. He buys her a washer machine, and one for me, too. He's a greenhorn, like Meyer and me, and yet he reads and writes English, and he makes money, too. And he has a big heart, Moe. But it's too busy. Too much pepper in it. Too much salt.

To live with him, I see Ida makes herself a shell like what grows around walnuts.

I guess I'm living long enough to see a nice American life has nightmares in it, like any other life. The funny thing is, once Ida has Celia, the bright rash under my navel, it goes away. I had this rash since a week or so after I went to the abortion doctor. Like a spread of strawberry jam it looked every morning I woke and didn't tell Meyer what I'd done. "What is it?" he asked me finally, with his eyes so kind I knew I could answer.

"It's a map of my sunken heart," I said. And I told him. He nodded. My husband understands the lot of women. I figured such love would make my rash go away, but still my belly burned red. Every remedy you can imagine, I tried it—cucumbers, oatmeal, clay. Nothing helped. Until Celia got born.

She doesn't have a blemish this girl, not a one. But her limbs are so scrawny and her eyes so dark and scared, when I look on her I wonder if I'm seeing the fear of more than one young girl.

M E Y E R and I, Mollie too, we go to Ida's every Shabbes, for dinner. Nineteen forty-one it is now. We all know that in the Old Country, times for the Jews are not good. We know by a feeling in the air, not by the American papers the men read, or the radio.

This one evening, I stand near Ida while she washes her lettuce. "My neighbor Judy Finkus keeps talking the Germans have a system now," she says, "to get rid of all the Jews. They made camps, the Nazis. Not for labor, but for death. They make the Jews like slaves. They have people dig their own graves, then the Germans give showers with poison or shoot their guns, and put the bodies in the pits, with some still alive."

Ida's voice now has the same weight as her lettuce. She's not washing it, just putting the dirty leaves into her salad bowl.

"She got her news in the *Forward,* Mrs. Finkus. She still reads it every day."

"Ya," I say. All of this I have heard before. "At the butcher's, Mrs. Shapiro told me about hands sticking out of windows on trains, reaching for air or water what never comes."

What do I do with such news? I wonder about my friend, Anya Davidson. We used to play together on Shabbes in Koretz, before I left to America. Her father was our rebbe. Just after Mollie was born, I heard word that the Cossacks made such a mess of Koretz, any Jews left there moved to Kiev. I heard the Davidsons moved there. So, now, what's happening to Anya and her family? What's happening to the Jews in Kiev? I wonder.

"So maybe," Ida says, "there's no God." She turns to put her salad on the table, and our eyes catch. "Do you ever ask Vitl what she thinks of this war, or what she thinks God is up to?"

"Sure," I say, "She tells me, 'Keep talking. Keep asking your questions. Keep feeling what you feel.' "

Ida starts to scrub her roasting pan. "That doesn't answer my question," she says.

My eyes, they wander. Onto Celia they catch. She is just ten winters now. She watches us from the next room, with small ears ready to hear everything. I give her a little smile and reach my arm out for her to come tuck into my side. "Ma," Ida asks just then, "would you go down to the basement for a can of tomatoes?"

Celia comes with me. Near the bottom of the stairs, she tugs my hand and whispers, "What does God do?"

I start to give her some kind of answer, but then there's Moe, leaning against Ida's washer machine. His arms he has folded on his chest. From one hand, a bottle peeks out. I know what it is in that bottle. I know also it won't do any sense to hide Celia from it—probably she has seen this already a hundred times. He has short shirtsleeves, and also it is unbuttoned at the neck this shirt. I think, *Kenehore,* may there be no evil eye, what muscles he has.

"Ha!" Moe says. "I can tell you all about God, Celia! God is God. But whiskey is something you can drink!" And from the quiet basement he lets out such a laugh—like that soldier from home had laughed from his big belly.

I don't have a hiding place to give her, Celia—a place where I could hold her and shush her. Even with her body so skinny she is too big for me to carry upstairs to a quiet room without everyone asking, what for? It would be a fuss. I still have the tomatoes to get, too. But now Celia looks like she can hardly walk. On the landing halfway up, I bend over, then sit on a stair and give her a squeeze.

It's all I can do.

"You know, Celia," Moe shouts, "a good Jew should drink so much he shouldn't see any difference between Mordecai and Haman!"

On Purim only, I think, not in the middle of December! Just then I catch a red blotch on Celia's leg—the left one, above the knee, just under the hem of her dress.

"Moe Zeitlin is Moe Zeitlin!" he goes on, singing to himself. "Moe Zeitlin is a good Jew!"

Ida, she hears him, she comes to the top of the stairs. With the light behind her, she looks like a dark ghost. *"Der biterer tropn,"* she says. "He's got whiskey."

"Ya," I says. For the moment, we all stay quiet. I stroke Celia's head and her back, stiff like a washboard. I wonder how she got this rash what looks like what I had after my abortion.

Ida, even in the shadow, looks so steady. With my arms around Celia, I remember when Ida came, my first who lived. I had such happiness that even my tatte got to smiling again. But when I took her to my chair by the river, Vitl would remind me of things other than dreamy happiness. "Even if the child lives," she would say, "soon enough she'll get too big for you to carry. She's for your arms now, sure. But a child does not remain a child forever."

So while Ida was a child, I learned to care for her like a tree on the street. I noticed her, I admired her. I made a decision to believe she'd get what she needed on windy days. I reminded myself her life was in God's hands.

From when she was a baby and I was pregnant again, with Mollie, I felt Ida didn't need me like other children did. Even before she was talking with words, somehow she could give me the idea, "Look, we're both women. We'll help each other out." It's a good thing, too. With all the children I had after all, I don't see how I would have managed without such a grown-up girl.

So now she has Moe for a husband; she has Rita—who can't wait to get out of her mother's house; and Celia—a pretty face with a scared heart. We also have this terrible war starting. I don't know what I have of use to give her,

Ida. But Celia is the one I keep my eye on—like once I kept my eye to the ocean.

"What's the rash on Celia's leg?" I ask Ida, when we are back to the kitchen.

"I don't know," she says. "It's been there awhile, like a stain. I've had two doctors look at it. They both say not to worry." Ida, she talks now like a river that's just gotten free of ice. "Once I saw Celia with a cool cloth on it," she says, "but she wouldn't talk about it. Whenever I ask her, she tells me to let her be. So, I let her be. Sometimes I think it's gone away, then I see it again. I tell myself, *loz kokhn biz oyf Shabbes*—let it cook 'til Shabbes. You used to say that, ya?"

"Ya," I say. "I still say it."

"But Ma," Ida says, tears coming down her cheeks, "since I married Moe, I've had no Shabbes."

From my bosom, I give her a tissue. "In your heart," I say, "you can make Shabbes."

FUN krume shidukhim aroys glaykhe kinder. From crooked matches come straight children. Rita, our first grandchild, she has a practical mind, like Ida. And like her father, she knows how to get what she wants. Already I see it, how she thinks to her future. To look on Rita makes me hopeful we'll see great-grandchildren yet.

And Celia. I've never met anybody who doesn't think Celia is the most beautiful child they've ever seen. Like a chiseled doll she looks, with skin pale as the sky before sunrise. Like she comes from another world, with everything about her soft.

Around a baby, if I just sit quiet, my insides get warm. I can feel the world spin. I hear the quiet that mixes with a roar, like when I put a shell to my ear. Well. To be with Celia, even as she gets older, is like this. Vitl tells me Celia wants only for me to sit near her with my own thoughts—while she is with her thoughts. It makes Ida nervous to sit like this, I think.

Me, I love to sit with Celia. Summers, on Ida's back porch, we sit. I rock, in the wicker chair. Celia hangs her legs over the wood, the floorboards, and I just look on her while she eyes the blackberry bushes behind the house. Practically a jungle it is, growing back there. So thick those bushes are, I don't think that ground ever sees a speck of sun, even in winter, when it's just branches making shade.

Celia, she's looking out there for something. She doesn't like anyone to touch her without permission, me included. I have a feeling she has a big something burning in her china doll body what she doesn't know where to put. Armies she has, ready to go off to war, living in a china doll body.

It aches me. Especially because I don't know what to do. All I know for doing is to let myself ache. She reminds me of the ocean, Celia, and the way I used to watch it, but really it was watching me. She reminds me of the waves that were little and calm. Because underneath, I knew they were wild.

Each Passover, I give the girls a quarter to run down to the corner market for an ice cream. "Don't let the neighbors see," I say when I put the coins in their hands. You know, on this holiday, ice cream's not kosher. But I want to give them a secret, something simple we can keep one to another.

"I HAVE ghosts," Celia says, one day while she is at my house, helping me to make latkes, potato pancakes.

"Ya? Goats?" I says; "What names are your goats, *Bubbele?*"

"GHOSTS!" she says at me; like she feels everything in her little body is *treyf,* dirty. With this big noise she makes, her skin gets tight—like ghosts are on different sides of her face, pulling skin.

Ay, my little Celia. Like a yeshiva boy, she walks into a room—shy. She never puts her hands to her hips or bunches her lips, like Ida does when she has a mad. Like Rita can do, real good. Celia is just a beauty to behold, in fine dresses even the Czar's daughter might not know from. Here, Celia has enough mad I think, she could kill somebody. It's such a big noise she makes, "GHOSTS!"

I am glad to hear it. "Ohhh, ghosts!" I say. "Ghosts! Come, tell me about your ghosts, Celia."

"NOOOO!" she says.

What's with her? I wish I could know. Like a chicken with a head cut off she acts, running between death and life. *Ach!* I must be crazy with such thinking. I want to give her a *glet,* a caress. But I don't want to put a scare on top of what she's had. "It's okay, Celia," I say. "Ya, ghosts, it's okay. I have ghosts what visit me, too. You tell me about yours only if you want."

She gets quiet. But she looks on me with a stare like you can't imagine. With a stare a gangster should buy, probably good as a bulletproof vest.

FROM mothering, Ida has big hurts. With Rita, it's like she doesn't care so much what her parents think. She has friends she likes, and a mind already making herself a family of her own, different from Moe and Ida and Celia. With Celia, Ida worries she can't give proper protection to such a delicate girl—who won't even let her mother give her a hug. No matter how Ida tries, Celia rolls her eyes. Ida frets she can't give her daughter any good at all. Not with Moe so crazy.

One night Mollie and I are there for dinner, just a few months after my beloved Meyer dies. Moe yells at Ida. Like one of those ambulance sirens that's broken and can't shut off. "You didn't get an easy man to live with," I tell her when we are in her kitchen alone for a minute, picking up a glass one of the girls has dropped and broken. "Oh, *a froy ken fartrogn a gantse velt*—a woman can stomach a whole world," she says. *"Arayngerekhnt dem sotn*—the devil included."

She says this so sturdy. I wonder, from where does she get such sturdiness? And then I see of course, it comes from not knowing what else to do. From not knowing how to talk to a child what has hell and heaven stirring together, right there in the belly of her soft body. Celia has eyes so dark I sometimes think they come from the Other World. She plays with the neighbor girls sometimes, that's good. But in this world, what is Celia's pleasure? Where is her place? Ida, I bet she wants to know this, too; Moe, I don't know what he knows at all.

"No matter what I do, it's never right," Ida says. "Not for Moe. Not for Rita. Not for Celia."

"If there's no right way with her," I say, "maybe also there's no wrong way."

I rest a hand to her arm. She has tears now; I think she's embarrassed. "This is my torture, Ma. Who knows why? And I've also gotten like Celia, nervous for people to touch me."

My lips bunch, I nod, I take my hand from her. I want she should know, with a day like this, still I can live.

1 9 8 6

HANNAH

EVEN though I finished that mythology course at the University of Michigan years ago, I still think a lot about Demeter and her daughter, Kore, whose name changed to Persephone when Hades brought her to the Underworld. I come upon a line the poet Adrienne Rich has written in her book *Of Woman Born,* "The loss of the daughter to the mother, the mother to the daughter, is the essential female tragedy"—as if it happens all the time.

Maybe I'm really not doing anything wrong.

Now, I've got a poem that feels hot in my hands, "Persephone's Lament." It's strange that I'm inspired by Greek mythology—not a Bible story. I'm not Greek, I'm Jewish. But maybe Demeter and Persephone can help me understand myself and Mom. Maybe even Karen and her mother.

It's three years since Karen died. At night, I often imagine her. The face I see is almost always her stony one, with enough anger to fuel a volcano; but for now, this mountain doesn't speak. Won't speak.

I called Becky Caplan last month, Karen's mother, and she said she's joined a support group for parents whose children committed suicide. It's helping her.

Is there a group for daughters of mothers like Mom?

———

"YOU'RE a nun!" Ava declares. She has just read my palm while I wait for Benjamin Katz, a high-school student who works behind the Bread & Circus deli counter, to stamp my potato salad with a price.

"Hannah's *Jewish!*" Ben yells. It's their bantering routine, which actually gives me a feeling of family. Some days I even look forward to it. And the truth is, Ava's not so far off the mark. It's been four years since my affair with Hal Riley. I go to the movies with Annie, my neighbor, every couple of months. I've gone on a few dates with men she's introduced me to from the theater. They have passion for their work, and I like that; but they drink so much beer while we're together, I can't tell who they really are. I told Annie if she knows a man who doesn't have to drink through his first date, I'd like to meet him. Until then, I'll keep to learning about being a woman—alone.

I visit Gram and Mollie a few times each year, insisting that they have old photographs on their kitchen tables when I arrive; I record our family stories on the pictures' backs. I spend my days teaching, buying my daily groceries, retreating home to nap or write, and dreaming of peace—with myself, with Mom, with Karen's face.

Meanwhile, I wake in the morning an hour before I need to, so I can lie in bed, doing nothing. I might write down a dream or a line to a poem. I come home after work and grocery shopping, put on Bach's *Sonatas for Unaccompanied Cello* (I have no television, despite one student's claim that this puts me "out of this world"), cook something that'll leave me with decent leftovers for a couple of days, read my students' stories or a novel while I eat.

Recently, because of a book I found at Bread & Circus, I've stopped eating sugar. Sugar might be what makes me so tired all the time; it might contribute to the intensity of my menstrual cramps. When I told Gram I'd cut it out of my diet, she said I reminded her of Grampa. In the forties, he decided that hotdogs and salami were dangerous, even the kosher kind. "And he turned out to be right," Gram said, adding, "I don't think sugar's ever done me any harm." I do feel at least a little silly taking away this basic American staple from my diet; but when I told Marie about it, she said a diet without sugar will force me to nourish myself. I like that idea.

Twice a year, I publish a four-page insert of Wild Women's stories in the *Tab,* the Cambridge weekly; we print five thousand extra copies and leave them in newsstands at the grocery stores. I'm always running into people who say they loved our last issue and can't wait for the next one.

When I ache for friendship, I walk down to New Words, the women's bookstore in Inman Square, or to the Grolier, which sells poetry in Harvard Square. If I'm lucky, I run into someone I know. Sometimes, if a stranger and I are eyeing the same book, we'll strike up a conversation.

I know I'm permeated with grief, and I don't make a great friend. At the Center, I don't share much of my own story with my students, but I don't have to hide my moodiness around them. We seem to agree that while we do our work, sadness is allowed.

Ava stares at me as if I'm a mystery she can't decipher.

Benjamin winks. I think he's trying to convey that he finds me sexy. *What can I say? That I'm a hermit? That I'm often intensely lonely? That I have a lot of debris to clean out?* Instead, I smile, shrug, and say, "Thanks, guys." I toss the potato salad they've given me into my handbasket.

I watch the seasons change. I notice winter linger, then leap into spring. I see the rust on cars, the degrees of gray and light in the sky. I notice the clothes my students wear—red sweatshirts, royal blue T-shirts, black jackets. I notice the cashier's mood at the grocery store. I hear neighbors fight in the apartment below mine. Like a black net, my grief from Karen's death and my mother's distance hang in the air, catching the moods and colors of my neighborhood I might otherwise miss.

Walking home from Bread & Circus with my groceries, I often see an old man, about seventy, walking toward his apartment building on Harvard Street. He's shorter than me, and round like a Pillsbury dough boy. He always wears a dark suit, and a rimmed hat like my grandfather might have worn in the fifties. I wonder where he walks from. He never carries anything. Sometimes his wife is with him. She's short, too, a little less round than he is. She wears maroon leather boots that look like they're straight from the Old Country—or a podiatrist. She wears these boots with an apron-covered shift in summer, or a tailored navy suit in winter. She walks with her hands behind her back. His are to his side.

I know they're Jewish, and I'm sure they know I am, too. It's the way they nod hello, ever so slightly.

————

"A N N I E—" I say into the phone. I always call her, rather than knock on her door, when I want to see her. The theater often keeps her up until one or two in the morning, so she sleeps as long as she can into the day—usually with another actor or a stagehand sharing her bed. Annie doesn't think sleeping alone is civilized. She explained this to me shortly after I moved in, before either of us knew how long I would sleep alone.

"I don't have *sex* with all of them," she explained, then went on to talk about her parents' deaths from a car accident when she was twenty, and the short marriage that ensued so she wouldn't have to live alone in the house she inherited. It lasted less than a year. Then she sold the house and used the money to finish a degree in drama.

"Hi," she says, into the phone. She's recognized my voice; she sounds awake.

"If you come over," I say, "you can hear my mother's voice. She left a message on my answering machine."

"Really? A message? What does she want?"

"You know, the usual," I respond with a flip tone. "Just to tell me that she loves me and doesn't want to talk."

"Oh, Hannah," Annie says, softly. "Hearing about your mother some days makes me grateful mine's dead."

By the time she's crossed our hallway, I can no longer hide that my heart's cracked open. Under my own doorway, I let myself cry on Annie's shoulders, feel the warmth of her soft breasts, then let her lead me to the answering machine that plays my mother's voice.

Hello, this is Mom. I'm glad I got your answering machine, because I just have a monologue here. I heard from Gram you're doing well at your teaching job. I'm calling to tell you that I'm proud of you. And I love you.

Uh, I see no reason for you to call me back.

After work and my daily trip to Bread & Circus, I read and type my students' stories, then photocopy them at Classic Copy on my way to work. In class, each woman reads her story aloud.

QUESTIONS FOR MY MOTHER
By Sharon Hamilton

At the age of seven my grandmother told me about my mother for the first time. She told me how she was nice and so pretty—like me. Not to brag about me. My grandmother said my mother used to sit up with me on the porch during nights, and sing to me for a long time. But things kind of changed when she had my little brother, because he died when he was still a little baby. My mom went kind of crazy on us. She left us for some man down South who wasn't even my brother's father.

I still talk to her on the phone sometimes. It's nothing special, just about boyfriends and do I have one. One time we talked for almost forty minutes. I wish I could have seen that phone bill of hers!

The last time we talked, there was one moment on the phone that left my mouth dry. My mother asked me can I forgive her for what she has done to me. She asked me not to hate her, but to give her one more chance.

I did not know what to say. My heart all of a sudden was jumping faster and faster like someone was chasing me with a gun. I couldn't even open my mouth. When I was not answering her, she asked, "Does the cat got your tongue or is it just you don't want to give me another chance?"

My mouth finally opened and I said, "Mom, I'll give you another chance, only if you apologize to my grandmother. She told me she loves you, but she still feels hurt for you leaving her." I told my mother I'll forgive her if she apologizes to her mom, 'cause that's the person she really hurt.

Next summer I am going down South to see her. It's been fifteen years. And I have some questions I'm going to ask her:

What did you do after you left Boston?

Was you thinking about my grandmother and me?

Do you still love us?
Are you proud that I'm your daughter?
Wanna make some corn fritters like I do with my grandmother?

EVEN with my new diet, my health has become precarious. I'm wiped out
each day after work, and have taken a few days off each month to stay home
and rest. The students I have this term have tough shells. Even four weeks into
the term, they need to be coaxed into speech. Maria Casiano told me today
she doesn't like our class because she doesn't like to think, and she doesn't like
to think because there are things she doesn't like to think about.

On paper, the women's stories are lush and revealing. But in the presence
of others, the class is divided between ones who are silent and those who are
belligerent. I don't see where or how to build a bridge. There's no discussion.
I suppose I could trust the silence and even the hostile glances I get when I
ask questions about what we read; but I ache to see friendships here.

I return home each afternoon with a weak voice, and eyes wanting sleep.
I trudge up the stairs to my apartment, unplug my phone 'til five o'clock so
I can sleep undisturbed before I wake to make my dinner. Sleeping feels like
part of my job, like digesting the day. It replenishes me enough to work a half
hour on my own poems before I read my students' stories, plan for the next
day's classes, and lay out my clothes for the morning.

I also have a rash on my forearms. Annie says it's eczema, and that a doctor would probably give me cortisone. She knows because her mother had it.
I don't want any cortisone, though some days the itching is so intense, that
rubbing it gives me an erotic charge. Some days I'm not bothered by it at all.
It's better after napping.

Meanwhile, I eat: baked potatoes, sauteed broccoli, thick slices of but-
tered rye bread, half a pound of broiled salmon. I worry that if I don't eat all
the time I'll lose weight. As it is, I'm a wisp of a woman. Why would a man
want me? There's hardly anything to pinch here.

My lips have begun to say *no* to all this food.

My belly says: Fill me. Help me. Fill me up *totally.*

I take the *American Heritage Dictionary* down from the shelf, look up *teuta,* the Indo-European root of "total." *Teuta* means "tribe." Its Latin root means "of the whole tribe."

Is my wanting—of food, of weight—rooted in desire to belong to a tribe? Am I part of the tribe of Wild Women? Are Gram and Mollie and I a tribe?

I LIE on a chiropractor's table, my lower back burning with stiffness—as if it's trapping heat. After missing four days in a row of work last week, I finally admitted to myself that my body isn't doing well, and called this man. Nancy Sullivan says he's helped her. "Are you a dancer?" he asks. "You've surely got the body for it." He's a large, strong man, frustrated that despite my small size, he can't crack my spine. "Petite women," he sighs. "You can be a challenge."

"As a kid I danced," I say. "Now I mainly keep to my living room floor. I don't like doing anyone else's steps."

"How about contact improvisation?"

"What's that?" I ask.

He tells me it looks like a cross between modern dance, tai chi, and wrestling. Usually it's done in duets. People play with weight—they let the momentum of weight lead the dance. There's no music. The dances look choreographed, but they're always made up on the spot. "My sister does it," he says. "She was a gymnast; and in contact, she can fly like she did as a kid, and she can lift men large as me, too."

"Oh," I say, genuinely interested—and just then, my back cracks.

I sign up for a beginner's class, and relearn the dancer's laws of gravity, friction, momentum. At one of my first contact jams, I dance with a man named Jason, who I figure is my age, maybe a few years older. Effortlessly, he lifts me over his head, then rests me on his shoulder. I feel like a glider in the air, until he says, "Hannah, you're not giving me your weight." Right there, flying toward the cathedral ceilings of a social hall in a Harvard Square church, I realize *I withhold my weight, even when I'm totally supported.* I let my ninety-eight pounds rest on Jason's shoulder.

"Every cell in your body holds water," he says. "That makes for a *heavy* body."

Returning me to the floor, he instructs: "Now push me. Otherwise it's like dancing without a partner. And don't let your mind go wandering off while we're in touch!"

I could fall in love with Jason, his verbal clarity, his perfect musculature, his ponytail. But he's gay.

One late winter afternoon, I enter the church twenty minutes into the jam. The Saturday sun filters through the beveled windows. I see a man lying face up on the wood floor near the heater. The rest he's allowing himself, his palms' caress of the floor, stirs me. I unlace my boots, quickly remove my coat and my socks. *I have to dance with this guy.*

I don't bother warming up. I walk over and stand with my heels about two inches from this man's knees. He's Japanese, my age, not much taller than me. I stand for two minutes, maybe four, facing the same direction he does. Slowly he lifts his left knee, the one closest to me, and leans it against the side of my right calf. Gently, I press back and keep pressing, until the fingertips of my right hand rise up in an arc that moves me toward the floor—while his left hand circles around his body, then strokes the length of mine.

For nearly an hour, we move in a fluid duet of weight and touch, pushing and playing like we're under water. *Replace your ambition with curiosity.* Jason once told me this, and now I might be experiencing it. Our dance ends with a simple, unmeditated stepping away from each other. I stare softly into the saddest eyes I've ever seen, not wanting to break our trance with words.

Eventually, I do. His name is Kiyo. His accent is thick, and as we walk across Harvard Square to Grendel's Den for dinner, I often have to ask him to repeat what he says. But I know he understands me. He lives in San Francisco. He's in Boston for a computer conference.

He tells me his father, an engineer, was involved in the attack on Pearl Harbor, then lost his first wife and two children in the bombing of Nagasaki. He married again—Kiyo's mother—and became a raging lunatic. "He hit my mother a lot," Kiyo says, once we return from the salad bar and begin to eat. "Very bad for me."

Oh dear, I think, slowly chewing my salad, uneasy that we've plunged so quickly from the grace of our dance into war stories.

"My father was disappointed," Kiyo says. "I had no ambition. Other boys had it." Just after he finished school, his father committed suicide.

As if his story is an offering, I nod, accept it, then take my turn. I tell him about Mom's refusal to speak with me; and that through a story I heard from my grandmother, I've begun to think that my mother's life—and maybe even her decision to cut me off—was shaped by the death of her first boyfriend, who survived a concentration camp because he was the sexual pet of a Nazi officer. I tell him about Karen, and her suicide. I tell him I write poetry, and that I teach at a women's center.

Kiyo nods. He is Japanese; I am a Jew. We're both descendants of a war that ended before we were born. While we linger at the restaurant, I realize that neither of us feels ready to say goodbye. I invite him to my apartment, knowing I might ask him to lie in my bed once we're there. I like his interest in me, and I'm curious to know more about him.

Soon enough, we lie in my bed like braided snakes, continuing our sensuous dance. His fingers touch me as if they're asking, *Who are you?* When I touch him, he just lies back, alert like a baby who's just begun to focus and see.

Then he moves to kiss me—like a famished animal set in front of fresh meat. "Wait," I say, turning away from his hunger. "That feels rough."

Kiyo's face turns stony. I don't want him to turn away, don't want him to think I've turned from him. But I can feel by his arms, now limp, that this is exactly what he perceives.

"You don't want intercourse," he says.

"Not tonight, anyway," I say, almost in tears for speaking so honestly with this man I will soon bid goodbye. "I just want you to hold me."

Kiyo sighs. "I've only done it twice," he says. "With you, I thought, maybe again."

I lie alone on my pillow, feeling a strange mix of repulsion and compassion. When we danced at the church, he was so extraordinarily gentle and graceful. Now in my bed, he wants to bite his way into lovemaking. "Sex wouldn't be right," I say. "Not for me." I must be a mystery to Kiyo. I told him it's been nearly four years since I've made love with anyone.

"I don't get it," he says. "You have a chance for love and you don't take it."

"Our connection feels *sensuous,*" I say, "not sexual."

"What does that mean?" he asks.

I sigh. I like being questioned like this. "I don't really know what it means," I say. "I like the way we danced. But I don't feel like making love."

"Plus," Kiyo says, "in two more days, I'll be gone for good."

"I know." I don't confess my doubts that I could really love anyone. We're all so full of flaws, of history we don't know how to touch.

TEN

---

1 9 4 1

FROM THE OTHER WORLD

LEAH

born c. 1869–1938

T H E ones with their feet on the ground, they say it is 1941. Me, I don't count anymore. But, four winters ago, I arrived to the Other World. And I sure don't miss hauling water.

Well, I decide to have a look, over my children now in Riga. My son-in-law Menachem Weinberg, my Masha's husband, he still works as a doctor. Also, he is the vice president at the Choral Synagogue on Gogola Street. He's a busy man. Plus, he has become nervous. His children, and Tamara's grandsons, all go to Jewish schools, but he knows the Germans are coming to Riga, and I think he doesn't see a way out.

The khevre kedishe, our Sacred Burial Society, is no longer allowed to operate. I'm dizzy, I tell you, looking on my people what can't honor its dead.

A L O N G the road into Riga comes a parade of Germans, with tanks. But Mr. Ilyitch, our landlord from Dvinsk, marches with them. Ya, there are other Russian men marching right with the Nazis. *Mr. Ilyitch! What are you doing?*

Ach! He wants to serve the winners. With his friends, Mr. Ilyitch pounds open the door to my Masha's house. Menachem, he is in bed—probably he hasn't slept for two days. He just got home from a family sick with fevers. *Ach, no!* They poke Menachem out of bed with the points of their rifles. They kick him, right in front of Masha and my granddaughter Ruchl. Now they kick my grandson Asher—just recently a bar mitzvah! The whole family they make march. More than two hundred Jews they make walk to the Choral Synagogue.

"*Es iz shreklekh, kinder meins,*" I whisper, "This is fearful, my children, very terrible. *Ikh vel aykh nit farlozn.* But I am with you. I won't abandon you."

I know Masha hears me, but I don't think she believes. She's in such a state she doesn't have room in her head for a mother's words.

Vey iz mir. I also wonder about Yeshia's children from his first marriage, and their families. In the stream of marchers, I have a hard time finding them. "Tamara!" I call out. "Chava!" But I don't see them, and I don't hear anything back.

Now the people are pushed into the shul. *Like matches in a tiny box,* I think, remembering a neighbor from Dvinsk, Mr. Rosenblum, who worked at the match factory—*just as I see the whole synagogue burst into flames.* Straight from the house of God, *my children go up in screams.* The Ruskies of Riga just watch. And they watch when a Nazi shoots down a woman who got left out of the shul. I have a wish for the dog to turn his rifle to me, too. Then I remember that won't do me any good. Because already I am in this Other World.

The sun sets, the sun rises. The sun sets, the sun rises. The Nazis and their Ruskie friends make a ghetto for the Jews left in Riga. It has a wall, so no one gets out. Here, I see Tamara with her family, looking for scraps of food. I see Perle Fineberg, my cousin Kayla's daughter who once had her eye on Moishe. Now she holds a little boy in her arms. She doesn't have even a cup of water to give him.

One day in November they take ten thousand Jews from this ghetto, and march them to the forest. Reb Mendel Sack is among them, the rebbe from Asher's yeshiva. The Nazis lift up their guns. Like hail on a field of ripe tomatoes, their bullets don't leave anybody standing.

One week later, it takes them two days, they kill the rest of my people. Fifteen thousand people in two days. What Jews are left in Latvia, they send to a concentration camp called Kaiserwald.

I hang over Riga, over the bodies of my grandchildren, my old friends and neighbors. I hang over the forest what I once visited with Daniel when he was a boy, over the blood of our rebbe, over the blood of Masha and Menachem. Like a cloud too black and thick to move, I hang.

I wait for them to join me. I wait. *Nothing happens.*

When a soul dies by fire or gunshot, does it go to the Other World a different way?

Does it go to yet another world?

ONCE you're dead, you're dead. Even the German boys and their mothers what I see here in the Other World—they're all dead, too. It makes me dizzy.

"Go to America," Rivke Plotkin tells me. "You still have people there. Don't you want to see life continue?"

Yes. Yes, I always wanted to see the palace my Moishe lives in, and his wife and his little girls, my granddaughters I never got to make blintzes for. Over America, I could have a look on Raisl and Daniel, too. So, I go.

My son's house is big like you can't imagine. Four rooms just for sleeping! A girl from a *goyishe* country, Ireland, lives in the attic to help Ida, Moishe's wife. That's a problem when you're rich enough to own a big house, I suppose—you have to be rich enough to pay someone to help you keep it clean. They get their heat from turning a knob, easy. Ida has a stove what makes different temperatures also by turning a knob. Moishe has a car he turns on with a little key. Like an emperor he sits in this car, comfortable. Doctors can come quick in these cars, and also they have a telephone to the doctor; to New York City if you have business.

Imagine it—a toilet, they call it—a nice porcelain thing on each floor of his house, takes everything away. I mean *everything!*

Then I spot the candlesticks I sent with Raisl on the dining room table, a big hand-carved table Moishe had men cart over from France. Nice it is, this table. A real king maybe has eaten on it. I remember when I gave Raisl those candlesticks to take to America. When I married Yeshia, they were like a present from his first wife. Her mother had given them to her. When I gave them to Raisl, I meant for her to keep them. But now I see, she gave them to Moishe, just like she gave her life for him.

Ach. I see my daughter sitting alone in her little room, just sitting. She sits sometimes with a radio, she calls it, and listens to music. She bakes challah for Ida, and some neighbors, too, to make a little money. Money for rent she gets from Moishe. Daniel, her son, has gone to the American army. To Japan, of all places. He writes her sometimes. Raisl. She sits alone. I wonder, would she like it that I look friendly on her?

And Moishe—he makes money, he has family, but Shabbes he has forgotten completely. Who needs a day for rest, I suppose, if you have fingers what can push buttons and make such magic happen, easy, every time easy. Ya, and if something funny happens, like you don't get your light or the hot air right away—well, if you act like now the world will end, people think you act normal; as though this is a good complaint for God to take care of right away.

It's no wonder I don't hear from Moishe. With electricity, water from a faucet, a car, what does a boy need from a mother in heaven? With all his American money, Moishe has got to thinking he doesn't need from God, either. Like he himself is Master of the Universe. And Ida, his wife—she doesn't have to worry or work for heat or water. But ha! She sure has worry enough for running her big house, and for making Moishe's books come out straight—worry and work what give her no pleasure. Even with that maid in her attic. Sure, I see she has troubles.

Every morning on smooth roads (including, do I have to say, on *Shabbes*) Moishe takes Ida in his car to his shop. He takes a smooth road with no trees, fast. News of the world he gets on a radio. Three or four times a day he listens to stories from all over. But these men from the box tell their stories without feeling. He has a radio in his car, at his shop, next to his bed. But yet he doesn't know the stories from Ida or the little girls. Certainly he doesn't talk with me, to hear what I have to say. You don't need electric wires to hear your own mother's voice! But Moishe already is an American businessman. I suppose he thinks different. At his shop, he works like a madman, bossing people. He reminds me a little of the Czar's officers.

And the two girls. The older one, Rita they call her, she is *zaftik,* a little plump. Nice. But already she has a mind she doesn't like her father. She has only twelve or thirteen winters, and she talks to him like he is stupid. Ha! She doesn't know anything what living was like for Moishe when he was a little boy, how hard he worked so she could live like a queen. The other one, Celia, she's a little skinny. She comes into a room like an angel, shy. But also, under her skin she burns hot coals. Actually, it concerns me. An innocent with a lot of fire, I'd call her. I don't see what she has to keep her feet on ground.

Rita is tough; but Celia makes me worry. Wide, wide eyes she has. And the face is so soft, you can't imagine. The face of an American princess Celia has, what doesn't know from scrubbing clothes in an icy river, or months of nothing but potatoes, or Cossacks taking away Jewish men.

Ida, she's a good mother, a good cook, a *balebatishe*—respectable. But most days now, she works at Moishe's shop. He makes like she has no choice. So the girls are left with that Irish woman.

Each of them in this house has her own closet yet, with more dresses than I can count. Here I have a bad feeling. Sure, it's wonderful my Moishe should have the money to buy for his wife and daughters so many outfits, each a different color. But in a year's time they will all be too small. The girls will again need new. They will get used to such fanciness. Sure, sure, it looks like Moishe has enough money to last forever, but who's to say? It makes me very nervous. If you have so many things, you think you don't need to ask God—or maybe anyone—for help.

Ach, what do I know? I am dead already. Still, for God, I have my words.

I T ' S near Hanukah, December, and the girls are almost ready for a little winter vacation. Rita has junior high; Celia is in the fifth grade. Girls going to school—this is a shock to me. But everything to me is a shock. Rita I see eats ham sandwiches with a *goyishe* girlfriend who lives next door. There's a wall of books in almost every house on this street like it's nothing. A phonograph that plays music. Ida, the richest woman I ever knew, is not happy. Not even a little bit happy.

Honestly, it's hard to make sense of things.

You don't get sick up here, since you don't have a body. But if it makes sense to you, I'll tell you what I see gives me a terrible taste in my mouth and a bad smell, something what lingers and can't be put out. I take a peek back to Riga. I don't see bodies now, but a proper burial I know my children didn't get. The Gentiles who were our neighbors once have taken from our houses what they wanted. I get a whirly, sick feeling, thinking on this—because so many people are glad we Jews are gone.

I go back to America. My eyes catch onto Celia. Ten years old she is. They're planning a party for her, another surprise for me—a party, for a girl's birthday yet, with cake and presents. Ida's sisters will all come and sing to her. But Celia doesn't smile about this.

Something is not right.

One evening, I see Celia choose her clothes for the next day. Then she gets into her bed, big enough we'd have slept three people and still had room to roll over. Ida comes in, pats her head, says, "Goodnight." When Celia turns out her light is when I get the feeling again, something here is *treyf.* Not kosher.

Her room is dark, but she keeps her eyes open and turns her head to her door. Small, stiff jerks she turns with, like the devil might be in her room. She keeps her comforter around her, close. All scrunched up with this cover she is.

Then who should come in but my Moishe. In he walks, and sits on her bed. "Where's my sugar?" Like a joker, he laughs. "Where's my kuchen?" But Celia is not laughing. No, her face gets hard, and she hugs her sleeping clothes, tight.

I nearly talk. I nearly say, "Here darling, come sit with me." But I know this would only scare her more, to hear from me. Just then Moishe lies down next to her, under her feather comforter. Celia has opened her eyes wide, with not even the eyelids to cover her. She gets so still, I don't see breathing.

I hear myself think, "I'll go back to Riga." But it's too late. Like Celia's eyes, mine are open.

Like she's his wife, Moishe wraps his arms around my granddaughter! "Oh, *here's* my sweet girl," he says.

He doesn't know *this is not right for Celia, this is not right* for a father to hold his daughter *like this.* Then, a *shande,* a shame, his privates get stiff. *His thing rubs on Celia's leg.*

"MOISHE!" I say. *"Her Uf! HER UF!!* Stop! STOP! Do you not see the scare in the child's body? *SHOYN Her Uf!* Stop NOW, I say!" But he doesn't hear me. He doesn't hear me at all.

"Kuchen, Celia," he says, and he presses himself against her again.

Celia, for her it's like when they put you in the grave, under a lot of dirt. Her little body gets heavier and lighter at the same time. She tries to get out of his arms. But Moishe, he doesn't even notice. "Such a sweet girl," he says again. "I could eat you!"

"MOISHE!" I scream so loud it blows the wind. The door to Celia's closet slams shut. But the only one who knows it's me is my mother, also here in the Other World. She comes to the room with me.

Ida's mother, Channa, she thinks she's waking up from a nightmare. But everything what she imagines and fears from her bed in Cleveland, Ohio, is what I see happening from the Other World.

Ida is in her kitchen, getting a cholent together that will be cooked while she and Moishe work at his shop the next day. Before she chops her onions, her eyes get blurry with tears, from where she doesn't know. She can't see for a minute, but she has the knife in her hand for cutting onions. When Rita comes to the kitchen to say she wants a glass of milk before she goes to bed, Ida feels dangerous—a blind woman with a knife. "Go sit at the table," Ida says crossly. Under her breath, Rita curses her own mother.

Celia, meanwhile, her eyes are closed now, her body looks like an old stone. Moishe, he pinches her cheek, hard enough it gets red. He thinks he is just saying goodnight, but his thing is on her leg! *Doesn't he notice this makes her want to die?*

Finally, Moishe gets out of Celia's bed, then he leaves her room. She turns her light back on, and goes to sit at her vanity. Into her looking glass she stares. Such a beautiful face Celia has, and hairs what curl like a baby's hand around a finger. Skin what glows like moonlight. She stares at her own rage. Then Rita comes to her sister's room, says, "What are you staying up for?" Celia doesn't talk, but turns out her light, closes her door, and goes back to bed.

To see what my son has become, it makes me feel dirty.

What did I do wrong? How did Moishe never learn to respect his wife and his daughters?

When I asked Raisl to lie with that Cossack, did I take from Moishe his choice to live? Did I take his knowing how to live properly?

I might be dead, but I have no place to hide. Not my son, not my shame.

THE next night I see Moishe go to Celia's room and open her door while she sits at her looking glass. She has a dress on, socks, shoes—even though it's time for her to sleep. Her hair, what she braided herself that morning, hangs behind her ears in two tails. She catches her father right away when he gets to her doorway. In her looking glass, they put their eyes to each other like they are nothing but eyes, waiting to see what will happen.

"Maybe I could invite her here, with us." I hear myself say this. But then I think, No. I can stand near her, is all.

My mind, *vey iz mir.* It has turned to chaos, trying to figure from where did Moishe learn to be a crazy man. Or is this the price of freedom for an American princess whose father lives because his mother asked his sister to lie down with a soldier? I remember Yeshia saying, "We study Torah not for answers, but for questions that upset us, that break our heads. So deeper things can come in." God wrestling, he called it. *But no one here is studying Torah.*

Oy! I make myself miserable. You can imagine, I am afraid to take my eye into the future. I can only stand near this girl. I don't think Celia has a feeling for me, but what do I know? For her, I have a feeling. For her I want to be near. Moishe, I have a feeling for him too, of course. I've never forgotten when he was little, and gave up his birthday kuchen so our family could have an easier winter. In America, he learned English and made a good business for himself. But I see, too, he has trouble forgiving what his sister did for him, what I asked her to do. *Ach.* I'm Moishe's mother. I gave him life. Then I took from him an important choice. Now, look at us.

Maybe, if I last, then Celia, too, can sit through her pain.

Now, she stands at her vanity with a stare into her mirror what makes her look like a powerful queen.

Moishe, he walks in like always, with a mind gone to who knows where. But right when he gets to her doorway, he sees this night is different. She holds his eyes by her stare to the mirror. God! Such a tortured beauty she is!

Moishe doesn't talk. He just looks into her eyes, her clear-minded gaze. Celia opens the drawer to her vanity and brings out a sharp knife, what must be from Ida's kitchen. Slowly, with the little hand that is learning to write, she brings the point toward her face, rests it between her eyes! She doesn't blink. *Blessed God.* She is letting him know if he doesn't stop his bed games, she will kill herself.

Moishe, after a short moment, he understands. His face bunches like a dead vegetable, and slowly, he nods. For a moment his eyes go to the ground in shame. He has given Celia the eye she wants, I think, the eye what knows she has talked truth.

1953-1967

CELIA

Born 1931

in Cleveland

THE afternoon before my seventh date with Leonard Gottlieb, I am twenty-one, a college graduate without a husband or a career plan. It's summer 1953. I dress in cigarette jeans and a navy sailor's sweater with a white stripe on the V-neck. I bring my hair around front, brush it against my breast, divide three long strands for a braid. I want to look nice for Leonard. He's a gentle man. He might be the man for me.

I remind myself of how he stayed alive through the war. When Karl Heydrich advanced on him, for sex, Leonard would imagine the Nazi was a musician; and he would imagine himself a musical instrument—a cello perhaps; another night a French horn. This is what he did to survive. And somehow, he didn't lose his love of music.

I let myself wish he'll propose marriage: I think we are kin.

When I had that car accident, I was nearly eleven. I woke in the hospital with a distinct aversion to Mother and Father, and patience for the faraway day when I could live on my own. Even with all my broken bones, I constructed an elaborate maze to shield myself from their touch.

Unlike so many other survivors, Leonard thinks his perpetrators were more stupid than cruel. He knows, as I do as Moe Zeitlin's daughter, there are times when one has no choice but to submit. If we marry, I think in these wistful moments I face myself in the mirror, we'll have a house where the only walls around are those you can see.

At five P.M., Father greets Leonard at our door. When Leonard hears that Mother needs some help, he quickly offers his. He's a buffoon, Father. "You know, you're pretty as a woman," he tells Leonard. "Some lucky woman's going to get a good housewife out of you!"

He's wounded my friend as much as that Nazi did. Leonard's long, dark lashes rest under his closed eyes for everyone else to see.

As we walk to Cain Park, I dare to reach for Leonard's hand. But I can't keep holding it, because I have no words to comfort him. I take back my hand. Perhaps he won't notice. Despite having just been insulted by my father—and perhaps because of my own ambivalence about touching—Leonard's tenderness with me seems to come from a bottomless well. But I have a new feeling: I don't want to marry someone so vulnerable.

I need a man who can handle my father.

BESIDES my grandmother, Channa, Leonard Gottlieb is probably the first person I am conscious of loving. Certainly he is the first person besides her with whom I feel comfortable enough to share an honest bit of my day. I like to hear him play the violin. I like the loudness of his orchestra—though I hear this only once. When he hangs himself shortly after our last date, perhaps because I know he'd sensed my rejection of him, and that it had played a part in his death, I push my caring for him out of my skin. Like water you wring out of a sponge, so the sponge can be useful again. I decide, too, to push away whatever remains of the girl in me. I squeeze out all of that—Mother's passivity; Father's explosions; Aunt Rose's unexplained, reticent stares; Channa's coaxing from me the stories I keep inside; and the newspapers' photographs of the bony figures that survived the war. They look more dead than alive, those people, and I am thin enough to see we resemble each other. I retreat to my room.

My father's explosions (like his periodic refusals to speak) come, I suppose, from knowing he had no way to help the family he left behind. One day just before I graduated from high school, I watched Father watch me pull a cigarette from my purse and smoke it. I knew he abhorred my spending money on such a useless item, and he abhorred the smell, too. I inhaled that moment as deeply as I could: without speaking, we agreed that my life was *my* choice, a choice over which neither he nor Mother has control.

With Leonard I can also be successful: for the most part, I can forget him.

WHEN my grandmother dies, about two years after Leonard, I despair for a while. I've graduated with a degree in education, but don't really want to teach. Rita and my friend Natalie have married and started new lives. I am still with my parents. I find myself stuck in my room, sometimes for hours at a time, knitting or reading. Channa was the only relative I'd really trusted. She'd taken the things I would tell her like rubies, and kept them quietly between us. Now that she's dead, I feel glad, in a way—because the stories she'd coaxed out of me have gone with her to the grave. No one will ever learn what I told her.

Mother insists I meet with Dr. Bartner, a psychiatrist. In his office, I realize I have desires and wants and I can act on them! I am not bound to my parents' house or to my father's whims. I see that lingering in Cleveland will not allow me to grow. In New York, I could eat ham and cheese sandwiches, attend lectures with real thinkers, and movies in different languages. I imagine there'd be a lot of jobs I could choose from. So, I charge off to New York.

When I meet Allan Schwartzman, waiting in line to see a movie—or, as we joke later, to meet *me*—my body turns on like a match struck against brick. Looking into his eyes, I can block out the rest of the world. My desire is for the power to hold him.

For the first several months we are together, we are delirious. Neither of us has experienced happiness before for longer than it takes to eat a slice of good pie; suddenly we have no concept or expectation of anything but happiness.

Of course everyone feels included in the world and open to it when they're in love. But for us it is miraculous. I've hardly spoken until now. Since my accident especially, but even before, I lived in a cocoon—that's more than fifteen years. Now, almost every day, Allan will take me in his arms, look me in the eyes and, as if each time is the first, say, "Has anyone ever told you you're beautiful?"

Of course, they have. But I've always shrugged it off—shrugged off the idea, shrugged off the people who say so. Whatever beauty others perceived so mismatched my internal life that, if anything, their comments amplified my feeling miserably thin and unattractive.

Actually, what I have with Allan is an experience of beauty. I radiate. I let off heat and I know it. I'm not gregarious, no. I am still a mouse. But I laugh with shopkeepers, even with my parents. When I return to Cleveland, I have a warm smile, even for Rose. I play with children in the grocery line. My arms begin to feel like an archer's, with an aim toward the golden bull's-eye: motherhood.

My infatuation with Allan doesn't last, of course. I never expected it would. Infatuation is not a lasting emotion. Unfortunately for Allan, on this score he is a fool.

N o w that I'm pregnant, I sit on the sofa, feel the completeness of the container I've created, the fullness of the baby's kicks, her caresses, their precision. I love feeling my belly stretch, and outgrowing my clothes. I love being big. I wrap a rose-colored shawl around us (the one Channa gave me before she died), prop up my feet on the ottoman, and let the baby run my day. The force of her grace is indisputable. Mesmerizing.

"You're developing a symbiotic relationship with him," Allan says in his social worker's voice. "That's not good."

"Uh huh," I answer. He's just background noise. I know the baby is a girl, one of the few times I have had an intuition and feel absolutely certain of it. I want a girl, of course—to name her after Channa.

Until I conceived this child, I lived with a constant ache—like a persistent, high-pitched tone. I sometimes wondered if this was the voice of God, attempting to communicate something to me. God meant nothing to me, of course. I don't think I've ever prayed in my life. I've hardly gone to temple— except to marry, perfunctorily, in a rabbi's office. I am not one for ceremony. I don't feel any less Jewish when I eat shrimp or lobster, or a grilled ham and cheese sandwich, for God's sake. As a child I liked going with my grandmother to the ladies' section of her synagogue. In the balcony, she and her friends would flatter me and gossip while the men prayed downstairs. Besides the high-pitched tone that nagged at me, that balcony's the closest I got to God. Which has been no loss to me.

With Hannah's birth, the buzzing goes away. Mothering her, I experience what I'm sure is a kind of holiness. Breastmilk might suit her, but mine never comes. I feed her formula at intervals regulated not by the clock but by her demands. Our communication is *amazing:* before she whimpers, I can tell that she is hungry. By the time she is four months, I offer her a bit of gruel from my fingertip, then wait for her to smile or bring a hand over her mouth—to let me know whether or not she likes the food and wants more.

In a way, it is strange to me—that this child wants my love; that I am moved to give it. I fear, of course, that with her remarkable sensitivity and expressiveness, she will sense my inner feelings as only Channa had been able; and that, unlike my grandmother, she will tell other people what she knows.

But she is a child, I remind myself. A baby without speech. Attending to her unique rhythms and desires, her *intelligence,* feeding her, then witnessing her emerge delighted at the end of another day, cooing in acknowledgment of our miraculous communication—this, I have no doubt, is a sacred life. Until Hannah, I'd had no idea how much love I had in me, how much I wanted to take care, take responsibility. And she received my care so purely, without conditions. My parents' love had always been conditional. I will never forget the day I saw Father offer Mother a ten-dollar bill for tennis lessons for Rita and me. While Mother reached out for it, he snatched it back, laughing at her and calling her greedy. She hadn't known his whims that day. That was often her crime.

And yet, I knew he loved her, loved me, too. Maybe just because he wanted us to know his whims. I never felt that she loved him—though she stayed in the marriage. And in my psychiatrist's office, I admitted that I loved my father. I loved my mother, too.

Now, with Hannah in my arms, I finally feel at home in the world. I *have purpose.*

———

H A N N A H is seven, watching me smoke one evening after dinner. Unaware of the dangers of tobacco, she innocently asks to try a puff of my cigarette. "Sure," I say. I don't hesitate an instant. She's as disgusted by this puff as I am pleased by it. Because now I know she'll never smoke.

Then she gets to third grade and learns about cancer. She comes home one afternoon while I sit at the kitchen table playing my solitary version of bridge, unbuttons her pea coat and hangs it on the hook, puts her papers in a stack on the table. "I want you to quit smoking," she declares. Her angelic face, framed by curls, looks too young for such seriousness.

"Sorry, my love," I say, trying to hold back my smile. "I can't do that."

She doesn't ask why; she just keeps looking me in the eyes. Squarely.

I sigh. I'll have to answer her with honesty, the startling variety. "I like to smoke, Hannah," I say. "It's simple as that. Plus, I'm addicted. I've smoked cigarettes almost twenty years. I need them."

"Maybe you could try an experiment," she says. "Just for a few days. Try not smoking."

"Doesn't work," I say. "I've tried. I know they're bad for me. But as soon as I'm done with my morning coffee, I need a cigarette."

"Oh, *Mom,*" she says, like I am a hopeless daughter, and she accepts me nonetheless.

A few days after this conversation, she leaves early for school. She says she has a special project. I sit down to coffee, spread my toast with cream cheese and blueberry preserves. "Okay, love, see you for lunch," I say. I trust her completely, of course.

When I finish my coffee, I cannot find my cigarettes.

They can't be in too many places: the bathroom, my purse, near the bed-stand, the Stiffel lamprest next to my knitting. It doesn't take me long to realize that Hannah has hidden them.

I call the school's principal immediately. "We have a family emergency," I tell him. "Hannah needs to return home." I say she'll likely return to class after lunch—we live only two blocks away.

When she walks in the door, unusually timid, I simply say, "First things first. Get my cigarettes." When she brings them to the kitchen, I light up right away. "You can't control me, Hannah," I explain. "I know smoking is bad for me. But I like it. I'm sure at some point you'll make choices about your life that I won't like. When you do, I'll try to stay out of your way."

She says, "Okay," angrily, and reaches for her coat to return to school.

I shake my head. "Not until after lunch."

Really, she's the only person over whom I've ever had any control.

---

TWELVE

1 9 8 6 - 1 9 8 7

HANNAH

I WAKE to the sound of street cleaners. Like a flock of pigeons, they cluck down Inman this third Monday morning of October with a parade of tow trucks and parking ticketers, poised to wreak havoc on the lives of decent people. By the time I grab a cardigan, pull sweatpants over my legs, find my Birkenstocks, and run downstairs, the Mahoney Brothers have already lifted the nose of my newly purchased eight-year-old Toyota. I see it roll away, toward Mass. Ave., with a ticket on my windshield that'll set me back at least fifty bucks.

It's an unusually warm day. But if I don't take a taxi to work, I'll be late to meet a photographer from the *Boston Globe.* I sent the features editor some of my students' stories, and asked if she'd like to publish them. Friday afternoon, the editor phoned to say she likes the idea and will send a man named Jonathan Lev to take pictures.

Over the weekend, I bought a loose-fitting, periwinkle vest for the occasion. It flows over my hips and black pants in a comfortable A-line. Maybe the women will say I look nice.

I walk through the Center's front door to find the photographer squatting in front of a camera on a tripod, posing students on the loveseat, the back of his head and denim jacket greeting me as I enter. *"Ohh!"* I blurt. I hadn't yet told anyone we'll be in the paper—and not all of them will be published, not this round, anyway. The photographer wasn't supposed to be here until nine-thirty, and it's only nine o'clock.

Jonathan Lev releases his hands from the camera, stands slowly as if directed by an armed robber, turns around. "Hi," he says warmly. He's about thirty, a few years older than me. Under his jacket, a gray rugby shirt is tucked neatly into the waist of his khakis. I figure his mother or a girlfriend gave him the maroon cashmere scarf. He smiles apologetically while he stands with his arms raised and looks a whole head down at me. "Hannah Felber?" he asks.

I nod, feel my lower lip hanging, my heart speeding up.

"My editor said you'd be expecting me." There's something familiar poking through his unabashed smile, friendly voice, and the way that maroon scarf hangs so gracefully around his neck.

"Yeah," I say, hearing my nervousness. "But I hadn't told my class about your being here yet."

"Ain't we huffy this morning," Talitha Whitmore declares. She folds her arms over her substantial breasts, tips her chin toward the right one, and raises both pupils toward mine. I know she thinks I've lost my marbles, but none of her stories will be published, and I wanted to tell her that gently.

Jonathan Lev hasn't left my gaze. His eyes are dark and brown, like my own. His nose is slightly hooked; his hair is short and thick, with a hint of curl. "What would you like?" he asks. He's respectfully raised his eyebrows with the question.

"I was hoping you'd get us writing—in our classroom—upstairs," I say, annoyed that I take note he wears no ring.

Jonathan bends to fold the legs of his tripod. "So let's go upstairs," he says.

Talitha leading our parade, we do.

From my satchel, I bring out an envelope of photographs taken the month after I was born, hoping to inspire the women to write their own birth stories. "Pictures of a young mother and her baby," I announce, spreading them out on our round table.

Celia's alone in the first picture, wearing a plaid kilt and a dark cardigan. She knows she is a queen: she lies on a plump sofa, propped up on pillows, with her lips slightly more extended than the Mona Lisa's. Her belly is flat already, although I was born just a few weeks before. *She's a mother, and she's glad the child that came to her is me. Any fool can see this, and that this is the kind of gladness that could never go away.* In the next one, I'm in the fancy carriage she pushes through a city park in Manhattan. She wears black cigarette jeans, and the same cardigan she wore with the kilt in the first picture. She's got so much gusto in her walk, you can see her slice the wind.

I look at these pictures and I know, *she loves me. She'll always love me. Whatever changed between us isn't about love.*

"Close your eyes," I tell my students, turning from the photographs, "and remember the day when you had your first baby." Each woman here has had at least one child, except for Rosie Martinez, who's seven months pregnant for the first time. "Rosie," I say, "just list the questions you walk around with these days. Then, all of you, pretend Jonathan Lev's not really here, and just write away."

"*You* try pretending he's not here," Carol Donnelly says. Her tongue reminds me of her sister's—Marianne, from my first class, four years ago.

The women giggle at Carol's sharp line and my blush, then get to work. While Jonathan quietly climbs onto a chair to photograph, I slip the pictures back into an envelope in my purse, then take my walk around the table to make individual contact with each woman. They work silently through the whole hour, until Talitha says, "You was a cute baby, Hannah," as if it's no big deal she's figured out what I'd meant to keep secret.

"Mm hmm," Maria Cordova says. "These stories are gonna be good. You better type them up."

I'm left alone with Jonathan Lev. "Who took the pictures?" he asks.

"I don't know," I say. "My father probably."

"Well, whoever took these pictures loved your mother." He wedges his camera and flash into a small pouch.

I feel as exposed as film that's been popped out of its plastic tube before development.

Jonathan swings his chunky bag to his backside, saying, "I think I got some nice shots. Good thing—it's a neat project." His flash is tucked into his pack, too; but I feel like it's still stinging me while his idea—*Whoever took these pictures loved your mother*—lingers like his smile.

I take the pictures of Mom and me as a baby to the copy shop, ask for a xerox of my favorite one, and tuck it into my wallet so I can look at it whenever I want.

I ARRIVE home at five o'clock and turn on the radio just in time for "All Things Considered." I lay down my groceries, and set a pot of water to boil so I can try quinoa, a South American grain Bread & Circus has started selling. There's one message on my answering machine:

Hannah, this is Gram. Uh, call me. My friend Sophie Greenberg, her granddaughter just met a nice man through a personal ad, she calls it. So call me.

"What should it say, Gram?" I ask as I sit down to my dinner and our call. I'm practically giddy—"Great young cook will provide meals in exchange for marriage and health insurance"?

"Why not?" she says.

"Because isn't that what you got from Grandpa? That's not what I want." I dwell on my memory of Jonathan Lev's profile while I argue with her, feeling resistant to marriage and motherhood, to letting go of my solitude and writerly routines.

"I suppose," Gram says. "But this man Sophie's granddaughter met isn't like Grampa. He washes their dishes. You could say in the ad you're looking for a man with housekeeping skills."

WHEN the story comes out in the *Globe* with a picture that everyone likes, I call the paper and leave a message for Jonathan.

He doesn't call back.

"I'll just forget him," I tell Annie.

"Really?" she asks, crossing her arms over her breasts to mimic me. "Sure doesn't look that way to me."

I phone again two weeks later.

Still no response.

REB Shuman, my neighbor, and Miriam, his wife, see my picture in the *Globe*. "We're proud of you," they say, as we walk together toward our apartment buildings from Bread & Circus. We know each other's names now. I know he's a rabbi, ordained in the Old Country, before the war began. Their children live in Brookline. They know I teach, and that my mother lives in Seattle.

"Tell me," I ask, "where do you walk from?"

"From shul," Reb Shuman says.

"From shul? But this is Cambridge. I thought all the synagogues were in Brookline."

"Temple Beth Shalom," Reb Shuman says. His accent is still thick with Yiddish, though he's been in this country since the war ended. He and Miriam both survived Auschwitz. "On Tremont Street," he says, "we have the shul. Three blocks from here. You should come. Whenever you want—you should come."

"Thanks," I say. "I'll see."

ON the Thursday before Memorial Day weekend, Nancy and I take the train to New York for a literacy conference at New York University. We unload our suitcases in a dorm room, then head to a seminar, *Journal Writing Techniques in the Multicultural Classroom*. Afterward, in the cafeteria, which doubles as a lobby for the conference, I tell Nancy I'd like to spend some time on the Lower East Side. "I haven't been there since I was little," I say, hoping she'll understand and excuse me.

Nancy looks at me quizzically, then affectionately scratches the top of my head. "Let me know if you stay out past nine," she says. "Or I'll worry."

"Okay!" I say, giving her a hug and a few samples of *Wild Women's Stories* to distribute at the conference.

I slip underground to the subway, and take the F Train to Delancey Street. Outside again, walking toward East Broadway, each pickle barrel, each apple strudel, every woman with a *babushke* and expressive hands makes me swell up and smile. *Just because I'm Jewish, I belong here. Each of these women might love me—or curse me.* At the Garden Dairy Cafeteria, I eat a dinner of potato latkes, and drink in the old people's accents and shuffles. I'm the only person here under sixty, and several of them nod to let me know they're glad I'm here.

At breakfast Friday morning, I ask Nancy if I can take another day to explore the city. "I have a long-lost relative who may still live here," I say. "I want to try to contact him." She empties a package of cinnamon oatmeal into a bowl and stirs boiling water into it. "Besides," I add, "I'm getting a lot of good ideas for writing assignments from walking around like this."

Nancy checks the collar of the jade green dress I figure she bought at Talbots to wear to the conference. She shakes her head at me with a grin she can't hold back. "And here I thought I'd have a weekend away from mothering," she teases. "Go ahead, girl. This *is* your hometown."

Late that afternoon, I stand at a phone booth just outside the Veselka, a diner at Second and Ninth. I lay the Manhattan White Pages against the booth's metal ledge, and open the book. There's only one Allan Schwartzman listed. Allan Schwartzman, it says, *LISW.*

As if the water level in each of my cells has begun to rock, I feel my balance erode. I hear the mysterious voice in my head gently ask, *What do you want here, Hannah?* while I keep a finger from my left hand pointed on Allan's number. *I want to hear what he knows about Mom,* I reply. *Other than that, I'm not sure. But I have to try this.* I lift the receiver, and dial.

A man answers with a voice that expects imminent disaster. "H-h-hello," he says.

"Hello," I say. "Is this Allan Schwartzman?"

"Yes."

"Do you have a daughter named Hannah?"

"Yes," he says, panicked, hungry. "Who is this?"

"This is Hannah."

"Hannah," he moans, a moan like an instrument out of tune. "Hannah."

Lightheaded, I lean against the wall of the booth.

"I've been *wanting* to see you," he says. "Where are you?"

"The East Village," I say.

"Where exactly?" he asks.

"Why?" I reply, suddenly cautious.

"Because I want to meet you! I've just finished with my patients."

"You mean *now?*"

"Yes," he says, as if there were no other time.

I don't know what to say. I don't know if I trust him enough to tell him where I am. "Where are *you?*" I ask, sobered by this realization.

"Union Square," he says.

That's maybe a half dozen blocks away. I had figured we'd just say hello on this pay phone here. "You want to see me *now?*" I ask again.

"Yes," he says. "How long will it take you to get to Broadway and Twelfth?"

"Maybe a half hour," I say. "But I'm not sure I can meet *now.*"

"What are you feeling, dear?" he asks. "What's happening?" His questions feel sweet and intrusive at once.

"I'm kind of dizzy."

"Uh huh," he says.

Is he clutching his *heart?*

"Give me forty-five minutes," I say quickly, returning the phone to its cradle, and wondering how we'll recognize each other.

MY father stands at the corner of Broadway and Twelfth Street, turning back and forth in a half circle, facing away from me. His back is hunched and broad. His arms and legs hang loosely from their sockets. He wears charcoal pants, a pale blue button-down shirt, loafers.

My heart quivers as I walk steadily toward the intersection, toward my father, and gaze at him without him seeing me. I savor the moment. He is thoroughly familiar. There's the Old Country in his weak and massive back, his loneliness, his shame. As he spins anxiously from left to right, I see his eagerness to love me.

Finally, he rotates a full circle. I don't quicken my pace. The evening has turned to dusk. Like offerings to the darkening sky, our smiles light up. Allan stands as still as a floodlight as I move toward him.

We have gone twenty years without each other. When we embrace, I feel my skin sparkle. We embrace for a long time, with my head buried in his chest. He has a slightly paunched belly, but I wouldn't say he's fat. He's about a head taller than me.

"Let me see your face," he says. He takes my head between his hands and tilts it toward his own, which is perfectly round. I'm squished in his hold. I don't think he knows it.

Our eyes catch and linger on each other's dark brown pupils: we know each other.

"Hannah," he whispers, closing his eyes, tucking my head under his chin. He gives me a squeeze, takes another look at my face. "Hannah," he says. "Hannah, Hannah."

Finally, my neck insists on a more natural angle, and I step away. Allan says, "I need something to eat."

We go to a deli where he can get a sandwich and we can talk. Once he learns that I'm a college graduate teaching writing in Cambridge, and that I have no boyfriend, Allan says, "Tell me about Celia."

"Can we wait a little while on that one?" I ask. Indeed, I've come to talk about her. But doesn't he have any questions for *me?*

Allan looks down at his roast beef sandwich to avoid my gaze. They divorced more than twenty years ago, in 1964, and haven't spoken since. In this moment, I realize he's never gotten over her. "She was very beautiful," he says, as if we've been confidants a long time. "And she was the most masochistic person I've ever met. She thrived on denying herself pleasure. She used to make me crazy. I remember one evening maybe a few weeks after you were born. She'd just put you to bed. She came into our living room and said, 'I'll leave you, eventually.' And then she marched on to the kitchen to wash dishes or something. It's true, I used to talk her into the ground. But—"

"What do you mean, 'talk her into the ground'? " I interrupt, startled by his quick storytelling—and aware I'm asking for more.

I know almost nothing about this man, and *he is my father.*

"I didn't know then how to relate to a woman other than how my father did, and he learned—" Allan stops midsentence. "What did Celia tell you about me, Hannah?"

"I know your parents are from Germany, and your mother was pregnant with you when they left."

"Did you hear if they'd waited any longer, we might never have gotten out?"

I shake my head, wanting to linger on this thread between our eyes, then take the bitterness wrapped around his voice and cradle it.

But Allan's chewing roast beef again, and talking. "My father served in the First World War for Germany, and he made good money, as an accountant. He could even buy my mother nice jewelry occasionally. They had a nice apartment, in Munich. They lost all that, and two siblings each, and all my grandparents died, in Dachau. They lost everything but what they had on their backs when they got on that boat to come to America. When they got here, because they didn't know English, the only job my father could get was cutting meat in a deli. They were pretty crazy when my sister and I were growing up. They didn't have the foggiest idea how to love a child."

Are you aware of what you're saying? I want to ask. *Are you aware that you're describing yourself, your parenting of* me?

"Your grandfather Moe wasn't any better," Allan continues. "But your mother, your mother was the most extraordinary woman I'd ever met. She was so daring. I used to tell her how much I admired her, her beauty, her composure, but it just didn't penetrate. My feelings were irrelevant to her."

I nod. I hold his words in my memory until I can make sense of them in my journal.

"You okay?" Allan asks cheerfully, as if we're old friends.

"I'm okay," I say. I feel blood speeding through me as if it's been drugged with the weight of new stories, and I look my father somberly in the eye. He quickly turns from my gaze, and calls the waiter for our check.

WE drive to his house in Westchester, forty minutes from the City. The suburb is dense with trees and houses. Compared with the others, the one Allan turns into looks small. "I'll warn you in advance," he says as he presses the genie and drives into the garage, "I keep the house scraggly. To protect it from break-ins."

He must have forgotten who raised me. Or maybe when they were married she didn't leave laundry on the dining room table. "You've been robbed?"

"Yeah," he says. "I seem to attract thieves. Last time they took my short-wave radio."

"Why don't you get an alarm system?"

"Well, I rent this place. The owner doesn't want to make the investment. Anyway, Judy and I are thinking of buying something together." Judy is his new lover, a lawyer with a teenaged daughter and son. Allan wants to introduce us sometime.

Ferns and ivy, half green, half shriveled and brown, hang from the ceiling and cover the large living room window that fronts the street. A worn maroon sofa sits in front of it. The dining table has a small pile of papers and a couple of coffee mugs.

"It's a nice place," I say.

"Yeah? Do you like it?"

"Mm hmm. It's comfortable."

I call the NYU dorm switchboard to leave a message for Nancy that I won't be back 'til Saturday morning. As I hang up the phone, my eye catches a stained-glass lampshade next to a rocking chair. "I made that," he says. "I have a workshop in the basement."

I smile. He's so hungry for my approval, he seems like a little kid.

I see how he and Celia could have shared a house. They both like nice things, and still their houses feel shlumpy. Allan has a pile of laundered socks on his dining table—just like Mom did when we lived in Shaker Heights.

"What's that canister—on the bookcase?"

"Your pick-up sticks," he says, smiling with tears in his eyes.

I slide into a downy, maroon chair. I keep feeling like I can't really trust this man, despite his tears, which feel more showy than real. *It's like he's asleep, and doesn't want to wake up. And where do I stand with him? Maybe if I ask him point blank, he'll wake up.*

"Allan," I ask, in the most neutral tone I can muster, "why didn't you stay around for my childhood?"

"Well, Hannah, uhn, look." He begins to clear a pile of papers from a coffee table in front of me. "I don't know that I had a choice. Celia wanted me out of the picture. My practice was just taking off. I was involved with a new woman. My parents were dying, making me crazy with demands here."

But wasn't I cute? Was it at all hard to let me go?

"I didn't have it in me to fight Celia," he continues. "Anyway, you were in Cleveland. I didn't know anybody there," he complains, as if this litany will absolve his incompetence—when actually, for me, he's highlighting it.

I close my eyes for a long minute, maybe two, to help me digest the evening, to let some quiet soothe us. That old voice speaks: *Be careful, Hannah. He might be a wimp, but he's not a bad man. He's never gotten in your way. You don't know what would've happened if he'd raised you. But he didn't—he let you go. Maybe that was best.*

When I open my eyes, I see Allan looking at me, afraid of me. I don't want to end our evening here. "Do you have pictures?" I ask.

He does. We head upstairs to his study. From the middle drawer of a captain's desk, Allan pulls out a standard, letter-size envelope, faded to the color ivory. He bunches his lips together like an old man without teeth, then hands me the envelope.

I receive the package as if it holds a strand of pearls. When I take out the pictures, indeed, they're strung together in a long row separated by perforations still intact after more than twenty-five years. "These were taken just after we married," Allan says. "Moe gave me the camera for a wedding present. It's still the one I use."

I barely hear his words. I've glued myself onto the images: Celia is posing playfully in front of a camera like a sensuous fashion model. She doesn't give a damn if her crossed eyes show. She stands above a lake surrounded by trees, each hand on a rough banister. She wears an Irish knit sweater I am sure she made herself, and winks—a subtle, sexy wink that drops my jaw.

In the next one, she lies in a big bed under ivory sheets. Blankets are strewn on the floor. You can see her face, glowing, even behind the hand that covers part of her lips. Maybe she's sucking the tip of a finger? A bare shoulder sneaks out from the sheet.

"I had no idea," I say.

"No idea of what?"

"That you were crazy about each other."

Allan pulls another envelope from his drawer, and out of it he takes a solitary picture. "I took this with the automatic timer," he says, handing it to me.

Celia's face is covered with cold cream. Her head is wrapped inside what looks like a shower cap with a tube growing out of it—a 1950s model hair dryer. Allan's chest is bare. He wears a shower cap. Looped in his ears, he's got plastic rings that hold up a shower curtain. They stand side by side, with deadpan faces like those of that famous farm couple with the pitchfork.

"I've never seen this side of her," I manage to say.

"Mm," he says. "Yeah. Those were really fun days."

"So what happened?" I ask. This time, it's me staring at him.

He sits back in his chair, sighs. "Celia came after me, when we first met. Man, did she. So we got married. She wanted a child immediately, but I wanted to finish grad school, get a practice going. 'You're a rich man,' she'd say—because Moe gave us money when we married. But I just wasn't ready. She'd ask, 'Why not?'

"I didn't have a good answer, I guess. So, we had you. For months after you were born, we just stared at you—for hours. You know, you were a miracle to us, Hannah. Neither of us had had much joy before. We couldn't believe we had someone as beautiful as you with us, every day.

"But then things got tense. One time, during a thunderstorm, you raced back into the house, bypassed your mother—who was sitting on the porch. Celia was really upset that you hadn't gone to her. I tried to tell her you just wanted to get inside, away from the storm. But she was devastated you hadn't gone to *her*. She wouldn't talk with me, because I'd thought it wasn't such a big deal." Allan shuffles the pens on his desk. "I guess you could say we soured," he says, staring at the dusty base of the pens' holder.

"And then one day she said she was leaving. If I had anything to say to her, I could go through her attorney. I was shocked. And her attorney, Safransky I think his name was—what a shyster-lawyer he was! The first time I met with him, he said, 'I want half your salary.' What a bastard he was—the kind that grabs you by the throat."

Through my dizziness, I feel keenly awake; and I feel like I'm dreaming. We sit together on the sofa in Allan's office. When he takes my hand in his, then hangs an arm around my shoulder, I begin to sob and heave. I can hardly breathe I cry so hard. I have no sense of time, but finally my breathing quiets. Allan says, "You surely didn't get much empathic parenting, Hannah. You've been lonely a long time."

I nod and begin to weep again. "She won't talk to me," I say.

"Oh, Hannah," he says. He caresses my shoulder and my head, gives me a big box of Kleenex, then sits back and folds his arms over his chest. "She's still crazy, isn't she?"

Allan's gone off into his own world. I bring my feet up onto his sofa and cross them, holding the Kleenex to my eyes.

"It's funny," he says, turning to me with a smile, just after I've let out a little whimper. "I don't know what to do for you."

I nod slowly when he says this—as if to clue me in on my own confusion.

Allan's neck looks like a doughnut, receiving the sinking weight of a prodigious head. He steps toward me for a goodnight squeeze. *I want his embrace; I don't.*

"We could stay up all night, dear, I'm sure," he says. "But I've got a full load of patients tomorrow. A couple of them are really difficult cases. I've got to get sleep."

I am so tired, I say, "Okay."

I SPEND the night on the pullout sofa in his study, and in the morning, Allan returns me to NYU. "I hope you come to New York again next year," he says. "I'd like to take you to dinner with Judy."

"A year?!" I ask, unable to withhold my disturbance that my own father wants to wait another year to see me.

Allan stares into the City while he responds to my outburst. "It's too much for me, Hannah. I didn't sleep last night—I kept thinking of things I'd do better to forget. I can't afford to open up the wounds."

My heart feels like a broken vase. My father looks so cowardly. *At least he's an honest coward.* "I hope you can understand, dear," he says, more quickly than I'd have liked. I'd have liked to offer him my understanding in *my* time. He pulls out his wallet, offers me two twenty-dollar bills, and forces a grin.

"No," I say, glaring at him, ready to close the door to his car. "Money won't comfort me."

THIRTEEN

1941

FROM THE OTHER WORLD
VITL

miscarried by Channa in 1900
in New York City

J U S T as I began to kick in the secure softness of my mother's warm waters, to feel the pitch of my nerves change as her emotions did, I had visions of the century to come. In Europe, I saw Jews lying in dirt like the remains of animals that had been eaten by other animals. Germans and Russians were strewn about, too. In America, I saw boxes with knobs and wires on tables where *Shabbes* candles or prayer shawls had once been kept. Ghosts talked from these boxes; but they weren't ancestor-ghosts. They spoke through electric wire. For much of what they needed, people had only to turn a button; they didn't call on God. A lot of people never knew their ancestors. A lot of people didn't even know how their own mother and father met.

In my visions, the people draped their forests and meadows with shrouds of black tar. They praised their cars for getting them from the start of a day to its end—the way observant souls once praised God. And they didn't even know they'd forgotten God.

The lids over my tiny new eyes remained closed. I felt afraid of the sensations I'd have in a human body if my inner visions came true. I didn't have faith I could tolerate the loneliness. I feared I would lose my love for God, shut off my senses, go numb.

If, on the other hand, I went to the Other World and witnessed the twentieth century from there, I trusted my soul would stay awake. I believed it might be possible to maintain my faith in the goodness of the universe.

It's easier from here. I see cycles, long spreads of time. Not time really—

but ripples, like in water. Tides that move gently, tides that move roughly, people on the verge of happiness, then confused and hurt because something they once knew has changed. I see movements on earth in a whole piece, with purpose and rhythm, hues that match.

Maybe it's an insult to give someone a dream, then take it away—like I did when I left my mother's womb. But here in the Other World, I can stand by her. I talked her through years during which she doubted her own decisions. After her abortion, she got a bright red rash in the shape of a fist just below her navel. For more than a decade, it itched her. It wouldn't go away. *"Red zikh arop fuhn hartsn,"* I used to tell her. "Speak it off. Don't go quiet on me about this."

She did speak. She cried her heart to me—about the baby she let go, about her worries for each child. Just after Celia came, the red marks finally went away.

But once Celia was born, my mother began to feel that something was really not right in the house of Moe and Ida. The house was filled with comforts, and always plenty of food. But to walk into it made Channa think *something is burning. Something is burning in Celia.* And she didn't know what to do about it. All her ideas to fix things would only have moved the fire to another place. And by then she knew, as we do here, that some fires cannot be controlled. They just need to burn their way to something else. People just have to find ways to live with the heat.

Now, from her husband and neighbors who read the Yiddish papers, Channa hears stories about ovens filling up—with *people.*

My mother's heart feels too heavy and hot. Like metal. One morning while she stands at her kitchen window drying dishes, looking out to the grape vines on the fence between her house and her neighbor's, she glances up, toward me.

"Is it true," she asks, "that all my friends what I left in Koretz are on trains without water—to ovens that gas them? That right under my nose, Celia is being tortured by her own father?"

"Yes," I have to say. And: "It's worse than what you hear."

"What do I do?" she asks.

What does a soul without sensations say to someone with a body? "He that has children in the cradle had best be at peace with the world," I tell her.

She rolls her eyes at me.

"Just feel what you feel," I say. "Make peace with yourself. Say what you think, keep saying it. Keep asking your questions that burn in your heart. Keep asking your children about their days. And meanwhile keep *Shabbes* and don't forget to praise God, even when His ways seem strange. All this," I assure her, "can come to good."

Maybe I sound reassuring; but I am the one who needs these words. I am the one who needs comfort.

"Take your breaths gently," I tell her.

Channa's eyes turn strong and hard. She aims them out her window. She's stopped drying her dishes. I fear that in her rage she might turn away from me. But instead, she asks, *"Why?* Why does this happen?"

As if looking at a field of corn withered by too much heat and not enough water, I see clusters of Jews walking into gas chambers, their limbs hanging like wilted ears on weakened stalks.

"It's beyond words," I say. "Silence your mouth from speaking of it, and your heart from trying to figure it out."

Channa, by now, she has faith in me; but this she does not like. She makes a face to let me know it—that after all my years of telling her to keep talking, to suggest silence now isn't right.

"I have no words," I say. "Some things can't be explained."

I realize my own helplessness. While people stand in long lines, naked, watching a sky fill with snow, too weak to dream of a warm stew, or the summer sun, what I tell her now seems useless.

These people—they feel like my brothers and sisters—have lost their desires; and yet some force keeps them going. I stare at this.

I look at the earth and see something like a riverbed, flowing with blood and bones. Now I doubt what I just told my mother. I need some help from God myself.

Channa dries her last dish. The next day, at Ida's, for dinner, she marches to Moe, sitting by his radio. "If your heart tears up from what you hear on

this radio," she says, "go write your President Roosevelt. Go give money to
your World Jewish Congress—they are trying to rescue some people. But *loz
zi op Celia!* Leave Celia alone!"

Moe doesn't bat an eye. Channa, she knows he could write a big check,
probably would; but something in him has shut off, gone numb. She marches
upstairs then, to Celia. The girl sits on her bed with its canopy, like a princess
with no place to go. "I know what I know," Channa says. "So don't you get
quiet on me. You have to talk about what your father's doing. You have to get
it off your chest!" Celia watches her grandmother fret, her eyes wide open, not
saying a word.

"You are part of the whole," I whisper to all of them. "Each piece of a
puzzle matters. To complete a puzzle, you need each little piece. When you
feel cut off, alone—it's okay. You're still part of the whole."

I need these good words for myself. "Embrace all that you know," I say.
"Everyone has the capacity to destroy another; and everyone has the capacity to heal."

Then I hear myself think, *Hitler and his men, too, they are wounded, but
they are also part of the whole.*

Well, at least I know now my mother listens to me. She looks up at me
like I am *meshugge.* Crazy.

FOURTEEN

1987-1988

HANNAH

W HY on earth did you call him?" Gram asks. We are on the phone for our Sunday call.

"Because he's *my father.*"

"That's no reason."

"What do you mean, 'that's no reason'?"

"Name one thing fatherly he's done for you, Hannah. Name one thing."

I might do best to get out of this argument quickly. I haven't heard from Allan since I returned to Cambridge, and I don't expect to. "He talked to me," I blurt. "Unlike some other parents."

"Sure! Now he talks. Now that you're grown. You weren't the easiest kid to raise, you know. And you were very expensive."

"As far as I know," I say, proud to hear such strong words from my own mouth, "nobody had to make too many sacrifices at my expense."

"I'm not so sure," Gram says.

"Oh, Ida," I sigh, somehow aware that she doesn't mean to hurt me—it's the topic that riles her. "I just wanted to know what he's like."

"I suppose."

"I'm not going to expect much from him. He pretty much spelled this out to me. So there's no need to rub it in. And I don't want to fight with you, especially about this."

"I suppose," she says again.

"Besides," I say, "I have other news."

"Well?" she says, as in *I'm waiting*. Gram always likes to hear news from me. I expect she'll find it strange, what I'm about to tell her; I hope she likes it, too.

"I'm changing my name," I say.

"You're changing your *name?*" she asks. "What kind of *meshugge* is that?"

"It's not *meshugge,*" I say.

"Well what are you going to call yourself, then?"

"Hannah Fried," I say, softly, enjoying how well these names sound together.

"That was my mother's name. Before she married."

"I know," I say.

"I never heard of that. A girl taking her great-grandmother's name."

"Does that mean you don't like it?" I ask.

"No," Gram says, surprised, it seems, at herself. "It means I'll need a little time to get used to it."

MY mother named me Hannah Lynn Schwartzman when I was born, at Mount Sinai Hospital on Fifth Avenue in New York City. Schwartzman came from my father—literally, it means black man. In the Old Country, Jews took this name for themselves to thwart the evil eye. If your name was already Blackman, they figured, the devil wouldn't bother you.

Deep artistry, this is, to protect yourself or someone you love with a name. When I was six, a guest at my Aunt Mollie's lunch table one Saturday, I complained about her chicken soup, which had noodles longer than I liked. "You're a *hanna pesl,*" she accused when I complained, a pest. And then she cut my noodles with such care, I knew she was glad to have me at her table.

When Grampa Moe teased me, I couldn't tell what he was after, I only knew I didn't like it. More than once he extended his strong arm to me and said, "Come here, little boy."

I was only four, and being called a boy put me in a spin of rage. "No No No No No No No *No No No!!!*" I shouted at him until I was sure he would stop. After my tantrum, I looked up at his face, and my mother's beside his.

They were speechless, awed that my young feminine force had stopped him from teasing me.

I was a *girl.* I was not a *boy.* Yet even then, underneath the teasing and the silence that held us all, I knew they loved me.

My mother said she knew I was a girl when she was pregnant with me. My middle name, Lynn, she said, came on the way to the hospital.

Hannah was the important part. It's the custom of Eastern European Jews to name a baby in memory of someone who was well loved. And Channa was the woman without whom, Mom told me, she would never have survived childhood. Mom made it through Channa's death only because she realized she could have a child and name it after her.

So my birth fulfilled my mother's desire. And in the eyes of my grandmother Ida—Channa's oldest child—and Mollie and their other siblings, and my mother's sister Rita, I could see how much they'd loved her. From an early age, I sensed their pleasure in Channa's memory, which came to them when they said my name. My family seemed a little lost without her. Their own flaws showed more now that she wasn't with them, even though she'd taken all their secrets with her to the grave. "I could do no wrong by her," my mother used to say. Then a warm smile would open her face, and she'd wink at me.

MY MOTHER NAMED ME DAISY
by Daisy Cochran

When my mother was still pregnant with me, she went on a picnic with my father. He picked about ten daisies and made a necklace for her. On the day I was born it was a hot one. Them flowers were smiling.

One day when I was nine, just before my stepfather adopted me and I became Hannah Felber, I squatted in my school library's biography section. Helen Keller, Abraham Lincoln, and Mark Twain were my favorites. I felt the familiarity of the books in my hands, the bindings soft from age, each page like a blade of grass I could stroke. In that dark corner, I realized I was a writer, and that I would use the pen name Hannah Fried, taking Channa's maiden name.

I told my mother my idea, which made her smile, and then I forgot about it. Norm adopted me, I took his name. My mother threw away all our home movies with Allan in them; on old report cards and the remaining announcements of my birth, I scratched out Schwartzman. On top of the scratches I wrote Felber, neatly as I could.

FEBRUARY 1988. It's Gram's eighty-sixth birthday. Rita and her husband Lester are here without Neil or Jay. Neil's become a stockbroker, with a young daughter and son; Jay's a CPA with a daughter. I can't say I'm surprised they're not coming; but I do feel sad about it, for Ida's sake. Celia's flown in alone from Seattle, since Norm doesn't like social gatherings. Mollie will come to dinner, along with Aunt Evelyn, and the ladies from Gram's mah-jongg club.

Ida wears a magenta Missoni dress my mother and Rita bought her for her birthday. "It's a wild color, Gram," I say. "You look great in it."

"Thank you," she says, as if I were a maid and had just handed over her morning roll with butter and coffee. From the living room, we hear Mom and Rita setting out silverware and napkins for the buffet. Aunt Rita talks proudly about her grandchildren, who have recently started school; Mom boasts that the Seattle Market has absolutely the best shopping a woman could want. I sense the lightness of their talk, their agreement not to bring up topics that would make either of them uneasy. Mom and I have kept distance between ourselves, politely nodding hello when we are in the same room, aware that our dance is closely watched.

Gram and I are in the kitchen, just before her friends arrive. From Sand's Deli, we ordered a platter of lox, smoked whitefish, corned beef, tomato slices, and dill pickles; baskets of bagels and sliced rye; small bowls of cream cheese and mustard, and a large bowl of potato salad. To augment the platter, I toss blanched green beans in a vinaigrette I make from lemon juice, olive oil, and Dijon mustard. When I spot an uncooked green bean on the counter, I bite into it.

"You're eating green beans *raw?*" Gram asks.

"Mm hmm," I say. "What's wrong with that?"

Like an aster at night, Gram's lips close up. "We sure do have some queers in this family," she says, and she leaves the kitchen.

Alone with a wide grin, I toss the blanched beans into the vinaigrette, shake my head in admiration of Ida, her language tart as a lemon.

WE'RE here for three days. Mom's staying with Gram; Rita and Lester are in a hotel. I'm with Mollie, who has rented a car for me to use this weekend. I sleep on the twin bed that was Channa's until she died. I bet the pale yellow sheets are the ones she slept on, too. After the party, Rita and Lester say they have an invitation to his cousin's house; Mom says it's the only night she can get together with her friend Henrietta. I'm relieved, actually, to have quiet time with Gram, and I volunteer to clean up—if Mom will take Mollie home. My mother's lips close up just like Gram's did when she saw me eating that raw green bean. "All right," she says.

After cleaning, I sit on one of the beige, paisley sofas in Gram's large living room. She's in her wing chair, which is upholstered in royal blue and white paisley. We just sit there. I can't tell if she feels tired, deserted, or pleased. "I like your friend Ruth," I say, "the one whose husband just died."

"Yes. She's a good woman."

"How do you know her?"

"Cards, mahjong. Hannah, would you get me a little dish of ice cream? I have a bad taste in my mouth."

"Sure," I say, and I get up for it.

"Thank you," she says. We sit without talking while she eats, then puts the empty bowl on the table beside her. Greek-looking gods are carved into its mahogany legs—my grandfather brought this table back from Europe before the war.

The phone rings in the kitchen, and I answer. It's Daniel Zeitlin, Rose's son. He's retired now, in Buffalo, where he used to run a medical supply business. Still grateful to Grampa for bringing him to America, he calls Gram each year on her birthday. I bring the receiver, with its long cord that can extend into the living room, to Gram.

"His daughter is pregnant," she says, giving the phone back to me so I can return it to the kitchen. "But she's not married."

I shrug.

"I suppose times change," Gram says. "And it is nice for Daniel that he'll have a grandchild." She gets up to rinse her bowl, then asks me to help her out of her dress. She's pleased, I think, with her day.

Mom returns from visiting Henrietta just as I'm about to leave. She glows as she takes off her coat and puts it over the side of a chair. My mother is not the kind who routinely hangs up her things. "She's amazing," Mom says, "as always." I can't tell if my mother's talking to Gram and me, too; or if she's pretending that I'm not in the room. "She's started her own antique business," Celia says. "In her basement."

"What's so amazing about that?" Gram asks.

"Oh, she has these lovely paintings, really unusual watercolors. She got them from a college student who's friends with her neighbor's son." I like hearing Mom admire art, and I wonder what she'd say about my Demeter and Persephone poems, even as I figure she wouldn't want to read them.

"Why didn't you bring one back with you if they're so nice? I could use some more paintings."

"Well, Mother, I don't know that they're your style." Her voice sounds suddenly demure, as if she's hurt Gram hasn't noticed that she has an interesting friend.

"So. Doesn't she have other ones?" Gram asks. "Doesn't she have paintings for me?"

"I didn't know you wanted paintings," Mom says, in a whisper. She sits on the loveseat to the side of the sofa and lights a cigarette.

Ida puts her lips together again, tight. I bet the taste in her mouth has gotten sour again. "You could have thought of me," she says.

I sit on a sofa, absorbing this volley, tense since my mother's return. "Oh Gram," I almost spit, "you're so selfish!"

Ida slumps in her regal chair. She rewraps her navy shawl around her shoulders. She looks smaller and larger to me all at once.

"She didn't mean it, Mom," Celia says, walking over to brush a hand on Gram's elbow.

Now I'm really confused. *Who's really angry at whom, and why?*

"She meant it," Gram says. "She meant it." She fights back tears, but they roll down her cheek, anyway.

I don't apologize. I just stay on the sofa, look out the window. Ida gazes on Leah's portrait, the one my grandfather hung probably fifty years ago above the fireplace mantel of their home. After about five minutes of silence, in which I feel a little regretful, but mostly angry, Gram leaves the living room without a word. It's just Mom and me now, which makes my stomach flutter. I keep my eye on the old, unlit cemetery across from Ida's complex. I hear Celia exhale a long puff. "We're all victims," she says. "Whatever."

"WOULD you like to go for a drink?" Mom asks over the phone. Mollie and I have just finished our dinner. I'm in her den, doodling with a new poem, watching the light fade over the apartment's courtyard. With Mom's invitation, my heart warms up, then seals itself. We've maintained civility by barely speaking to each other this weekend. Now, it's her last night here.

"Sure," I say, wondering what she means by "a drink." Could it be alcohol? Except for a small glass of Manischevitz at Passover, I've never seen my mother drink liquor. And even though my cooking repertoire has expanded, I haven't been drawn to wine.

We meet at a bar in the Ramada Inn near I-271 and Chagrin. A candle burns in the middle of each table, keeping the place dimly lit. The chairs are maroon velvet. Like a graceful bird with a burden, Mom's hand moves slowly, removes cigarettes from her bag. She lights up. "A screwdriver," she tells the waitress, sliding matches back into her purse.

"Tomato juice," I say. Between the time the cocktail waitress takes our order and returns with drinks, neither of us says a word. I focus on the candle. Mom looks at the furniture and at the wall of liquor bottles behind the bartender. I've rarely been in a place like this—a bar. We're conspicuous here.

Mom takes a swig of her drink, then clears her throat. "I'd like to start over," she says.

I nod, slowly, not sure what she means. I'm afraid to ask, and I want to bring my right foot onto the chair and curl up; but I know I should sit properly here, with my feet on the floor.

"I'd like to forget everything that's happened since you left Cleveland," she says.

I know she's making a peace offering here. For years, I've said that's all I want. But how could I pretend that we've been talking all this time? "I don't know that I can do that, Mom," I say.

We're silent again. She takes several puffs from her cigarette. I drink my juice. Like the inside of a womb, the bar is dark. *My memory is too good and too active to forget seven painful years. Maybe she means we could* forgive *each other?* Both of my hands, one on top of the other, grip my small glass. In this moment, it's all I have to hold.

"I'd like to be a family again, Hannah," she says. "That's what I'm asking."

"I want that too," I say. And I do want that. But I don't know what she means by "family," what she expects of me. "I need to know what I can count on," I say.

"I'd like to depend on you without being dependent on you."

I'm still confused. "What does that mean?" I ask, as gracefully as I can, still hearing my voice's demanding tone.

"Exactly what it says."

I feel like we're in a chess match, without a king to capture. My strategy is to save my integrity. And I feel monstrous at our table, like a potent force I'm not sure I can control. My mother sits two feet from me, of uncertain power, thirty years older, gripping a slender, fresh, white Pall Mall.

"I need to be myself, Mom. Even if that means saying or doing things you're not comfortable with."

"That's what loving is," she says, "as I understand it." Honestly I believe she's rooting for me, as I am for her. But something's in our way. *Maybe, if we keep at this, we'll find out what.*

I nod, slowly, heavily. My glass is almost empty. The wedge of lemon that came with my drink swims now in a shallow pool of red juice. I look up at Mom's soft, brown eyes, noticing, perhaps for the first time, how scared she is. "I've made a decision recently," I say. "I'd like to share it with you."

"Go ahead."

"I've changed my last name to Fried," I say. I don't expect her to love this idea, at first; but I hope she'll like how connected I feel to Gramma Channa, her favorite relative. "Remember as a kid I wanted—"

"My God," she says, interrupting me. "I open up a little bit to you, and you try to destroy me."

We get deathly quiet again. Inside myself, I feel a strange, uneasy power. Minutes pass. I wish I could move around, but the sides of this chair don't give me much room. I want her to see what I see. I want her to see how much I love Channa, and how much I love *her*.

When Mom calls the waitress for another screwdriver, my organs contract. *She wants to make herself drunk.* I figure these are the second and third drinks I've seen Mom take—the first was at my cousin Neil's wedding, ten years ago. I realize there's not much I can do now but watch her.

She takes a long swallow, says, "You don't want to be in my family."

"That's not true," I say, maintaining a low enough voice so we don't attract attention. "Hannah is the name you gave me, after your grandmother; I'm taking her maiden name because I love all the stories you and Gram and Aunt Mollie have told me about her, about our matrilineal line."

"I don't know what that means, 'matrilineal line.' "

"It means—"

"No—no—I don't want to know. *I can't.*" She takes a long drag from her cigarette. "Just stop." Her voice is weak and desperate. I realize that Mom's not invincible as I've always imagined. Especially in the face of my own will-fulness.

Norm Felber was good to me, but he's not my father, I remind myself. Felber is not my true name. I don't feel connected to the name Schwartzman, either. I keep quiet. I slurp the tomato juice still in my glass, then suck the lemon wedge. I won't weaken, though it seems to mean making myself cold.

"My God," Mom says, as if she's reading my thoughts. "You think you can get by without a father—without a man!"

"That's *not* what I'm saying." Though I do get by without men. I'd like to be close with one, if he were the right one. I almost say this aloud; but like everything else I say, it might offend her. So I keep quiet.

We leave the bar, and walk into the winter night toward our cars. Mom lights a match for a new cigarette, and inhales as if she hopes the tobacco will revitalize her. As she waves her match in the air to extinguish it, I feel suddenly desperate that we don't hug goodbye, aware that I've passed up her offer to make peace.

MY mother leaves a day before I do. When I phone from Mollie's to bid her goodbye, Gram says she's outside for a smoke, she'll tell Mom to call me back. But the next call that comes is from Ida. "So what are we doing for dinner?" she asks me.

"You mean you want to have dinner with me?" I ask, realizing that Mom's left without calling me, and feeling tender about my last remarks to Gram.

"Of course, Hannah! What are you asking *that* for?"

"What about Mollie?"

"I don't care!" Gram harrumphs. "She can eat with us! But I was expecting you'd spend your last night with *me.*"

Gram's either forgotten my rude remark about her selfishness or forgiven it. Maybe both. "Okay," I say, hiding my surprise. "We'll pick you up at five-thirty."

"Good," she says. "And honestly, Hannah, Celia's left. What's the problem?"

In the face of Gram's strong voice, I feel called to speak my own. "We haven't exactly had a lot of grace in the last few days," I say. "I thought you'd still be mad at me."

"Well, I was mad!" she says. "But now it's water over the dam."

I STAY with Gram for the night, sleep beside her in my grandfather's old bed. In the morning, as I ready my bags to return to Boston, Gram hands me two twenty-dollar bills. "And," she says, "I have something else for you." She leads me into the kitchen, to her closet—stuffed with paper bags from the supermarket, laundry detergent, shelves of canned tuna, salmon, and whole tomatoes. She bends down into the closet's world. *"Ach,"* she says. I can feel her lips curl. "What a mess. Here. Take this." She hands me a clunky pot I've never seen before. "What a piece of junk," she says. "I don't know why I hold on to it."

"So, why do you?"

"It was my sister Bessie's. I got it last year when she died."

"Do you have use for it?" I ask.

"No."

"So give it away."

"All right. Put it on the counter."

While I do that, she fishes out a large wooden chopping bowl from under the paper bags. The wood is old and golden. "This was my mother's," she says. "I thought you might want it."

"Wow," I say. "It's beautiful."

"Ya. You know I can practically taste the gefilte fish she ground up in that bowl. She used to bring it to me when I couldn't eat anything else."

"Oh?" I ask. "When was that?"

"When Celia had her accident. That was a hard time—for everybody." I stand quietly with the bowl while Gram continues fishing in her closet. "So, go put it with your luggage. Use it in good health. And help me get all these bags back in."

I smile quietly at her. "Thanks," I say. "It's about the best present you could have given me. This weekend especially."

The bowl feels like a gift from Channa herself, like an *okay* that I have taken her name. I place it beside me as I drive my rented car back to the airport, feeling like I have a companion.

LIZA Bailey leans her side against my back, rests her head on mine. Liza's my height, but plumper. I bend over slowly, delighting in the strength and softness of her torso as she rolls her front side onto my back, and lets me lift her gently. Once her feet return to the floor, she slides down the length of me— as if I'm a tree trunk. Then I'm on the floor, too, and we're rolling over each other like monkeys.

Liza is in her early forties, a therapist at a Cambridge elementary school.

She has two teenagers of her own. When our dance is over, we rest together. I savor the kindness of her large, maternal hands on my head and back, let my fingers linger in her short, gray, straight hair.

"Mm," Liza says. "That was great."

"Yeah," I say. Speaking has broken our trance. I begin sitting up, thinking I might have another dance before I head home. Near the edge of the stage, where we all leave our bags and coats, I've heard the clicks of a camera. Jason had announced at the beginning of the jam that a friend of his was coming who wanted to photograph us, unless anyone objected.

I look up and see that it's Jonathan Lev, the *Globe* photographer who never returned my calls; whose observations moved me to contact my father. I quickly tuck my head in Liza's belly. "You okay, hon?" she asks.

"Uhn," I mumble. "I know that photographer."

"He's smiling at you."

"Uhn," I say again, nervous that I feel stirred at the sight of this man— and he never even returned my calls.

I glance up long enough to see that he is staring at me.

I check out what I'm wearing—a big white T-shirt with the neck cut out over a black ballet-neck top and slightly baggy purple pants that don't reach my ankles. My hair is pulled up in a bun. Against my neck and ears, I feel curls coming out. Slowly, I get up from my nest with Liza to say hello.

"Hi," Jonathan says warmly. He seems more shy than I've remembered. "Hannah Felber, isn't it?"

"Used to be Felber," I say, noticing the intent of his gaze, and that he's wearing the same maroon scarf he wore to photograph my class. "I've changed my last name to Fried."

"You've married?" he asks. This possibility seems to disappoint him—I think.

"No," I explain. "I've taken my great-grandmother's maiden name."

"Oh," Jonathan says. He puts his camera down and takes a seat on the ledge, as if to signal he's got a leisurely conversation in mind. "That sounds like a good story."

I smile complacently. "It is," I say.

"It's beautiful watching you dance. You get into some pretty amazing shapes."

Unless he has a good reason for never calling me back, I don't want to hear that. "Thank you," I say curtly.

"You know, I owe you thanks," he says.

I tilt my head inquisitively, admitting to myself that I have not dismissed this man.

"A few months after I did that shoot of you and your students, I had lunch with my mother. She's not far away—in Concord, but we don't get together very often. Usually we have a very awkward time—we're both pretty quiet. But what you did with your class inspired me to ask her about my birth." I hoist myself onto the ledge, on the other side of Jonathan's camera. "My mother had a stillbirth—a girl—after my brother, before I was born," he continues, "and I never knew about it. So now I know. And it's really helped me that I know, and my mother, too. We're getting along a lot more easily."

"That's nice," I say. "Thanks for telling me."

"You're welcome," he says, lingering over my eyes.

Get his home phone number, that old voice in my head announces.

What for? I counter.

Just get the number, the voice says, exasperated.

"Would you like to trade phone numbers?" Jonathan asks. "Maybe we could go to a movie sometime."

"Sure," I say, decidedly holding back a smile. "You know I've given you mine before. I left it with your secretary at the *Globe* when I called to say I liked the picture you took of my class."

"Really?" Jonathan asks. He scrunches his eyebrows together. "You know I went away the month after I did that shoot. I don't remember getting the message."

I just say, "Mm."

"Gee," he says, "I'm sorry."

I get a feeling he really is. "Apology accepted," I say, smiling warmly and reaching for the notepad I always keep in my bag.

FIFTEEN

1941

CHANNA

A LMOST to the Other World Celia is. All plastered up she lies, our *sheyne meydl.* Everything's broken and covered with plaster. Her neck is also broken. The doctors say she should lie still. They made a warning to Ida and Moe, she might not live. And we shouldn't touch her. The plaster only can touch her. It makes me remember my arms what ached and felt lost from the rest of my body when I couldn't hold my baby Vitl.

When I look on Ida, *ach.* It's so hard for a mother when she can't give herself over to her child. The Holy One, He gives a mother the hardest job when he gives her nothing to do.

So, what happened?

It was just a few days after she told me she had the ghosts. Mr. Griffin, Ida's neighbor, was driving out of his driveway backwards, but he didn't see Celia. She was playing with another girl, in the street, even though of course Moe yelled to her not to do this from when she could understand words. Ida I have also heard tell the girls never to play in the street. Well, this day Celia took a jump near Mr. Griffin's Chevy, just when he was starting it up. So bloody our Celia got, Ida says it looked like the blood of a birth—in snow.

She broke a lot of bones. The neck is the worst, the doctor says. One arm is flattened—like a butcher makes a pancake with veal breast. Her eyes have gone the way of the cross. Cross-eyes, they call them. If you can imagine everything broken, you can get the picture good enough.

Ida never was much for talking, but now her quiet makes me think on Celia's quiet. She just sits by Celia's bed, with her eyes always open, and a heart heavy. Sure, she has two closets of her own coats and dresses, more vases than she has flowers, and paintings of all colors from France yet. But, she says, she doesn't give a damn about these things.

Ida. My blessed-by-God child. And Celia. I know, those doctors might make miracles for her bones. But. Those ghosts what she has—for them, the doctors have nothing.

Nineteen forty-one it is. Late December. By now, my Meyer and Moe too, they read the papers like it's food they haven't seen in three months. Every day they read like this. "To find out about the Jews, you have to search," Meyer says, "like a scientist."

I think, if you don't know what is happening in the Old Country, you have turned deaf ears to the world, and blind eyes. Nobody gets a letter from over there anymore. And my Vitl, whom I have talked to by now forty years, she doesn't talk much, either. Or I don't know how to hear her good. I'm sure she knows things what are happening. But when I ask about the Old Country, she talks to me about my granddaughter. "Celia must make the choice," Vitl says. "Does she want to live? Does she want to die?"

"I know this," I tell her. And also I tell her, up in her heaven, "It seems to me you in the Other World must give some help here. You in the Other World must also make some decisions: Do you want her here with us, or up there with you? If you give a girl of ten years such a decision," I tell Vitl, "you must also give her some help."

Meanwhile, about Anya Davidson, we do not exchange words. Not about Kiev, either, or Lodz, or Riga. About Koretz, I already know. It hasn't been Koretz since about 1910, on account of the Cossacks. On that little plot of land, there are no more Jews.

I rest my eyes on Celia. A mystery she is. She's had more comforts in her life than I could have dreamed when I was a new mother, making wishes for my children. And she don't seem to care for living like a princess. Well, now she's shattered to pieces. Now we can just give her quiet.

I peek under her covers while she sleeps, to see about the rash now on her arm, the one she didn't break. It's between her little wrist and her elbow, ashy and red, making me think of the light from a candle on a windy night.

Maybe, this night, Celia will make it through.

SIXTEEN

1988

HANNAH

B ECKY?" I say into the phone, at ease, finally, with calling her by her first name, rather than Mrs. Caplan. "It's Hannah."

"Hannah Fried?" she asks, affectionately. "It's so nice to hear you."

I hold the phone to my ear and see Karen's face in the wires between Cleveland and Boston; when I hear Becky's motherly affection for me, I nearly cry. I wonder if our friendship is okay with Karen. I wonder who fills Becky's well. I know she still goes to a support group. And Joe, her son, still lives in California; but he and his wife had a daughter last year, Andrea. "Just hearing her cry in the background while I talk with Joe," Becky says, "just that gives me pleasure."

The Caplans were in California the last time I was in Cleveland; it's been a few months since we've talked. "How are you?" Becky asks warmly. Still, even with Andrea's birth, I hear despair in her voice. I imagine it will never go away.

"Well," I say, wondering if it's too much to ask for her attention, "I'm going to dinner next Sunday with this man named Jonathan."

"Oh, really? Who is he?"

"He's a photographer," I say. "I met him two years ago, when he took the picture of my class for the *Boston Globe.*"

"That sounds nice."

"Mm," I say. "But you know, I don't know if this is a date, or what."

"Well, that's okay. You can have a nice dinner. You don't have to decide the rest of your life over dinner."

"Yeah," I say, nodding. "That's good."

"Let me know how it goes, okay?" Becky asks. "I tell you, Hannah. If you get together with a nice man, I want to hear about it. It would make me so happy."

TWENTY minutes before Jonathan Lev and I agreed to meet, I arrive at the India Palace in Central Square. It's early April, a Sunday evening, still cool enough to warrant long underwear. I'm wearing rayon pants with a green and black print of small flowers—they're slightly baggy and cropped neatly above my ankles; a green jersey shirt with a jewel neckline; and a barely fitted, black wool jacket that drapes just past my waist. I've rolled its sleeves up above my wrists.

My hair is short now, cut every three and a half weeks, so the back never grows long enough to curl. Denise Porch, a black woman in her mid-twenties, who dresses in bright colors, with belts and purses that always seem to match, looked me up and down last week and declared, "Now, you just need a little lipstick." Annie likes my new style, too. "Before," she said, "everything about you *fit fit fit*. This is civilized. This is looser."

The waiter shows me a table, and I sit so I face the door. I look through the menu and find a dish that looks good; then I pull Denise's folder out of my purse. I can edit one of her stories for our next newspaper insert, which comes out in a couple of weeks.

JESUS, MY BROTHER'S FRIEND
by Denise Porch

Last week, for my grandmother's birthday, we had Kentucky Fried Chicken. My brother Kevin brought a friend of his, Jesus. They both in school for car mechanic. Jesus have a little beard, just like the real one. He look at me all dinner long. He don't say nothing, but he look and look. He teach a little song to my girls.

I ain't no fool. I see he's real nice looking. I see he likes me. I look back.

Then I wait for him to call on me. But he don't. And I think, I have to ask Kevin about Jesus. And that means everybody will know I like him.

"I bet a lot of women have a story like this," I'd written earlier on the top margin of Denise's paper. "The way you tell it makes me curious to find out what's going to happen. If we publish this, do you want to change your name, and Kevin and Jesus' names?"

"Keep the names," she wrote back last week. " 'Cause now Jesus is calling. A lot."

When I look up, Jonathan's coming toward me, wearing a maroon T-shirt under a charcoal V-neck sweater, and jeans. He's got a manila envelope tucked in his left arm. "Hi," he says, smiling warmly, taking his chair.

"Hi," I say, annoyed by how good he looks in his clothes. *Mom would like how good he is with colors.* I'm annoyed, too, to be a little nervous, and glad to have the task of returning Denise's folder to my purse.

Jonathan turns to the family sitting next to us, to acknowledge the stares of their little boy, who looks about three. Their eyes lock in a sustained, silent note until the boy breaks it with a staccato giggle and begins eating again.

Jonathan turns back to me and smiles, shyly. His hair is crisply short; his face looks freshly shaved. He's slowly rocking the edge of the manila envelope he's been carrying against the palm of his left hand, and I wonder if he's uneasy meeting me (or anyone) without a camera. "This is for you," he says.

"Thank you," I say, hearing the rigidity in my voice, and how similar it is to Mom's and Gram's.

From the envelope, I draw out an eight-by-ten print of me and the wild women he photographed two years ago.

"This is nice," I say, as casually as I can, sliding the picture back into the envelope. "Thank you."

"You're welcome," Jonathan says. "After I saw you at the jam, I spotted the last issue of your magazine. I really liked it. I mean—I *really* liked it. The stories felt so real to me, like the women were talking to me comfortably about their most intimate secrets. I strive to get intimacy like that in my pictures, but usually, I don't get close."

"Yeah." I nod. "I learn a lot from how my students write." *So we're having dinner because he's interested in my work, not because he's interested in* me.

"I thought if you had some photographs," Jonathan offers, "you could include them with the stories."

I nod and shrug at the same time. This could be a great idea, but I'm hesitant to say so.

"Maybe you could publish photographs of the women's families and homes."

"Maybe," I say—even as I wonder whether or not to use the photograph he just gave me in the upcoming issue. *I don't really know how to talk with a man—how much to give, how much to take. Aunt Mollie once said she never learned that, either.*

Before Jonathan slips into his menu, he focuses intently on me—just for a moment.

"I already know what I want," I say quickly, as if to answer a question he's not asking.

"Oh," he says. "Sure."

Maybe this is how photographers look at people: with a lingering gaze. I like it. And it makes me nervous.

A wispy waiter in a white, button-down shirt takes our orders. "So where'd you go those couple of weeks after you photographed us?"

"Christ in the Desert Monastery," he says. "New Mexico."

"A *monastery?* I thought you were Jewish."

Jonathan nods. "Born Jewish," he says. "But I've never been to a synagogue that feels peaceful."

I shrug. He looks sincere, but maybe he's presumptuous. "How many synagogues have you been to?" I ask, remembering the one I visited in Switzerland.

"Not that many," Jonathan says. I can't tell if he's embarrassed by this or not. "But I sure don't know a Jewish place where I can be alone and not have to talk to people when I see them; at Christ in the Desert, the others are there for solitude, too. I also love the desert's horizon."

I imagine telling Annie he goes on vacation to be alone—and I hear her response as clear as if she's at the table: *I've always said you'll marry someone who'll live next door to you, in an adjacent condominium.*

"So what do you do there?" I ask, dismissing that marriage thought.

"I take really long walks," Jonathan says. "I photograph, if I feel like it. Sometimes I just nap."

"For three weeks?" I'm fixed on the gentle hook of his nose, the proportioned length and width of his chest, the fineness of his fingers. There's Jewishness in his mannerisms, like the subtle shrug of his head to the side after he's expressed an idea, even if he doesn't like being Jewish. His movements are familiar to me.

"That's usually how long I need to get anywhere," he says.

I raise my eyebrows, unsure of his meaning.

"I spend a lot of time meditating before I start taking pictures. After getting assignments from my boss at the *Globe* every day, it takes me a while to see what I'm drawn to photographing on my own. Sometimes I have to simmer a long time."

Oh, God! He meditates. That's so New Age.

Why don't you give this guy a chance? some other voice counters.

"Do you meditate here, too?" I ask curiously.

Jonathan nods. "But it's different here, because of my job. I usually have to be somewhere a half hour ago. And you," he asks, "do you meditate?"

"No," I say, realizing that meditating might be to him what journal writing is to me. "But I live without a television."

"Oh!" he laughs. "That qualifies you."

While our waiter places warm plates of food in front of us, I think about the time I spend sitting quietly on a stuffed chair in my living room, not doing anything, not even writing or reading. And when I visit Gram, we sit on her sofa for days—not even talking, just sitting.

Jonathan keeps his soft gaze on my face until it takes him to the pakora balls on my side plate. "Help yourself," I say.

———————

TUESDAY, just two nights later, Jonathan phones to invite me to dinner at his apartment on Thursday.

"Sorry," I say. "The next issue of *Wild Women's Stories* is due at the printer on Friday. I'm really busy."

"Oh," Jonathan says. "Okay. How about Friday night?"

"Uhn," I grunt, hearing my own confusion. *I like this guy, but I don't know what he wants with me. We've only had one dinner, but still, if I knew what he wanted, wouldn't that make everything easier?*

"Is that a no, thanks?" he asks.

"No," I say. "That's not what I mean. What if I call you when I'm done?"

"Okay," he says. "Sure. I'll look forward to it."

"MARIE," I call, clutching the phone, hoping it'll ooze wisdom, "there's this guy, Jonathan, and we've had dinner."

"Is that a problem?" she asks. I know she's smiling widely right now. Marie's been living happily with a landscaper for five years now.

"Well, I like him. But I'm so belligerent whenever we're together. It's like he's done something wrong before he's even opened his mouth—and so I don't like *myself* when I'm with him."

"Mm," she says. "Time to make the bridge again."

"The bridge?"

"Yes," she says kindly. "I remember saying this shortly after we met, and you'd read me one of your poems. I mean the bridge between the woman in you who's a bitch, and the woman in you who's sensitive and tender."

"Oh," I whisper. "Ohhhh. I do remember." I'm taken again, away from what Marie calls "the drama" toward noticing I've been sucking in my belly—even though I'm much more comfortable when I let it breathe. Lately, when I tell Marie about missing Mom, she sighs and tells me that my mother might be endlessly strange and fascinating, but that I need to give my attention to myself—to how I relate with myself.

Marie continues. "You know that picture you sent me with your new haircut? I just looked at it the other day, and it's like your lower half and your upper half have two different personalities. It's like your legs are ready to march forward, and your head and shoulders are stuck waiting for perfection that probably won't ever come. If you bridge these parts, Hannah, you can move forward in one piece. And gee whiz," she adds. "You're getting to know another person. That's really *sweet*. Savor it!"

I hang up, nodding. *If I know how to help my students write intimate stories, why don't I know how to make friends with a man?*

ASSIGNMENT: Tell a story about your family's old ways and new ways.

OLD WAYS AND NEW WAYS
by Sokkeo Sao

Before 1975, my life was very peaceful. My father was a teacher at our school. Everyone respected him. I lived with my older brother and two younger sisters. We honored our grandmother. She died peacefully, while she was sleeping.

In 1975, the killing started in my country. The Khmer Rouge killed my father. Then they took my family to work in the rice fields. The children and parents were separated. Since that day, I have not seen my mother.

My brother and sisters and I worked from before the sun made light until after we could see only stars. We grew the rice, but we could not eat it. My young sisters died because they did not have enough food.

In 1981, when I arrived in this country, I lived with my brother and his wife. They have three children.

I want to become a teacher. But my brother wants me to follow the old Cambodian ways. He thinks I should get married. He thinks I should not go to school.

———

T H E new issue of *Wild Women's Stories* is ready to go to the printer—after I call Jonathan for permission to use his photograph, and to invite him for dinner on Saturday.

April 1988

 Nervous. Queasy belly. Keep wondering what it would be like to wrap my arms around Jonathan's chest, and tuck the top of my head on his shoulder. Feeling very small. Like he wouldn't have much to hold if he held me.

"W H A T did you *do* to this chicken?" Jonathan asks. He's spooning the juices from the serving platter onto his plate.

"I marinated it," I say.

"Yeah," he says, "but what's in the marinade?"

"Orange juice, grated onion, garlic, and salt."

"Wow," Jonathan says. "I'll have to try it."

"You cook?" I ask.

"Well, I've never made anything like *this;* but I have roasted a chicken before. Maybe next time I'll have you for dinner?"

"Maybe," I say.

After dinner, we move to my living room area, and I flip on *Kind of Blue*, a Miles Davis tape I borrowed nearly a month ago from Annie. I offer the stuffed chair across from the loveseat to Jonathan. I'm sure if Annie were here coaching me, she'd say, *"What harm is there in sitting next to him?"* Call me the Queen of Hesitancy, but I still don't know if I'm the only one who wanted to reach across the table while we ate, and hold hands.

We sit quietly with cups of tea. Jonathan scans the titles in the bookcase just beside the loveseat. I catch him noticing the menorah on my highest shelf, and the photographs of Leah, Channa, Ida, and Karen and her mother. I've also got a picture of Mom and me taken by Allan—which Jonathan saw that first day at the center. I follow his scan and realize *I don't have any pictures of men here.*

"If you like quiet so much," I ask, after we've shared about a minute of it, "how come you live in Boston and work at the *Globe?*"

Jonathan takes a moment to respond. "That's the tension. I've got this one ambitious part who loves photographing and meeting all the people I get to meet at the *Globe*—and another part who just wants quiet. On my best days, I get to travel in both worlds."

"And on your less-than-best days?"

"I obsess on wishing I'll photograph something that will really surprise me. The shots I take for the paper don't do that. The ones I take in New Mexico sometimes do; but I made my best stuff almost ten years ago, just after I graduated college. I've been kind of stuck creatively since then, since I've had this job." Jonathan shrugs, a delicate shrug I might have missed if I'd blinked.

Miles Davis's tape ends, and we hear the din of my refrigerator. Then its fan goes off, and we hear the wind whirl against my building. It's barely eight o'clock. "Let's go take a walk," I suggest. "Maybe down to the river."

"Sure," Jonathan says. "That sounds good." From the coat rack near my front door, he takes his maroon scarf and wraps it around his neck.

"Do you ever go anywhere without that scarf?" I ask.

"It's warm," he says. "On a cool night, a scarf is a good thing, don't you think?"

"Yeahhhh," I say, still curious about where it came from, noticing the play in my voice. "But it feels like there's more to it than that."

"My father gave it to me. We were having lunch one day, something we rarely do, and I had a little cold and he just gave it to me—it was his scarf."

"Oh," I say, zipping up my down vest. "That's sweet."

"I guess it meant a lot to me," Jonathan says. "My father doesn't usually give me much."

As we leave my building's front door, Reb and Miriam Shuman are heading toward their apartment. They have the same smiles and subtle nods for me that they usually do. "Good Shabbes," they say, in unison.

"Good Shabbes," I smile.

SEVENTEEN

1941-1943

IDA

A *FOYLN iz gut tsu shikn nokh dem malekhamoves.* Send a lazy man to fetch the Angel of Death.

She hovers. It's three weeks since the accident. Just now the doctor starts to give her pupils her minute of light for the day. I don't miss a motion. I see her weary eyes go to different directions. I see them scan me, then the room, then the casts and bandages they tied up to hold her body still. Slowly she looks at these things, one at a time. Then her eyelids close, like heavy covers. They carry the weight of the world over eyes that say, *Being dead has got to be better.*

For the first time in his life, Moe's not going to the shop. He paces around the hospital like he's winding it up with his feet. My mother and Mollie have taken Rita. Somebody brings me food. Last night when a nurse took away the tray, I realized I hadn't even looked to see what I ate—my eyes are constantly fixed on Celia.

My loving her feels like medicine. I make every cell in my body give Celia its attention. Then my mind wanders: *If I'd been out in the yard with her, this never would have happened. I should have taken her for lunch on Saturdays. I should have taken her to shul! I could have left Moe and moved back with my parents for a while*—though I know enough to know a bookkeeper's salary isn't enough to support a woman with two girls. Sometimes, I hook onto these things, and I can't let go. There's so much I haven't prevented in her young life.

Whether she lives or dies, I need her to know I love her. *My life depends on loving you, Celia, you who have always been out of my reach.*

I keep to my chair near her bed. *If you want to live, Celia, you can live.*

My mother lays a hand on my shoulder and looks at Celia with her kind eyes that love a dozen children and grandchildren, us included. Pa's here, too, though his health is worrisome. "I just want you to know," he says, several times at least, "I always think you're a good mother."

Each time he says this, tears come—I can't hold back. When I can manage it, I tell him thanks.

Does he know that the fires that have burned my guts all these years with Moe have made their way to Celia?

"*El nah refah nah lah,*" I hear Pa say. *God, please heal her, please.* It's like my face just got washed to hear this prayer. I remember Rabbi Silver talking about it, our people's first-known prayer for healing. Moses said it when his sister got leprosy, and *she got better.*

I close my eyes. "*El nah refah nah lah,*" I say. "*El nah refah nah lah.*"

I t ' s like a moonlit bath sitting here, not knowing what will happen, waiting. I talk to my grandmothers. They're the ones in the Other World who once were mothers, and who know me. I ask for them to help us. My grandfathers both died when I was young, but I pray for them to love us, too. Because I know that Celia's coming to life again will take more than earthly hands; it'll take more than my earthly wanting of her. "If prayers worked," Moe's always said, "they'd hire people to do them." Before the accident, I giggled every time he said it. But I do pray. With Celia here, it's the only thing I can do.

O n e morning last week, the doctor left her eyes unpatched for nearly an hour. Like normal, Celia scanned the room. But when she cast her eyes on me, she glared—like she held light from the dead. In that moment she pierced me with those fiery eyes, I knew: I might not be such a good mother, but Celia will live through this. She'll live as long as she wants. Her broken body will mend.

It's like she had a visit to the Other World. She's brought back something sour and mysterious, something I don't understand. Her face reminds me of Rose's now—a stone that would glisten if only it were wet. Rose-Raisl, my sister-in-law who never talks. She keeps a world inside her lips, and doesn't let it spin.

But Celia's home now, breathing, even seeing and walking again. She's still fragile. And she has a new, hard edge, maybe even a touch of Moe's crazy meanness to keep her going. It's just a touch—like a parsley sprig you might put to the side of a plate. It may never get eaten, but still it changes the look of a platter.

Getting Celia to eat something is still my biggest challenge in the day. Each time she does it, I say thanks to Ma's baby, Vitl—as if she has something to do with Celia's swallowing what I offer. This whole thing has made me a little crazy, I suppose.

And Moe. You know how some people can eat half a chicken, two baked potatoes, apple pie à la mode, and then they want another slice of the pie, with more ice cream yet? Moe is like this now, and not just about food, but with money, too. More so than before. We both know Celia's going to have scars left over from the accident, and I suppose it worries him.

I'm sure he blames me for her playing in the street that day, right near Mr. Griffin's car. At night, after the girls have gone to bed, we sit together in the living room. Moe listens to his radio or reads the papers. I knit an afghan or read my Hadassah magazine. Sometimes, when he's ready for bed, he just up and leaves the room and turns off the light switch—with me still here in the dark, like I'm nothing.

I close my eyes each time, take in my loneliness. Whatever words are at my tongue, I swallow. It's like he puts his pain in my lap—every night. Evenings, when we get home from the shop, I holler for Rita and Celia to help me set the table while Irene gets an hour to herself, and Moe looks through the mail or the afternoon paper. Often, he looks up from his reading and catches my eyes, just like he did my first day at the shop. *Don't leave me.* That's what his eyes seem to say. *I need you.*

I suck my tongue, I feel the hard seal of my lips. I give the littlest nod. *Here we go again,* I think, *another whole conversation, without a sound.*

I suppose it startles him that I don't blow up. But it doesn't take a genius
to realize he's tortured. Sure. Because his money doesn't help his family here
or there a damn. Here he has a daughter who practically walked right in
front of a moving car; and while he lives like a king, everybody he left in Riga
is getting marched to hell. I know he knows what's happening to his sister and
the rest of his family, but he doesn't want to believe it, this news we get only
in the Jewish papers, and then only in snippets. "Send your money to the
World Jewish Congress," I tell him—they're the brave ones who report on the
exterminations. "It's something you can do that's useful. It'll make you feel
better." But when I talk like this, he just dismisses me with a swift wave of
hand, like I'm a fly.

What a mess. Rose's son and Bessie's husband off to war—to Japan, of
all places; Celia almost dead, now back to life; Moe not knowing how to live
with what he knows about his family in the Old Country. Me surrounded by
things nice enough for a museum—those seaside paintings and the still life
of the flowers in a gold vase, for example. He bought those in Paris. He
stopped there on his way back from visiting his mother.

Sure, sure, they're pretty things. But big deal. All those painted sailors cast
their eyes at me, a woman unhappy in her own home. Nothing is really beautiful to me these days. Except Celia. It gives me a queasy feeling sometimes,
seeing all her features come together inside a perfect, uncreased oval—despite
the accident. Each time I look, her face catches me off guard, and draws me
toward her.

I see the mysterious part of her now. Part of that mystery is wanting to
know how to help her enjoy her prettiness. I suppose I might as well wish for
enjoying all the fine things hanging from the walls here. I might as well wish
for enjoying myself with Moe.

Just last Sunday, he said we should go to the movies, and bring my sister Mollie. He said this with his eyes to the girls of course, because to me he
doesn't usually talk. Rita, she rolled her eyes, she turned her nose up. You can
practically hear her count to herself how much time left she has in this house.
Celia, when Moe and I don't speak to each other, she stands real still.

Her bones are so skinny, her face so pale. She glows. And those crossed
eyes. I wonder if she sees double what we see. Watching her watch us, it rips

my heart more than whatever Moe does or says. She's like a measuring stick, Celia, tallying up how bad a mother I am. That's what I think when I see her watch our silence and our fights.

Anyway, I got Celia ready for this movie, and phoned Mollie to say we'd pick her up in an hour. Moe dropped us off at the theater, and we ladies stood in line to buy tickets while he parked the car. Then he took our place, and we went to wait in the lobby. The boy at the popcorn booth knew Rita, apparently; it was sweet to see him take an interest in us, her family. We had a nice time. But today, when Moe left my allowance for groceries and piano lessons and such for the girls, he subtracted the cost of Mollie's movie ticket—as if she was *my* guest, not *ours*.

LAST Saturday, my mother, the girls, and I went to Shaker Square for lunch. I went to the ladies' room for a moment alone. As I sat in my stall, I heard a woman washing her hands tell her friend she'd had an afternoon with the devil. I realized, I've *lived* with the devil, sixteen years. *A froy ken fartrogn a gantse velt*—a woman can carry a whole world. I thought that my first day at the shop. And now I know: *arayngerekhnt dem sotn*—the devil included.

I can't see living without him, dammit. How would I make ends meet? Maybe I have too much sense to leave him and find out. Maybe I should forget about sense. And the girls. I worry for them, although Rita just asked if she can help me cook, because she wants to learn how. And Celia has special eyeglasses that help her see; and she has taken an interest in school. Whatever I do as a mother, I suppose, my job gets done: they grow.

EIGHTEEN

1 9 8 8

HANNAH

JONATHAN lives on Magazine Street in Cambridgeport, just a few blocks from the Wild Women's Center. His apartment's on the second floor of what was once a large, single-family Victorian house.

A dark brown corduroy sofa faces me as I enter. There's a rocking chair across from it, and an unusual coffee table sporting photography books and magazines. When I ask, he says the tabletop was once his grandmother's pastry board. Jonathan shellacked it, and nailed it into a metal base.

One wall has two large windows and several plants hanging at a variety of levels. Another is half lined with books, and half displaying, at eye level, three photographs of a New Mexico horizon on different days. The room is softly lit, with a square sisal rug under the furniture. "There's no clutter," I blurt.

Jonathan smiles sheepishly. "I had fair warning you were coming."

His rooms are connected by a long hallway. The wood floors are old and dark. The kitchen is tiny, with a window looking out onto a basketball court. The bedroom is large enough for a desk and a dresser.

He's made fish stew for dinner. Standing a few inches apart in his tiny kitchen, ladling stew into bowls, we ask each other about our days. It's evening, but Jonathan's face looks newly shaved. *If he held me, my head would tuck just under his chin.* He must have showered before I arrived—his hair is a little wet and smells of minty soap. He wears a large gray T-shirt, which hangs over his jeans. His arms look strong and gentle. His hair is dark, very short, and barely curly. He rests his whole hand on the middle of my back to signal me toward his living room, and keeps it there long enough for me to take a deep breath.

In the living room, I take the sofa and he sits in the rocking chair. The task of eating quiets my body. "I like the stew," I say.

"Thanks," Jonathan says.

"Where'd you learn to cook?"

As if he doesn't want either of us to be impressed by the fact that he can, Jonathan shrugs. "I lived in a sort of community house when I was in college, and we each had a night for making dinner."

I get the idea there are lots of things he does well: photograph, cook, make tables, and yet he's not impressed by these skills.

"What else do you do besides teach?" Jonathan asks, once our bowls are empty.

"I'm working on some poems in the voices of Demeter and Persephone."

"Isn't Persephone the one who spends half her time in Hades?"

"Mm hmm," I say, pleased he's heard of her. "Demeter's daughter."

Jonathan raises his eyebrows. "You'll have to remind me."

"Sure," I say. "Demeter was the goddess of fertility, and the mother of Persephone—I don't know if anybody knows who Persephone's father was. Hades abducted Persephone—he raped her—just when she came of age, and brought her to the Underworld to be his bride. Demeter got really depressed, and said she wouldn't let the rain fall until she could see her daughter again. Everything got barren and wintry—until the gods worked out a deal that Persephone would spend half her time in Hades, and half her time with her mother, on Earth."

"So mother-daughter relationships are seasonal," Jonathan muses.

"Yes," I say, lingering on the word *yes*. *Is my relationship with Mom seasonal? That would make sense—we had a beautiful spring; now we're in winter. Will it shift again to warmer weather?*

Jonathan gets up to clear our dishes, unaware, it seems, that his insight has touched me. I watch him take our empty bowls to the kitchen and stand to look at the books on his shelf. I don't recognize the writers—Jim Harrison, Gurney Norman, and a poet named Gregory Orr.

"That was helpful," I say, when he returns, "what you said."

"Really?" Jonathan smiles. He wraps his arms around me in a quick hug, like a kid might do, then lingers. *Once people get comfortable with each other, do the seasons change? Is that what this myth is about? Is that why Hades is part of it?* "I'm so glad," he says.

He lets go of our embrace, and we both sit on the sofa. *Does he know I want him to hold me?* "You know," Jonathan begins, "once when I was making really bad pictures, I went back to my first teacher at Mass. College, and he said, 'You're in Hades. Don't fight it. It'll pass—and some day you'll see how this time is fruitful.' "

We sit awhile, just taking in the idea. *Maybe I'm in Hades now.* "Maybe I could write poems in Hades' voice, too," I blurt, realizing that Jonathan is still with me, listening. "But just the thought of trying feels like I'd be inviting darkness."

Jonathan smiles affectionately and raises his eyebrows. "Why would that stop you?"

"I don't know," I say. His question has startled me.

He reaches for my hand. "I'm sorry, Hannah—I'm no master of this stuff. But for me the issue isn't about avoiding darkness. Isn't it about being true to the poems? Besides, you don't seem like the kind of person who'd avoid something just because it might take you to Hades."

We're still holding hands. I feel the unusual softness of his palm, and my eyes close. Then our fingers begin moving, slowly, in a sensuous dance. Oh God. *This is kindness. This is what I've been avoiding. This is a man being interested in me.*

Jonathan brings his other hand toward me, and it lands on my thigh. I bring my right knee over his left thigh, and then we catch each other in the eyes. Up close, his face is actually round. *I don't know if I'm a bitch or a sensitive woman right now, but I'd like to curl up in his lap.*

Jonathan touches the side of my face, my hair. I bring my legs over his, rest my head on his shoulder. His lap is like a graceful bowl. I close my eyes, feel the soft heat between us. Then I lift my head toward Jonathan's. Like unopened daisies leaning on each other before dawn, our lips come together and rest.

———————

I PHONE Gram. "Well," she says. "It's about time. He sounds like a nice boy. Is he tall?"

"Oh, Ida," I say, shaking my head. "He's five-eleven." Her question is really a code. It means *Is he Jewish?*

"All right," she says. *"And?"*

"And does he have a nice job?"

"Ya," she says.

"He's a photographer at the *Boston Globe,*" I say. "And he's never been married."

"Sounds good," she says. "Keep me posted." By her systems, with what she knows of Jonathan, there are no snags.

"Sure," I say. For all her wanting me to have a man in my life, I expected her to throw a party once he arrived. Instead, she asks me about the weather in Boston.

MOTHER'S Day morning, Jonathan and I lie in my bed after making love. "Gotta call my grandmother," I say, "and my Aunt Mollie."

"Not your mother?" Jonathan asks.

I can almost feel him wondering if my mother's dead. "My mom and I don't really talk," I say, quietly. "It's been this way for a long time."

Jonathan rolls to his side so he can look at me. "I know my mother loves me," I say, anxious about how he'll receive my story, tucking the sheet up to my collarbone to keep warm. "But for seven years, since around the time I turned twenty-one, she's rarely talked to me." *He's still looking at me. He hasn't turned away.* "She adored me in that way Jewish mothers are famous for," I continue, noticing the numbness in my voice, not knowing how to let it go. "She gave me an incredibly creative childhood, and maybe she lived it more vicariously than was sane. Anyway, one day she snapped. She says she can't handle my presence." Jonathan scooches closer to me, lays his arm across my breasts so that his left hand grasps the upper part of my right arm.

"She says she can't handle that I changed my name to Fried, either—Fried was my great-grandmother Channa's name before she married. She gave me the name Hannah because she loved her grandmother more than anyone." Now I've said everything, although I haven't felt anything—like Marie sometimes notices I do when I read my poetry to her.

"Why *did* you change your name?" Jonathan asks.

"Because I don't really feel connected to either my father or my stepfather," I say. "And my great-grandmother feels like she's around me all the time."

"If you ever got married, would you take your husband's name?"

"No," I practically blurt. "No way."

"You're a bundle, Hannah Fried."

"Yeah," I say, figuring he's ready to leave now.

But he doesn't. "It sounds like you do spend time in Hades," Jonathan says, wrapping his arms and legs around mine.

"Mm hmm," I say. I nod and begin to cry, and lean against his side.

"Just let me hold you," Jonathan says. "Let's just be quiet for a while."

And then for an hour, we drift in and out of sleep.

"HANNAH Fried must have herself a boyfriend," Lucia Langley tells her friend Masline a few days later, just as they leave the classroom. "She's looking mighty *healthy.*" Her voice is loud enough for me to hear, with a Jamaican lilt that could be admiring or condescending or both.

Eileen O'Toole, a chunky Irish woman in her mid-twenties, stands behind her chair until we're the last ones in the room. She rarely speaks in class, though her intent gaze on me signals that she pays attention. I know from her stories that she grew up in South Boston, and started high school just when black and Puerto Rican teenagers were being bussed into her neighborhood. She dropped out because she felt so unsafe at school—desegregation made the place violent. She married a man from Somerville, had two kids before she was twenty, and worked her way up to the position of manager at Lechmere Sales; but she never got her GED.

"Your assignments are not teaching me English," Eileen says. Her anger sounds more like a whine.

I nod, pensively. I think she means to say, *My intimate stories are not your business.* "Are you saying you'd prefer I pay more attention to grammar?"

"You don't pay *any* attention to grammar!" she blurts.

I nod again. I know people need to write clearly and understandably, maybe as much as they need to know how to drive a car. But isn't it better, I wonder, for someone to start with believing they have a story worth telling, rather than with inhibitions about "proper" English?

"It's my experience," I reply, "that good writing comes mostly from writing a lot, not from dwelling on where a comma goes or how a word is spelled."

Eileen purses her lips together.

"When writers focus on grammar, they can get lost in *that*. They can lose focus on the story itself."

Eileen sucks on the inside of her cheek. I can't tell if she's weighing what I've said, or simply rejecting it.

"How's your throat?" I ask, remembering that she missed class last week.

"My throat is fine," she declares. "My *eyes* were infected. They are now fine."

I nod, almost shamefully, for not having remembered correctly.

On the first Sunday in June, Jonathan and I bike along the Charles to Auburndale Park, on the border of Newton and Watertown, for a picnic. While we spread out the towel Jonathan has brought, I realize the tension I've been feeling since we left my house isn't imaginary—he's avoiding my eyes. And he's so businesslike about spreading out our picnic. He hasn't stopped to hug me, even once.

Finally, he begins to talk. "You remember when I told you that learning about the baby who was born before me helped my relationship with my parents?"

"Yes," I say.

"Well, it helped with my *mother*. But my father . . . my father's a scientist. He treats everything by logic. And I don't know how to talk with him."

I giggle.

"Hannah . . ." he says, so sweetly that I want to roll into a ball with him, right here on this old blue towel. "It's not funny."

"Did something happen," I ask, "with your father?"

"Yeah. Sort of. I told him about you. And all he wanted to know is if you're Jewish, and whether or not your parents are still married."

"That's wonderful, Jonathan!" I say with a hearty laugh. "You can give him my grandmother's number."

My mother answers the phone with a low, subdued tone, more low than melancholy.

"Mom?" My voice floats in the vacuum between us.

"Mom?" I say again.

"Why are you calling me?" Her voice is still low and calm.

"I wanted to talk to you."

"Why are you doing this, Hannah, banging your head against a wall?" *I know it's breaking the rules, calling her. But hearing her voice gives me a feeling of reality.* "You have every right to call yourself what you want," she says— she's said this a handful of times already. "But *I* can't handle your changing your name. I cannot handle talking to you."

I sit at my desk and look out at a web of lush maples. It's June. I hold the phone to the side of my face and wonder if I'm crazy—because what she's just asked makes sense to me: *Why are you doing this, Hannah, banging your head against a wall?*

My forehead slides into the palm of my free hand. Mom doesn't seem bothered by my pause. "It's just that I want to talk with you sometimes," I say.

"But what would we talk about?" She is genuinely unsure.

"I don't know, Mom," I moan, knowing I'd really like to tell her about Jonathan, and send her the newest issue of *Wild Women's Stories.* "You're my *mother.* I'm your *daughter.*"

"Ri-ight," she says pensively, "I'm a mother, you're a daughter. But we have nothing to talk about."

I'm quiet again, engulfed by this hole without words. *Doesn't she want to hear about me?*

"I'm hanging up now," she says. And she does, leaving me alone with my desk and my heavy head.

WHEN I ask, Gram tells me, "It wasn't good with them, Celia and Allan."

"Oh?"

"If they'd stayed married, someone would've gotten killed."

"What do you *mean?*"

"I mean they behaved like enemies, not man and wife."

"Uhn," I grunt.

"I shouldn't have told you," she says, aware, I'm sure, of the tenderness around my heart.

"Oh, but it helps me, Gram."

"What do you mean, it helps?"

"It helps me understand why Mom hasn't been able to be with me. You know when Mollie rubs you the wrong way, and you say if you could just get it off your chest and tell me, you'd feel better?"

"Yes," she says, matter-of-factly.

I begin crying. "Do you think Mom's ever gotten stuff off her chest?"

"I don't know," Gram says. Her voice is concerned now. "How do we reach her?"

"I think all we can do is love her and wait until she says she wants to be reached."

"Hannah," Gram says, "you're getting wise!"

"I know—so why haven't I married yet?" As soon as the words are on their way out of my mouth, I'm sorry about them, sorry I've nixed her compliment.

"I wasn't thinking that," Gram replies benevolently. "Honestly. I was wondering when you're coming again for a visit."

NINETEEN

1953 - 1959

IDA

I T's July 1953. Rita and Lester have moved to New York with Neil, their new baby. Lester got a good job there with an insurance company. Celia's got a college degree now, but she hasn't gone to one school yet, to apply for a job. Well, no matter. It's not for me to understand. I'm happy to have a relaxing evening and watch the television.

It's a quiet evening. I've sliced a capon, put the cole slaw in the fridge to cool, found a small platter for the potatoes. It's time to sit in my easy chair. I've made my dents in this chair, plopping onto it day after day for a precious five minutes, maybe ten, not moving, before I call everyone for dinner. Celia's usually in her room at this hour. Who knows what she does in there—knit? Read maybe? Once she comes, we wait for Moe. He's at the radio. He's always needed the news. The discovery of his sister and her children or his half brothers could be announced, just like the State of Israel was in '48. Or the stock market might move.

Oh, the things I tolerate with that man! Twenty-six years now—waking every morning at five, getting in the car next to him, then zooming downtown to the shop while dawn breaks. He doesn't know how to sit still, Moe. All day long I work the books while the plumbers come, buy their pipes and faucets for the day. I don't know why any of them come back; he's as nasty to them as he is to me. Maybe they return for the same reason I stay: there's no other place to go.

Anyway, here it is before dinner. The sun's still up; there's no relief from the summer heat. Celia comes to my little sitting corner off the dining room. She isn't a girl anymore. She's a striking young woman—striking, I suppose, because for all her aloofness, the way she wears a simple blouse and skirt has real class. She looks like someone who'd have interesting things to say. "Miriam Gold's invited me to a picnic," she says, with no trace of emotion in her face that I can see, "for the Fourth of July."

"Well, that's *wonderful,*" I say. I feel like a mother whose child has just learned to ride a bicycle. "Miriam Gold's the girl from Ohio State?"

She nods her head a little. "You don't seem very happy about it," I say. "How come?"

She shrugs. She says another girl will pick her up before dinner tomorrow. "What'll you wear?" I ask.

"I'll take my gray sweater."

"That's a *shmate,* Celia." I don't hide my irritation. What's wrong with her? She has so many pretty sweaters.

"It'll be fine, Mother."

So that ends that conversation. She leaves me to set the table. Well, maybe she'll meet someone. Won't that be something, if she gets her heart touched.

With Rita, I've never had it easy, but at least I know she's fine, in New York, starting a family. Celia, though, she lives in another world. A few words a day she offers me. Even before the accident, she was like this. There was no talking to her. Like Moe, I suppose, only he blows up periodically. I think Celia hopes her quiet will keep her from getting noticed. Her blood heats up, but a boil I've never seen. We might have a siren going off through our neighborhood, but she doesn't turn her head. Something's not right, not natural. All I can do is ache about it.

SOMETHING nice must've happened at her party, because Celia's eyes have been dancing for nearly three days. 'Course I don't dare say anything.

Tonight she's offered to help me set the table. "I have a date tomorrow night," she says, neatly folding the napkins under each of our forks. Her voice, of course, sounds as enthusiastic as the weather reporter on the radio.

"Sure," I say, as if she's asked my permission, though she hasn't. "I'd like to meet him."

She says, "Uh-huh." And I get the message: She doesn't want to discuss the matter.

So, the doorbell rings the next night; Moe answers. I'm sure Celia hasn't told him. He's not talking to me these days, nothing unusual. So even if I'd tried to tell him, he'd have turned a deaf ear. Well, here stands Prince Charming. "You are Mr. Zeitlin?" he asks, polite as can be.

Moe must be as startled as I am, because he gets a little soft. "Ya," he says, a little timid.

"I'm Leonard Gottlieb," the man says. "I'm here for Celia." His accent, I learn, is Czech. He has soft, quick eyes—they make me think he's had a good education somewhere. I imagine he's nearly thirty. For his name alone, I take a liking to him. Gottlieb was my grandmother's name before she married. God-loving, I think it means. But there's plenty more to like. He brings me a bag of fresh peaches, which he says he picked himself from a tree in his yard.

The next day from my neighbor Mrs. Birnbaum I learn he was in a camp, the only one in his family who didn't perish. Mrs. Birnbaum knows because her husband is in the Cleveland orchestra, and so is this boy. He plays the violin.

When he got to the camp he was seventeen. He was put in their chamber ensemble. It boggles the mind that human beings would want a little string music after their work with the gas chambers. Well, that's how this boy survived. As far as Mrs. Birnbaum knows, whatever family he had perished. Frankly, we don't know too many of these new immigrants, though I hear the women are good dressmakers. I don't think there are too many of them who make their living as a musician now, like Leonard.

I can see why Celia's picked him. He's a classic beauty, anybody can tell that. Excepting himself, I think. Which is just like Celia. Stick her in front of a mirror and she just wonders and looks—not for beauty, I imagine, but

to see if somebody's home. And if so, who? I catch her doing this sometimes—staring in her mirror. This boy Leonard, I'll bet he does the same
thing. With him, I figure, his is the craziness that comes from sitting on a
comfortable chair in a death camp.

So they take to going to the theater, on nights when Leonard doesn't play
music. I haven't enjoyed much in my life, but seeing them together, this is a
pleasure. Not just because I'm glad to see Celia with someone—of course I
am—but they're like pansies going walking. Each one looks so pretty. And
even from that first night, they look so comfortable together. Like a couple
that's been married thirty years and still feels glad about it, in a quiet way.
There aren't those nervous sparks flying. They're just good-looking, and their
clothes match, too. Like they came from the same seed.

One day after they've dated four or five times or so, Mrs. Birnbaum tells
me she heard those Nazis got more from Leonard than a little Mozart. So. His
chair in their camps had pins in it. I don't really know what to make of it. I
feel gas in my stomach, sharp. I see pictures of Leonard naked, a boy yet, with
a big German getting pleasure . . . from behind. Then, after, giving Leonard
a meal that keeps him alive another day. Celia has plans to go out with him
tonight. I don't breathe a word.

Moe answers again when he comes by. It makes me nervous, I can't say
why. I suppose Leonard reminds Moe of his lost family—and of his own
greenhorn days. When Leonard hears I need help bringing in the bushel of
peppers we bought earlier that day, and offers to help, Moe says, "Some lucky
woman's going to get a good housewife out of you."

Men ken fun im tseplatst vern! A person could burst their guts from listening to him!

Well. Who knows what they talk about, Celia and Leonard. She comes
home quiet, her usual. But a few days later, Leonard is dead. In his landlady's
garage he hanged himself. Mrs. Levine is the landlady's name, she says he left
his room neat as a pin. His clothes he had folded with a note they should go
to the refugees; and on his desk, the only paper had our phone number and
Celia's name.

Celia. Celia, Celia. She spends the rest of the summer in her room.
Sometimes I get afraid I might find her dead, too. She's quieter now, if you

can imagine. Or maybe it's me. I've gotten quieter with my questions to her. When Rita comes to visit us with her baby, Neil, it's the only time I see Celia lift her eyelids.

She's not like those that carry the world on their shoulders. She's more like a bird, hollow bones. She can disappear any moment, and even when she's around, she's so light. Leonard was like that.

He died *Erev Shabbes,* Leonard. That gives me pause. Since I married Moe, Shabbes has lived near me each week like a thread I might not have noticed. But I do notice.

Moe has us at the shop on Shabbes—even I call it Saturday now. But I look for that Shabbes thread all the time, cling to it even, like a strand I can play with, gracefully, in my own hands. Sometimes I feel this grace in the moment after waking: I don't yet have a thought in my head, and haven't opened an eye to see if Moe has risen.

Leonard's death makes me realize that Celia has never known *Shabbes.* Rita either, of course. I never offered it to them, a day of nothing but rest. From what I can see, neither of them has ways to make living in this world a little sweet, like I did, ages ago, with my moonlit baths. I could blame Moe for it, but I feel the responsibility.

I feel the consequences too. The evening we learned about Leonard, I put a hand on Celia's shoulder. She said, "Don't. I don't want to be touched."

"Oh—" I say, startled. My lips part to make that "oh" sound. They hang open; there is nothing sweet to take in. I close my lips, seal them. My hand slips from her shoulder to my bosom. It rests underneath, like it is waiting for milk to pour. Milk, or maybe blood.

When she refuses it, the love I give Celia bounces back at me like rocks. To keep going, I'll have to leave the child alone. If I don't, nothing of me will remain.

AFTER Leonard, the only pleasure I see Celia have is when she has one of her long sucking draws on a cigarette. Well, I don't know if I'd call it pleasure. Maybe satisfaction's a better word. She also lets go her frown a bit when she's around my mother. I suppose she has a little pleasure there.

A college education my daughter has, and no want of anything. It's hard to be a mother to such a girl. Moe of course is very anxious she'll become an old maid. I care about this too, but really I just want to see her involved with *something.* I'd like to see her interested in a job or another person. But she just eats, dresses herself, goes downtown to look through department stores, and returns with nothing to say. She goes to her room after dinner without a sign of being lonely—to me it looks like she doesn't care if she lives or dies.

Until my mother passes away. One evening, Ma went to bed a little earlier than usual, then died in her sleep. Sitting shiva that week in Mollie's living room, I scanned the faces of each of my sisters, their children, too, and I knew each person felt the glue that'd held them together was gone. There wasn't anyone to take Ma's place—someone who'd pull out of us the stories that soured our hearts until we spoke them; who made each person feel special.

Most of us went on with our lives of course. But not Celia. For the first time, I saw a hole in her, a pain she couldn't hide. For months, I got the feeling that if I spoke to her, she might burst into tears. For better or worse, something would have to change.

Ma died in the spring, just before Passover. A few weeks ago I finally suggested to Celia that she meet with a psychiatrist, a Dr. Bartner. I heard about him a couple years ago from one of my club ladies, and quietly kept his name. With Celia's gloom, this doctor was all I could think of. I guess she didn't have good reason not to go.

Sure enough, she comes back from her meetings a different person. She's quiet still of course, Celia's quiet. But she walks in with a glow to her, like her blood's fired up. It looks like joy to me, whatever it is. I feel a little lighter myself, seeing her this way.

Of course I don't let on. Today, staying in my spot at the stove, I just say, *"Nu?"*

"I've decided to go to New York," she says, with a little turn of the lips, I suppose you could call it a smile. "I'll get a teaching job. I'd like to phone Pearl and Eli tonight to ask if I could stay with them."

Pearl's my oldest girlfriend—from when I lived with my parents on Kinsman. Her husband Eli got work in New York shortly after they married, and they still live there. But we stay in touch; we're still close enough that she knows I don't feel so easy with Moe—or the girls. Rita and Lester are in New York, too, but they're in the suburbs, on Long Island. And Celia says she wants to be close to the Village.

I stop my stirring in the barley soup and look at her. Now I have a smile I can't hide. "Celia, you talk like a girl with a strong mind. I think that's wonderful," I say.

She smiles back at me! For a moment it looks like she's opened that wall she built and let me in. My mother's voice is still fresh in my thinking. *"Efsher vet zi emetsn trefn,"* she says. "Maybe she'll meet someone."

Maybe, maybe. Out loud to Celia, of course, I don't say a thing.

THE night she meets Allan Schwartzman, Pearl's with her. Pearl's a talker. The first chance she has, she tells me all about it. Celia and Pearl go to the movies with a woman my daughter knows from the school where she now teaches the third grade. In her evenings, this woman studies psychology. So they're standing in line to buy their tickets when Allan comes over. He's in the same course as Celia's friend. He comes over to say a book she'd told him about has helped him with some report he's writing.

Pearl says I wouldn't have believed it, the way Celia starts talking with him. "Like water from the faucet, her words came out," Pearl says. "Easy." She tells me Celia asked him what his report was about.

"Longings of the soul," he says.

If it was me, I would have rolled my eyes. But it wasn't me. "Like a match struck against brick," Pearl says, "Celia lights up. She looks at him like they are the only two in the world. She sucks her tongue and brings her eyebrows together and says, 'Mm. That sounds really interesting.'"

Through his wire-rimmed glasses, this Allan smiles. And says something like, "I'll go for coffee any time with a woman interested in the soul."

Where Celia got interest in such a subject, I'll never know. It's the first I've heard of it. But Pearl says I'd have been amazed to see her unlatch her purse, find a pen and blank paper without letting go her gaze on him. "Let me give you my number," she tells him.

Pearl, she wondered if the young women around them might ask Celia for lessons.

AFTER that, Rita is the one who tells me about their romance. She and Celia are friendly now. "She's delirious," Rita reports, after Allan has proposed marriage. "He tells her she's beautiful—and it sounds like she believes him. She poses like a model for a fashion magazine, and lets him take pictures of her. She even sent me one. She says she jokes with the children in her class. She thinks maybe she's a flower that took a really long time to bloom."

When you live long, you can see everything.

FOR the first five minutes, I like Allan very much. I can admit it. He seems to take a genuine interest in Celia, in Moe, me even. He asks questions, says things he's been thinking that what I just said reminds him of.

But then, all of a sudden I feel like I'm in quicksand or something, with all his psychology talk. And as often as he can, he gets in a story about his mother being an evil woman who tried to poison him, and it's lucky he's alive. You know, once because she put a splash of sherry in a chicken sauce just when a doctor'd told him not to have any liquor while his liver was a little weak.

She is *meshugge* that woman, I'll agree. The first time she has Celia for dinner, which is after she and Allan are engaged, it comes out that Celia has false teeth. She got them shortly after Leonard died—just didn't have a strong enough set to begin with, the dentist said. Though I always wondered if it was from the way she barely ate as a child, or if it had something to do with her accident. "What else about her is false?" this Mrs. Schwartzman asks.

Can you imagine? I do feel badly for her, she barely got out from the Nazis, and lost the family who stayed in the Old Country—both her parents and at least a sister I think. But to talk like this to her future daughter-in-law?

Allan, I think he honestly believes he is the world's most unfortunate person. I feel badly for him, too. But he bugs me. I can just see him walking into a boxing ring with a big smile saying, "I'm the loser."

I guess everybody gets their pleasure, somehow.

I WAKE with a dream. *"Ikh nem aykh,"* a voice whispers, "I embrace you."

Mame-loshn it talks, this voice, Yiddish. With Ma gone, we hardly speak it anymore. Moe and I almost always use English; the same with my sisters and me. Of course there are always things that can't be expressed but in Yiddish. And sometimes, like when I want to curse him and I don't want my girls to understand, I use it.

Anyway, this dream has a woman's arm reaching from one side of a river to another. It makes me shake my head. "This can't be done," I tell the arm, "you'll hurt yourself." But then I watch the arm grow long, real long. Enough to make it to the river's other side.

I wake feeling like I live in a circle, and then I feel the circle turn into a spiral which moves, up and down. I have a strong feeling Ma's Vitl is the one talking in the background. Ma feels near, too.

Even after dinner, washing dishes, I have still a warm feeling from that circle. Irene has stopped working for us. I look out over the sink and see the moon. I haven't noticed it in a month of Sundays. It's just a sliver tonight, new like a clean ladle, ready to scoop something big. Probably years have passed that I haven't noticed it. That's sure strange—because of course I've always had dishes to wash, always had that big window over the sink that has me facing east.

Between the moon and my dream, I think something's about to happen. Moe has the news blasting away as usual, the TV and the radio going at once so he won't miss a thing, and it doesn't bother me a wink this evening. That's how good I feel.

Just after I dry the last dish and put it away, the phone rings. "Hello, Mother," Celia says, but with something in her voice I've never heard before. Happiness, I suppose I could call it.

"Well, hello," I say. "What brings you to call in the middle of the week?"

Moe must've realized it's Celia, he's already upstairs to listen on the other phone.

"I'm pregnant," she says, in a voice that has the strength of the midday sun. A smile starts to grow in me, very slowly at first.

"Oh, Celia," I say. I feel like a braided ring of warm apple kuchen. "That's"—wonderful, I'm about to say; but Moe has begun to carry on like a crazy man.

"Ay-ay-ay! Ikh gey aroys fun di keylim!" he shouts—"I'm flipping out of my vessel! In my whole life I did not hear such good news!"

Well, it gets me to giggling out loud, his crazy antics; Celia, too. Then Allan gets on the phone. "What do you say, Moe," he says, "should we pass around a box of cigars?"

I just keep quiet and smile. Because this news is a miracle. A real miracle. Rita had two kids by the time Celia married, and I've had my fun as a grandmother there. But with Celia, with all those years she didn't eat, I never expected she'd have children. Even when she married, I didn't picture her as a mother, with a child. I figured a long time ago her organs wouldn't work.

Also, as I understand it, being a mother means having an unzipped heart twenty-four hours a day for the rest of your life; and I just hadn't been able to imagine this with Celia.

As I fall to sleep I hear that voice again, *"Ikh nem aykh arum,"* it says, like it did in my morning dream, "I embrace you. I embrace you all."

TWENTY

1959

FROM THE OTHER WORLD
LEONARD GOTTLIEB

1925–1953

born in Prague

CELIA, I always wanted to tell you what I was thinking that last night. Before, when I've tried to reach you, I've ended up thinking, what's the use? Well, maybe, with this child growing inside you, you'll help me let the past rest.

You remember that last night together? Don't say you have no memories. When you lie to a dead man, well, it scars your own heart.

So, that last night. I said hello to your parents. Your father said I'd make a good housewife. I figured he'd heard about Karl and me. You knew about him, of course. I was so ashamed, Celia. Can you imagine?

Do you know even, what is shame?

Ach.

Well, so. We walked. From your parents' house on Shannon, down Taylor Road to Lax & Mandel's Bakery. It was a Thursday night, they were open a little late because it would be *Shabbes* the next evening. The whole way to the bakery we didn't talk. You were so soothing to me. Such a comfort. The dirty cobwebs inside myself felt smaller and smaller. People nodded at us when they passed—like to look on us made them happy. I felt good just to be out walking, under the sky, still warm, still light. You were at peace then too, ya?

You pointed out a window above the toy store; you told me your Aunt Rose lived there, your father's sister, but there was no need to pay a visit. "With Rose," you said, "there's never anything to say."

We kept walking. At the bakery, we bought *mon kuchen,* poppyseed cakes. The lady gave the bag to you, then we walked on to Cain Park, still quiet together. You were calm, like always, then you took my hand. The air was so humid, thick it was, the way Cleveland always is in summer. Like a bird flying through my mind, I had a thought. *I want to marry Celia.* I loved to be with you and feel peace. My hands were all sweating, but your hand was soft. Dry and soft and warm.

With Karl, who made me in Theresienstadt like his wife, my hands would sweat, too.

Maybe you noticed I got nervous. You turned to me. You didn't smile but you squeezed my hand a pinch. Oh, Celia. I wanted to tell you about Karl, and how my hands used to sweat and shake with him. I felt so ashamed they sweat with you, too. I had told you stories from Theresienstadt, but I never told you about after Theresienstadt. Ever since I left the camp and arrived in America, I couldn't get hard. I didn't know if I could give you children. I felt a little peace—for me a little peace is a lot of peace—because I thought I could tell you. I thought maybe you could be happy, like I could be, if we just held each other. Or maybe your father would know a good doctor.

Once you took your hand away, I couldn't get words out. My mind was like violin strings, tangled. Some pulled tight, too tight. Some like noodles. Nothing good for music.

We got nearer to the park, and there were more people near us. I think it was an Ibsen play that night. "Let's go up on the hill," you said. "There's a bench there. We could have privacy."

"Sure," I said. "Let's."

Ach, I was such a mess. I thought you wanted to kiss. I never wanted to be with Karl, but being with him—because he gave me food—maybe saved my life. *He risked his life to have relations with me. Anyone caught with a Jew could be shot.* I wanted to kiss you. But I couldn't think of a thing more scary. And here you were—calm, calm. How do you make such calm? I wanted to ask you. Are you inside also calm?

There were all these things going on in my thinking when I tripped on those stones and fell. You were under me when I landed—my head was in your lap. I looked up and your face mixed in the dusk light with the treetops. It looked to me like God's own Symphony Hall. Your hair was a little messy. You felt so gentle and soft, Celia. When I took your hand and put it to my heart so you could hear how wild I was inside, *oy*.

I didn't know what I was doing, but I wanted you should know what was happening. I guess, I wanted to share myself. Your face was so beautiful, Celia. Your mouth was open a little from being startled. That's why I reached my hand to your cheek. Your mouth became a straight line, not a smile, not a frown. Other days, your mouth like that was soothing to me. But not this time.

I noticed your crossed eyes. Crossed eyes, a flat mouth, and calm, so much calm. Hands so soft to me they felt more like breasts. Suddenly I felt myself get stiff, I couldn't believe it. I didn't think anymore. I just wanted to be inside you.

I put your hand to my pants because that's what I knew. That's what Karl liked. Over and over he had me do this, bring his hand to my pants. Oh Celia, Celia, it was so terrible with Karl, so bad, every time. It was terrible because he gave me what I prayed for. When I first got to the camp, everything looked so bleak, I prayed, God, if only I could make music, hear the sweetness of a bow against a tight string, I could continue. I could get through another day and survive. Then I got to be in the little orchestra that played for Karl. He said he liked my playing, and he liked me, too. I believed him. I played for him. I tried to love the music while I played. When he touched me, I remembered the music. And here I was, taking your hand and moving it. Just what he'd done to me.

But your face, even your eyes with different directions, your face was calm. Like earth at the bottom of graves.

"You feel scared," you said.

I couldn't talk. I let a little bit of tears come out. I was so ashamed. Did you know it? You rocked me a little, back and forth—now I think it wasn't to comfort me, but because you needed a new position on the dirt. "I don't know if I can give you children, Celia," I said. "But we could adopt." Once I said it, I started to whimper.

"Okay," you said. You said it like you'd had enough. I tried to let it be enough. I knew somehow you weren't going to say what you thought about a family with me.

"Celia," I said. "What is peace? Where do you get such peace?"

You laughed and said, "I have never known it."

"But I feel it with you."

"Then it's your peace," you said.

I felt like I was in the middle of a symphony, so many notes and rhythms, but no conductor, no other musicians. The way you talked felt like a game—like the game Karl had played on me. But you were Jewish, a Jewish woman, and so beautiful. I had been thinking, with you I could live. I could live with what happened in the camp and with Karl, even all what I lost of my family, and I could make a home with you. Children, too, of course. We could adopt. But this evening I saw you could live without me. I could die and you wouldn't care much.

I had pictures of hearts in my head. Karl's heart was soft for me, open. It had in it a little boy's tiny hands, what reached out for my hands. Then your heart. I saw a box covered with locks, no keys. I couldn't see a picture where you'd let me in to touch you.

Like your eyes, whatever you said, everything I felt was crossed. I heard myself think, "Celia is cruel." But this was really crazy. "Leonard Gottlieb, he's the cruel one"—I had this thought, too. Only this one I couldn't deny.

I felt such disgust for myself.

I KNOW now, we missed a chance. But I still feel friendly with you, Celia. I see the love you live with—for the girl you carry in your belly. I see you burning off the locks around your heart. So you can let this soul touch you, I think.

What can I say, Celia? I can say it makes me happy. I can say *mazl tov*, and *l'chaim*. To life.

HANNAH

S HERRY Johnson, a black woman as petite as I am, with a blue head-band dividing the front and back of her head, lingers after our Friday afternoon class in July while I assemble my papers and put them in my bag. Sherry and her five-year-old son, Anthony, live with her mother's mother. She's twenty-three, and supports herself with a night job at Dunkin' Donuts so she can spend days with her son. "I depend on myself," she tells me.

What a sweet kid.

Kid? *I'm* only twenty-eight!

I slide my bag's long black leather straps over my shoulder as we walk together toward my office. "I'm out of my grandmother's house," Sherry says. " 'Cause she made some rule I can't have no boyfriend under her roof, and she says some man called for me over the weekend. Now Anthony and I got no place to live."

Sherry's one of my favorite students. I give her a hug, for which she stays limp. I feel so helpless. Do I give her my phone number? "I got myself a caseworker this morning, before I came here," she says, relieving me some. "She's a decent lady, I think."

Once she leaves my office, I realize I can hardly wait for seven P.M., when Jonathan will walk in my door and embrace me, and I can let go of the week in his arms.

———

JONATHAN arrives for dinner with a line in his forehead I've never noticed before. He hands me the bunch of basil I requested, and a stem of oncidium, then puts his hands back into the pockets of his jeans. "Can we sit down on the sofa for a bit?" he asks quietly.

"Why don't we go to the bedroom," I suggest. "Lie down?" It won't take long to get dinner ready tonight. The menu is leftovers.

"Okay," he says, tipping his head a little, making me realize it might be awhile before I tell him about Sherry Johnson.

We land in a spoon position, his chest to my back, his right hand on my heart, my hand over his hand. We lie there, almost dozing off. After about ten minutes, I finally ask, "What's happening?"

He sighs. "Last February, probably a month before we ran into each other at the contact jam, I saw an announcement in *ArtForum*—a painter in a little village in New Mexico published an ad that he was looking for some-one to live in his house for a year, and take care of his dogs. The house doesn't have plumbing or electricity, and the nearest neighbor is a half a mile away. I sent him a letter saying I was interested. It seemed like a good idea—to take off for a year. After a couple of months of not hearing from him, I forgot about it.

"Last night," Jonathan continues, "he called me. He said I can have the house."

"Last night," I repeat, sitting up to poise myself for the implications, "a man you've never met said you can have his house in New Mexico—a house which you've never seen, which you know has no electricity or plumbing."

"He wants me there in three weeks," Jonathan says. "And if we like each other, I can stay for a year, rent free."

"He wants you there in three weeks. For a year."

Jonathan nods. He sits up, too, and I see that line dividing his forehead again. I grab the pillow behind me, pull it out, and whack it over his head. "It's wonderful news!" I say, moving onto my knees so I can get leverage in my attack. "And I hate it!"

Jonathan shields his face with his arms. "I don't want to leave you!" he shouts. "I think I even want to live with you! And I also want to know what it's like to live without running water or electricity!"

"Man!" I say. "You talk a mouthful! *You want to live with me?*"

"Yes," he says, looking me straight in the eyes.

A smile I can't stop spreads across my face.

Jonathan tips his head.

I bite my lip and cry. "I think I might want to live with you, too."

We lie back down, and rest our lips together, our mouths barely open. After a while, I lay my head on Jonathan's shoulder. "Now, how's it going to work for us to live together while you move to New Mexico?"

"I don't know," Jonathan says. "I don't know." He sits up again. I sense him wanting to reach for my hand, and holding back. "I've definitely got a chance to do my own art right now—to find out what my own art *is*. I mean, since I can't even have a darkroom without electricity, who knows, maybe I'll paint. Maybe I won't do anything. I just know I'll be in a totally unfamiliar place. Last night, talking with the owner, he said it's still untamed land. All of that appeals to me. If I give it up, I'll be pretty pissed at myself."

I know I can't interfere with Jonathan's choices about his life, about what he needs to do for his own creativity. I wouldn't want anyone to interfere with my choices. And sure, I've always thought I'd want a man who knows himself. But damn! It feels like Mom or even Allan walking out on me all over again, right when the intimacy between us feels strongest.

I strike a pillow gently over Jonathan's legs. "This makes me mad!" I say. "We were just starting to talk about your coming with me to Cleveland at Thanksgiving to meet Ida. What about *that?*"

"I guess I'm just not ready for it, Hannah. I'm just not."

"Uhn," I grunt, and plop myself back down. I can't even think of an argument to what he's saying. "I hate this!"

"Well, what makes you so sure you want to live with *me?*"

"I'm not!" I say. "But right now, the chance of it feels taken away."

Jonathan stretches out on the bed next to me. He just lies there, quietly, with closed eyes. Slowly, I curl against him, and let him hold me while I cry. When my tears subside, I turn toward him for the most passionate kiss of my life.

———

SHERRY'S here today, three days after Jonathan left for New Mexico, really strung out. She didn't show for two weeks, and I feared I might never see her again. I fretted that I hadn't given her my number. *"I deserve better than this,"* she rants, breathless, the white bow in her headband bobbing while we wait in my office for her caseworker to return her call. *"I don't do no drugs. I don't deserve this. My boyfriend'll be out of jail on the thirteenth, next month. You know he was abused when he was real small. His sister told me his stepfather messed with him. I've been rehabilitating him; I'll live with him. But if he don't act right, forget it. We met just a little while before he went in, but he says I'm all he needs."*

Oh God. I think she's over the edge.

"I'm the only one who visits him. His family don't ever go. Costs me forty dollars to get out there. Can I have a cigarette? I don't need counseling. I just need my own place. I'm an emergency—you think they could do *something!"*

I ask if she'd like to write down a list of what she needs now; she says no. I offer to sit with her quietly for a minute, and she refuses this, too. I want to help her find even a small respite from her problems, but I don't sense we're making contact at all. I feel scared about what might become of Sherry—scared about what's already become of her—and scared of getting into more than I can handle. Nancy is out today. So I just listen. I feel her crazy pent-up-ness and know I won't give her my phone number. She isn't telling her stories to *me,* though she is telling and retelling them. She's telling them like she's building a wall around herself, *brick brick keep out brick keep out another brick brick keep out keep out.*

But what if I'm all she has?

I ask if we could think of things that might relieve the pressure on her, even a tiny bit. She looks me straight in the eyes, and speaks in a steady voice. "My son and I just need our own place," she says.

I nod. I feel helpless and tense. Nodding feels like all I can honestly offer.

"GRAM," I say somberly into the phone, sitting on my sofa, tightly balled, "three of my poems have been accepted by the *Antioch Review.*"

"Mazl tov," she says. "Congratulations."

"Thanks," I say.

"What's the *Antioch Review?*"

"It's a literary journal."

"So why do you sound so miserable?"

"Mm," I say, relieved at her recognition of my heaviness. "I guess I miss Jonathan, and then I called Mom, to ask her if I could send her the *Wild Women's Stories.* She said she'd rather I didn't."

"Ach," Gram says. "This is *meshugge."*

We're both quiet for a long moment. "Did she give a reason?" Gram asks.

"Not really," I sniffle. "She said something like, 'I don't want to spend my time stamping approval on your work.' "

"Somebody's got to give," Gram says.

"What do you recommend?" I ask. "I have tried everything I know."

"Maybe you should drop it," she says. "Forget about it. Move on."

I uncurl from my fetal position, lay my head against the side arm of my sofa, and wonder if these are the permissive words I've waited for since Mom first told me, eight years ago, to leave her house.

"Gram?" I ask, perching on the sofa's edge as I form the words to my question. "What do you mean, 'drop it'?"

Her TV flicks off. "I mean you've spent enough time trying to change this situation," she says, "and it hasn't changed. So, maybe it's time to accept it."

"You mean don't do anything?"

"Ya, sure," she says. "Seems to me something else must matter besides your mother. Sure, you had nice attention from her for a while. But she's not God, you know."

"She's not God . . ."

"Lekh lekha, Hannah," Gram says, almost impatiently, quoting God's words to Abraham. *"Go to yourself.* You do a real nice job with those ladies' stories. You're publishing some poems. Let yourself have a little happiness."

"Gram . . ." I warn.

"What?" she asks innocently.

"The poems are about a Greek goddess and her daughter; but they're also about Mom and me."

"So?"

"Mom would probably be offended if she read them. She gets upset when you tell me she's gone to Las Vegas for a weekend to play bridge. I don't really know what she'd do if she saw herself in print."

Gram's quiet. I wonder if she's preparing to tell me to keep everything in my file cabinet until all my relatives are dead.

"I think you should put your mind to something else," she says. She speaks with a softness that feels like an embrace.

"You mean something besides poetry?"

"No," she says. "I mean something besides looking for your mother's approval."

ANNIE suggests we spend a day in Plymouth, where the Cape begins. She knows I've been blue. I'm still whirling from Gram's idea that I stop being so obsessed with Mom, and I don't feel very connected to my students right now. When I first started teaching, I practically drank their stories—about motherhood, being a girlfriend, being a daughter. But now it's like reading woeful tale after woeful tale. I don't see the purpose anymore. Plus, I haven't heard from Jonathan in nearly two weeks.

Annie and I haven't spent much time together since she and Neil Shuster, a painter who waits tables in the Square, started sleeping together regularly last summer. In her boxy blue Fiat, we drive south on Route 3 in silence. Once we pass Quincy, the traffic thins. I love the quiet, the last of the colored leaves, even thinking through what stories I might publish in the spring edition of *Wild Women's Stories*.

Then we reach Pembroke, and Annie begins a monologue of complaints about the other actors at the Rep. *"Bozos,"* she declares. "Everybody just wants their face on the *Globe's* front page. They haven't figured out that their art is dying and *USA Today* won't be interested. If it weren't for Neil, I'd probably go mad."

I'd expected her to nurture *me* on this trip—but I'm the one listening.

"Annie—can we just have quiet?"

"I'm just telling you what's going on with me."

"I know," I say. "And I know I'm being difficult. But right now I need some quiet."

"Let's just get to the beach," she says.

"All right," I agree.

We park near White Horse Beach, on a street marked PRIVATE—NO PARKING. The mid-November air is almost warm, in the fifties; but the wind is wild, and the sky is gray and mournful. I take the windbreaker Annie hands me from her trunk, zip it over my down vest, and head down old, wooden steps to the beach. We're the only ones here.

Alone, I make my way to a jetty of whale-size boulders. The wind whips a succession of bitter lashes while I walk out to the jetty's edge. "I know you can hear me," I say. The words tumble out of me. "I know you can hear me," I tell Mom and Allan again. My voice, louder than its normal pitch, sounds barely like a whisper in the face of these crashing waves. I scream: *"I know you can hear me!"* Seaspray or tears glisten on my face—I'm not sure which. *"I KNOW YOU'RE BOTH JERKS. AND I CAN LIVE WITH THAT! BUT I WANT TO LOVE YOU!! I HATE IT THAT WHENEVER I TRY, YOU JUST SMASH ME!! BUT I KNOW I'M LOVABLE!! I CAN LOVE OTHER PEOPLE!! I CAN LET OTHER PEOPLE LOVE ME!!"*

Spent, I wrap my arms around myself and let the ocean spray me with its replenishing mist.

DRIVING home, Annie turns on a tape of Ben Webster's *Ballads*, partly, I'm sure, to ease the silence between us. Finally I ask, "Can we talk about what's going on?"

"Sure," she says. She turns down the stereo.

"I've been angry," I say. "I thought it was about Jonathan leaving, but now I think it's about my parents. Maybe it's stupid, but I didn't really know it 'til we got to the beach."

"What were you doing at the end of the jetty?" she asks. I notice she's not wearing any lipstick today. Since she's been with Neil, she's stopped wearing neon altogether. "I couldn't make out what you were saying, but it occurred to me that if you're ever in danger, you could attack with your voice."

I crack a fond grin. "I was screaming at my parents," I say. "To myself, too, I guess."

"Are you still afraid you're not lovable?" she asks. I confided this to Annie after my weekend with Kiyo, the Japanese contact dancer. Since Jonathan's left, I've found myself wondering about it again.

Before I can answer, Annie blurts out, "It is still the *stupidest* thinking I've ever heard! Don't you know that everybody's got baggage?! And, shit, Hannah, whenever you're a jerk to me, you bring it up before I do! You *listen!* You've loved all those women at the Wild Women's Center for *years!* And you cook like a regular grandmother! Just because you got a couple of weird parents and a lover who needs to do a little self-exploration you think you're unlovable? Really!"

She turns the stereo off.

"So I guess you're settling the matter once and for all?" I ask.

Annie gives me her warmest, most compassionate smile. "Oh, if I could do that, Hannah, I'd be the happiest woman in all of Massachusetts. I know these things take time. Especially with you."

"Hello," Jonathan says. It's ten o'clock in the morning in Cambridge, the middle of January, a Monday. My Monday classes don't start until after noon.

"Hi," I say.

"You're still in bed?" he asks.

"I woke up early to write," I say. "I've just come back in here for a little rest. And it's really cold, even with two sweaters. How come you're calling?" Usually, he doesn't call me on a weekday, when I don't have much time to talk.

"It's so beautiful here," Jonathan says, lingering on the words, "and so cold. I miss you."

"Mm," I say, remembering how I shivered in his outhouse on bitter December mornings when I visited him for a week last month. I'd look out through the peephole of the outhouse door, and at the barren trees lined up along the frozen creek, and realize how much I've taken for granted in my life, and how much I haven't yet seen. "If you were in my bed right now," I grin, "we'd both be a lot warmer."

"If you were in *my* bed," Jonathan teases, "we'd both be a lot warmer."

"Mm," I say again.

"Hannah," Jonathan says, "I want you to come live here."

"In New Mexico?"

"Yes," Jonathan says. "I want you to come live here with *me.*"

"Gee," I say. I suddenly feel a wave of heat.

"I really like what's happening here with my photography, with the way I'm seeing things. I don't want to go back to Boston. And I really miss you."

I take a long, quiet moment to drink in his words, his invitation. "I don't have a quick yes or no," I say.

"I like that," he says. "I mean—does this mean you're open to the idea?"

"Yeah," I say, surprised. "I guess so." I feel how far away he is, in an adobe house in the desert, while I'm in the heart of urban Boston.

"I'd need a job," I say. "And I'd probably prefer a house with indoor plumbing."

Jonathan laughs. "I could consider that."

"Well, okay," I say, grinning. "So then we both have things to think about."

"I JUST feel like calling," Gram says, that evening. "You know, perk myself up a little."

"Gosh," I say, "that's nice to hear."

"Ya," she says. Then: "Uh, Hannah? Now I don't believe 'psychic.' But this morning, I turned to the obituary section in the paper, and I *looked* for Rothman."

"Yes . . . ?" I ask, a smile already emerging on my lips.

"Well, Irene Rothman died yesterday. She was a friend when we lived on Shannon Road."

"And you found her obituary in the paper?"

"I did. Isn't that strange? You know my mother talked with her baby, Vitl, for a long time; but usually I don't believe that business—life after death."

"Mm," I say. "You remember when my neighbor Mrs. Slater died—that older woman in my building? I got groceries for her when the weather was so bad last winter. I hadn't seen her for a couple of weeks when she died, and then I dreamed about her a few times. It felt like we were saying goodbye."

"Uh huh," Gram says, sort of meekly. "It just seems so strange to me, that I knew."

"Well," I say. "Like you've said before, you have a good intuition."

"Yes, I do." Her voice has become confident again. "Well, do you remember Irene?"

"Not really."

"She was a talker. She liked to argue things to a point. One time Moe and I were there for dinner, and you know how Grampa could be, he just up and called her a foolish woman—for no reason that I could see. *I* didn't think she was foolish. I always liked what she had to say. But anyway, she wouldn't have anything to do with Moe after that. She and I stayed friendly. She knew what I had to live with. But if she had a dinner party or something with husbands, I wasn't invited on account of Grampa. You know, Irene's the first of us to go. It kind of brings things close to home."

"You mean about your own dying?"

"Yes."

We hold the phone quietly, just to take in this thought. "Gram," I say. "When you die, I'm going to keep talking to you."

"Well," she says. "I'll try to answer."

Dear Jonathan,

   Last night my grandmother called. She talked about dying, and I realized I want to be with her through that. If I move to New Mexico now, I think she and I would both feel like I was moving too far away from her. It surprises me to realize this, but I don't want to move anywhere while my grandmother's still alive.

                                        I love you,
                                        Hannah

I dance with Jason at the contact improvisation jam. "Push me," he says. "Let me know your weight."

I dance full out. I lift him several times during our dance, surprising myself. At least twice I don't realize I'm carrying him—it feels that easy. Jason gives me an unusual, big smile when we complete our dance. "You're taking responsibility for your weight," he says. "And your extensions are going really far; that's lovely. Sometimes they're a little rigid—you could let your extensions be more flowing.

"But you're doing great." He winks, in a smile that makes me realize he thinks I'm a good dancer. "You're getting grounded."

TWENTY-TWO

1 9 8 9

FROM THE OTHER WORLD

RAISL

c. 1891–1971

born in Dvinsk, Latvia

I AM the raisin on the bottom of your challah: burnt. Maybe I was un-cooked once. But once you're burnt, you're burnt.

Why did I give myself to that Cossack?

Because in that moment, saying no to my mother would have taken more chutzpah, more nerve.

Because it meant our family would get a little bit of freedom.

Because the bread I'd been baking was almost done. Our dinner was al-most ready. I had clothes to mend, but that felt like lazy work. To be with-out real work the night before my brother was to leave us, the thought alone made me nervous. Real work got me up in the morning. To lie with that Cos-sack took real work.

So, I got a lot more work. I got a son without a father. I got a brother who could save me from the Nazis, but not look me in the eyes.

I used to eat those burnt raisins, the ones nobody else would eat. I got to liking them, actually. No matter how burnt they were, no matter—always I could taste the sweetness in those raisins.

Most people don't know about it.

TWENTY-THREE

1989

CELIA

H ANNAH was an exceptional child. From when she could talk, and she talked earlier than most children, she spoke with an unusual awareness of me. Months before I began to acknowledge even to myself that I wanted to divorce Allan, she said, "You and Daddy don't share your room nice." She didn't say that we *should;* she didn't say that we *could;* she simply stated that we *didn't.*

Mother spent the last month of the marriage in our spare bedroom, then drove with me on the trip back to Cleveland. I went back with her because I had the wherewithal to know I'd need relations after divorcing, in 1964; and I had no other place to go. My parents weren't exactly my favorite people, but they were what I had. When we pulled into their drive, exhausted from the tumult of those last days with Allan and the ten-hour trip, Hannah was still awake and talking; her ramblings had kept us alert enough to drive safely. Father came out to the car. He was so happy to see her—awake yet—he did a jig. I felt afraid that he might harm her, even though he was supportive of the divorce. He'd expressed rage at Allan I hadn't been able to feel.

I felt devastated by the divorce, even though I was the one who asked for it. Divorce is rough. To call Hannah a source of comfort and pleasure during that period puts it mildly. She moved me to get out of bed.

Father was also taken with Hannah, which gave me a new kind of control over him. She delighted him the way soft-boiled eggs do someone who's lived on bread and water for a decade, though I found myself not wanting to leave her alone with him.

One evening, probably only a week or two after we'd arrived back in Clevcland— we were still staying with my parents—Hannah and I went upstairs to give her a bath. Afterward, she stood stark naked in her perfect, nearly four-year-old body. Soft, wet curls combed out to the middle of her shoulder blades. I got on my knees to help her step into her pajamas while she began a story about her imaginary friend, Lily. Suddenly, she stopped talking. Her eyes grew sharp and focused.

I turned around: Father stood in the doorway. What could he possibly have needed that couldn't wait?! There was another bathroom downstairs! I felt furious, but I couldn't speak. My blood seemed to get redder, if that makes sense. And I felt woozy, too, and couldn't say a word. I wanted to close my eyes. I wanted to sleep.

Hannah didn't bat an eye. "Don't be in here," she said.

Like flies on a window, we three hung together until Father turned around and left. A surge of joy shot through me: I felt as though I'd kicked him out myself.

"I just told Grampa, 'Don't be in here,' " Hannah glowed.

"You did," I smiled. "I heard you."

"If he comes back in here before I'm dressed, I'm gonna say it again."

I hugged her to me. "Good idea," I said.

Witnessing her gave me a sense of power: I, too, could tell Father what I wanted, what was really on my mind. I could cross my arms over my chest, tell him to give me ten thousand dollars, tell him not to play jokes on Hannah. I could tell him to take us all out for dinner if I felt we needed a break from routine.

Around Hannah, even Mother got quiet in a peaceful way; and Father began to express a kind of loving I'd never seen before—certainly not from him. I myself felt a pure kind of happiness in her presence. What can I say? I have felt pure happiness twice in my life. The evening I met Leonard I felt it, though it didn't last. This time after the divorce, when I lived alone with Hannah, was my second time.

————

I THINK Hannah is more beautiful than I ever was. Her beauty is not merely physical. Hers comes from something internal, some wisdom or acceptance she has about being herself, alive and human. But her face nearly always had pimples. When she was a teenager I used to notice her looking in the mirror, imagining her face free of acne. It was like she knew she was beautiful; that her core, her essence, was bold and pure. But she had a mask of blotches she couldn't peel off.

I blamed myself for them. It was my ugliness she'd swallowed from my mothering of her. Even though I think Hannah came to accept her sensitive skin, the sight of it continued to torture me. It reminded me of my own war.

I used to search for pimples when I was young, for something that would declare that what I felt inside was true. I got small rashes occasionally, insignificant, especially because they would appear on skin always covered by clothing. Pimples never appeared. When Hannah's did, it meant she wasn't that different from me after all. I lived with this. I took her to dermatologists; they gave her pills that didn't help. She stopped taking them her first year in college, before I left Cleveland.

I couldn't help her, I hadn't been able to help myself. I passed on to her whatever filth I felt was mine only; and I still don't know if she can fend for herself. Either way, I hope her beauty makes its way through.

When she was sixteen, in Switzerland for the summer, she hesitantly asked my permission to stay another week. She worried I'd feel hurt that she didn't want to rush home to me after two months away. "I don't need to have you physically," I told her. "I have you emotionally—which is all I need." And there she was, lovely as the day is long, every day, for nearly twenty blissful years.

Looking back, I can see that Hannah mesmerized me—and I possessed her, too, in a way I suppose was not healthy. It took me awhile to learn that such closeness with a child is unwise, even when I am the parent, and Hannah the child.

When she began college, I worried, of course, that I might lose her—that she'd stop needing me. I could handle her living away from me; that wasn't the issue. But her dependence on my response to her every written word, my adoration of her, my *approval*—without her need of my responses, what would I be?

In my fiftieth year—the year she turned twenty—I came to a place where I couldn't fathom my life without her. I also recognized that she had chosen a writer's world, with the past as her source. Oh, I'm sure she'd bristle to hear me say that; and I know about those fertility poems she writes. But the fact is, she dwells with the ancestors. I could never enter that world and survive.

I often feel disgusted with myself. I created a dependency between us that I could not defend; can't defend. Hannah is not meant to be dependent. Tough love, that's what this is.

THE week before Hannah's visit to Cleveland—the week all this insanity began—Natalie phoned. Besides Henrietta, my bridge partner, Natalie Harrison's probably the only friend I've ever given a damn about. We went to college together. I hadn't heard from her in five years, not unusual for us. "I'm divorcing Gerard," she said, "and moving to California. The East Coast doesn't need me anymore." Her parents were both dead, her brothers apparently felt a woman without children wasn't worthy of an invitation to dinner, and they didn't even know she'd left Gerard.

Natalie had a miscarriage and then a stillbirth with her first husband, right around the time Hannah was born. We've never talked about it. I suppose it's what kept us from talking more often—she'd met my daughter, seen the delight between us, enjoyed Hannah herself. I always knew it must have pained her not to have a child of her own.

I think it was our second year at Ohio State that we met. In those days, I still said only what I had to to get by. I hadn't really talked to anybody. One morning in the cafeteria, Natalie and I were at the same table drinking coffee. There must have been other girls with us, though I don't remember them now. My eye had caught onto her toast. *"You have butter underneath the cream cheese,"* I said—like noticing this had brought me out of a long, deep sleep.

"Yes," she said. She had flaming red hair, cropped short, making her look boyish and feminine at the same time. Then she wore a simple navy dress that on her tall figure looked more formal than collegiate. "My whole family eats it this way. Would you like a bite?"

For me, this was a considerable conversation. God—I was so shy in those years. "Not now," I said.

Later, of course, Natalie told me it took her everything she had to keep from laughing out loud. Instead, she asked my name, and told me hers. She asked what classes I was taking, what my major was. When I told her education, she said, "That sounds like the studies of a lady with plans for supporting herself."

I must have let out a giggle, the first of many I would have with her. "I don't have plans," I said.

It's still a miracle to me that I talked so much that day, and then that we became friends. She couldn't be more outgoing, Natalie. I couldn't have been more shy. And yet, we're friends.

When she phoned that week before Hannah's visit, five years had passed since our last call. She still had the uncanny ability to make me laugh—in this case about her second failed marriage, her whimsical move West, and her invitation to join her. "You're crazy, Nat," I said.

But the next morning, I woke with a realization: *I could leave Cleveland.* Hannah was perfectly happy in Ann Arbor, and, I figured, would never return to Cleveland to live. Mother was past seventy-five by then, but fully capable of caring for herself. She had enough money to pay for whatever help she wanted.

I could leave Norm behind, too. We'd been married almost fifteen years. He'd never prodded or questioned me to change, be other than who I am, even the way I was with Hannah. Believe me, plenty of people tried to change that, especially once I let her go off in the world, alone, to Switzerland for example. But Norm had adopted her, which kept Allan out of our lives; and he helped financially in her upbringing, too. He'd given us normalcy, I suppose. After Allan, that took on considerable meaning.

Because of Norm's income, and my earnings from teaching, I was able to use the money I got from Father for Hannah's education. Norm and I talked about adopting a child since he couldn't have his own; but those conversations just petered out.

Natalie had gotten me thinking on the wild side. I had to admit, Norm wasn't the man of my dreams; and with Hannah grown, I could do whatever I wanted. I didn't need to stay with Norm, or Mother, in *Cleveland.*

Besides that, with Father's death, I had a substantial inheritance to enjoy. This was all a little disorienting.

WHEN Hannah arrived for the weekend just after I'd spoken with Natalie, I felt myself move automatically into the delicious rhythm of looking forward to showing her the sweater I was knitting (for her, of course); to hearing stories about her dropout friends; to sharing the article on Alvin Ailey I'd just read in the Sunday *Times* magazine. To discussing how her money was holding up.

She was primed for these conversations, too. But I also wanted to tell her—*I might make an adventure of my life!*

Then she said something to Norm, and started talking about that writing teacher. Something snapped in me. *I woke up:* it was time for both of us to see that *I* had a life. I had decisions I had made, was making. Until this moment, we'd been so oriented to *her,* to her bloody writing, and now this teacher she'd just fallen for. *WHAT ABOUT ME?*

I suddenly could not stand to look at her. After twenty years of pouring boundless love into her, I'd had enough. I felt saturated. Absolutely full of mothering her. I immediately began calculating how many rows of that sweater I was knitting I'd have to rip out in order to size it for myself.

I'd put my whole life into her, and she hadn't even noticed. She could actually forget me—without even noticing that I have a life!

What had I seen in her that I had adored so much?

When I asked myself this question, which was more than once in the months and years that followed, I could only see how naive she was. She thinks she can live however she pleases, without a man or even a roommate, and write *poetry.* She has no concept of reality, of nine to five, of right and wrong, men and women, of *what it takes to be a mother.*

I'll take responsibility here. I always let her live as she chose; but that weekend, I decided she would do it without my support.

I helped fill out her tax forms that year, but I wouldn't give her another cent. Hannah needed to learn that money does not come easily. Ha. The way she spent money on artichokes and almond butter her first year away from home required a part-time job. I tried very hard not to worry about it.

Until I bowed out, she had no idea how much reassurance it takes to live the life I had given her, how much reassurance I gave her every single day of her life. In two decades, I hadn't entered a supermarket, a clothing store, or read a newspaper—without considering what was there for Hannah. She was on my mind every single moment those twenty years—and then look! She walked out of the door and discarded our Felber family's name.

I knew in that instant she'd make it her business to learn the stories I nearly killed myself to forget. She'd write them down, *publish* them if she could. Her almost magical capacity to draw stories out of thin air flashed before me: I knew she could do whatever she set her mind to doing.

And I knew she wouldn't need me.

HANNAH'S first visit to Seattle, Norm and I were driving her around the city with his nieces, Lynda and Darlene. God knows why, they started talking about pimples—*Hannah's* pimples. "Could you take pills?" one of the girls asked, clearly flustered.

Hannah giggled and said, "You're telling me you think without pimples I'd be pretty."

I saw Mount Rainier looking really spectacular, not a cloud around it, which was very unusual, and I pointed this out. Right. That was my response to this conversation: change it. Later, she made this a criminal offense.

"Oh, Hannah, you bloody well can't tell black from white," I said. "Of course Darlene had the right idea. Do you want me to say it, too? You're *ugly!* Your pimples are offensive!"

Not exactly the thing a mother wants to say to a daughter. But it was all I had. She'd boxed me in. She'd asked for it.

————

AT the memory of Hannah's voice, I feel myself move, habitually, to call her and ask, "Have all your W-2s come in? Did you see *The Year of Living Dangerously* yet? Do you have a favorite sweater in Kaffe Fassett's new book?"

I can't pose any of these questions. They'd be deadly for me. I shouldn't even hear the name Hannah. Because I gave my life for this child. And now, for her sake, I have to give her up.

Maybe I'm crazy. But I don't think so. I'm seeing more clearly than I have in my whole life. I think I'd like a drink, actually, to make a toast to this clarity. If Natalie were here, she'd see my happiness and clink glasses. She wouldn't ask questions.

And if to Hannah or anyone else my decisions appear those of a madwoman, I don't give a damn. If they do, it won't make me act any differently. I know now, I must make my own life. Either that, or I'll go under.

MAYBE I began turning ugly around the time I married Norm. Allan was out of the picture—Norm had adopted Hannah by then. I figured I'd be in Cleveland for good. I had a suburban lifestyle, stability. I had problems, certainly; but they were ones I could live with.

When Hannah left for college, my skin began to turn dull, kind of gray—like the Seattle sky, come to think of it. I gained a little weight. I had always cut my own hair; in those days especially, it looked like it.

I went through hell those first five or six years without her. But now, I can say comfortably, I've come to some internal peace. I am a wretch to look at by most standards—and I don't give a damn.

A few years ago, I cleaned out our closets. I threw away the albums Hannah made after her summer adventures, and whatever journals she wrote in childhood and left with me. I'm sure if she knew, she'd feel these things were not mine to destroy. I suppose I can agree on this, morally speaking. But at the time, it was a true move for me. I did not want her remnants around.

A few weeks after this particular day—and it took a long one to storm through the closets and weed out what was hers—I spoke with a bridge player who works as a forester. We were talking about the big fires sweeping the West that year. I was alarmed by them, the damage to nature. "These fires bring good, too," he explained to me. "Like, the pinecone lodge—when it gets old, its veins get large, and beetles can creep in and kill the tree. But when fire destroys it, the intense heat opens the cones—which is where the seeds are. For a lot of plants, fire's the only way to regeneration."

So then I began to consider that all this madness between us has been exactly about that: regeneration. The more I think about this, the more it makes sense.

I remember sitting with her in my bed or at the kitchen table, on the sofa after Norm had gone to sleep. Our talk satisfied me in ways nothing compares to. I felt at home in the world. I felt useful. We talked about people. People Hannah babysat for, neighbors, her friends, people I worked with in the furniture store's accounting department, relatives.

We always saw eye-to-eye. When the KKK wanted to march through Skokie, that Jewish suburb outside Chicago, we were aghast at their nerve and the ACLU's for defending them. A few days after first discussing this, we shyly confessed to each other we had changed our minds; that the Klan had the right to march. Just as I have the right, despite what my sister Rita thinks, not to speak to Hannah.

I'VE heard that in the *ketuba,* the Jewish marriage contract, the man agrees to pay certain sums in the event of divorce. So on the day you make your vows, you also consider, seriously, that the marriage might end. I don't even remember now if Allan and I signed a *ketuba.* If we did I have no idea what we did with it when we divorced. But perhaps just the tradition of it prepared me for the possibility that our relationship might not last.

With Norm, I'm sure we didn't have a *ketuba.*

Anyway, what I'm getting to is that with a child, there's no such sobering document—from what I know. Maybe there should be.

When Hannah was born, that empty space I'd ached with dissolved. Perhaps that ache was my wanting some spiritual experience, some experience of godliness. Who knows. What I do know is that Hannah filled this space—

until the moment she demeaned Norm, called him a housewife as casually as Father had labeled Leonard.

I looked at her and saw the dark worlds of my childhood, Leonard's years in Theresienstadt and his suicide, all meet with the holy life I'd known as a mother. With this word, housewife, the life I'd sealed away suddenly unzipped—in vibrant textures and colors too raw and bold, I felt, for me to survive. I also had to recognize that Hannah was no angel.

Yet once again, I felt my own desire—to survive. The first time, of course, was after my childhood accident. And I suppose I felt it briefly when I decided to leave Allan. Now again, with my passion to live, all the muck of my life was exposed. I felt weak. I knew too well that a little bit of darkness could open into an endless abyss, and in fact, that's what happened. This past decade, I let my wretchedness ooze out. I became convinced that Hannah was possessed by the dead, carried along somehow by spirits from the Other World, that she *wanted* this. When she changed her last name to Fried, a name that died out in our family three generations before her, I saw that my idea was confirmed.

Hannah got her stories through no help from me. She learned of the comforts I received while the world of our ancestors was being destroyed. By now, I imagine, she's heard about Leonard. God knows who told her. I presume she knows that I love her; and that I had no other way to survive to old age than to turn my attention from her—the only person I ever cared about enough to want to stay alive for—toward myself.

Well. I've needed these years, all of them, to get to this place where good and evil can spiral together and not make me whirl.

Once I heard a woman say, "When one becomes a mother, suicide's no longer an option." I suppose this woman would say it's not an option to refuse your child. But I've never seen that I refused Hannah. No, what I did was opt for myself. I opted for finding a way to love this life without using motherhood as my anchor.

LAST week, I took my car to the shop for new brakes and an oil change. It was a Thursday, Norm's day for volunteering with Habitat for Humanity. Angelo, our mechanic, offered to drive me to my bridge game. In his truck, the radio announced the fall of the Berlin Wall. Trying, I suppose, to connect with this news—and with me—Angelo asked about the Holocaust. "Did you lose family?"

"Yes," I said. I thought of Masha, Father's sister, and her daughter Ruchl, who was born a few years before me. She once made me a picture book about her life in Riga, about the dress her mother had made for her with my father's money. I was entranced by Ruchl's drawings. I kept the book near my bed.

With the war, we stopped hearing from them of course, and when I returned home from the months in the hospital after my accident, the book from Ruchl was gone. I never asked what happened to it, or to them.

But back to my mechanic. "Man," he said, "what did those people do for God in those camps? A God like that I'd *disown*."

The word came out to me in bright lights. Because my mother once accused me of that, of disowning Hannah, when of course I tried to tell her, that isn't true. A day doesn't go by I don't think of her.

Once, I heard a rabbi say, *Silence your heart from figuring it out.* Maybe it was the only religious thing I ever caught all those days I sat with my grandmother in the balcony of her shul. It's stayed with me. *Silence your heart from figuring it out.*

Maybe, if I'm lucky, Hannah knows this now, too.

TWENTY-FOUR

1989–1990

HANNAH

Dear Hannah,

Your decision makes complete sense; and your letter makes me crazy. I mean, what about us? *You don't say anything about us.*

I love you,
Jonathan

It's a Sunday, the middle of February. I've spent the day doing laundry; reading *Ghost Dance,* a novel by Carole Maso about a schizophrenic poet and her daughter; and replying to Jonathan's letter. Annie and I have a date to go to dinner at six at the S & L Deli in Inman Square.

Dear Jonathan,

I might be a quick decision maker, and I still feel that staying in Boston now is what I need to do; but your invitation made me realize that I could leave Boston someday. And that I might want to live with you—even in New Mexico.

This scares me, because all I really have to bring to living with another person—with you—are cooking skills and a decade of solitude.

I don't know if this should prevent me from daring to live with you, but it makes me nervous.

I wasn't ignoring us in my letter. I was just feeling scared.

love,

Hannah

I lean against the corner of my sofa, and remember the intense cramps I had the first time I got my period after Jonathan and I became lovers. He lay in bed with me the whole long day, just held me and brought me tea or whatever else I wanted—*and my cramps didn't feel as strong.* I remember the thrill I felt just from tracing the curve of his nose. He said he loved it that lying on top of his belly soothed me; it made him feel useful.

I glance at my clock and realize it's time to meet Annie for dinner.

Just before I leave my apartment to knock on her door, I slip into my bathroom to scrutinize myself in the mirror. All day, over the black pants I usually wear to contact improvisation jams, I've worn an oversized forest green T-shirt, and my favorite earrings. They're squiggly, silver dangles, made in Israel. Karen got them for me just before we left for college.

I stand in front of the long mirror, behind my bathroom door. *My left earring is missing.* Both my hands reach up to cover my ears, and I feel panic dart around inside me. Okay, I think, I did laundry today. I head down to the basement, to the washers and dryers, scanning the three flights of stairs for silver. In the laundry room, I search around and inside the machines.

There's nothing here.

I trudge back upstairs, looking more slowly, still not finding anything. My favorite memory of Karen is the day she gave me these earrings. We'd met for a picnic at the Shaker lake near the high school, just two days before I left for Ann Arbor. She had an almost motherly glow when she gave me this little box and said I could always have our friendship with us, just by looking at these earrings.

I feel my face turn stony—like Karen's—when the missing one still doesn't turn up in the crevices of my loveseat, or around the clean clothes I've put away. When Annie knocks to pick me up for dinner, I warn her, "I'm in a bad mood. I know this is just a thing. But *Karen* gave them to me! And they were my *favorites.*"

Annie sees my eyes bulging out and gives me a hug. "Maybe you could make a necklace out of the one that's left," she says.

"No!" I whine. "They're *earrings.*"

"All right," she says. "Make a sign that you lost one, and put it in the laundry room with your phone number. We can post it on our way to the diner."

"But I already looked all over the laundry room."

"Hannah—what is it your Aunt Mollie calls you? A *hanna pesl?* A pain?"

I nod, sheepishly.

"Yeah," she says. "I can see why she calls you that."

February 24, 1989

> *I hate Annie Kingston. Everything in her life is lovely. Everything is fine. Why share my grief with her? Yesterday, when I said, "I'm having a hard time," she said, "Everybody does, now and then." That makes me crazy! That makes me not trust her! I wish she'd just tell me honestly that she's sick of my grief.*

FOR two months, I wake with my head aching, pee that burns, my vagina feeling dirty and itchy: I wake angry. I want to return to bed, to sleep, though I'm not tired. I don't know WHAT TO DO with this stuckness. *Pound pillows,* I think. But I don't. I feel too stuck to try.

I go to the kitchen. A few days ago I replaced the battery in the clock. Yesterday I realized this new battery must have extra juice, because after twenty-four hours, against my watch, the clock was twenty minutes fast. But I keep glancing at it, expecting it to tell me the true time. If it's so hard to adjust to a clock with a bad battery, no wonder I've needed almost ten years to swallow my mother's changed tune.

I take a Granny Smith apple from my fruit bowl, eat it. Then I start another. I feel bloated. My lips are tightly closed now. They say *enough.*

What do I want?! I want a place where I belong. I want more time for writing poetry. After years of feeling like the Center is where I feel most at home in the world, where I feel wanted, where I love hearing what people have to say—I feel uneasy there. Eileen O'Toole still gives me dirty looks in class; Sherry Johnson hasn't shown in two months. Nancy says that government cutbacks may force the Center to close within a year. And Gram says she's "getting tired." Her tone makes me think that she's trying to tell me she's not going to live forever.

Last week, Jonathan sent me a collage made of rusted tin cans he found in the arroyo behind his house. He hammered them into old wood, and formed an image somehow of a coyote roaming at the base of a mountain, with a full moon overhead. He also told me about Georgia O'Keeffe. He's been reading about her. "She said she was absolutely terrified every single moment of her life," Jonathan wrote. "And that it never stopped her from doing a single thing she wanted to do."

I like his collage. I like the quote from Georgia O'Keeffe. *Does this mean I want to live with him? Does this mean I want to live in New Mexico?*

DREAM

In the library, I read a book about my mother when she was young. She lived with Marilyn Monroe on my grandfather's bed. The year I was born, things changed. Books and beds turned to logs. Everything burned. Marilyn and my mother stopped being friends. Walking home from the library, I see Marilyn. She's drunk or crazy, maybe both. She can't see me. When I reach the beginning of my street, I see that my neighborhood's in flames. Other people are near me. I don't trust them much, but I go with them into the fire. I know this is the direction that will lead me to safety. I look past the flames and see a beautiful young girl dancing a wonderful dance. Her choreographer gives her a lot of hope.

IT's the middle of March, spring break. In Cleveland, the sky is gray. From the airport, I ride the rapid transit toward Ida's suburban apartment. The other passengers move slowly to their seats. Each person who boards makes eye contact with me, and often gives a "How you doin'?" to our driver. Just last year the ride felt like a long cruise through garbage dumps; but now the banks we ride along are kept clean, even grassy. Drying laundry threads together the downtown neighborhoods.

I rest an arm against my suitcase, filled with my journal, a small box of pastels, my camera, and two one-pound bags of granola from Bread & Circus. The one for Ida has dried blueberries in it; the one for Mollie is fat free.

At the Terminal Tower, I lug my suitcase upstairs and down to get to the suburban trolley. I make this visit at least three times a year now. Rolling into the last stop, Van Aken, I spot Ida's ten-year-old blue Nova in the parking lot, her crown of white hair sticking out above the steering wheel. As I cross the tracks and head toward her, she slides to the passenger seat, keeping her eye on me as if to ensure the safety of my crossing.

"Hello," I say, happy to see her, opening the back door for my suitcase, then the front one to take my place in the driver's seat.

"Hello," she says matter-of-factly. Ida Zeitlin is not a sentimental woman.

"I have to move the seat up," I say, getting down to business myself.

"All right," she says.

"One, two, three!" As far as this bench goes, we pull forward.

"There's no room for my legs, Hannah!"

"Well, Gram, I have shorter legs than you. And if I'm the one driving, I need to reach the pedals."

Through her nostrils, she lets out a long sigh.

I grip the wheel, shift into reverse, notice that her odometer still has only sixteen thousand miles on it. She must hardly leave home. When we're talking on the phone, *I love this woman.* But being right next to her exacerbates my own rigidity, dammit. I start my countdown: four and a half days to go.

"I see we're not getting off on the right foot," Ida says.

"No," I say. "But that doesn't mean we have to stay that way."

"I suppose," she says. She folds her hands over her purse and tells me to turn up the heat.

———

MY grandmother's tongue could be made of diamonds. She can slice me up cleaner than knives. In the middle of the afternoon, I return from the dentist with a load of fresh vegetables in my arms. "*Nu,* so?" she asks, before I close the door. "How much?"

"Honestly, Ida," I say. "Give me a minute."

I take off my coat, hang it in the closet, find a place in the freezer for her ice cream while she goes back to her crossword puzzle. She doesn't mind waiting, once she knows I'll give her attention. I return to the living room, sit in one of the blue wing chairs. "I spent nineteen dollars and sixty-four cents on groceries, and the dentist's bill came to a hundred and five dollars."

Gram clucks her tongue against the roof of her mouth. "Do you know how much it costs me when you visit? Including the plane ticket, it's at least four hundred dollars! Every time!"

"And I'm worth every penny, right, Gram?"

"I'm not so sure." Her words come from an ancient, sour place. They sting.

"I'm going to take a nap," I say now, boring my eyes into hers, hoping she feels hurt some, too.

I sleep soundly for nearly two hours. When I wake, I hear the creak of Gram's bed parallel to mine. She's been napping, too.

I take my cardigan from the bedpost. "How's your mouth?" Gram asks.

"Almost back to normal," I say.

"Good," she says.

"What about you?"

"Ya, I like a little nap."

"What time is it?" I ask.

"Nearly five. I'll go put dinner on the table. I've got gefilte fish."

"Wow," I say. "One of my favorites."

"I *know,*" she says. "That's why I made it."

I get out of bed and rinse my face in the hall bathroom, which is mine for the week. Above the loveseat, I notice Leah Zeitlin's hawk-eyed portrait, and think how peaceful she is in the darkness that surrounds her.

———

"I just don't understand why you're not more established, Hannah. You've been teaching for eight years. You should be able to afford your own doctor bills. You should own a house by now." It's late afternoon, my third day here, and we're once again sitting in her living room, watching the sun set over the cemetery across the street.

I sigh. "We've been through this before, Gram. Teachers don't get paid decently as it is; and because I'm not a regular teacher, I have to pay for my own health insurance. And if a poet gets paid more than one hundred dollars a year for poetry, the IRS gets suspicious."

"So why don't you get a regular job? Sonia Finkel has a grandson who's a high-school science teacher, and he even gets dental insurance."

"Well, *mazl tov* to Sonia Finkel's grandson. He probably sees a hundred and twenty kids every day. If I had that many students, I wouldn't be able to get to know *any* of them. And I'd be way too exhausted to publish anything like the *Wild Women's Stories,* or to write my own poetry."

"I don't know, Hannah. Other teachers help their students with yearbooks and such."

"I know," I say. "And I don't know how they do it. I honestly don't know how."

"Well, for heaven's sake, you should find something that pays you well and doesn't exhaust you."

"You know what, Gram?" I say, standing up, because the smell of her roasted chicken signals it's time to steam the cauliflower.

Ida clasps her hands together and turns toward me on the sofa. "What?"

"From now on, every time you imply something negative about my work or finances, I'm going to charge you a dollar."

"I'm not worried," she says crisply. "I can afford it."

Until I am in the kitchen and out of her view, I hold back my wide grin. I cut the white head into florets, toss them in the steamer. I take her chicken out of the oven, knick a piece off the bone for a taste. I shake my head. What did she *do* to this bird? I *watched* her prepare it. She rinsed it, put it in the

Pyrex dish, sprinkled it with salt and garlic powder. And it's the best chicken I've ever eaten.

"Your wealth inspires me, Ida Zeitlin," I holler into the living room. "I'm going to use up all your frozen corn, and the parsley. We'll buy more tomorrow."

"*All* of it? You have to use *a whole package* of corn?"

"Yep," I say, "the whole package."

MORNING. I wake to Ida's profile, her finely chiseled face, her breasts showing through her white gown. Her thick glasses rest on the nightstand. Under the old, pale yellow sheets and pea-green wool blankets, her long legs are folded like a lamb's. The foot peeking out shows toenails as thick as wood.

I rest in Grampa's bed, three feet away, the bedcovers' warmth a protective halo. I see my grandmother's smooth skin, and her white hair curled near the nape of her neck. *What kept her so soft in the house that Grampa built? Each day Moe woke in this bed, did he notice her soft lines and want to touch them?*

At dawn, Gram reaches for her eyeglasses and her old robe, and heads for the kitchen. She starts her morning with a scouring pad and the pot I burned last night and left to soak.

I follow her. From a high cupboard, I take down a crystal bowl. She turns from the sink to watch me; she utters no sound until I am down from the stepstool, filling the bowl with fruit.

"What are you doing?" she asks.

"I say we set our table as if we are queens."

She purses her lips, shakes her head like it needs to be balanced again, presses her weight back into the pot's last burn. Finally, when the pot emerges from her soapy bath shiny, stainless, she says, "Well. If you're going to have that bowl for fruit, you ought to get the good silver out, and bowls from my good dishes, too."

I smile—a small, hesitant smile.

"You know Loehmann's has an outlet here now," Ida says, "in Euclid, I think."

"Oh?" After her complaints about the grocery and dental bills, I don't want to sound too interested in the shopping spree she is offering.

Later, we leave the breakfast dishes in the sink, and move to the TV room. I'm rereading a novel I sent her two months ago, Louise Erdrich's *Love Medicine;* Ida just sits quietly, sometimes with her eyes closed. Except for the nightly news, while I'm visiting, she keeps the TV off.

"Well," she says, "I thought we could go out this afternoon. Maybe even go to Sand's for dinner. I'd like a corned beef sandwich."

"That sounds like a nice day," I say, trying to tone down my glee at the prospect of buying clothes.

"Before we do anything, though, I need to stop at Dr. Stadtler's. I get a B-12 shot, you know. Once a month. It doesn't take five minutes."

"That sounds fine," I say, folding my book and laying it on the floor so we can talk.

We let the quiet soothe us. We hear the refrigerator hum, the low din of traffic.

"Mother has a new job," she says, meaning Celia. Gram knows I don't talk with Mom for more than a minute or two every couple of years; my news of Seattle comes through her.

"Oh?" I say.

"She has a job taking care of a new baby. Darlene went back to work, and she asked Celia to look after her son."

"She has a job taking care of a baby?"

Gram nods, one of those really small up-and-down nods, letting me know she finds the situation weird, too. "She says she loves it. Five days a week, all day, while the parents are working."

"You know she once told me her favorite thing in the world is taking care of a baby. Because she can communicate without having to talk."

"I suppose," Gram says, her eyebrows full of doubt. "You know, I still miss her," Gram says. "I wish she'd never left Cleveland. To this day I don't understand why she had to move clear across the country—to *Seattle."*

Gram has brought the thumb and index finger of her right hand to knead her jaw; her left hand tucks under her right elbow to support it. Sitting with her on this sofa has made my own joints creaky and stiff. I stretch my legs out in front of me and my arms—palms flexed up—to the ceiling.

"I know why Mom moved," I say.

"Why?" Gram asks—as if the word is a steak she's plopped in front of me on a platter.

"She had to get away from me. She wrote me that with their new address when they moved."

Gram indulges the quiet again for a few moments. "Celia's not well, is she?"

"Oh, Gram," I say. "It's easy to say that. It helps me some, actually, to tell myself that she's not well-balanced when I try to come up with reasons why she won't talk to me. But there's stuff about her that's so *sane*. That's what drives me crazy—I always have this strong feeling that her craziness makes sense."

"Mmm," Ida says. "I think I sort of felt like that when she was growing up. In those years her not talking made sense to me, on account of Grampa. With his crazy antics ruling the house, what kind of person would want to talk?" Gram uncrosses her legs and recrosses them. A gust of wind blows against the building. The curtains rustle a little, and when they settle, the room seems softer.

"Ach," she says. "What's the use? I don't think I was such a good mother to her, myself."

For a while, each of us takes in the weight of her last words. Finally, I ask, "Can you tell me more about Mom and Allan's relationship?"

Gram looks at me sitting cross-legged on her sofa, as if to gauge my capacity for knowing certain things. "One of the last times I visited you before the divorce," she says, turning her gaze away from me to allow us each a little privacy, "I heard that so-called father of yours, and your mother. He was forcing her. I heard it through the walls."

She's given me a full plate to swallow and digest. "I was three at the time?" I ask, wanting to know exactly what the ingredients are here, conscious that I'm postponing whatever I feel.

"Something like that."

"What else did you hear?" I ask.

"Oh, I don't know, Hannah," Gram says, rising from the sofa to dress for the day. "It's water over the dam.

"And another thing," she hollers from her bedroom, "I've told you enough about Celia. It's time you started telling *me* stories. Like about Jonathan for instance."

"I don't know that there's anything to tell," I say, following her path to the shower. "He's in New Mexico, walking through dried riverbeds and making collages. We write letters, and talk on the phone."

"He must like you an *awful* lot."

I raise my eyebrows, bite my lip. "Yeah," I say. "I think he does."

I REST a clean washcloth on the high plastic stool in Gram's shower stall, lay a clean towel on the counter in front of her sink, then help her find the water's right temperature. After her shower, she calls out, "Hannah, I'm ready!" I dry her back and neck, her legs and feet, then stand behind her so she can slide her arms into her white terrycloth robe.

"Why don't I give you a massage," I ask, just before she readies herself to dress.

"I've never had a massage," Gram says.

"That's okay," I say. "I'll talk you through it."

Like a cat waiting to be stroked, she lies down on her bed. "Do you miss Grampa?" I ask, placing her arms along her sides.

"No," she says succinctly. "I hardly think about him."

"You've sure changed a lot since he's died." I lay my hands gently in the middle of her back.

"Oh? How so?"

"Well, you let yourself enjoy things more—like corned beef, for example. And even though you complain a lot about all the money you spend now, I get the feeling you're glad to be doing it."

"Maybe," she says.

"Grampa'll be gone nine years this summer," I say.

"Yes," she says, as in, *So what?*

"Okay," I say, gently swirling hand lotion into her back. "Soften your tongue. Soften your scalp."

I'm surprised by how silky her skin is—maybe I'd expected her to be calloused, crusty, like her words can be. But only the soles of her feet are dry and rough.

"Mm," Gram says. Her breathing is deep and heavy.

"Feel the relationship between the top of your spine and the bottom," I say.

At this suggestion, Gram's looks up at me like I'm nuts. When our eyes meet, she rolls into a wave of uncontrollable giggles. *"Vey iz mir!"* she shouts, "Moe should see this! And Mollie."

I burst into a hearty giggle myself, and land on her bed, spooned, with my arms securely wrapped around her exquisite softness, our laughter billowing out of us like bubbles from a kid blowing soap.

WE stand at the cashier's counter at Loehmann's while she adds up two sweaters, two pairs of pants, and a scarf. "Ninety-two dollars and forty-three cents," the woman says.

Ida has pulled her checkbook from her purse and begun to write. But then she pauses. "That's not right," she says, looking the woman in the eye.

The cashier looks like a reliable woman near fifty. "I can add it up again," she says politely.

Gram says, "It shouldn't be more than ninety dollars."

I hover near the counter, nervous and embarrassed, my eyes on the clothes folded neatly in tissue paper.

Then the cashier looks up from her calculator with a startling grin. "You're right," she says. "Eighty-nine seventy-two."

"Ya," Gram says. She writes the check matter-of-factly, then tells me she'll stop in the ladies' room while I wait for my package.

"She's eighty-eight!" I tell the cashier. When we get to the car, I plant a kiss on Gram's cheek.

"What's that for?" she asks.

"For being wonderful," I say.

"Well," she says, "someday soon I hope you're able to buy clothes for yourself."

I tip my head as if to accuse her of wrecking the moment.

"Was that a dollar comment?" she asks.

"Yep," I say, turning the ignition. "I think so."

LEAVING the Wild Women's Center one day in early January, Josie asks me if I'm going to type the stories everyone wrote today. I'd asked them to describe a person they know who feels at home in the world—or one who doesn't. Honestly, I'd rather work on my poems than type students' stories tonight. "Mm," I tell Josie, feeling guilty and honest, "I forgot to ask people's permission."

"Too good to waste," she says, in the first show of care I've seen from her since she started at the Center last fall. Eileen O'Toole is just leaving class while Josie is lobbying for me to type these stories; her head is bowed as if she's hiding something and wanting to leave the room quickly.

As soon as I get home, I set my students' stories out on my table.

MY DAUGHTER
by Eileen O'Toole

My daughter is not at home in the world. She is not at home with me. We used to do puzzles together and laugh sometimes. But now, if I am in her bedroom, she goes to the parlor to watch TV. If I am in the parlor, she goes to her bedroom. I don't know if she has friends, but she never brings them home.

Her name is Kathleen, and she is ten. I think she steals from the drug store near us, because I see her eating candy bars sometimes that I did not buy.

My husband says I shouldn't worry, but I do. I especially worry that she doesn't trust me. About a year ago, I was having a hard time, and I sent her to my mother's house. I think my mother is an alcoholic. Some-

times she can't stop drinking. Maybe something happened there? All I
know is when Kathy came back home, she was not at home with me.

I should not have left my daughter alone with my mother. Because
I know my mother drinks, and I know she shouldn't have a young child
around her when she's drunk.

I should have sent Kathy to a friend's house.

I change the names in the stories, and type them up, feeling lucky that I
know Eileen and the other women, too. *At the Wild Women's Center, I am at*
home in the world. In the morning, I photocopy the pages; and at the beginning of class, I return each woman's paper with a note. To Eileen, I write:

Dear Eileen,

Your story really touches me, because I have spent many days not at
home with my *mother.*

It seems like Kathleen is really hurting about something. I think that
must be one of the hardest things for a mother—to see that your child is
hurting. Especially when you don't know what you can do to stop it.

For me, knowing that someone cares enough to watch me and hold
me in their heart helps me feel at home in the world. And it sure sounds
to me like that's what you do with Kathleen.

I know of a summer writing program for kids your daughter's age,
and if you'd like, I can get you their number. I could also get a list of
counselors who work with families whose mothers study at the Center.

I think you are a brave writer, and a brave mother.

Sincerely,
Hannah

Just when we begin to read the stories aloud, Lucia Langley passes a note
to my lap. Usually, she sits at least several chairs away from me in our circle,
next to her friend Masline. Often, they lean their heads together and return
to their upright posture nodding, nearly in unison. Each time, I figure they've
found another fault with my teaching—though one or the other of them

might comment on a story after they've conferred. Today, Lucia sits next to me. "Do you die from diabeetees?" her note asks. "Yesterday, my husband learnt that he has it."

My goodness, I realize, *she must trust me.*

"People with diabetes need to eat a special diet," I scribble back. "And sometimes they take shots to balance their blood. Then, usually, they can live normal lives."

Masline is reading aloud a story about a woman whose sister is not at home in this world. Their mother died when the author was fifteen, and the sister was six. It's Josie's story. "I did my best with her," Josie wrote. "I kept her with me til she was eighteen, which was three years ago. I sewed her real nice clothes. I always asked her every day how was school and how is it with her friends. But still, she is not at home in this world. She is in bed all the time, and I swear, she must steal whatever food she eats, because she sure don't make any money that I can see. I tell you, just by how much my heart aches, I KNOW I AM IN THIS WORLD."

When I look up, Josie's dark eyes are waiting for mine. She reaches for a tissue in her purse, and nods to me, slowly, as if to signal she's *in this class,* and glad to be.

TWENTY-FIVE

1991

FROM THE OTHER WORLD
CHANNA

1880–1956

W HEN my time of life came, my body by then was strong like a rock. The hot flashes went through me like God's lightning. They started around the time Celia was born—just as Evelyn, my youngest, was getting old enough to cook a good meal without my help. That was a good thing. Because by then, on a lot of days, I just wanted to take a seat and rest. I'd be working away at the stove or the sink, and feel the pressure in me rise up. I'd take a pause and feel myself wobble. Back and forth I moved, unsteady like I might be in a dream, or back on the boat what took me from the Old Country. My breasts and my belly would turn heavy, then light.

Moe, my rich son-in-law, he got me a washer. So, I lost my day of scrubbing in the basement, which helped. But also I lost my place to sing. Then I wondered if the pressure wasn't just my time of life, but if I was dizzy or shocked—for people still in the Old Country. I knew something for them was also changing. I knew they had pressure. It was the beginning of the upheaval, of course.

Most of my children had left the house by then. They had their own families. With that and the washer Moe got me, I didn't have so much to do. Then Celia got born. She brought me a new kind of work.

With my children, the work was in stretching my belly, squeezing them out; then with my arms, I held them through sicknesses, scrubbed their clothes, cooked. It was the work of muscle. With Celia, my job went from working the muscles to holding them back. I tried not to be tight. Because I ached to hold Celia; but like Vitl, she wouldn't come into my arms. Even though she was right next to me.

This gave me a grief. My arms hurt, sometimes more than they had from a day of scrubbing clothes. The older Celia got, the more I watched her with an ache. I lived with it.

Of course when Meyer died, that was a big change. To sleep alone felt strange—like it did to cook without a thought to his taste for food; and to have the soft touch of children only, not a man's embrace. I thought when he died we might talk like I do with Vitl. But the truth is, I couldn't tell after a while whether the voice I talked with was his or hers.

HANNAH, my namesake, my *taskele,* I know you know I've kept my eye on you—while you grew in your mother's belly; while you grew in her house. I saw you wanting to know and love the world beyond what Celia knew. I watched your mother give you room for that as much as she could; I saw you wanting more. More than she could make room for. I saw you wanting to use your heart. Which means, of course, it has to break open a lot.

Sometimes you get to know your heart by not using it. You, you were born wanting to use it—to a woman who spent her life trying not to. Think kindly on your mother: she was afraid that you might know, as she did, the feel of love gone sour. She loves you, Hannah; she just couldn't stand to feel all she felt, to watch you feel any pain, to see your big eyes on her when she felt shattered.

And what does someone get from loving people who are trying to sleep through certain feelings—like they want to sleep through history? They learn that condemning people doesn't really change anything. They come to know what God said to Moses at the burning bush: *the place where you are standing is holy.*

ONCE Celia had you in her belly, she changed. Before you arrived, she would let nothing into her arms unless she knew she could move it away. Also of course, she didn't let anybody hold her. She lived inside herself. In a small dark corner of her spine, I used to think. Moe, your grandfather, he always gave her nice clothes, then college, and she also got her own car. Moe made sure of these things. And Celia made sure she kept herself from need or want of anything.

That is, until she went crazy for Allan, your father—for that boy Leonard, too, I always thought. Her chemicals got stirred when she was with those boys. It was sweet with her and Allan; I used to think they gave each other comfort. He was such a scared boy. When he was just finishing high school, he used to see the pictures in the paper of the naked bodies from the camps, piled high like garbage. His parents had left the Old Country just before the upheaval. Pregnant with him, his mother was, on their boat to America. Allan knew, it could have been his parents in those pictures. *It could have been him.* But no, it was his aunts and uncles and cousins.

Ach. What he saw, and what he didn't see. What he didn't see was the hunger in those Nazi boys—way back behind their eyes, eyes gone flat. They wanted a life with order to it. But they got mixed up. They couldn't tell the truth about themselves anymore.

Well, like a lot of men I know, your father got to feeling there was no God for the Jews. He was also a romantic, with a big hunger to make the world a place for love what always smells like kuchen right out of the oven. Your world has plenty of love in it already of course; but it doesn't always smell like kuchen.

He was scared of girls, Allan. And he was sensitive, too. He would see a girl and want to comfort her. He would see in her eyes such a big hunger to be held. He had the same eyes in his own mirror, of course, but he saw only the gray hairs starting to come out, and the shame that still he hadn't really loved a girl. To make friends, he didn't know how.

Well, he went to make himself a social worker—not to learn himself how to make friends, but to give people the comfort he couldn't make for himself.

So then he met with Celia, Celia our girl so hungry for love she had made herself think she didn't need it. Until she met Allan. Celia, she had never been with a man, but it didn't take long for her to get into this one's lap. "Are you a virgin?" she asked Allan, after they had been on a few dates.

Allan, he had her in his arms, on a bed. He had his face on her shoulder. She moved her soft fingers on the hard muscle parts of his arm. From the Other World, I saw them in that ocean of comfort, deep. You think you'll never get out of that ocean. But of course, you get to choppy water soon enough; and then you can't remember love.

"No," he said, "but it's probably not what you think. Do you want to know?"

"Yes," she said, real clear. She took his face into her hands and looked him in the eyes yet.

So, he told her about a day he had in the Village. "I'd just bought myself a salami sandwich," he said. "I had another lonely evening ahead of me, with my books. A girl came up to me, she couldn't have been sixteen. She looked so lonely and sweet. 'You want a good evening, mister?' this girl said. 'I can give you a good evening.' "

"Oh yeah?" Allan said, and he asked the girl for her name. It just came out of him, this talking to her. Maybe at first it was like a game. Her name was Alice. She took your father to a room maybe a block from Washington Square. "God," he was thinking, "this girl's ten years younger than me, and she knows more about the birds and the bees than I do." He felt embarrassed for that. But he looked into her eyes, and kept seeing her sadness.

When they got to the rented room, he asked her if she'd like a massage. She looked at him like he was kind of crazy, but she shrugged her shoulders and said, "Okay." I think she liked it, the massage. Afterward, Allan asked her if she had dreams for herself, you know, besides working the streets. Well, she poured her heart out to him. Told Allan her whole life's story. And then she undressed him, and took him inside her. He felt like he'd really given her something, not just money, from listening to her talk. He felt that he'd loved her.

Celia, she squeezed Allan tighter when he'd finished his story. He could hardly believe it. "You still want to be with me?" he said.

"Yes," she said, clear again like when she said she wanted to hear his story.

"Why would you love a man who lost his virginity to a prostitute?" he asked.

"It's so beautiful," she said, "your hunger. You've got a beautiful, monstrous hunger—to comfort the whole world."

Ach. We get nervous up here with love words like that. You know, they make like a Grand Canyon in the body, they scoop out a big hole—with no telling what will fill it up.

H E would make her breakfast—pancakes with blueberries, or eggs scrambled with lox on rye toast. I saw him once take her picture with rollers in her hair. He said, "Even right now, you look ravishing."

So, we got to see Celia could giggle. And she would touch him. Really put her arms around him, come to him from behind and lay her hands on his chest.

It was sweet, ya. But it was all sugar, you know, not what keeps a marriage going. By now, Celia had her idea to make a baby with Allan; so she needed him. But he wanted first to finish his schooling—I think because he wanted to start a family on his money, not Moe's. So, they had their different wants. The sex with them got funny. She wouldn't be with him except in the middle of her month. Allan complained about that so much that for a while she wouldn't let him touch her, even to try for a baby. I used to watch them and wish they had a way to talk about these things. His psychology classes were telling him if you have such problems, it's a sickness. So, fine, let it be a sickness; but at some point, every marriage has its hard time in the bed.

Well, one night, Celia felt sad, she couldn't tell about what. She let Allan just hold her. And out of that night of comfort, she got her pregnant belly.

This really stirred her up, to carry a baby. On the outside, she got more beautiful. Anybody could pick her out, easy—just like when you look to the sky at night, some stars catch your eye first. She *glowed*. Celia might have said it was you glowing, and she took from you to make herself shine. Some days when she sat in front of her vanity with the big mirror, even she could see and feel for herself she looked like a princess. So, she didn't need Allan now to tell her she was beautiful—she could see for herself.

Still, some days she felt *treyf,* ugly. She got an infection in her privates, real bad itching what made her tired in the day and kept her awake at night.

So now she had more reason to keep her and Allan from their together time in the bed. Celia, she didn't mind that. She was happy just to dream for your future. She knew you were a girl, and she made you in her mind a princess who would know how to talk about what she wanted. Allan, it was hard for him, not to have together time with his wife. He's one of those men who don't feel okay really, except when he's inside a woman.

Then Celia got the scary dreams of babies trying to swim for themselves, and she couldn't help them, because she didn't know how to swim. *Sheyne meydl,* she didn't have tolerance for a mother who couldn't help her child. Especially when she was the mother.

Around the last month, you got very active. And big, too. Celia could hardly move. She felt such worries. She started to realize she would have to do for you. Take care of you. But she thought she couldn't do it. Because all her life Moe and Ida had done her taking care; and she had kept herself inside herself. She loved you before you were born, but she wasn't sure she wanted to open up for someone.

Celia didn't have anyone to talk to who could really listen, like my Vitl always can listen. Celia didn't talk so much when I was alive; now that I'm dead, well, she doesn't talk much at all. To babies she cares for, she talks sometimes about her own heart—before they understand English.

One day, in her last month with you, Celia felt such worries, and aches in the bones, in the neck, she could hardly move. She climbed to the attic with ideas that to climb stairs would be good exercise, maybe help her. But when she got to the little window and sat nearby, she started to wonder about jumping.

We watched her, you know, we stayed nearby—Vitl and me, and Moe's mother, Leah. Leonard came, too. He's a good soul, Leonard. He really loved her. And also, of course, we watched on you.

You moved slowly inside her, you had a rhythm like the water at the beach when it's gentle. You rocked yourself. She was trying to shut you off, to shut off the whole world so she could jump, but you kept rocking.

She had her plans for doing her labor natural; she went to those breathing classes. Allan, too. To me, it was *meshugge*—classes in breathing, and a hospital for having a baby yet, where they get nervous if you make screams, where they have machines and shots what do nothing for a woman what just needs a kind eye nearby, and someone telling her she is good and what she does is exactly right, now go gentle or push hard.

When she got to the hospital, already she'd been having the contractions a few hours. The moon was nearly full. She put her eyes to Allan, for help. "The lucky doctor's going to get my favorite view of you," he said.

Your father was so troubled and scared. He was really thinking he didn't have the strength to watch his wife labor with nothing to help her but to look her in the eyes. Celia had a panic then. I suppose because some part of her had taken to believing they would be together, always, that she'd never be alone. And here in her broken waters, she saw how each soul lives alone with its own feeling. Sure, you watch each other a lot; but everyone has their own seeing and thinking.

Allan panicked too. All he had to do was sit with Celia, give her a kind eye. But this seemed useless to him. She got real scared, Celia. Whatever opening she'd started to make for you to come through, she closed it back up. Leah, she has a lot of chutzpah, she *plotzed* herself right onto Celia. "Make your mind, Celia," Leah says. "Do you want to die; do you want to be with us? Or do you want to live?"

She can sound harsh, Leah. She likes a quick decision. I like it, sometimes. But I thought, for now, Celia needs a gentle voice. "Whatever you choose," I told her, "the baby will go with you."

We watched her. We didn't miss a motion. She went inside herself, it looked like she made some peace. "The baby wants to live," she whispered.

Leah, she made a sigh. It moved the curtains in the room. That got the doctor nervous, to see a curtain blow from nowhere. He didn't even check to see if Celia was opening up again. He gave her the shot to take away her feeling and put her to sleep. Allan, he started to make like a chicken with a head cut off. Naturally, a nurse took him to a room with other fathers. And when Celia woke from her labor and saw him, through her foggy mind she had a clear thought: as soon as she could get by without Allan, she'd leave him.

For you, she had to make a choice: to shut you out, keep you outside herself; or she could let her heart open, take you in. You know it, Hannah, she took you. She took you in without any walls at all.

And then, of course, she built them. *Ach.* What a thing to watch. From here, it wasn't easy. Our comfort came from knowing if you survived those walls your mother built, and if you could let yourself love other people—then, well, then despite all the ones our family lost in the last hundred years, and all the tears we've held back, well, then maybe something of us would continue.

She did her best, Hannah, you know that.

I know you hear me, Hannah. I know you know we all have our eye on you.

And another thing. I like this Jonathan Lev.

TWENTY-SIX

1991

HANNAH

I RETURN home from a contact jam to find my answering machine blinking like a friend waving hello. "This is Gram," Ida's message declares. "Call me as late as you want."

"Hi," I say, returning her call before my jacket is off. "What's happening?"

It's May, two months since my last visit to Cleveland. We talk almost every evening now, after dinner. She likes to ask about Jonathan. I think she worries about him. I didn't call her earlier tonight because I was running late for the jam.

"Well," she says, her voice steady and focused, "my stomach ache turns out to be cancer."

"Oh, Gram," I say, sitting down slowly on my old stuffed chair. "I wish I was with you right now." We hold our phones silently.

Then slowly, she explains that her doctor wants her to go to the hospital for some more tests, maybe surgery. "To tell the truth, I'm not sure I want to go through with an operation."

"I can understand that," I say, split between wanting to support her and not wanting to lose her. "What does the doctor want to test?"

"Ach," she says, disgusted. "Those doctors would be happy to test me till I'm blue in the face."

"Loz kokhn biz oyf Shabbes," I say, her mother's expression, now one of my favorites, though I don't exactly observe the Sabbath—"Let it cook until Shabbes."

"I have let it cook!" she says. "I've let it cook all day. I know what's going on, and I don't need a bunch of tests to prove it!"

Tears stream into a gentle smile I can't hold back. "Oh, Gram," I cry, "I love you."

She doesn't miss a beat: "So when will you come?"

"Well, I'd been planning for Memorial Day weekend," I say. "In about three weeks. How's that?"

"I suppose."

"You want me to come sooner?"

"I want someone with me," she says. "And not a paid someone. Celia said she'd come in for a week, and Rita for the one after that."

"So I'll come after Rita," I say, knowing the Wild Women's Center can get by without me for a week.

"Oh, great," Gram says. "That's what I hoped you'd say."

"I want one of our hugs, Gram," I say. "I'll be counting the days 'til I come."

"I hope I make it," she says. Her voice is meek.

I want to ask, *What are you talking about?* But instead I say, "How about we do this like we always do—one day at a time."

"Okay," she says. "And don't forget to call me tomorrow night."

I hang up the phone, curl up in my bed with my jacket still on, and sob.

By the time I arrive in Cleveland two weeks later, Gram's been in the hospital for five days. She stopped eating once she learned her diagnosis, and became too weak to move around on her own. Rita is still in town, and my mother is due to return later in the day. They're staying in Gram's apartment; I'll stay at Mollie's.

From the airport, I take the rapid transit to Shaker Square, then a taxi to Suburban Hospital. It's just after lunch. A nurse directs me to her room. "I think she's sleeping," the woman tells me. "Her daughter just left." *Aunt Rita,* I realize. I place my suitcase near a green vinyl armchair, then walk slowly to the side of her bed, glad it's just the two of us here.

"Get some lotion," Gram says, through closed eyes. "I want a massage."

"How do you know it's me?" I ask, giggling. When she doesn't respond, I just head to the nurse's station.

Returning to her room, I close the door, take a seat at the edge of her bed, and squeeze a little lotion onto my fingertips. Gently, I swirl around her cheeks. The skin is so dry, small flakes fall into my fingers like from pie crust. Mixed with the lotion, they form something like paste. After her cheeks, I caress each ear. Then I take my grandmother's right hand, and squeeze down the length of each finger.

"Harder," Ida says. "Get a little blood going."

Her body feels brittle and light, like a bird's.

"Roll me to my side," she says. "Do my back." Her voice is a little blurry, but her thinking's keen and clear.

I lift the covers, push away a tube, then roll her so she faces the window. I untie the bow at the neck of her gown. Beginning at her shoulders, Ida's back is hunched. *How much has this back carried? How long has it been hunched? What else have I not noticed?*

I reach for the lotion on the tray table. "This might feel cold for a minute," I say.

Gram mumbles back, "Uhn."

I caress the length of her spine, make swirls out to the edges of her back until my hands and her back are no longer cool. I feel the fragile warmth her body makes, and slide in beside her. I fold my left arm between my breasts and Ida's back; I lay my right arm over hers. My eyes get moist. I let them close. I lay my hand on her head, feeling her old, white hair.

We lie like this maybe a half hour. Then I slip out of Gram's bed, roll her onto her back again, pull a yellow chair up to the bedside, and prop my knees against the metal frame. I take out my journal, hold it in my lap, and watch my grandmother breathe.

A MAN in a navy suit comes into the room carrying a flat black box with buttons. He's a large man. Ida must hear him walk in—she opens her eyes. "No," she says, even before he opens his mouth. "No TV."

The man looks puzzled. "I have cable," he says.

I turn my head from Gram to meet the man's eyes. "She's the boss in this room," I say. "No TV."

The man looks for a moment like he doesn't know what to do, but then he aims his box to the television. It makes a poof sound, and he leaves. Ida's body rises a little under her blanket, falls gracefully, rises again.

I ARRIVE at Aunt Mollie's at 6:30. She's still an elegant, graceful woman; but at eighty-seven, her movements are decidedly slow. A year ago, she fell and broke her hip. She walks with a three-pronged cane and rarely gets out these days; she no longer bothers to dye her hair. The day Ida was admitted to the hospital, a neighbor drove her across town for a visit. "We kissed each other," Gram told me. "Which for us is pretty good." Mollie and Gram are the only ones of our family still living in Cleveland. Bessie and their cousins, Abie and Sol, died years before; Evelyn and Jeremy have gone to be near their children in other cities.

When I ask Mollie if she wants my help with dinner, she says, "Just put your things in Ma's room"—the spare room she still attributes to her mother. "And make sure you keep it neat." Then she gives me a wink. "If you're well behaved, I'll let you wash the dishes."

We sit down to cold chicken and applesauce, steamed broccoli, and challah from Lax & Mandel's—the same dinner Mollie prepared for me when I occasionally spent nights with her twenty-five years ago. "Only I don't make my own applesauce anymore," she says, in case I can't tell the difference between Mott's and her homemade variety. "I don't have the patience to peel apples."

We eat quietly. Mollie dips each bite of skin-free chicken into applesauce. "I thought I'd tell you," she says, "since your grandmother probably didn't, the day I visited her at the hospital, we talked about you. She said, 'We're lucky to have Hannah.'"

"*Really?*" I ask.

She smiles at me directly. "Really," she says, dabbing her lips with her napkin so I can see her clean smile.

After washing our dishes, I phone Gram's apartment. Aunt Rita answers. "Hi," I say. "It's Hannah."

"What can I do for you?" she says bruskly.

"Hard day."

"Right," Rita says.

"How are you?" I ask.

"Fine. Are you aware Gram has refused treatment and most of the food she's been offered since she heard her diagnosis?"

I close my eyes, swallowing this news, which Gram first hinted to me two weeks ago. "Yes," I say. "Is Celia in yet?"

"Yes," she says. "Celia! Telephone!"

"Hello," a sluggish voice says.

"Mom, hi. It's Hannah."

"What do you want?"

"I'm planning to be in Gram's room by eleven tomorrow. Will you be there then? I mean, could you be there?"

"I don't need to hear this," she says.

"But Mom, we don't have to talk or anything. We could just be together."

"I'm not going to do this your way, Hannah!"

"Bye-bye, then," I say quickly, so I can hang up before she does.

"*I hate her!*" I practically spit, pacing Mollie's living room, grunting and making other weird noises.

"What happened?" Mollie asks.

"Mom said she doesn't need to hear I'll be in Gram's room tomorrow."

"Oh," Mollie says. "That must hurt."

"Yeah!" I say. "I'm angry enough to pace for the rest of the night."

"You'll drive me crazy if you do that," she says. "Why don't you scour my bathtub instead."

"Sure," I say, noticing an oncoming grunt, not wanting it to turn into a giggle. "That's a great idea."

IN the morning, I wake on Mollie's pull-out sofa, feeling stiff and numb. My eyelids are cracked with dry, red streaks. Methodically, I turn to the yellow pages for a chiropractor.

"A *chiropractor?*" Mollie asks. "What kind of a girl goes to a *chiropractor?*"

"Mollie," I say, "this is how I take care of myself. Maybe we shouldn't discuss it."

"I suppose," she says. "You don't drink coffee in the morning, either, do you?"

I shake my head no. "I'll get to the kitchen in a minute. I'll make my own breakfast."

THE chiropractor takes my head gently into his hands, massages its base, then turns my head quickly. Down my neck, I hear popping sounds. He shapes my torso into a spiral, cracks my back. When I stand up from his table, I feel dizzy.

"Why don't you sit for a minute," he suggests.

"Yeah," I say, noticing I feel like I'm carrying a bucket of water near my heart.

"Are you okay?" he asks.

"It's just my heart," I say, wishing I could make a joke. But I start crying so hard I end up a heap on his table again, moistening with tears.

"MOLLIE sends her love," I say, kissing Ida's forehead.

Gram nods, faintly.

"She wanted to come, but she worried about walking outside—it's slippery today with the rain."

"Tell her it's all right," Gram says, sweetly. "She's a good sister."

I take off my jacket, pull up the chair. "Do you want a massage today?"

"No," Gram says. "Just sit on the edge of the bed here." I make myself comfortable. "Your mother and Rita were just here."

"Oh?"

"They didn't stay long. I was sort of hoping you'd be here together."

I nod. "I talked to Mom last night," I say, tears trickling down my cheeks. "She doesn't want to see me, Gram."

Gram nods, closes her eyes.

"It hurts," I whisper.

"Loz es lign," Ida says. Her eyes are closed.

"Loz es lign?"

"Let it lie. Silence your heart from trying to figure it out. And move on." I lace my right hand in hers. "You can still have a good life," Gram says. Her words come out in the slow, measured pace of her breath.

We rest in these words, as if they've become part of the air, for most of the afternoon. I sit at the edge of her bed, my hand on her hand, watching the softness of her face. I watch her breath become softer and quieter. When an aide peeks in the room with a tray of food, I wave her away. The mid-afternoon sun beams into the room in stripes.

"Going," Gram says.

"Am I going?" I ask, wanting her to know I'm staying with her at least through the dinner hour.

She doesn't say anything.

"Oh," I say, tears now moistening not just my eyes, but my cheeks, too, my lips, even my sweater. "You're going."

RITA and Mom sit together in the funeral parlor, mumbling. "He was impossible," Rita says.

"She should've left him," Mom agrees.

I wonder if they know we all hear them. I can only see the back of Mom's head, her hair shorter and whiter than it was when I saw her last, at Gram's birthday party. It's still unruly. Sometimes, when she turns to Aunt Rita, I can see her profile. Her face has several dark moles on it, daring me to care that she might not be well. She's plump now, too. Not as plump as Aunt Rita, but her slenderness is lost, in the folds of a gray tent dress. Still, it's the scowl on her face that startles me: she must not let *anybody* in.

Uncle Lester and Norm sit beside Aunt Rita and Mom; Aunt Mollie's on Uncle Lester's right. Behind them, I sit with Jay and Neil and their wives.

Three of Gram's friends have come, one with a cane, one in a walker.

"She was a devoted wife and mother," the rabbi says. It's a young rabbi who never knew my grandparents. I feel indignant that Gram's getting short shrift in this eulogy. I'd like to get up in front of that pulpit and say what she was like to *me. She wasn't afraid of telling the truth or hearing it. Sitting qui-etly on her sofa felt like heaven. Her head and her heart were connected. She had beautiful skin. She cooked with magic. She knew about reciprocity. She took her-self for driving lessons when she was in her seventies. She loved Celia and me at the same time.*

"Oh, Ida sure was proud of you," Sophie Greenberg says, as we leave the funeral parlor for the parking lot. "We heard all about your work with those women, helping them to write their stories."

"Thank you," I say. "I loved her." Gram's friends meet me with glisten-ing eyes, giving me respite from the tension I feel between Mom and me. Mom steps into the car that will take her to the cemetery, and closes the door. Then from behind the window, she turns her face toward me, and mouths hello.

"She mouthed hello!" I turn toward Mollie, almost bursting at Mom's small gesture. "Isn't that wonderful?"

"When you get home," Aunt Mollie says, while we sit in the limousine that follows Mom and Rita's to the cemetery, "write me a list of what you want from Ida's. And don't be bashful about it. Put down everything you want. I'll get the list to Rita."

TWENTY - SEVEN

1 9 9 1

HANNAH

On my way to Bread & Circus a few days after returning to Cambridge, I meet Reb and Miriam Shuman walking down Harvard Street. "To the grocery store?" Reb Shuman asks.

I nod. I wonder if they notice my sadness.

"We're going to shul," Miriam says. "If you want to see it, maybe this would be a good time."

"Okay," I say. "Sure."

Almost as soon as we enter, the sanctuary's simplicity and warmth remind me of the synagogue I visited fifteen years ago in Switzerland. The walls are painted a soft white, the pews are mahogany, the ark holding the Torah is draped by a maroon velvet curtain with the Ten Commandments embroidered into it, in gold. My sadness has a place in here. We stand for a while, noticing the soft light coming through the colored glass windows. *I bet Jonathan would like it.* Miriam explains that in their shul, men and women can sit separately, in the Orthodox tradition—or together, in the modern one. She motions for me to take a seat in a middle row, between her and her husband.

"You don't feel so good?" Reb Shuman asks.

I nod, bite my lip. "But it's beautiful here."

"Very peaceful," Miriam says.

"My grandmother just died," I whisper, "and my mother—" I can't finish the sentence. Really, I don't know how to describe her—or me, or the way we relate, or what it means now that Gram is gone.

"El nah refah nah lah," Reb Shuman says, as if he understands everything from my fragmented sentence. I know he's speaking in Hebrew, and even though I don't understand the words, they soothe me.

Miriam nods. "Do you know what it means?" she asks.

I shake my head.

"God, please heal her, please," Reb Shuman says. "Moses said it for his sister Miriam when she had leprosy."

"Can you say it again?" I ask.

"El nah refah nah lah," they say in unison.

Then Miriam pats my knee. *"Ana el nah refah nah lah-nu.* God, please heal us, please," she says.

I start to sob. "Ya," Reb Shuman says. "That's the one you need to say."

I REMEMBER summers, the time I usually wasn't home, the lawn my mother weeded every day. She planted flowers on its borders when we first moved in—white daisies and black-eyed Susans. In September, she squeezed the dried heads between her thumb and forefinger, intensifying the reseeding, ensuring the next summer's crop. After a few years, the flowers in our borders stood out among the manicured lawns of Shaker Heights. In July, our yard looked lush. I think of Celia like this, actually: around a sharp outline, she blazes into wildness.

It's nearly summer again now, 1991. On my kitchen table, I spread out a red paisley cloth that Gram gave me last year. I'm working on yet another issue of *Wild Women's Stories*—my last, I told Nancy. These stories have given me courage over the years; and teaching has helped me see that the kind of attention I give my students is like what Mom once gave me. I feel ready now for different work—I might like to write for a newspaper or a magazine; and I'd like to have a garden.

I catch Gram's straightforward gaze in a photograph I took almost five years ago. She's in her royal blue robe; her white hair glows.

Oh, Ida. You've been dead six weeks. I miss you.

SOME nights, until I was eleven, maybe twelve, Mom would sit on the edge of my bed and cradle me in her lap. We'd sing together, way out of tune. Whenever I tell people about my mother, that I love her and have rarely spoken with her in ten years, they often twist their faces—sometimes their torsos, too—as if they've gone to a place outside of what they know as possible. "*Why?*" they ask me.

God knows, I've spent this decade driven by that question. My responses to it have changed, often. At this juncture, they blend together to form a mysterious climate that has become my familiar: my mother was born at an apex in Jewish history—at the beginning of the Old World's annihilation, and, in the New World, the beginning of an unprecedented rise in many Jews' standard of material living. I don't think Celia ever had desire to learn our personal ancestry; I did. She loved mothering me. That's no secret, even when she got lost in it, and had to step far away from me to find her own life. And I needed to see that neither mothering nor loving has its source in the woman who gave birth to me. Like Persephone, who was considered Queen of the Underworld before Hades took her away from Demeter, maybe my separation from Celia has rightness to it. Maybe my years in solitude do, too.

Demeter and Persephone have shown me that every mother and daughter in civilization go through some kind of separation. Like weather, there is no logic to loving, except that we change. We're dealt earthquakes, sometimes violent tornados—evolutions that come without warning or reason. After all these years, missing my mother still drives me daily in search of reasons to live. I'm beginning to cherish the search now, even more than I cherish my mother, or the other treasures I find.

Celia. *La ciel,* the sky, the ceiling, my Celia, sealed up.

One woman can be so many different things. A mother, the *American Heritage Dictionary* says, is "a woman who conceives, gives birth to, or raises and nurtures a child." Well, I got that. "A creative source; an origin." I got this, too. And there's also *"Vulgar slang:* Something considered extraordinary, as in disagreeableness, size, or intensity."

My mother gave me life. My father did, too. I am forever grateful.

————

"HELLO," a woman with a strong German accent says from my answering machine, just after I've returned home from work, "this is Ilse Schaubach. I maybe have your earring." She lives in the building adjacent to mine, which shares the same basement laundry room. *What is a German woman doing with the Israeli earring Karen gave me—Karen whose mother survived the Holocaust; Karen who didn't survive?*

"Ya, please, come in." Ilse smiles warmly, almost exuberantly, when I arrive at her door. On the phone she told me she's an art historian; she's in Cambridge for a year to teach at Radcliffe. She must be at least sixty, and I immediately realize that she would have been alive during the war. She's a few inches taller than me, and heftier; she has short, straight, gray hair, and blue eyes. The brightness of the blue startles me; the sadness they hold is unmistakable.

"I found it stuck on my shirt," Ilse says, handing me my earring. "I didn't wear this shirt for several months. Today I wore it, and I remembered the sign you had up there. I remembered your name, and in the phone book, I looked up your number."

"Thank you," I say, enclosing the new-found earring in my hand, with its mate, before I slip the wires into my ears. "Thank you so much. Someone I loved very much gave me these earrings."

"I'm so glad you've got them back," Ilse says. "They're good on you."

I look up to her kind, generous face, and notice the warm apartment behind her—a green velvet sofa with a matching armchair, lots of plants and books. There are probably a half dozen drawings on the wall I can see. The one I recognize is by Käthe Kollwitz.

When Ilse catches me staring at it, she asks in a quiet voice, "You are Jewish?"

Our eyes latch. I nod slowly, feeling the world in my nod, wondering how she knows.

Humbly, Ilse tips her head to the side. "Your earrings look like they could be from Israel," she explains. "And your name."

We stand quietly in her doorway, and just stare at each other, German and Jew, not talking or touching. *She's old enough to be my mother.* Like a bullet, a tear pops out of my eye. Ilse's eyes tear, too—and then our faces break open with tentative smiles. "Would you stay for tea?" she asks. "I would like that very much."

"Ya," I say. "I'd really like that."

THERE'S a gentle breeze today, a Sunday. I take my bicycle out from my basement locker, ride down Western Ave. until I get to the path along the Charles. I ride all the way to Watertown Square, then walk my bike past old brick buildings that once were textile factories. There are woods behind them.

I lean my bike against a lush maple, then lay my cheek against the smooth skin of a prostrate trunk. I nestle my knee and the inside of a thigh against a stable branch. My arms hang along the trunk's wide girth. My ear rests on a raised knot in the wood. I rest and I wait—for smells as delicate and mysterious as my mother's. And I listen—for winds that carry Ida's voice, or Channa's, Leah's, maybe Aunt Rose's or Vitl's. For the earth beneath this tree. For the earth beneath that earth.

After I bike home, I push my file cabinet into the hallway. There. Now the main room has more space. I pull the dirty sheets off my bed, take them down to the laundry room. I give the gerbera daisies I bought myself three days ago fresh water, put them back on my desk. I wipe the counter, chop an onion to start a soup, glance at the last collage I received from Jonathan. It's a rusted heart, with the words *return used* just under the heart. "This collage came together without any planning or thinking from me," he wrote. "It feels like a message from whoever it is who gives us a heart when we're born: *return it well used.* Like your grandmother did, from all you've said."

I've read this note probably twice a day since it arrived nearly three weeks ago.

Spritzing rose water onto my face, noticing how long my curls have become, and that I like them this way, even as one hangs over my forehead and reaches for my right eye, I hear the phone ring. I dry my hands quickly on the towel near the sink, wonder if Jonathan's on the other end. In New Mexico now, it's early afternoon.

"Hello, this is Celia," she says, then clears her throat. "I mean, this is Mom. How are you?"

"Uhh," I say, startled, groping for a response to her simple question. "Surprised."

"Mm hmm," she says. She's in complete control.

"What brings you to call?" I ask, feeling suddenly woozy. I pull the seat out from under my kitchen table and sit down slowly.

"I'm gambling," she says. "I'm at Lake Tahoe."

"Uh huh," I say. "What's Lake Tahoe?" I stand back up, pick up the blue Handiwipe draped over my faucet, notice the stains on my toaster oven. *If I keep moving this cloth while I talk to her, I'll have something to hold on to.*

"I'm at an all-night casino. I wasn't sleeping at home, so I came here. I haven't really slept in ten years, you know. Here, there's always a place to go with lights on, other people. I don't even have to go outside. I can just go from my room to the casino."

This is my mom? This is my first confidante, the woman who sent me to Europe before I could drive? My first teacher, my mother who cultivated daisies and preferred weeding a lawn to watching TV? This is my mystery, my majesty, my mother?

"Mom," I say, "why are you calling?"

"I slept a little bit last night. I woke with a dream."

"Oh," I say. I feel stunned, even scared, about what she might reveal; and I feel ready to hear it.

She's stopped talking again. I hear Muzak in the background, slot machines, the squeals of winners and losers.

"Mom?"

"I'm here," she says, in the voice of the grounded mother I knew as a child.

"What did you dream?"

"Yes."

I hear her light up a cigarette, exhale her first puff. I sit back down at my kitchen table, surprised to find myself welcoming the sound of her smoke, the rest it allows between her words.

"Channa came to me, my grandmother. You know I always called her

Channa. She took me to the back of my house—Gram and Grampa's house—to the porch. Channa and and I used to sit on the edge of it, dangling our legs." Mom's voice sounds declarative. She's using all her powers to tell me this story. Of course, I remember that porch myself. At the end of the summer, before Gram and Grampa moved from Cleveland Heights to Shaker, Mom and I would sit on it and smell the grapes that grew wild along the fence between my grandparents' house and their neighbors'.

"I probably felt more at home on that porch than any place I'd ever been—until you were born. Then I was a mother. *Your* mother. And even when you were at school or away for the summer, I finally had something—some*one*—who needed my attention." She says this as if she's never stopped giving me her attention. I've got an arm around myself now, waiting for what'll come next.

"In my dream, I was on the edge of the porch, and Channa came out from the grapes. I ran up to her and started asking how she was, saying how good she looked—much younger than I remembered. I mean I actually felt happy. I was seeing Channa, my Bubbe Channa."

"Your bubbe?" I interrupt.

"Sure," she says, as if she's always used Yiddish, "that's Yiddish, for grandmother."

I don't bother to say *I know that.*

"But Channa wouldn't answer my questions," Mom says, in a voice that's newly tender, almost humble. "She wouldn't talk to me."

She takes another draw from her cigarette, and I wonder if she's holding back tears. I've never heard her sob—that morning after I called Norm a housewife, she wept into her hands, but without a sound. The tears I sense she's holding back now might make a lot of noise—even in her casino.

We hold out, on the wire, until she can speak again. "This made me feel a little crazy," Mom continues, "that Channa wouldn't talk, and she knew it made me crazy. But she still wouldn't talk. I started to cry, and I woke up crying. Then, she began talking—when I woke up. It was crazy. She said I had to call you. She said it's time for us to eat together."

My eyes have begun to splay a soothing waterfall onto my face, past the cheekbones, around my nose, over my lips.

I sit in the quiet between us, feeling my slow-sweet trickle of tears. *Our silence has always been this sacred.*

I don't hear anything now except the sounds of the casino. "Mom?"

"Ya," she says, subdued. "I'm just thinking."

"Can you say what?"

"I miss my grandmother."

"Oh," I say. "Mm." I let my hum linger while the slot machines, like fire-crackers, keep punctuating our conversation.

"I asked Rita to send you that moldy trunk from Russia you told Aunt Mollie you wanted from Gram. You should get it any day now, though I can't imagine what you'd want with it. We double-bagged everything else you wanted in plastic, so it wouldn't get moldy."

"Really?" I ask. "Everything?"

"Yes," Mom says. *"The Settlement Cookbook*—it's falling apart, you know. That green bowl Rita figured was large enough to hold a pasta salad for fifteen people—"

"That was Channa's," I say.

"Whatever. We even let you have the silver candlesticks from my Grandmother Leah."

"Oh, Mom!" I say, unable to contain myself.

"Ya," she says, delighted, it seems, to be telling me about all these gifts. "You get the still life you wanted that Grampa brought back from Europe before I was born, and we threw in Ida's pearls, too. Everything's wrapped in that old afghan Ida made at least ten years ago."

"Oh, Mom," I sigh. "Wow! I mean, *thanks.*"

"Right," she says, perfunctory again. "And you know, it didn't get past us that there weren't too many photographs left."

I let out a nervous giggle.

"Well," Mom says. "I'm going back to my hotel room. I'd like some quiet. Maybe I'll even sleep."

She's stopped our conversation so quickly, I feel jolted. "Mom," I ask, "can we talk again in the next day or two?"

"I don't know, Hannah. I'm not sure if I'll keep sleeping so well and waking up like this, you know what I mean?"

"Sort of," I say. I notice I'm not quite as pushy as I might have been a few years ago. "But if you could keep me posted, that'd make things a lot easier for me."

"You're still an insistent daughter," Mom says. I'm sure she's smiling when she says it.

"I'll take that as a compliment," I say.

"Perhaps," Mom says.

I'm wearing an enormous grin. I hang up the phone, ladle a bowl of lentil soup, and sit down at my table, covered with Gram's paisley cloth. The window ledge beside the table is lined with photos—of Ida and Mollie; of Channa; of Celia and me when I was a toddler. There are self-portraits of Wild Women, and Jonathan's heart collage. As I slurp my soup, I remember a carpenter once telling me that he'd lined his great-uncle's trunk with cedar panels—and wiped out the smell of mold. *I could ask him to do that with Channa's trunk. I could pack my dishes in it—and Leah's silver candlesticks—when I move to New Mexico. Jonathan and I could use it as an end table.* I head back to the stove for more soup, sensing the beginning of a poem about making this old trunk into a table while I dream of heading west.

Ikh hob brokhes oyf mayn kop, I smile. There are blessings on my head.

ACKNOWLEDGMENTS

E IGHT years ago, I decided I wanted to write a novel. "You have no money," a voice in my head said.

"Well," another voice countered, "you could give your attention to that. Or, you could give attention to writing."

I chose to focus on this novel, and found myself propelled into an adventure beyond my wildest dreams.

During the first three years, I sustained myself primarily by housesitting. For giving me their homes while they traveled, I thank Tom Adler, Ruth Alpert, Nora Bailey, Shelly Batt, Julianne Blake, Steve Cohen and Pauline Kenny, Mary Charlotte Domandi, Michael Finney, Ellen Fox, Douglas Johnson, Norman Johnson, Judy Moore and Bob Kraichnan, Susan and Phil LeCuyer, Catherine Macken, Melanie Mitchel, Joan O'Donnell, Laurie Richadone, and Saz Richardson. And another thanks to Ruth Alpert, who called my tenacity in housesitting a triumph when I felt it was a shame.

Many people gave me money: Ester Barfi, Sallie Bingham, Julianne Blake, Lisa Bloom and Richard Frankel, Leona Bronstein, Savitri Clarke, Marty Cohen, Steve Cohen and Pauline Kenny, Deborah Dineen, Donna and Bill Fishbein, Cynthia Frude, the late George Geiger, Evy and Larry Gordon, Nancy Hurlbut, Anita Jamieson, the late Mary Krasovitz, Bill Krupman, Bob Levin, the late Fred Preuss, Jennie and Karl Preuss, Arden Reed, Saz Richardson, and Anonymous (two). *THANK YOU.* And thanks to Larry Ogan, director of the Santa Fe Council for the Arts, for kindly and efficiently administering many of these grants.

I am also very grateful to the Ludwig Vogelstein Foundation and the Western States Arts Federation for their generous support.

Conversations with Lisa Bloom and Deborah Dineen over the last twenty years have knitted together the pieces of my daily life. I look forward to more! For reminding me about the power of rest and listening to stories like there is nothing better to do on this whole earth, I am indebted to Brooke Pyeatt, and eagerly awaiting his novel. And I am grateful to Pauline Kenny, who generously gave this project her resourcefulness and enthusiasm.

For their stories, encouragement, and friendship, I thank Shelly Batt, Sallie Bingham, Kathy McGuire Bouwman, Bridgit Brown, Marty Cohen, Marge Edelson, Dietl Giloi, Evy and Larry Gordon, Rebecca Green, Anita Jamieson, Rabbi Nahum Ward Lev, Rabbi Ben Morrow, David Moss, Michael Nunnally, Louisa Putnam, Virginia Pyeatt, Arden Reed, Saz Richardson, Ruth Rosen, Don Sale, Joe and Sandra Samora, Sylvia Segal, Penny Street, Michael Tierney, and Rabbi Gershon Winkler.

For responding kindly and efficiently to numerous questions, I thank the Reference Department of the Santa Fe Public Library. Thanks to Dave Ewars, whose computer knowhow saved this novel one day; and to Steve Terrell of the *Santa Fe New Mexican,* who generously informed me about Neil Young. Kathleen Lewis Loeks connected me to Bob Levin, whose desire for the birth of this book nourished it and me for years.

Yehudis Fishman, Rabbi Zush Margolin, Gitl Viswanath, and Moe Zimmerberg gave me indispensable help with Yiddish.

Hunter Beaumont, Marty Cohen, Gary Weston deWalt, Rebecca Friedman, Ellen Kleiner, Dennis Jarrett, Ann Mason, and Brooke Pyeatt, my first editors, brought this story into their psyches while it was still young. Their passionate support and deft pens gave the book clarity and cohesion. I cannot thank them enough.

Stephany Evans of the Imprint Agency graciously connected me to Donna Downing at Pam Bernstein and Associates. *Thank you, Donna,* for loving this novel, and for giving it more than one chance.

For their insights, integrity, and zeal, I thank my editor Celina Spiegel, and Erin Bush, her assistant. I also feel privileged to work with copyeditor Martha Ramsey and book jacket designer Honi Werner—and the whole team at Riverhead Books.

My gratitude, my whole heart.